PRAISE FOR JOEY W. HILL'S VAMPIRE QUEEN NOVELS

Vampire Trinity

"Only Joey W. Hill can make me yearn for blood and fangs."

—*Romance Junkies*

"One amazingly phenomenal sexy novel that will keep the pages turning, your imagination running, your dreams carnally vivid and your partner very happy."

—*Bitten by Books*

"A Joyfully Recommended Read . . . Joey W. Hill impresses me with every word she writes."

—*Joyfully Reviewed*

"Ms. Hill is a talented writer with a style that can only be deemed exclusively hers . . . All of the books in this series are ardently poignant romances at their finest."

—*Risqué Reviews*

Vampire Mistress

"Keep a fan and a glass of ice water handy; this one will raise your temperature."

—*Romantic Times*

"The Vampire Queen novels are more than a reader ever needs to indulge in a world where connection with the characters is amazingly intense and all-consuming, leaving you very, very satisfied."

—*Fresh Fiction*

Beloved Vampire

"Lock the door, turn off the television and hide the phone before starting this book, because it's impossible to put down! . . . The story is full of action, intrigue, danger, history and sexual tension . . . This is definitely a keeper!"

—*Romantic Times*

"This has to be the best vampire novel I've read in a very long time! Joey W. Hill has outdone herself . . . [I] couldn't put it down and didn't want it to end."

—*ParaNormal Romance*

continued . . .

A Vampire's Claim

"Had me in its thrall. Joey W. Hill pulled me in and didn't let me go."

—*Joyfully Reviewed*

"*A Vampire's Claim* is so ardent with action and sex you won't remember to breathe . . . another stunning installment in her vampire series."

—*TwoLips Reviews*

"Sure to enthrall and delight not only existing Hill fans, but also those new to her writing."

—*Romantic Times*

"A great vampire romance . . . [an] enticing, invigorating thriller."

—*The Best Reviews*

Mark of the Vampire Queen

"Superb . . . This is erotica at its best with lots of sizzle and a love that is truly sacrificial. Joey W. Hill continues to grow as a stunning storyteller."

—*A Romance Review*

"Packs a powerful punch."

—*TwoLips Reviews*

"Hill never ceases to amaze us . . . She keeps you riveted to your seat and leaves you longing for more with each sentence."

—*Night Owl Romance*

"Dark and richly romantic."

—*Romantic Times*

"Fans of erotic romantic fantasy will relish [it]."

—*The Best Reviews*

The Vampire Queen's Servant

"Should come with a warning: intensely sexy, sensual story that will hold you hostage until the final word is read. The story line is fresh and unique, complete with a twist."

—*Romantic Times*

"Hot, kinky, sweating, hard-pounding, oh-my-god-is-it-hot-in-here-or-is-it-just-me sex . . . so compelling it just grabs you deep inside."

—*TwoLips Reviews*

MORE PRAISE FOR THE NOVELS OF JOEY W. HILL

"Everything Joey W. Hill writes just rocks my world." —Jaci Burton

"Sweet yet erotic . . . will linger in your heart long after the story is over."
—*Sensual Romance Reviews*

"One of the finest, most erotic love stories I've ever read. Reading this book was a physical experience because it pushes through every other plane until you feel it in your marrow." —Shelby Reed, author of *Holiday Inn*

"The perfect blend of suspense and romance." —*The Road to Romance*

"Wonderful . . . the sex is hot, very HOT, [and] more than a little kinky . . . erotic romance that touches the heart and mind as well as the libido."
—*Scribes World*

"A beautifully told story of true love, magic and strength . . . a wondrous tale . . . A must-read." —*Romance Junkies*

"A passionate, poignant tale . . . the sex was emotional and charged with meaning . . . yet another must-read story from the ever-talented Joey W. Hill." —*Just Erotic Romance Reviews*

"This is not only a keeper but one you will want to run out and tell your friends about." —*Fallen Angel Reviews*

"Not for the closed-minded. And it's definitely not for those who like their erotica soft." —*A Romance Review*

Berkley Heat titles by Joey W. Hill

THE VAMPIRE QUEEN'S SERVANT
THE MARK OF THE VAMPIRE QUEEN
A VAMPIRE'S CLAIM
BELOVED VAMPIRE
VAMPIRE MISTRESS
VAMPIRE TRINITY
VAMPIRE INSTINCT
BOUND BY THE VAMPIRE QUEEN

Berkley Sensation titles by Joey W. Hill

A MERMAID'S KISS
A WITCH'S BEAUTY
A MERMAID'S RANSOM

Anthologies

LACED WITH DESIRE
(with Jaci Burton, Jasmine Haynes, and Denise Rossetti)

UNLACED
(with Jaci Burton, Jasmine Haynes, and Denise Rossetti)

Bound by the Vampire Queen

Joey W. Hill

HEAT BOOKS
New York

THE BERKLEY PUBLISHING GROUP
Published by the Penguin Group
Penguin Group (USA) Inc.
375 Hudson Street, New York, New York 10014, USA
Penguin Group (Canada), 90 Eglinton Avenue East, Suite 700, Toronto, Ontario M4P 2Y3, Canada
(a division of Pearson Penguin Canada Inc.)
Penguin Books Ltd., 80 Strand, London WC2R 0RL, England
Penguin Group Ireland, 25 St. Stephen's Green, Dublin 2, Ireland (a division of Penguin Books Ltd.)
Penguin Group (Australia), 250 Camberwell Road, Camberwell, Victoria 3124, Australia
(a division of Pearson Australia Group Pty. Ltd.)
Penguin Books India Pvt. Ltd., 11 Community Centre, Panchsheel Park, New Delhi—110 017, India
Penguin Group (NZ), 67 Apollo Drive, Rosedale, Auckland 0632, New Zealand
(a division of Pearson New Zealand Ltd.)
Penguin Books (South Africa) (Pty.) Ltd., 24 Sturdee Avenue, Rosebank, Johannesburg 2196,
South Africa

Penguin Books Ltd., Registered Offices: 80 Strand, London WC2R 0RL, England

This book is an original publication of The Berkley Publishing Group.

Cover illustration by Don Sipley.
Cover design by George Long.

PRINTING HISTORY
Heat trade paperback edition / December 2011

Library of Congress Cataloging-in-Publication Data

Hill, Joey W.
Bound by a vampire queen / Joey W. Hill. — Heat trade paperback ed.
p. cm. — (The vampire queen series ; bk. 8)
ISBN 978-0-425-24344-2
1. Vampires—Fiction. I. Title.
PS3608.I4343B58 2011
813'.6—dc22
2011004515

PRINTED IN THE UNITED STATES OF AMERICA

10 9 8 7 6 5 4 3 2 1

Acknowledgments

In past books, I have thanked those invaluable folks who have contributed to the books in terms of production, research, critiquing, suggestions and overall moral support for the process, all vital things to help an author offer the best book possible. However, equally important are those who read the books, who take them into their hearts and become so enthusiastic about them that they spread the word and share that love with others, contributing greatly to the success of the books.

Thank you always and forever to my readers, who are so generous in this regard. You give me so very much, more than I can express, and I treasure the chances I've had to meet you through email and face-to-face, sharing the joy of reading and writing this genre.

A very, very special thank-you to those who have volunteered to do even more, actively promoting the books merely because of your passion for them. This includes Terry, who started the very first Yahoo! fan group, and Jaime, Sandy and Kat, who helped with its ultimate transformation into the Joey W. Hill fan forum. I'm amazed with what you've done with the idea and what it's become. And a huge shout-out to the Femme Fatales for their tireless "street team" work!

Last but not at all least, to Karen, who has taken on the daunting task of creating a series bible for the Vampire Queen series, something I've never had the time to do (and therefore has led to some humorous and sometimes painful gaffes in the books. If you haven't noticed, then just ignore that statement—*grin*). She has tried to keep me out of trouble in this book and going forward. As always, any mistakes made, despite her heroic efforts, are all mine.

I wish I could list everyone, but please know I owe all my readers so much. Thank you for everything!

Bound by the Vampire Queen

1

JACOB squatted on his booted heels on a mountain of broken concrete. Looking down the slope of rock and across a thicket of ruined foliage, he wondered how hard it was to pull off a fairy's wings. He'd sure as hell like the chance to find out.

His lady and Fae Lord Keldwyn were a few hundred yards away, standing next to the clump of twisted trees where the verandah used to be. She called it the mangrove, evidence of her macabre sense of humor, given that the trees used to be a pack of rabid vampires. That is, before she turned them into future firewood, and crushed the surrounding marble and concrete like popcorn.

Thanks to his ability to be in her mind, Jacob could easily hear their conversation. Which was why he was envisioning wing extraction. Of course, since Keldwyn's wings were currently concealed, Jacob would settle for breaking a limb or two.

"As long as you had no true grasp of Fae power," Keldwyn was saying, "the court had no interest in you. You were like solitary elementals; pixies, dryads, gnomes. The peasantry of our kind. Less than that, even, because of your inferior vampire blood."

Through his lady's mind, Jacob watched the Fae lord's eyes, like onyx and pale moonstone, slide over the center tree. The shape of the trunk was undeniably like the tortured body of the male vampire trapped within it. One large aboveground root kinked up like a leg, in a futile struggle to push out of its prison.

"But this, and the potential of your parentage, has set your future course. The Unseelie queen demands you come before her, for assessment and possible acknowledgment. If she determines that you are significant, you will be made a member of her court, one of her subjects, required to attend her will as she deems appropriate."

"What are they saying?" The question came from Lord Mason, sitting at a lower point on the pile of debris. He had his elbows braced on a jagged slab of what used to be the veranda steps. His long legs were stretched out, ankles crossed.

"He's saying he misses us. That he wants us to come join the conversation." Jacob rose, and with a couple of graceful leaps, was on the ground near Mason's polished riding boots.

"The same tight-assed bastard who said 'the vampires need to wait here,' like we were lepers?" Mason arched a brow.

Jacob gave him a grim smile. When Keldwyn had issued that curt directive, not even by a twitch had Mason reacted to being treated like chattel on his own estate. Of course, that wasn't surprising. Though Jacob had warned Mason of the Fae's contempt for vampires, Mason had dealt with plenty of egos in his own world. Hadn't they all? Jacob's lip curled at the thought.

"Yeah, he's had a change of heart. He's feeling all warm and fuzzy about us now."

Mason snorted, but Jacob knew neither of them gave a rat's ass what Keldwyn thought. Lyssa was their mutual main concern. As such, when he headed toward the mangrove, he was aware of Mason rising to follow him at a sauntering pace, ostensibly to check his surviving roses, but Jacob knew he had his back. A Fae might be able to kick a vampire's ass any day of the week, but kicking two of them, as well as dealing with Lyssa, might be more than Keldwyn wanted to do. He'd muss his perfect hair, after all.

Jacob. Easy. Lyssa spoke in his mind. *Let's see where this goes.*

I'm ever obedient to your will, my lady.

He felt the touch of wry humor, saw it flash through her jade green eyes as her gaze flickered his way. Still, he meant it. He wasn't as good at poker faces as Mason, but he could keep his mouth shut when needed.

As Keldwyn noted their approach, his expression got sour. Lyssa spoke before he could say anything, however.

"And if I prefer to remain solitary?"

Unlike him, his lady had an exceptional talent for not revealing anything about her true thoughts on a matter, so Jacob knew the edge to her voice was deliberate. Keldwyn turned his gaze back to her.

"Then you should not have done this." He nodded at the trees. "This is dark magic, with a clear Unseelie signature. Your father had blood from both the Seelie and Unseelie courts, so it remains to be seen if your abilities will stay in the realm of one court or expand to both. However, as of now, you've made an indelible mark on the Unseelie queen's universe, and so her eye is turned toward you. This is not an invitation. If you choose to refuse it like one, you will not have months to live like a fugitive in the woods as you did when the vampires shunned you. The queen will destroy all you hold dear. She can have you brought to her in chains and keep you as a pet at her feet, until she feels you understand obedience."

Keldwyn's voice was flat, his gaze utterly impersonal. Even so, Jacob sensed something beneath that, an elusive sense of urgency, enough to underscore and make his words unsettling truth, not a goading threat.

Ever since they'd met Keldwyn, months ago, this was the way it had been. Jacob's gut was always on high alert around the pointy-eared bastard, scanning for something that felt not quite . . . right. Of course, Jacob had Irish roots, and before her death, his mother had regaled him with bedtime stories of the Fae. Fascinating, beautiful and wondrous, they were also capricious, unpredictable and morally neutral at best. At worst, they could be and do things much like Keldwyn had just described the Fae queen doing. In short, it was best to give anything smacking of them a wide berth.

I am part Fae, Sir Vagabond. Lyssa's amusement was evident in the thought. *I think you have lost that chance.*

Because of his background as Renaissance Faire knight, drifter and vampire hunter, it was her preferred endearment for him when she was in a good mood. Less frequently—usually when she was reminiscing much further back—she sometimes called him Sir Knight, recalling his past life as such. Regardless, he was glad she was calm about this, but then Lyssa had fought in the Territory Wars and seen a thousand years of crises. She tended to consider a matter carefully before getting too excited about things.

Mason, with a similar relaxed mien but one Jacob knew could conceal a panther about to tear into the soft underbelly of his prey, had taken a seat on a wrought-iron bench. He stretched a powerful arm across the back, propping one boot against the base. Like Jacob, Mason kept his amber eyes trained on the Fae. Keldwyn continued to ignore them both.

"To go to her court, you will have to cross into the Fae world. She won't simply throw open the gate. She will want to test your mettle, see if you can find your way to it. I am not allowed to point the way, but she did not forbid a useful suggestion."

Lyssa cocked her head. "You're playing a dangerous game with her intent."

Keldwyn shrugged. "Our ways are tricky. A step left, when the dance seems meant to go right. You may have powers like ours"—he glanced toward the grove again—"but you do not yet know the way our minds work. We are creatures of random chaos. It is why our paths separated from humans and vampires so long ago. Because of their violent natures, they need order and structure. We do not."

"Yet the Fae have a court and a queen. Two courts, even."

"We have our own etiquette. It's just far less predictable."

"There are time distortions between the Fae world and ours," Lyssa said. "What if I go there for a day and return to find a hundred years have passed here?"

"The queen is capable of managing such things. If you please her, it will not be a concern. Do you wish my suggestion or not?"

Not. Though I'd be happy to give him a suggestion or two.

Lyssa's lips quirked at Jacob's thought, but otherwise her face remained serene. "Of course, Lord Keldwyn."

"Entrances to the Fae world used to be fairly easy to find. In-between places or times. Crossroads, forks in the road, stream edges, midnight or noon, equinoxes. The mists. Such circumstances are still required for an opening, but in your case the will of the Fae queen must be aligned with it as well. Bring an offering that impresses her, and she will make the crossing an easier one."

Keldwyn's focus moved back to that largest tree. "I walk in your world, in the places of old Earth, deep forests such as where we met. However, because of my age and strength, I can visit places like your cities, observing certain precautions. Our young are not so resilient. If, through foolish curiosity, they wander too deeply into the human world, and keep their soles too long on the things of earth men have made into their tools—concrete, steel, brick—the young Fae weakens. When their magic is dangerously sapped, their base instinct is to transform, as many of us can, into a pure earth form to regenerate. A tree, a plant, a stone."

Keldwyn's gaze shifted to the necklace Lyssa wore, chunks of amber. Some of them had tiny fossilized creatures inside. The center pendant was a smooth teardrop of jade, speckled like a bird's egg. It reflected the color of her intent eyes.

"But that is a trap," he continued. "Once they are in that form, it becomes their prison. Only the touch of a Fae, one who has enough strength for it, can release them. Even then, the young will need to be taken out of your world of iron and structure, back to the Fae world, before their strength can truly regenerate."

"So you want me to free someone to impress the queen."

Keldwyn lifted a shoulder. "There is one, a dryad, lost to our world over two decades ago. The queen bore her affection and was grieved to lose her, but where she is, no pure Fae can reclaim her. The risk is too great, and the queen forbade anyone to try, because of the chance we might reveal ourselves. However, you are as yet outside our world, our laws. If you succeed, I am certain a gateway in the proper in-between setting would open for you."

Lyssa considered him. "You are ever helpful, Lord Keldwyn. Where is this Fae located?"

"In the city you made your home before your fall from grace with the Council. Atlanta. In a place surrounded with broken asphalt. I do not know her condition, but even near death, a dryad can live for a long time inside the shelter of a tree. I cannot give you the exact location, but she is in the downtown area, the decaying, crime-ridden parts. Perhaps in what you call a parking lot, or an older, abandoned area?"

"That narrows it down," Jacob noted dryly.

Keldwyn shot him a glance. "Yes. I expect you will have to spend some time finding the right place. But you cannot take too long. The queen will not wait beyond the next full moon on your attendance. Samhain approaches and other events of importance take place in the Fae world. At that point, she will get tired of your fumbling attempts to find a gateway and bring you to her. In that case, the crossing will be a far more unpleasant experience."

Because it already sounds like the perfect vacation hot spot now.

~

Once his message was delivered, Keldwyn headed back toward the forest, making it obvious he intended to depart, irrespective of whether they had further questions or need of him. It wouldn't matter regardless, Jacob knew. He didn't serve their interests, but that of an unknown monarch. And his own.

Though Lyssa asked Mason to remain at the grove, Jacob stayed a close step behind her, and she didn't discourage him. When they reached the edge of the forest, Keldwyn paused, those onyx eyes settling back on Lyssa's face after a brief flicker at Jacob's. "Long ago," he said, "a woodsman fell in love with a beautiful and mysterious girl he found in the forest. She agreed to marry him on one condition. She had to leave him from midnight to dawn every night, and he couldn't ask her whereabouts or try to follow her. Since he loved her, he agreed. They were very happy, for a time."

He paused. "Eventually, they had a child together. Since the woodsman had been busy with his trade, upon the child's birth they only had an old cradle loaned to them by the village wise woman. One night, while his wife was gone, he couldn't sleep, for he never slept well without her. He decided he'd pick out a tree to make a new cradle. Putting their daughter on his back, he carried her into the woods. Not too far away, he found one that was perfect, the wood so smooth beneath his fingers. The baby smiled and laughed when he touched the tree, reaching toward it, so he was sure it was the right one. He chopped it down and made the cradle in that one fateful night."

Now his gaze shifted back to Jacob, flat, unreadable. "His wife was a hamadryad, her life essence connected to a specific tree. To maintain that life essence, she had to return to a tree form for a certain amount of time every night. As I'm sure you guessed, he mistakenly killed her to make a resting place for their child. Fae lore is filled with many such cautionary tales about the wisdom of love between the species."

"Perhaps if she'd just told him who and what she was, it never would have happened. Honesty is the best policy and all that," Jacob suggested. As he met Lyssa's bemused green eyes, he thought of how much he liked the porcelain smoothness of her face, the delicate features. "The problem I have with that old folktale," he added, "is how long he accepted her being gone at that time of night. When it comes to love, you don't accept rationing. Over time, you want it all. He would have followed her."

"He would have lost her that much sooner." Keldwyn's lip curled. "The Fae can make man or vampire believe what they want them to believe. For instance, you believe you and the Lady Lyssa are meant to be together forever. That you can have a happily ever after, like the fairy tales humans have bastardized. But in the end, if her path lies in our world, you and the half-breed infant will be left behind. Just like the woodsman and his daughter."

Despite Lyssa's sudden stillness, a warning, Jacob stepped forward. He and Keldwyn were of like height, though the compressed energy of the male Fae was like standing within the incineration range of a star. It didn't matter. Jacob was a ticking bomb himself. "At some point," he said quietly, "you *will* acknowledge Lady Lyssa's son."

"Not as long as he is yours as well. Lyssa, you would do well to tell your servant to stand down, before there's one more tree out there. One that can be snapped like kindling."

Jacob, there's a time for this. Go back to Mason. I need a few minutes of privacy, and I do not want you to listen in.

It was a firm order, but there was also a caress behind it, telling him she was quietly pleased he'd stood up for her and Kane. He rarely doubted her wisdom, though there were times it was hard to stomach, like now. He nodded to Keldwyn, his jaw tight. "I've said my peace."

Turning, he sketched a bow to his lady. *I'll respect your wishes, but I'll be close, my lady. I don't trust your welfare to him. Not now, not ever.*

He returned to his place on the concrete rubble, finding Mason back in his own place there. Though he gave him a nod, Jacob kept his attention trained on Lyssa and Keldwyn. They spoke for only a few moments, and he could tell nothing from their expressions. At length, Keldwyn vanished into the rainforest.

"I'll leave you two to talk," Mason said, correctly interpreting the mood as Lyssa moved back toward them. "We'll discuss plans shortly."

Jacob watched his lady come toward him, all sensual grace in slacks and a cream-colored blouse open at the throat. Her long black hair was clipped at her nape, the hip-length strands playing around her shoulders and the nip of her waist. She was so fine-boned and petite, the result of her Asian vampire mother, but only a fool would ignore the royal power that emanated from those jade eyes. The fact of her bare feet didn't impact that in the slightest. Of late, she seemed to prefer direct contact with the earth, another indication of the changes happening with her Fae blood. She looked pensive.

"Figuring out his motives is like trying to spear a fish with a straw," he remarked.

Taking a seat on one of the lower concrete pieces, she crossed her legs and stretched her arms back to brace herself. Turning her face to the wind, she closed her eyes.

"Yes," she said simply. Her velvet voice could caress a man's skin, her vampire allure in perfect complement to the Fae. Though he was resigned to her ability to arouse with nothing more than her voice or her scent, long practice and intense servant training allowed him to focus past it, particularly when it was incidental, not targeted. When she *wanted* to arouse him, a battle against an army of Keldwyns would be easier than resistance. Her lips curved, telling him she'd registered his thought, though the pensive look remained. The private conversation with the Fae lord had bothered her.

"I know you don't believe his motives. Or his story about the dryad trapped in Atlanta."

"As a queen, I know there are certain things you do and don't do. The Fae monarch has many to do her bidding. If she was truly fond of this dryad, she would have sent someone after her long ago, even if she could not risk herself. I think it far more likely the queen imprisoned the girl there as a punishment, and Keldwyn has his own reasons for wanting us to free her, perhaps to rouse the queen's ire, challenge her."

"But you still think we should do it."

She glanced up at him from under thick, dark lashes. "You already know that."

"Which is why it wasn't a question."

His tone won an imperious arch of her brow, but she nodded. "Keldwyn is duplicitous, secretive. However, every piece of advice he's given us contains a certain degree of wisdom. If I am able to release her and bring her to the queen, doing what another Fae can't or won't dare to do, then there is a status to that even if I anger her."

Jacob snorted. "Only another queen would think about it that way."

"But that is how I need to come to her. Not as a supplicant, but as an equal."

He slid down next to her. Stretching out his legs, he rested on his elbows, tangling his fingers in a lock of her long hair. As he twined it around his fingers, he gave it a tug. She laid her palm on his abdomen, slipping her fingers beneath his T-shirt to trace the ridges of muscle. Jacob didn't want to say it, but he knew he had to do so.

"You are superior in all ways, my lady, but what if your new powers are *not* equal to hers? What if she feels compelled to teach you a painful lesson? Set you back on your heels for freeing this Fae girl?"

"That's a risk I must take. Far better to appear assertive in such a situation than meek and scraping." One long-nailed finger teased beneath the denim waistband, tracing his bare hip bone. "And that applies not only to queens. Not too long ago, I remember an insolent young man who presented himself to be my servant. Respect he had, but not an ounce of true submission."

Jacob gave a half chuckle. "Yeah, and I remember how *that* night went. I got my ass kicked."

"But it turned out all right in the end, didn't it?"

He looked up at her. Despite her Fae abilities, he could still get the jump on her with his vampire speed. Sometimes. Like now. In a blink, he'd moved them off the concrete and down below the mangroves, into the cultivated gardens where there was a patch of soft grass. He'd left her on top, but had her pulled down against his chest, his arm around her back, his mouth warm on hers. She stirred against him, and he felt her pleasure with his body against the softer curves of her own. His cock hardened as her own flesh dampened, readying itself for him.

Even when he'd been a third-mark human servant, he'd had the senses to smell her arousal. A third-mark was equipped to mostly keep up with a vampire's insatiable carnal appetities. Now that he was a vampire, he had those appetites in spades himself. So her arousal was an irresistible perfume, an acceptable invitation to deal with the tension of the past couple hours.

But more needed to be said first. Seeing it in his lady's eyes, he braced himself, pretty sure he wasn't going to like whatever it was.

Lyssa pushed herself up, straddling his hips, but flattened her palms on his chest, a mute order to stay where he was. "Jacob, you know you're staying here."

"Like hell."

She pressed her lips into a thin line. "You sound more like your brother, Gideon, than the servant Thomas trained so well for me."

"Gideon and I have more in common that most people realize. Particularly Gideon." His eyes didn't waver. "I'm going with you."

"We both know how the Fae feel about vampires. It's very likely the doorway won't open for you, even if we manage to free this dryad and bring her along."

"Is that what Keldwyn told you when you had your private conversation?"

Not exactly.

~

When Jacob rejoined Mason, Lyssa hadn't watched him go, though she usually took great pleasure in the attractive flex of muscle in all the right places, the warrior's grace and power enhanced by the vampire blood.

Keldwyn lifted a shoulder. "You counsel your servant wisely, Lady Lyssa."

"Don't flatter yourself overmuch, my lord. Call it a challenge to Fae superiority all you wish. I know male posturing, regardless of the species."

He lifted a brow. "What is it you wish to say to me that required this private audience?"

"It wasn't Fae allure or any power of mine that convinced Jacob we were meant to be together. He convinced *me*."

"Then you are as much a fool as he is. Many things change, but not someone's fundamental nature. It matters not what species they are."

"That is my point, exactly. And Jacob's."

He studied her for another moment, then inclined his head. "I wish you well, Lady Lyssa. As always."

When he disappeared from view in a blink of time, she didn't bother to try and track him as she had when he'd first started visiting them. Unlike vampires, it wasn't speed that gave him that ability, but a Fae's capacity to blend. He could be within a stride of her, cloaked not only in the colors of the forest, but its scents and life energy, a perfect chameleon. So, anticipating he was still close enough to hear her, she spoke, taking the final word.

"Better a fool in his arms, my lord, than a lonely Fae who haunts the forests and doesn't know how to smile. I wish you well. Also as always."

RETURNING to the present, she knew she wouldn't be able to convince Jacob the Fae world was closed to him, mainly because she didn't know that for certain herself. He'd had exceptional intuition long before he had the ability to delve into her mind. Demonstrating it now, he closed his hands over hers on his chest, with enough pressure that her blood stirred at the challenge. "Even before I became a vampire, lying to me usually didn't work out so well for you, my lady."

"Take care that you don't overestimate what you know of me, Sir Vagabond." But her mouth softened. "Jacob, there's Kane to consider. Would you abandon him?"

Letting out an oath, he set her aside, getting to his feet. "That's unfair, and you know it."

"I never said I was fair. If Keldwyn is not telling the truth about the time distortion, or if I don't survive this, or can't get back for any reason, Kane needs one parent in his life. We both know how critical it is to have at least one blood parent watching over a vampire infant. As great as our feelings are for each other, he is the summation of those feelings. He comes first."

Jacob strode a few paces away, his fists clenched. After a long moment, they eased and she heard his dry chuckle. "You almost had me, my lady." He glanced over his shoulder, those blue eyes shrewd. "What would Kane think of me if I didn't do everything to protect his mother? We both know Mason is just as capable as I am of protecting Kane. More so perhaps, though I'll deny it if you feed his overinflated ego. Plus, Kane has an uncle who will defend him to the death. An uncle who—by some unprecedented miracle or freakish aberration in the universe—is the bonded servant of one of the most powerful vampires either of us know. This has nothing to do with Kane, and everything to do with you protecting me. I thought we were past that."

"As much as we are past you always trying to protect me?" She rose. From the stubborn set of his jaw, she knew her eyes were flashing fire. "Set aside your damned code of chivalry, Jacob. It's far more likely you could be killed in the Fae world. What if we step through that doorway at night, and it's bright daylight on their side, with no cover in sight? That's the capricious type of cruelty the Fae excel at."

"Then they'll have barbecued vampire fumigating their pretty, sparkly world."

Now it was her turn to curse. He looked impressed by the sound of it, the number of syllables. "What was that?"

"A particularly virulent oath Mason taught me, years ago. I just insulted twelve generations of your obstinate Irish heritage."

That made him smile. The handsome charm of it never failed to make her heart trip a little faster, but now her reaction made her frown, at herself as much as at him. "Earlier, when you challenged Keldwyn, you said, 'Lady Lyssa's son.' Not 'our son' or 'my son.' Why did you say it that way?"

He sobered, eyes becoming flint. "It's the lesson a human servant learns early, my lady. Keldwyn doesn't view me as an equal, no more than the Council did when I was human. However, I can challenge him—or them—on your behalf. It suits my purpose to do just that, in every instance where you suffer insult."

When he spoke like this, he reminded her of a medieval courtier. After he'd stopped working for his brother as a vampire hunter, he'd traveled with a Ren Faire, but the Faire hadn't taught him the principles of chivalry and honor. Those things were magnets already lodged in his soul, elements of a past life drawing him to the circuit. She remembered the knight who had moved over her in the dim light of a desert tent centuries ago, making her feel his strength and fragility at once—

and her own. She'd never forgotten that knight's eyes, the soul they revealed. A few hundred years later, that soul had stared at her out of Jacob's blue eyes. As a result, she'd embraced the unlikely idea of taking a former vampire hunter, drifter and Ren Faire player as her next full servant. And the fact he was easy on a woman's eyes had only helped the decision.

His hair had once possessed copper highlights from the sun, but as a vampire, the reddish brown had become a deeper bronze color. Loose, it fell to his shoulders. When she met him, he'd also had a trimmed moustache and short beard, so like the medieval knight's she'd shivered, remembering the feel of them and his firm lips against her skin. Jacob's nose had been broken at least once and retained that interesting shape even after she turned him, but of course it was his eyes that arrested. Fine, reddish-blond lashes framing the vivid blue color. A *stubborn*, vivid blue.

When he spoke like he did now, she could do nothing to change his mind. It overwhelmed her with anger, despair and love for him, all at once. As he moved back in her direction, recognizing it, she wouldn't let the last take precedence, not when she had a point to prove.

She backed away from him. The stillness that entered his gaze warned he could leap forward, use vampire speed to catch her. But he didn't. Not yet. He slowed his steps, matching her pace. It was a deliberate tracking maneuver, guaranteed to bring another element into their shared tension. She had no problem using the irresistible attraction between them to make her case, though she didn't deny there was far more to it. Just as his determination to follow her no matter where she went could go hand in hand with the sexual predator taking him over now.

Moving out of the low hedge garden in which they'd been arguing, she stepped into a sculpted maze that had been created out of lattice walls taller than Jacob. Along the edges of the winding gravel paths were a variety of whimsical ground flowers. Occasionally an oval window opening allowed her to get a better view of the other paths. Otherwise, the walls were solidly covered by lush vines coated with dark, shiny leaves and white trumpet-shaped blooms as wide as her hand.

As she turned a corner and moved out of view, he followed her with those unhurried steps, his booted feet crunching the gravel.

For many years, she'd been able to transform into the winged gargoyle creature that proved her Fae blood. Each time she did that, the Fae magic had stirred within her soul, but she hadn't recognized its potential. It had been like starlight she could see, but too far out of her reach to comprehend its true essence, the heat and power signified by that glimmering light.

That had been fine. Dormant Fae power meant that it had never attracted the attention of the purist-minded Vampire Council.

Then things had changed. Jacob had been human, her third-marked servant. She'd illegally turned him to save his life. In doing so, she'd dumped most of her considerable vampire powers into him by accident. The thirty-year-old male, who should have had only a fledgling's grasp of a vampire's strength and speed, had instead acquired the skills of a thousand-year-old one. And Lady Lyssa's Fae powers had started to wake, with wild and unpredictable results.

Such energy had a mind of its own, and a way of pulling the soul into its purpose. As she stayed one turn ahead of him, glimpsing him for a breath each time, that primitive desire kept growing.

At the center of the maze, she found a carved trellis of heavy oak. The archway piece looked like a pair of muscular stallions leaping in opposite directions. The four posts had been driven deep into the ground to stand fast against the pressure of the thick root stalks that twined around them. As the foliage reached the top of the trellis, the vines twisted along wood pieces that created a starburst of symmetrical spokes connecting to the closest set of maze walls. This was the anchor point and birthplace of all the foliage that covered the maze.

When she stopped on the other side of the trellis, she could feel the energy of such a place, a tangle of nature and symbols, the circle, the wheel, the deep rooting into the earth. It unfurled a craving inside of her, and she opened herself to it. It was a part of her, a set of new magical limbs and senses, and she could do remarkable things with them. Her loss of vampire abilities had left her reeling, but she'd been propelled up close and personal into this new galaxy, so much power at her fingertips.

Though she got tired of moving so carefully, when she'd turned the invading vampires into a new arbor for Mason's garden, she'd contacted Keldwyn. While she obviously had a great deal of raw power ready to call, her use of it at this point was far more intuitive than learned. She understood power enough not to be irresponsible about it. But this moment wasn't about being responsible.

Perhaps she was a child who'd not yet mastered running, but she could careen out of control and it would still be thrilling, her blood surging with youthful invincibility. It had been a very long time since she'd felt that way, and having Jacob here with her only spurred it.

She hadn't been surprised that Jacob had taken it upon himself to join the conversation with Keldwyn when he did, to provide a physical show of support before Keldwyn's imperiousness. Even so, she decided it might be time to remind him who held the reins on their relationship. For her own pleasure as much as for the lesson.

He'd halted on the opposite side of the trellis. Now, his gaze locking with hers, he stepped to the right to follow her in a circle around it, a far-more-adult version of ring-around-the-rosy. A bench was built inside of the trellis. In his mind, she saw them both naked on it, her straddling him, holding either side of the trellis as if restrained, yet using it as a bracing point to shove herself down on him. It underscored the point that they were bound together, locked into one purpose, one soul. She answered that challenge with one of her own, no less intense.

With his precognitive ability, Jacob sensed the change before it happened, but her magical reach was greater than his speed. He sprang back, but the roots snaked out from the trellis, cinching around his biceps. They slammed him against the right side of the frame, flush against the crossed oak pieces. Capturing his wrists, they drew his arms up, tightening in swift loops and knots so that he was arched against the wood, making his body an offering to her. Another speared out to loop around his throat, holding it fast. Others wrapped around his legs, all the way up his thighs. The surface of the strong roots was rough enough to cut through the thin denim of his jeans in several places, biting into his flesh, tempting her to taste.

She was still enough of a vampire to savor Jacob's blood. But a servant savored a vampire's blood as well, and she was both, wasn't she? When she'd turned him and lost her vampire powers, she'd been pregnant and nearly defenseless for a short time period. Jacob had redefined being a servant then. He was there to protect and care for her, no matter if that meant he had to reverse their roles. He'd marked her as a full servant.

Though that meant he could delve deeply into her mind, whether she willed it or no, he didn't do that unless she invited him to do so, as she had during her conversation with Keldwyn.

Well, amend that. He didn't do it except when he thought her well-being was more important than her orders. Her presumptuous, delectable servant.

"With all those fine muscles, you might be strong enough to tear loose," she purred. Moving closer, she savored the danger in his vibrant blue eyes. "But Mason does love this trellis, and we've already done quite a bit of damage to his property."

Trailing her fingers down his sternum, she registered the rapid beat of his heart. "Can you submit to me, as you did when I was your vampire Mistress?"

"You've never stopped being my Mistress, my lady." His mouth was taut with a perilous desire that made her tremble low in her belly. "Even when I found you in the forest, your body weak and carrying my son."

No matter the role he played with Keldwyn, now the possessiveness was there in full force, his reminder of the claim he'd put upon her that no other male ever had. It got her even hotter. "There's nothing I won't do for you," he said. "Except let you leave me behind again. You'll have to kill me to do that. You *will* kill me if you do that."

Since she knew it was the truth, it was like a knife twisting hard in her heart, tempering the moment with far more than violent lust and predatory games. That knife was always there, ready to stab her with the likelihood of losing him in the dangerous life they led. But she didn't want to give herself to painful sentiment. She didn't want the softening of his mouth, the compassion in his eyes as he registered her feelings. It wasn't tenderness she craved right now. If things weren't going to go her way in this, she was going to exact a price for it.

He recognized her shift, whether through vampire mind games, his own intuition or the fact they seemed to share the same soul. The softness disappeared into a far more feral expression as he bared sharp fangs at her. Crimson light glinted in his eyes.

"Show me that upper hand, my lady. Do your worst."

He was irresistible, the beautiful layers of muscle, firm skin, blood and bone. The heat of an aroused male. Sliding behind him, she put her knee on the bench. Reaching through the cross pieces, she threaded her hands beneath his T-shirt. She started at his armpits, enjoying the sense of those layers over his rib cage, down to his waist. Because of his stretched position, the jeans had fallen lower so she could tease the bare hip bone. From the very beginning, she'd liked that look and preferred him without underwear. Knowing that, he honored her desire as often as possible. She couldn't see his front, but it was a familiar path, her knuckles following a straight line from his hip bone to the upper thigh, though the line was disrupted by his arousal, the fabric straining.

It made her press her lips together, wanting to taste. She thought about letting her fingers wander over to stroke that engorged organ. Instead, she drew back and changed her target. The leaves brushed her forearms as she found his lower back with both hands. Pressing her thumbs into the shallow valley there, she dropped her grip to his ass, sliding into the loose hold of the jeans to take hold of the firm buttocks and squeeze. His muscles flexed in reaction, tension strumming up his thighs.

"You are the most beautiful man," she murmured. "In my dreams about you, I'm still fully vampire. I have you stretched and chained on a table before me, naked and vulnerable. I've torn into your flesh, devouring you bite by bite as if I'm a ravenous monster. I bathe in your blood, shuddering with desire, and then the blood becomes tendrils like these vines, winding around me, my limbs, my throat, binding me to you . . ."

Rising onto her knees, she reached through higher openings to settle her grip below where the vine collared him. Her fingers teased the strong column of his throat, knowing how erogenous a zone it was for both a vampire and servant. "I drown and shatter at once, dying from the pleasure, the lack of air."

"My lady." His rough voice betrayed a need matching hers.

"You understand the meaning of the dream. We will die together, because we are the same being. The hunger will never abate. Knowing that truth doesn't make me accept putting you in danger any more gracefully, Sir Vagabond."

"Then you know how I feel, my lady. Come be one with me. If I don't get inside you, I'm going to die right here, right now."

It gave her a painful smile, even as her inner muscles contracted eagerly, wanting the same. She slipped off the bench. Despite her urgency, she stepped out far enough that he could watch her as she approached him straight on. The sway of her hips, the tilt of her head and arch of her back were all designed to catch a man's gaze. But she liked the way he looked at her, how he saw those things as part of everything she was, not just the purely sexual being she was right now. Everything she was . . . all of it was for one particular male. For him.

He made no apologies for being in her mind right now. Those fangs were sharp and glistening, his eyes like blue lasers. "Now, my lady," he demanded, his fingers curling in his bindings.

She placed her fingertips on his chest, a tiny pressure. Dug her nails through the thin cotton, and then lower, until she found the hem and raised the shirt. Keeping her upper body away from him, she nevertheless stepped onto his booted feet and pressed her lower body to him, feeling his cock against her belly. Using a tight grip on a handful of his jeans, fingers curved in a belt loop, she rubbed, enjoying the feeling as he growled low in his throat. She dug her nails further into his flesh, pushing the shirt up to the base of his throat. When she put her mouth on his skin, her hair fell down over her shoulder to caress him as the wind blew it against his abdomen.

Tell me how you will fuck me, Jacob.

Deep . . . hard . . . I want to claim you to the point of blood and pain. I want to push you far beyond that, give you so much pleasure it takes you into a place beyond fear. I can smell how wet you are. Your cunt is dripping for me. I want it.

She bit him hard enough to leave marks, tasting the salt of his flesh. In her Fae form, she not only had fangs but also talons that could tear his flesh. They had, in the past. She'd licked away the blood as the wounds healed, as he quivered beneath her, as his cock spurted inside of her. Though he was not a natural submissive, he served her and so understood the way of it, an instinct that could command his body when she desired it.

She teased him further, bending her knees for a sinuous dance against him, dragging her breasts over his abdomen, then lower, pressing aroused nipples against what was beneath the denim. Shifting her hold, she fished out the switchblade he kept in his front pocket, caressing the impressive organ within tempting distance of the weapon. As she flipped open the blade and used it to cut the T-shirt away from him, he followed her every move with a man's lust and a warrior's alertness, a thrilling combination. She recognized the stillness that held him now. He was done playing. He was waiting for opportunity, and it only excited her more.

Tearing the rest of the cotton away, she attacked his flesh anew, keeping her head tucked beneath his jaw as she tasted, bit, licked. When she was a vampire, she'd given him the second mark around his nipple, and though the scar was no longer there, the memory was, such that he always shuddered hard when she mouthed him there. Then she went back down, sinking to her knees to press her mouth over the brand above his hip bone, dragging on the waistband to pull the jeans even lower. The brand was a cross, a symbol of faith she'd placed there herself.

"Take off your clothes, Lyssa. Let me see you."

He did that sometimes, called her familiar, always in deeply intimate moments like this. It was an indicator of the unpredictable nature of their relationship, the exchanges of power, determining who would surrender and when the next battle would be. She wanted him to see her. Restrained as he was, she could torture him to madness with the way she unbuttoned her blouse, letting it fall open to reveal the cream-colored bra, which pushed up her small breasts. The cups were low enough to expose the areolas. The blue color of his eyes was black in the darkness of their shared desire. As she shrugged out of the blouse and released the bra, her nipples got even tighter, bared to his gaze.

Then she slid out of the slacks, taking the matching panties with them. He tilted his head, as much as his restraint would allow, and focused on them, compelling her to bring them up to his face. He inhaled the scent, the tip of his tongue darting forth to register how her arousal had soaked the crotch.

"All for you," she whispered. "You can merely look at me, and my body readies itself."

"My lady," he said again, and this time instead of an honorific, he was saying it as it was meant. *My* lady. His love, his heart. His temptress, his tormenter.

It was when he combined everything that way, engaging her heart, mind, body and soul, that she was most vulnerable to him, most off her guard. So she wasn't ready when, in a flash of movement, he pulled free of the vines on his left arm, breaking their hold with a screech of splintered wood from Mason's trellis. That arm banded around her waist, yanked her body fully to him, high enough that her pussy pressed against the hard ridges of his abdomen. Her knees landed against the openings of the trellis, finding a desperate brace as he sank his fangs into her throat.

She cried out at the pleasure and agony of it, because he always seemed to know just how gentle or not she needed him to be. He bit down like he was an animal taking her flesh, drinking deep out of that frantically pounding artery. The flow was so thick that some escaped in a heated trickle over her collar bone, flowing down to her breast.

Let me go, my lady. Let me have the ability to pleasure you fully.

Perhaps I like my vampire like this. A partially caged beast, proving his ferocity and passion to me while still under my control.

As he swallowed her blood, a throaty chuckle vibrated against her flesh. *Then put my cock inside your needy pussy, my lady. I'll prove what a wild beast can do for you.*

He refused to relinquish his hold on her throat, so she had to work her hands down between them blindly to open his jeans, but she used his banded arm around her back for leverage. When he sprang hot and hard into her hands, she caressed and squeezed him, his pre-cum slippery on her palm.

Jacob . . . She was getting lightheaded, but she didn't want him to stop.

Though he'd inherited her abilities, he was still a very young vampire, capable of being goaded into full bloodlust. Moments like these could be particularly dangerous for them, because everything disappeared but this. She knew she would fully surrender to his ferocity, let him drain her, because she would give him everything. There was a destructive part of her that no longer feared death, only losing those few, precious things that meant the most to her. And yet it was when she was most careless of her life that his protective instincts overcame his savagery, his yin to her yang.

Because of the powers she'd transferred to him, it was as if there was an essence of her will that he could grasp, to help call himself back. Which might explain why she had less will with him than she'd ever had with a servant—he'd taken some of it from her. Of course, she knew that wasn't the whole truth of it, but she wasn't going to give him the satisfaction of admitting it. Giving him her life was one thing. Female pride was another.

Lean back, my lady. Now. His fangs eased, a split second, and she pulled free. Lifting his free arm, he took firm hold of the trellis, a self-restraint. His fingers were trembling, his eyes flickering with that red glow. Though he made a noise of protest, a warning, she reached toward that hand, molded her slim fingers over his. She loosened his grip, turned it so they were palm to palm. Slowly, their fingers tangled as his heart rate modulated and his eyes came back to blue. The vines slipped away so he was fully free, and his other arm came around her hips, giving her support again. Moving to the center of the trellis, he sank down on the bench with her straddling him. She was fully naked, while his jeans were raked to his thighs, the tatters of his shirt barely on his shoulders. She moaned as he sank deep inside of her. Watching his face, she saw his jaw tighten in a similar reaction of pleasure and fierce need.

Close your eyes, Jacob. Lean forward and lick the rest of the blood away. Slow, easy.

She had to close her eyes when he did it. Then she began to move, a gradual rise and fall, aided by the constriction of his arm over her hips. When he suckled the blood away, his powerful body trembled, bloodlust warring with his love for her, his ever present need to care for her. She knew which would win. In a thousand years, she'd never trusted anyone the way she trusted Jacob Green. If the day ever came that he did kill her, it would be because she'd offered her life to him freely, knowing it was meant to be.

I love you, my lady.

Before she could reply, he lifted his head and brought her mouth to his. She tasted herself as he caught her in the demanding kiss, channeling the bloodlust into something else entirely. He thrust up deep into her channel, as he'd promised. Her fingers pressed into the cuts left by the vines in his throat, his biceps, and he let out that feral growl again.

Love your cunt . . . could fuck you forever.

Male need taking over, finesse gone. She threw her head back, hair lashing her buttocks and his knees as he dipped his head and covered her nipple, sucking it in, scoring it with fangs, a sensual threat. When she clamped down on him, he thrust even more violently into her, her slim body banded in the restraint of his arms. Slipping her legs out from their folded position, she locked them around his hips and dropped to a deeper angle of penetration, one that increased her sounds of need. He gripped her ass, fingers bruising, pushing her down on him, again and again. The fire in her belly expanded, the orgasm coming, driving up from their joining.

Come for me, my lady. Make me come . . .

She would let him give the order this time, because it matched her own desire. Her pussy was already spasming, and as she gave herself to it, the long, low cry that split from her throat grew higher, more frenetic. She held him fiercely, determined to have her way as well.

Come, Jacob. Come for your Mistress.

His thighs were hard columns, his booted feet pressed into the earth beneath them. As the earth responded to their magic, the energy they raised, she twined it around them, made it part of their shared orgasm, driving them even higher. The shiny leaves became even shinier, the moon sliver whiter. The ocean pounded louder in the distance, and the stars seemed closer. The whole world was connected to this magic. She rode the wave of it with him, twisting, turning, lost in the pleasure of it, screaming as he spurted inside of her, his seed bathing her cervix, teasing her over another pinnacle. Though she already had her arms wrapped around his shoulders, she pressed her face against his skull and held him even closer, reveling in the equal lock his body had on her, all that need and desire culminating in one moment that shattered them both.

~

When the world reoriented itself, he nuzzled her throat. "You shouldn't push me that way, my lady."

Stroking the reddish-brown strands of hair back from his strong face, she gathered it on his shoulders with one hand and tugged, giving him a feline smile. He sighed. "I know. I might as well tell you not to breathe."

He rose, still holding her by the waist, but let her feet touch the ground when he'd moved the necessary several steps to her clothes. Hitching up his jeans, he refastened them, then picked up her blouse, slacks and underwear. "Mason and Jessica are coming," he said as he helped her dress. He left the slacks half zipped to hold them on her hips as he buttoned her blouse and then tucked in the tails for her, his hands caressing her curves as he did so.

"Is that why you have a sudden urge to make sure I'm dressed?" She gave him an arch look. "You're not wearing a shirt."

"Someone destroyed it, so you'll just have to deal with Jessica ogling my manly chest. I think it's best we don't test that bloodlust problem of mine too much around Mason."

She let out a ladylike snort. "Males are so predictable."

"Perhaps, but not as much as women like to think we are." Mason emerged from the darkness. As Jacob had sensed, Jessica was with him. Her gaze flickered over Jacob carefully, but despite what he'd said, he knew she was gauging things other than his half-dressed state. The scent of blood and violent sex lingered in the area, and both of those things would make her wary. Though she'd been around Jacob enough to be more at ease with him, Mason's human servant was always wary around vampires other than her Master.

It was understandable, since she'd spent five years as the second-marked servant of a vampire who'd tortured her in ways that should have destroyed her mind, and nearly did. Only Mason's third-marking of her, and the bond that had formed between them, had salvaged what was left. It hadn't taken Jacob long to understand the vampire's devotion to his fragile servant. She had the courage and endurance of a whole Spartan legion, and the fact that she depended on Mason's strength and love to manage in the vampire world didn't diminish that accomplishment one bit. If anything, it just made the powerful vampire all the more dedicated to her.

It was like that with a remarkable woman. Jacob glanced at Lyssa. Sometimes a man would destroy the universe to win one smile from her. Fortunately, tonight such drastic measures weren't needed. The third member of Jess and Mason's party was more than capable of winning smiles, and making Jess a little more relaxed. Having an armful of toddler could do that.

Kane had a passion for female hair. Jessica had been growing hers out, to Mason's immense pleasure, and the chestnut brown locks were past her shoulders, long enough for Kane to secure an iron grip. He looked cranky, which didn't bode well for the universe after all. The second he registered Lyssa's presence, his piercing wail split the air, loud enough to spook Mason's horses on the other side of the estate.

Hungry, Jessica mouthed with a half smile.

"Tyrant," Jacob informed his son. He took the child from Jessica to pass him to Lyssa since his lady, even without her full vampire powers, still made Jess more uneasy than Jacob. Kane flailed, screwing up his face to scream some more. "Yeah, yeah, I know. I'm not the one you want right now. Little Judas."

"He's gnawed on me a couple times, but I'm obviously not to his liking," Jessica said with a half smile. "He didn't want more of the blood mix, so I figured he was ready for a meal fresh from his mother."

Lyssa nodded. They'd moved out of the maze but there were several benches placed among the landscaping. Sinking down on one of them, she turned away, enough to cloak herself in the shadows as she slipped off the blouse and removed the bra again. Usually she wore darker colors, since she'd learned that wearing pale colors when nursing a child on blood was inadvisable.

With Lyssa being Fae and a vampire of reduced capacity, they hadn't been sure if her blood could nourish Kane. Often a vampire child with a non-vampire mother had to be nursed on a mix of the father's blood with human formula, so Lord Brian had shown them how to measure that out, reinforced with a vitamin elixir. Fortunately, it appeared both her blood and the blood mix were acceptable to Kane. However, as he'd just demonstrated, his preference could vary, but the baby was thriving, the most important thing to all of them. When possible, born vampires were nursed far beyond their human counterparts, until they reached the age of three. It seemed to help their mental and physical development.

Jacob placed the child in her arms so Kane could sink his tiny, kittenlike fangs into the curve just above the nipple, drawing on the veins there. After Lyssa settled him, she made sure her pale skin was still mostly in shadow. Despite her teasing, she didn't see any reason to provoke Jacob's territorial instincts around Mason. As an alpha, he'd had them long before he was a vampire, and that bloodlust was still detectable, though on low simmer.

She glanced toward him. Whether or not he'd read that from her mind, he was giving her that lazy, heavy-lidded look that made her think of what they'd just shared. When Kane bit into her breast, innocently enough, the stimulation reminded her of Jacob biting her just below, around the nipple itself. A shudder went through her, dual reaction of mother and lover. Jacob's lips curved in that dangerous smile. He'd folded her blouse and the bra, putting them next to her, though she'd noted how he rubbed his thumb over the heat that lingered in one of the soft cups.

The way he flipped so easily between lover and father was irresistibly sexy. When Kane let a trickle escape, Jacob anticipated him, using his ruined T-shirt to cradle the breast and blot away the escaped blood so it couldn't drip onto her slacks. "No table manners at all," he clucked reprovingly.

Mason had turned tactfully away, leaning against the corner post of the lattice maze. As he drew Jessica against his front so they could look out toward the ocean, Lyssa heard him murmur to his servant.

"I'm thinking I might replace the veranda with a saltwater pond. Pipe the water in from the ocean. It would be like having a wave pool in the backyard. Would you like that, *habiba*?"

"You know I would," Jessica replied softly, the sweep of his thumb along the outside of her right breast obviously distracting her, if the way she was biting her bottom lip and lifting her chin, a response to arousal, were any indication. Seeing it, Mason's tone became huskier.

"I like the idea of looking out the window just before dusk, seeing you disrobe and stroke through the water, your beautiful body tempting me to come out once the sun sets."

"Good idea. The pond," Jacob remarked. "Can't blow up a body of water. Well, you can, but it doesn't require as much reconstruction. Not like a marble veranda."

Jessica sent him an amused look, even as Mason bared fangs in his general direction. Jacob shot Lyssa a breathtaking grin. Touching Kane's head with a father's tenderness, he knelt to place a kiss on her breast, right above the baby's mouth, a brush of contact. Then he sat back on his heels to watch them both. If the world stopped turning, Lyssa knew she would be content, locked forever in a moment like this. Such things never lasted long enough.

"I've already talked to my pilot. We can leave in the morning if you wish." When Mason glanced toward her, he shrugged. "I assume I'm going with you. You'll need as much help as possible if you're going into the Fae world."

She rolled her eyes. "Goddess save me from honorable men who think a woman can't do anything by herself. I've barely agreed to let Jacob go with me. I appreciate the offer, Mason, but I won't give you an excuse to dodge Council meetings."

"Excellent attempt to provoke my temper and change the subject. But I know you too well." He gave a half chuckle. As he did, he dipped his head to tease Jessica's throat with tongue and fangs. Her breath whispered out, thready, then sucked back in on a quick catch. Lyssa noted then that he'd made his own use of the shadows. He'd apparently commanded her to slide her fingers beneath the short gauzy skirt she was wearing and was idly watching her play with herself through the thin cloth. When it came to sex, male vampires were more than capable of multitasking. Lyssa could smell Jess's unique scent on the wind. So could Jacob. It stirred his blood, despite the fact he'd spilled himself only moments earlier in Lyssa.

Damn vampire appetites. His rueful look gave her a quick flash of amusement.

"You need backup, my lady," Mason added.

"I've agreed to Jacob's going. You will not be going with me, Mason. That's final."

"You think I'm a child you can order around?" Those amber eyes glinted.

"Hardly. You're the vampire we're trusting with our son while we're gone."

That stopped whatever he was about to say and stilled Jessica, both of them forgetting modesty as they looked toward her in surprise. When Lyssa freed a now-sleepy Kane from her breast, Jacob leaned forward, blocking the view. He teased the twin punctures closed with his mouth and gave the silken skin a more personal cleaning. It caused a catch in her throat, a sound much like Jessica had made, masturbating herself for Mason's pleasure.

When Jacob raised his face, the hair over his forehead brushed her lips. She gazed at him with a mixture of tender exasperation and desire. *Male vampires and their insatiable needs, indeed. You feed off of one another. Behave, so I can have this conversation with Mason.*

Offering an unrepentant look, he dried the area with his T-shirt and slipped her bra back on to her body. Since he had to lean into her to fasten it in the back, she let her lips touch his shoulder. When she shrugged back into her blouse, he took a far quieter Kane from her arms, offering his free hand to help her rise. Lyssa faced Mason. "You know better than anyone what happens to a vampire child not protected in our world."

Shadows crossed the male vampire's gaze. "I was fortunate in your patronage, my lady." The stiffness to his tone came from the pain of memory.

"I will always wish you'd had it much earlier." The regret was there, but then she arched a brow, giving him her usual haughty look. "You wouldn't have turned out so surly and difficult."

"Yes. Having your gentle nature and flexibility in my life earlier would have been such a great influence on me." He snorted.

Lyssa almost smiled, but then her gaze shifted to Jess. "Kane is very fond of you already. I know you will protect him with your life if needed."

"Yes, my lady." The girl seemed overcome by the vote of confidence, but when she looked toward the baby, her expression eased. "He's so stubborn and fierce, he could fight off enemies all by himself."

"With his lungs alone," Mason noted. "She's already playing tag with him, building up his strength. He'll be walking more than crawling in no time. He doesn't like not being able to catch her."

"Predator instinct." Jacob chuckled. "As inevitable as rain."

"Indeed." His lady slanted him an ironic glance, even as her fingers settled on the bite mark at her throat, drawing his attention to that sensual reminder. For all that she teased him about his appetites, Jacob knew she was a master . . . or mistress, as it were, at keeping those appetites gnawing. He knew that was the way she liked it.

Mason sighed. "You outmaneuvered me. As capable as Jacob is, I do wish you had more reinforcements. However . . ." He offered a more formal bow. "I am deeply honored. Your son shall be safe with us."

"Thank you." Lyssa reached out, pressed his hand. "Don't worry about us. Based on what Brian has said, even an army of vampires couldn't defeat the magic of a handful of Fae. Our greatest weapon will be our wits. That's one weapon I wield fairly well without reinforcement."

"With a skill that makes a man's blood run cold," Mason acknowledged. But as he briefly met Jacob's gaze, Jacob saw his own concerns reflected there. "You better be back before our next Council meeting," Mason said lightly. "Else we'll have to take Kane along. He's likely to stage a coup to overrun Council."

"Do your own dirty work." Lyssa gave him a fond look, then returned her attention to her son. He leaned backward over Jacob's arm to grab a strand of her hair that the breeze had carried over his tender head. "We leave tomorrow night. If all goes well, we should be back before that next meeting."

MANY in the vampire world thought Lady Lyssa was aloof, a woman hard to read. She was, but Jacob knew exactly what saying good-bye to their child cost her. The following night, he drew Mason and Jessica away while she took one last stroll with Kane in her arms. They went to a statuary garden on the northwest side of the estate. All the sculptures were creatures, and Kane had a typical toddler's passion for animals. When Lyssa put him on a miniature horse, he was smiling up at her, waving his arms and holding a strand of her dark hair in either hand as if they were the horse's reins. Jacob was close enough to see her, though he was also in her mind. He knew she wouldn't mind him there for this. He'd said his good-bye to Kane as well, but Kane had a unique sense of the two of them, even when only one was present, and they'd take every moment they could with him before they had to go.

"You be very good for Lord Mason and Jessica," his lady murmured, stroking his back and balancing him so he wouldn't topple off the horse. "They will teach you many wonderful things and take excellent care of you."

She hesitated then. When a wave of emotion surged forth, Jacob almost went to her. She battled it back down, not wanting Kane to sense it, of course, but Jacob knew her eyes were wet. She'd lived through a lot of things, including the loss of another child, centuries ago. She knew better than anyone that every day could be the last, that this journey might be one from which they wouldn't return. It wasn't a dramatic observation; just the way their lives were. Usually she shut herself down to handle such realities. However, staring into the face of the child that was one half of herself, who expected she'd always be there because that was the oblivious faith the young had, she lost a grip on those shields. Leaning down, she kissed his head, pressing her lips hard to his fine cap of hair, her own curtaining him as she gave him her touch, her scent.

"Go to her," Jacob said to Jess. "She'll want to leave him playing there, so he won't see us go."

The girl nodded, moved down the slope. Jacob sensed Mason at his shoulder.

"You know," the older vampire said. "My relationship with Jessica is . . . complicated. Far beyond the rules of the Vampire Council—fuck all of them."

Jacob bared his fangs in a feral grin, appreciating Mason even as his eyes remained on his lady. "However," Mason continued, "if prizes were going to be handed out for the most complex and hard-to-understand vampire-servant relationship, you and Lyssa would win that ribbon hands down. You know that."

"What? She has vampire blood, but she's not technically a vampire anymore. And I used to be human, and should have a fledgling's skills, but I have hers instead. What's complicated about that?" Jacob shot him a wry look.

"And she's your fully marked servant."

"I fully marked her. She's not my servant."

"Jacob." Mason drew the younger man's attention with the serious note. "You know how I feel about Lyssa. It would take far more than the loss of her vampire powers to make me view Lady Elyssa Ameratsu Yamato Wentworth as anything less than the dangerous force of nature she can be. I don't mean any disrespect to her."

"I know." Jacob shifted. "But it's not merely sentiment, Mason. You've seen her come out of the forest in her Fae form, transition back to human, so to speak. And while I hope your gaze has not lingered too long before she puts on her robe, I'm sure you've noticed it. She doesn't have a servant's mark. But I still have mine."

All third-marked servants bore a skin mark, a spontaneous occurrence when the final serum was administered. Jacob, whose vampire transition should have eliminated his full-servant mark, still bore the silver fossil-like serpent imprint up the line of his spine. Some things were beyond the ken of man or vampire, but Mason knew that in everything he was or did, Jacob saw himself as Lyssa's servant. Her protector, her lover, whatever she needed.

While Jacob observed that belief privately as well as publicly, there was a practical purpose for the public side. Only three vampires and their trusted servants—Mason and Jess among them—knew that Lyssa had lost her vampire abilities from that turning. That kind of vulnerability was dangerous as hell in their world.

Jacob's background as a trained fighter had helped him gain command of Lyssa's former strengths relatively quickly, though he still had the occasional bout with a fledgling's bloodlust if he got pissed off. However, as much confidence as Mason had in Jacob—those strengths being a formidable combination with his unshakable loyalty and courage—he found the knowledge of Lyssa's own burgeoning Fae skills an additional and considerable reassurance. One could never have too many weapons in the arsenal.

Unfortunately, the Fae Queen's summons meant that Lyssa's growing gifts had opened herself up to dangers from the other side of her family tree.

Mason put his hand on his shoulder. "All I'm trying to say is, she means a great deal to me. If there's anything I can do . . ."

"You'll be the first I call. As well as Gideon. We'll come back, Mason. Never underestimate her."

"I don't. I never underestimate either one of you."

~

Jacob hoped that was true. He had a great many concerns related to a trip to the Fae world and the things that could go awry, but first they had to find a needle in a haystack. Though finding an actual needle in a haystack was probably easier than locating a dryad in downtown Atlanta.

Lyssa passed most of her time on the plane sleeping, stretched out on the comfortable cushions, her head pillowed on his thigh. She'd spent most of the daylight hours before Jacob and Kane woke talking to Jessica about the child's care, but he knew that wasn't the only reason she sought refuge in oblivion.

They'd slipped away while the baby was occupied with Jessica. His last glimpse of his son was his face screwed up in concentration as Jessica showed him how to press his heels into the concrete horse's sides. Even while dozing, Lyssa kept her hand linked with his, that connecting pressure a reinforcement for both of them. It was the first time since Kane's birth that they'd been away from him. While the blood connection allowed them to locate or communicate with him, he would do better for Jessica and Mason if they didn't use that link too often, like any child being left with trusted guardians for the first time.

When they arrived in Atlanta around eight in the evening, they sent him a warm good "morning" and the emotional equivalent of a hug, but not wanting to distress him, they left it at that.

Elijah Ingram, the majordomo for Lyssa's estate, was guardian for his young grandson John, whose bedtime was ironically 8:30 p.m., shortly after Kane was getting up. As a result, Jacob had told Ingram to leave Lyssa's car at the private airstrip and Jacob would drive them back to the mansion.

They'd visited her Atlanta home a couple times since the Council had rescinded Lyssa's fugitive status. That had occurred just prior to Kane's birth, thanks to the efforts of Lord Brian, Lord Mason and other friends Lyssa had that could influence Council mind-set. While the Council still hadn't decided Lyssa's new status, she had free use of her properties once again. Lord Richard, a friend and territory overlord in her Region, had been designated acting Region Master. He'd made it clear to Council he would concede the role back to Lyssa if and when they decided to restore it to her. Through a communication with Lyssa, he'd also stated he considered her an honored guest in the Region, not bound by the requirements of other subjects under his control.

Given what he knew of Richard's ambitious and sometimes ruthless nature, Jacob was surprised, but he supposed he shouldn't be. His lady inspired loyalty in unexpected places, probably because she was never less than who she was. After greeting the dogs, Lyssa's pack of Irish wolfhounds, they joined Elijah in the kitchen. The fifty-something former chauffeur, whose steady nerves and military skills had landed him in this unlikely role as Lyssa's estate manager, was slicing ham and tomatoes for John's lunch box. As he did that, he briefed them on the mundane estate business that had occurred while they were away. Whiskers, the kitten Jacob had rescued from the inner workings of Lyssa's Mercedes and that John had adopted, was perched on top of the refrigerator, watching the food preparations keenly. "You jump from there onto this cutting board, and I'm going to dice up cat for lunch," Ingram promised. Then he grunted, put aside the knife.

"That reminds me. Your mail's all on your desk, but I thought you'd want to see this one pretty soon after you arrived."

Jacob straddled the stool behind her, so he saw the Council seal on the envelope Elijah offered. As she broke the seal and scanned the contents, her sudden tension tightened screws in his chest. She handed it over to Jacob, her gaze unreadable.

Dropping past the bullshit preamble, Jacob reread the key paragraphs twice.

It has come to our attention that you require assistance in the protection of your newborn son. As you know, vampire infants are rare in our world and the son of our queen would be of particular significance. A strong vampire parent is needed to safeguard that life. Your former servant is still a fledgling, and while you have demonstrated some capabilities, a Fae and a fledgling are not the appropriate primary guardian for a vampire child.

No mention of her vampire blood at all. Someone had found out about the loss of her vampire powers and let it slip to Council. It wouldn't be Brian, Mason or Debra, he was sure, which left him clueless as to how it had been discovered. He met her gaze, then returned to the letter.

You are therefore required to appear before Council at its next scheduled meeting, where this matter will be determined. In light of your former position among us, we will of course consider your input in this matter, but we know you will submit to our guidance for what is best for your child. You may be assured you will still have a presence in his life, particularly if you accept relocating to a more closely supervised location. It may be necessary for your fledgling servant to serve a time in the household of another Region Master or overlord, as is our custom for accommodating newly made vampires.

As always, we wish you well—

She'd been on the run from the Council before, but at a time when the governing body had been in disarray and not greatly inclined to pursue them. Plus, Kane had been protected inside her body. Being fugitives with a vampire child barely out of his infancy would be entirely different.

At Lyssa's nod, he passed it to Elijah, knowing the majordomo should be in the loop. "Mason's not on the letterhead yet. I expect that's a good thing."

It was a reminder to them both that the newest member of the Council was a strong ally. But it wasn't enough. Mason was already beholdened to Council for their tolerance of Jessica, who'd committed the usually unpardonable crime of killing her previous vampire master. While Jacob suspected the male vampire and his brave servant wouldn't give a rat's ass about that if they knew Lyssa was being threatened, Lyssa wouldn't want to repay Mason's loyalty by putting him in the same position they faced if she could help it.

The flicker in her eyes, a subtle gesture, told him he had permission to see what way her mind was going. Her Fae powers were impressive and growing, but she didn't yet have a predictable command of them. If she couldn't disprove the leak that she'd lost her vampire powers, then they didn't have a lot of options, not in the short term. She knew they couldn't risk coming before Council where they'd be outnumbered. They might indeed succeed in taking Kane, and she wouldn't risk that.

"So instead of going in a more enlightened direction, they've decided to tighten the reins."

"We shouldn't be surprised," she said. "Mason implied as much, based on the documents he's been reviewing on recent Council decisions. There was the mess involving Stephen's betrayal of Council, and Lady Barbra's suspected involvement in it."

"His next Council meeting will be Mason's first as a full member." Though Jacob offered it as a point in their favor, it didn't ease the pale strain in her face.

"He can't fight the entire Council. Call him. Tell him if we're delayed, he should not take Kane to that meeting under any circumstances. Provisions should be made . . ."

"I'll take care of it, my lady." Jacob nodded firmly. "They won't get near him."

Her fingers were white on the table edge. Elijah looked between them. "Can you postpone your trip to this Otherworld?"

"No." Lyssa tightened her jaw. "Lord Keldwyn made it clear that they will come looking for us. That would be just as dangerous for Kane. Perhaps more so."

"Trapped between two crappy choices." The majordomo passed a ham sandwich to Lyssa. "Sounds like a normal week for you two."

If the Council had remained in the dark about her loss of vampire powers, Mason would have been able to do what he'd intended. Recommend she be reinstated in an advisory capacity to the Council, where they could honor and benefit from her wisdom and strength, as they had for decades. Jacob knew she'd nursed that quiet hope herself, even though she hadn't put as much faith in it as he and Mason had. Still, feeling anger on her behalf, he reached out, touched her hand.

"Power is the true currency with vampires." She lifted a shoulder. "I'll pen a neutral response to this before we embark on our quest tomorrow. A great many things may change before that part of things is over. It's best not to commit to a course of action until then." She glanced at Ingram. "Were you able to work on the project we called about?"

"Yes, John helped. No surprise that the boy's actually much better than his grandpa on the computer." Ingram wiped his hands on a towel and slid a folder to her. "I spoke to the visitors' center in Atlanta, a couple historic societies, even some of the garden clubs. While they had nothing definite, they gave us some leads and we drove around a bit, took some pictures. John also helped me put some links to satellite photos in the file that might be likely spots for what you're seeking." Taking a computer tablet out of the kitchen desk, he laid it at her elbow.

"Our needle in a haystack?" Jacob asked. "The dryad in a tree?"

"We'll see." She sighed, turning on the screen. "We'll study these, and head out to look ourselves tomorrow night. After you've had your vampire beauty sleep."

"That's right. Us young vamps need more rest than you old—"

Jacob was quick enough to have his hand off the butcher block before the knife stabbed into the wood where it had rested. Fingers flexing on the blade, she lifted an eyebrow, her jade eyes gleaming. "Don't get too confident, fledgling. Age and experience are more than capable of taking you down a peg or two."

He grinned, glad to see the flash of temper in her gaze. "I never forget, my lady."

Ingram cleared his throat. "I'd forgotten vampire flirting is a little more extreme. Or perhaps that's just the two of you," he added dryly. Carefully retrieving the knife, he began slicing again.

~

Later that night, after taking care of some other more mundane business for her, Jacob went looking for his lady. From the way she'd looked after digesting that note, he knew she'd be walking in her rose garden, and that was where he found her.

Ingram had taken good care of the plants, keeping tabs on the landscaping crew who maintained them. Like Jacob, he understood the significance of the spot to her. For loving and impregnating a vampire, Lyssa's father, a Fae lord even more powerful than Keldwyn, had been turned into a rose bush. He was then planted in the desert to wither and die. That had all happened a thousand years ago, before Lyssa was born. When she'd been hiding in the mountains and still carrying Kane, Keldwyn had given her an enchanted rose that came from her father's transmuted form. It was now suspended under glass in her bedroom here, but she'd known the story long before she'd received the rose, and so had always cultivated exotic, delicate roses in her father's honor.

She'd avoided going to the nursery entirely, and he knew it wasn't because she missed Kane. As he watched her from the doorway of the solarium, he could see it happening. She was shedding that part of herself. It was in how she walked through her rose garden in that slow, methodical way, her back straightening, chin lifting unconsciously. She was drawing her shields around herself, repatching any armor that the past months had softened or dented. She was becoming Queen of the Far East Clan again, right before his eyes. And Jacob knew what that required from him.

Though some might call her months as a fugitive in the Appalachians a hardship, once they'd been reunited there, neither of them had viewed it that way. Not long after they'd met, he remembered a vulnerable moment where she'd spoken of her longing to simply exist. Not as a queen, but as a creature of the forest, nothing required of her but to be. As such, in those forest months, they had been merely Lyssa and Jacob, one's strengths filling in for the other's weaknesses, whenever needed, so that they could survive and be together.

Even after they'd returned to Atlanta, with the limbo state of the Council not being sure what to do with her, they'd been able to hold on to that, unmolested by vampire affairs. Until the attack on Mason's estate had drawn the attention of the Fae queen. While he was sad to see those times about to disappear, perhaps he was cut out of the same fabric as she was, because it was a passing moment. He could feel himself changing as well, aligning back to the concentrated focus of a servant. Not just guardian and lover, but the being whose role was anticipating her needs at all levels. The knight and samurai that were his past, but also part of his present, were resurrecting, getting ready to defend and care for his liege lady.

His somber thoughts were broken by a smile at her entourage. Bran, her Irish wolfhound, stalked so close to her side that her hand rested with relaxed ease on his wiry head. Whiskers trailed in their wake, making occasional spectacular leaps at Bran's tail as it swayed with his stately stalk. Now that Ingram and John lived on Lyssa's property, Bran had developed a tolerance pact with the cat, ignoring her most of the time. However, Mr. Ingram was careful to keep the feline inside when Bran's siblings were running loose on the estate.

"Because what one dog will do to a cat is a different matter from what a pack will do," the fifty-something majordomo had observed earlier.

"A universal truth," Lyssa murmured. That moment had been the beginning of her mood shift.

At dusk on the following day, they'd start seeking the whereabouts of a dryad trapped somewhere among the concrete, glass and asphalt of downtown Atlanta. But tonight, Jacob watched his lady draw strength from the brown earth beneath her bare feet. When she at last stopped in the inner circle of her garden, where the plants were oldest, those that bloomed with the sweetest, deepest fragrance, she lowered herself to the ground gracefully, sitting on one hip. She wore one of the older skirts she used for her gardening, an oversized Renaissance shirt loose over it. The shirt had belonged to Rex, her former husband. An unsettling choice, but Jacob understood that as well. Another reminder of what she had to become again, from a time when she'd had to be more guarded than she'd ever been, her emotions locked behind a fortress to protect what she held dear.

In the kitchen with Ingram, he'd seen the sharp, calculating intelligence she'd always possessed. But he also had a window to the scars that had lingered inside her from the events of the past couple of years, things those white knuckles on the table had betrayed.

When he'd met her, his lady's confidence had been unshakable. Even now, he'd put his money on her against the intelligence or brutality of most opponents. However, something had shifted. She was more unsure of herself, afraid of the consequences of her actions. Her irritation with that, with her inability to overcome two years' worth of traumatic events to reclaim that steady core of certainty, was severe. She viewed it as a liability to her, to him and to their son. It made her savagely angry with herself. So when it became unbearable, she paced, hoping to find what he knew only time and other, as yet unknowable factors, could bring back to her.

What he could give her was his unshakable faith that it would happen. His confidence could be hers. Feeling her frustration getting beyond what he could bear to let her handle alone, he moved into the garden, came to her. As he sank to his heels, he slid his arms around her, and was glad when she laid her head on his biceps, though her hands stayed compressed in her lap. "I hate this shirt," he said. Nudging her head to the side, he gave her the sharp edge of his fangs, underscoring how fervently he felt about it. She shivered in his arms, a sweet coil of desire moving through her. She wasn't wearing a bra beneath the loose shirt and he cupped her breasts, the peaks pressing into his palms. "I'm going to make it disappear one day, I swear to God."

"You'd never destroy it." She drew in a breath as he punctured her skin, drawing out a sweet, small drop of blood, teasing the artery with his tongue. "You understand too well why I keep it."

"I wish there was no reason for you to keep it." She was silent at that, and he changed tactics. He hummed against her skin, until her shoulders relaxed somewhat. "What is that?" she asked.

"'Stand by Me,' by Ben E. King. Surely you've heard it." He told her the words, spoke the opening lyrics. How he'd stand by her when the night came, when all was dark. Her lips curved.

"Actually, since you're a vampire, it would *have* to be dark. So I am not overly impressed."

He chuckled, pressed a kiss to her temple. "If the world crumbles, I'll be here, my lady."

"I know." She hooked her hands over his forearm. "Would Keldwyn lie about the time distortion?"

"According to lore, the Fae don't lie. They're master word manipulators. Either way, we're faced with an impossible choice, just as you said."

She sighed. "It begins again, Jacob. We must be queen and servant once more."

"Yes, my lady. Though you are always my Mistress. That never changes. Only the face of it does."

He knew something else about her that no one else did, except perhaps Mason. A thousand years gave her great wisdom, great strength. But it was also a long, long time to live. A long, long time to be a queen and endure loss and betrayal, to see death and hate resurrecting in her life, challenging her over and over again. Thomas, her former servant, believed Jacob had come to her in three different lifetimes, whenever she was in greatest need of him. There were times Jacob thought the Delilah virus she'd barely survived had only been the catalyst of that rebirth, that the true danger to her was the unbearable weight of time.

Other than the Delilah virus, the Ennui, a wasting and self-destructive apathy, was the only disease that could impact vampires. When they met, she'd dismissed the idea that Ennui would ever affect her. *"I've seen things, Jacob. I've met Chinese dragons whose whiskers feel like feathers when they brush them across your face. I've seen wars begin and end. Seen people do so many things I didn't expect, and many things I did expect, and dreaded. That is why the Ennui does not affect me . . . Life can be intensely amazing, or quietly desperate, as Thoreau said. If you wake each day with a genuine awareness which allows you to appreciate everything as if you were seeing it for the very first time . . . or the last."*

But he also knew such a mental illness could hit when a person's defenses were low, and she'd taken so many emotional blows these past few years . . .

You are worrying for me. You know I worry about nothing when you are at my side.

"Yes, my lady." He smiled against her skin. "Apparently, you don't need a vampire's ability to be able to read my mind."

"You rarely close your mind to me. Though you could do that anytime you wished now, as a vampire."

"But never as your servant."

"I think we are the most confusing relationship the vampire world has ever experienced. Certainly the most confusing one I've ever experienced."

That made him laugh outright, but he nodded toward two rose bushes. Bran lay between them, a look of sufferance on his face as Whiskers occupied the valley between the dog's shoulders in a neat bread loaf shape, purring. "There are other, far more confusing relationships, my lady. The world is a mysterious place."

4

BASED on what Keldwyn had said about the dryad's possible condition when freed, they'd told Ingram that, when they located her, they would be going straight from her tree to the nearest possible Fae portal. However, any hopes that might happen the first night, or even the second, came to naught. On the third night, after they sent their usual mental greeting to Kane upon his rising, and set out at dark to resume their search, Lyssa had only one comment.

"When we finally find this dryad, I never want to see the underbelly of Atlanta again."

Jacob grunted. He was driving tonight, at the wheel of Lyssa's Mercedes. They'd repeatedly gone through all the photos and information that John and Elijah had gathered, but it had narrowed things down little. "Still a needle in a haystack," he said, glancing at the handheld screen his lady was scrolling through.

"Ye of little faith," she said. "While you were getting dressed, I was thinking. Keldwyn did give us some clues. A twenty-year-old tree, downtown, but not in a park. Surrounded by asphalt or concrete."

"Which narrows it down to a few thousand trees. A lot of businesses have trees in their landscaping."

"Only this tree wouldn't fit the landscaping, not necessarily. She was trapped there, so wherever she froze, for lack of better word, it should stand out. And the lore says dryads favored certain types of trees. Oaks, hawthorne, rowan. But this is also a female dryad." She studied the satellite photo in her hand, but her mind wasn't on it. "Son of a bitch."

"My lady?"

She smiled, a bit grimly. "I think Keldwyn gave us another, quite significant clue. Have you ever known him to volunteer a story, like he did about the cradle?"

"You mean when he was being an ass, telling us in a not-so-round-about way that we don't belong together?"

"That was the distraction. Males think with their cocks far too often." She teased his knee with her long fingernails. "I looked up the story. The tree was a willow."

Capturing her hand, he kissed it. "I defer to your estrogen-driven logic, my lady. And please tell me that narrows things down so we won't be forced to endure Atlanta traffic one more night. Otherwise, tomorrow night we're having Ingram drive and we'll put John in a sleeping bag in the limo. We'll call it camping in style."

She consulted the handheld again. "There are about seven businesses and four medians we've not yet visited that might have trees that fit the description. I also have about thirty other possibilities, but those eleven are my first choices."

"Well, read them out then, and we'll see what we can find."

None of the locations held the tree. Though they found several willows, when Lyssa laid her hand upon them, nothing happened other than the disruption of some ant trails along the trunk. They discussed the possibility that she might not have the power Keldwyn had intimated was necessary to release the spirit, but Jacob thought it more likely that they hadn't found the tree. Something didn't feel quite right about the ones they approached. His intuition, or what Lyssa called his psychic sense or his precognition, was attuned to certain situations, and this was one of them. It was like radar, and he could tell practically before they got out of their car each time that the targeted tree wasn't the right one. However, since they'd never freed a dryad before, he didn't dissuade Lyssa from touching each one, just to be sure.

By three-thirty in the morning, they were running out of night, and trees that fit the parameters. "Now I've *really* seen far more of this section of the city than I ever wanted to see," Lyssa commented, sitting on the car hood.

Jacob handed her a coffee he'd bought from a convenience store and propped his hips next to her. The convenience store had a locked entrance and a pickup window, heavy bars on it and the doors. Graffiti was scrawled on the walls of the buildings along the side street where they'd parked. Since their search had been limited to the lower-income area of downtown Atlanta, each night they'd gotten their share of sidelong, calculating looks from human predators, but direct stares from both male vampire and queen had made those gazes avert fairly quickly, the petty criminals recognizing far bigger threats.

"I've got an idea," Jacob said abruptly. "Hell, it's worth a shot."

Straightening, he studied their surroundings, then turned, listening. His nostrils flared, taking in a scent. Lyssa watched that extraordinary stillness settle over him, something that happened when a vampire was focusing all his senses, reaching out far beyond mortal abilities. It not only underscored the fact he was no longer fully human, but how dangerous a predator he could be. She supposed it was one of those vagaries of female nature, that such a thing could stir her loins as well as her blood. Picking up on it instantly, he gave her a sidelong glance. "A fine time to distract me, my lady," he murmured. "And such an image. Right here on the hood?"

"I trust you can enjoy the fantasy and exercise some self-control," she returned evenly. "What are you about?"

"When computers and garden clubs fail, there's a better source of information, the kind that only a former drifter and vampire hunter would know." He held out a hand. "Care to take a little walk with me? A female presence might be useful, even one as intimidating as yours."

"As long as I can bring my coffee."

"I wouldn't be brave enough to pry it from you, my lady."

She gave him a narrow look, but slipped her fingers in the crook of his arm, letting him escort her down the side street. Despite his teasing, he liked seeing her enjoy the coffee. Since becoming more Fae than vampire, she'd been able to actually eat, versus frugal sampling. Though his reserved lady would never be accused of gluttony, she had discovered some things were more addictive than others.

One night, on an earlier trip to Atlanta, she'd made herself sick on a one-pound box of buttercream chocolates she'd polished off herself. She'd been curled up in her favorite chair, reading. With Kane sleeping in a nest of pillows nearby, he'd stretched out on his stomach on the floor with his latest batch of comics, featuring new episodes of The Losers and Iron Man. He'd been close enough that she could rest her dainty feet on his backside, her preferred footstool so she could knead him with her toes like a satisfied feline. Whiskers had curled up in the small of his back, Bran lying to the left of his lady's chair.

Jacob had been vaguely aware of the crinkle of the box liner as she reached for each chocolate, but neither of them had tracked how many she was eating until her fingers felt their way over the foil of an empty box. Later that evening, he'd held her hair back from her face as she threw up. He'd found it a tender experience, no matter how annoyed she'd been with him for feeling that way. After her stomach had settled down, for the next few nights her blood had possessed a delightfully sweet taste.

Since then, she'd been able to exercise a little more control, but he liked seeing her indulge in such pleasures, like her penchant for coffee. Now he squeezed her hand, seeing the corner of her pretty mouth twitch at the memories he was giving her.

He took her down several smaller, less well-paved streets, until they were moving in dank, poorly lit alleys between buildings. There they found Dumpsters, more graffiti, the smell of garbage and unwashed humans. Several of them. Jacob stopped, listening again.

Lyssa realized they were being watched, but stayed silent, knowing he was aware of it as well.

"I'm not going to hurt anyone, I promise." He raised his voice. "I need information. Whether you can help me or not, I'll pay you for your time and honesty."

Silence. Giving Lyssa's hand a squeeze, Jacob moved forward, nodding toward his target on the far side of the Dumpster. She answered with a shift of her body, showing she'd located the other two and had his back.

A tiny growl became a whimper, a dog struggling to make a noise against the hand clamped around the snout. Jacob dropped to a squat from his six-foot height, within a couple paces of the shadowed corner the Dumpster provided. He tented his fingers on the pavement, despite the questionable debris beneath them. "I won't hurt you, ma'am. All right? I'm looking for something, and if you've lived down here awhile, I think you'll know where it is. You probably see things a lot of people don't."

There was the sound of newspaper being crumpled by movement, and Lyssa saw a shift in those shadows. However, she left that one to Jacob, turning to face the two men who stepped out of the gloom on the other side of the Dumpster. They appeared to be about Ingram's age. Both were dressed in worn, layered clothing of dull colors. Their unshaven, thin faces and unkempt hair beneath grimy bill caps, the watchful, not entirely stable expressions, were the signature of the career urban homeless. One held a metal pipe, the other a length of board with nails stuck through the end, a crude mace. "Leave Essie alone," the one with the pipe said in a voice roughened by outdoor living and smoker's cough. "Don't no one ever come down here in the middle of the night who don't mean trouble."

"Well, now someone has," Lyssa said, holding him in her gaze. "We're seeking a tree. A very special tree."

Whatever they'd been expecting, it was obviously not that. As they exchanged a look, she extended the coffee. "I've only taken a little. Would you like the rest?"

"I don't sleep when I drink coffee. Pete'll take it though. He drinks it like a fish." Pipe Guy jerked his head at the other man.

Lyssa stepped closer, aware of Jacob's careful attention on them and Pete's tight hold on that lifted board. However, she stepped inside its range without fear. With or without vampire intuition, she had a pretty good grasp of human motives. She kept her gaze on Pete's, not in challenge, but to show him her intentions. As he warily took the cup from her, she noted the cracked skin on his knuckles.

A creak of metal made her glance right. The woman Jacob had addressed was hobbling into the dim light with the help of a rusty shopping cart. She was much older than the men, perhaps in her seventies, or perhaps the elements were harsher on a woman's thinner skin. Whatever story had put the men on the streets, this woman was here due to mental disorder. It was in the furtive way she looked at them as she muttered to herself and the little dog. Lyssa suspected schizophrenia that had dovetailed into dementia as she got older, exacerbated by poor nutrition. Fear emanated from her, but also a belligerent streak of independence that had her clutching the small mixed-breed dog and jutting her chin at Jacob.

"You won't make me tell you nothing. I know about your kind. What you want, what you see. You won't get into my head."

Jacob had worn a light jacket over his T-shirt and jeans. It covered the nine-millimeter and six-inch army knife he carried, along with a couple very well-sharpened stakes. He was vampire, but he never stopped having the mind-set of a vampire hunter, and he went nowhere with Lyssa where he wasn't armed. But in this instance, he was carrying something more effective, something he'd picked up at the convenience store. Fishing them out of his pockets under Essie's suspicious stare, he extended the chocolate bar and pack of peanut butter crackers, one of his favorite personal combinations before he'd become a vampire. He'd probably intended to have a taste and then offer the rest to Lyssa.

Throughout the centuries, Lyssa had seen unimaginable poverty and deprivation. As awful as it was, homelessness in twenty-first-century Atlanta was nowhere as bad as it could get for a human being. But it still stirred her pity, to see such shadowdwellers, lost to the world through their own madness or other trauma and circumstances they couldn't or wouldn't resolve. The woman she was looking at had been on the streets for a long time. Over that time, she'd probably been raped, beaten, her belongings stolen again and again.

As much as it stirred *her* heart, the man handing the chocolate to Essie had a chivalrous streak a mile wide. Leaving the woman here, in these circumstances, would go against everything Jacob believed was right, but he would do it, because she knew he saw the same thing Lyssa did. This was the only place Essie would live, the only life her madness would let her embrace. This was all she had, the world she knew. But he could give her his respect, and the chance to feel valued.

"Have you seen the tree?" he asked. "It will stand out. It has a special magic, an unexpected beauty."

She'd let the dog down. Jacob stayed in his nonintimidating squat while the terrier mix sniffed suspiciously at his ankles. "Your dog probably enjoys the shade there in summer. It's a willow tree. It looks like a beautiful slender woman, her hair rippling in the breeze."

The woman opened the chocolate, sniffed it, then hid it in one of her pockets. She was continuing to mumble to herself unintelligibly.

"He crazy as Essie," Pipe Guy said to his companion. That one nodded agreeably, propped on his spiked board, sipping the coffee. But Lyssa had seen the gaze they exchanged.

They know what you're talking about, Jacob.

"I saw her," Essie said abruptly. Leaning forward, she seized Jacob by the lapel of his jacket, peering into his face. The two men tensed, but Jacob lifted open hands, showing he wouldn't react with violence.

"So long . . . younger then. More teeth." She cackled, showing a mouth full of decay. Lyssa detected the odor at this distance, and knew Jacob was getting a direct blast. But he didn't move, focused on Essie's expressive face. "She ran. Ran like ballerina, so pretty. So graceful. Dancing through alley. Like girl with red shoes. Fairy tale. Tiny, delicate little butterfly wings, so she moved just over the ground, not very high. They were too small. They couldn't carry her off and away, above their heads. Bad men run after her." She frowned then, her grip tightening. "Why you hurt her? What's wrong with you?"

"It wasn't me," Jacob assured her. "If I was there, I would have helped. I would have protected her."

"She protected herself," Essie declared proudly, straightening. Her dog settled at her ankles, looking hopefully at the peanut butter crackers she still held in one fist. "She turns corner . . . boom, she gone. She gone away. They don't know where she go. Only a tree left in that place. A tree . . . And sometimes I see her in it. She sways in the wind, like you say. A beautiful, beautiful dancer . . . but so sad."

She spread her arms and rocked back and forth on her feet, swaying like the tree. When she overbalanced and Jacob reached out to steady her, she petted his jacket, the way she'd pet her dog. "Pretty, pretty. Bad men come and go. But the tree, she there . . ."

"Where? Essie?" Jacob touched her face lightly, bringing her eyes to his intent ones. "Can you show me where?"

~

Getting Essie going in the right direction took a little time, since she wouldn't go without her shopping cart, and she wouldn't go in a car. Her two companions also insisted on going, marching at Jacob and

Lyssa's back, unlikely body guards for their eccentric friend. However, when Lyssa dropped back to join them, Jacob experienced his usual admiration for how easily his lady interacted with any strata of humanity. Though she had pointed out his intuitive gifts many times, her own natural perceptiveness was unparalleled. Males might respond to her beauty, but when she wished to do so, she could offer a warmth, a genuine interest, that disarmed them entirely.

In no time, Essie's companions were telling her stories of their lives, despite the fact that Pete, having a bad stutter, had let Pipe Guy do his talking up to now. When she placed her hands on their elbows, as if she was letting herself be escorted by them, they were hooked. Disjointed and unlikely as some of the tales they relayed sounded, there were obvious wretched truths interwoven into them. Time and hard living had made the truth more difficult to recall . . . or they wanted it that way, preferring their imaginations.

Meanwhile, Essie kept up a running prattle between herself, her dog, and sometimes threw things at Jacob that didn't seem to require response. Which was good, because after her fairly lucid moment, her current commentary was as cryptic as Sanskrit. Their progress was slow, for sometimes she clung to his arm, then abruptly shoved him away and accused him of trying to take advantage of her. After that, she might wander in circles around her cart for a few moments, shouting incomprehensibly and rummaging through her things. When she wound down, studying him with bewildered eyes, he would gently remind her of the tree, and she would resume their trek with a sense of purpose.

You are cutting it close to dawn, Sir Vagabond.

I'm all right. Though he could feel the sun's approach. In addition to the occasional attack of bloodlust, he still had a fledgling's increased vulnerability to the approaching daylight. Whereas Lyssa had been able to step into shelter a moment's breath from dawn without any problem, it was near impossible for him to comfortably be above ground less than an hour before the sun's rising. However, he'd deal with some discomfort. They were too close.

If we have to do so, we can come back tomorrow, Jacob. We'll find her again.

But Essie might not remember the tree tomorrow.

"Here, *here*." Essie clamped down on his arm. Her pace increased as she dragged him down a narrow, pitch-dark alley that smelled of offal and several rat carcasses, remains left by feline alley scavengers. Sometimes, if impressions were strong enough, his precog senses worked in reverse, calling up past images. This place was overrun with lingering impressions of violence. Needles discarded, a man kicked almost to death. He'd dragged himself a few feet, only to die in a pile of garbage. There was still a scrap of police tape in that pile. A hooker had been gang raped, beaten. Others had brought johns here, let themselves be pounded against the wall. One had knelt in garbage to suck her clients off for just a few dollars, whatever she could get for her next cocaine fix.

He'd stopped, reeling from all the images. It was a place that had seen so much evil, it collected it, made a barrier of it.

"Jacob." Lyssa was at his elbow, touching him.

"Where?" He spoke in a hoarse voice, trying not to sound threatening. "Where is the tree?"

Essie's eyes were round, pale green pools in the darkness, but she pointed. "Back there. This is terrible, terrible place. But sometimes we're brave. Sometimes we come, when it's daylight. We don't come at night, but you're here." She caught Jacob's arm abruptly, fingers digging in. "Don't disappear. I brought you here, like you said. Don't leave me and my friends here."

"No." He shook his head. "I won't."

Glancing down at Lyssa, he nodded, reassurance that he was all right. Because she was here. Her eyes warmed, her hand closing around his. They moved forward together.

The end of the alley opened up into a barren area, once a parking lot for the clump of abandoned businesses that formed a square around it. The pavement was broken pieces and gravel. A scattering of strawlike grass and weeds pushed through the cracks. More garbage and syringes. Because taller office buildings shadowed the area, Jacob could see there was little room for sunlight, but meager shards would get through.

It was like a well. The evil pushing in behind them and the buildings and fencing before them made it claustrophobic. A cheerless steel and concrete cage for a beautiful, exotic creature.

Dear Goddess. No wonder she couldn't get back home.

Jacob nodded again, but he couldn't take his gaze from the one feature that obviously didn't belong, what had drawn Essie and her companions here during daylight hours, despite the horrid nature of the place. Now that they'd found her, he wondered that they'd even gotten out of the car to check the other trees. Though his and Lyssa's senses were far more advanced than humans', he marveled that no one other than a trio of homeless people had called out the unique quality of the willow that had survived here.

The roots had gone into that broken pavement, taken hold. During their trek here, Essie had mumbled "starlight, starbright" several times, and now he knew she wasn't aimlessly reciting a nursery rhyme. With those advanced senses, he could see the tree's aura. Blue and green fire sparkled in the darkness, limning the slender layers of leaves that rustled in the scrap of wind that found its way into this dank funnel of existence. The willow was perhaps fifteen feet tall, the trunk ironically the diameter of a shapely woman's waist, such that he could easily put his arms around it. Even in this soulless place, the tree had attracted life. Birds nestled up in those branches, giving quiet cheeps. Crickets sawed among the leaves.

There seemed to be less trash and drug paraphernalia near the tree, and he wondered if Essie and her friends had tried to honor the tree spirit by doing what they could to improve her space, or the more unsavory elements had unconsciously respected the barrier around it.

Being a former vampire hunter, he considered himself reasonably exposed to paranormal things. Then he'd met Keldwyn. The first time he'd seen the Fae lord in the deep forest, Jacob had been focused on Lyssa's protection, on his need to find her. Even so, some part of him had registered the wonder of being in the presence of a creature connected so deeply to Nature's magic.

Keldwyn had said the Fae withdrew from the mortal world when humans began taking it over with their buildings and fences, with their need for order and control. In the stark contrast between what Jacob saw before him and the dark landscape around it, he saw why their two worlds would never reunite in the same way. It was a gift they'd all lost, that would never be theirs again. It made his throat thicken and tears sting his eyes.

Your Irish is showing, my love. But though she saw and felt it differently with her vast years, she understood. Her hand gripped his.

They moved forward again. Sensing something unexpected might be about to happen, Essie and her friends held back.

"You know . . ." Lyssa spoke in a low voice. "We were so focused on finding her, I didn't consider what to do once we actually free her."

"I'm not sure there's a section on the Internet about how to feed, water and care for your liberated dryad." Jacob grimaced. "We'll figure it out. Let's just see if your touch works its magic this time."

As they reached the tree, he held a curtain of slender branches to the side, allowing Lyssa to step beneath the canopy. That aural energy shimmered over his arm. Glancing up, he saw a tiny cadre of moonlit-colored moths dance upward to a higher elevation to avoid the intruders. They moved toward the sliver of fading moonlight partially obscured by the silhouettes of the leaves. His eyesight was good enough to see a spider web the size and shape of a perfectly round quarter. The occupant was so small that it took Jacob's vampire eyes to detect the pencil-tip-sized body, the eight, tiny threadlike legs.

As they reached the trunk, he dropped to his heels, holding Lyssa's one hand as she reached out with the other. She laid it on a curve in the trunk that was reminiscent of a woman's shoulder, the shallow dip above it the swanlike curve of neck. When she paused, Jacob saw her attention directed inward, as if she were listening to a whispered voice. Dipping into her head, he sensed an oscillating surge of energy, the taste of her Fae magic as it was stirred by the presence of this tree like a spoon dipped into slow flowing honey.

A vibration of response shuddered through the tree, down through the roots under his feet. Distress, like a sleeper woken from a nightmare. Terror, and all of it female. Reacting without thought, he laid his palm below Lyssa's, adding to the calm energy she was pouring into the tree, since she of course was detecting the same thing he was.

The vibration got denser, implosive, and then everything went still. The crickets were silent, the moths gone. Jacob heard the tiny peep of one bird, a question, followed by more silence. He met Lyssa's eyes, and so he saw them widen before he felt the touch.

The bark shimmered over his hand. It distorted, smoothed, then became slim long fingers that overlapped his, testing. When the root beneath his boot twitched, he moved it. The trunk quivered, a cambered section becoming a bare leg. The visible root edge sculpted into the tiny, delicate foot.

Jacob rose, turning his hand over so the dryad's fingers rested in his palm. Gently—as gently as if he held one of those moths, afraid to dust their wings with his flesh and take away their ability to fly—he closed his fingers on hers. Lyssa was gripping the other hand. In sync, they backed up, drawing the fairy out of the trunk's hold like Excalibur from the stone, with all the same awe.

As she came out, the trunk twisted and molded back into a closed shape, one far smoother than when it had held her body in its embrace. Jacob looked into large, almond-shaped eyes the color of gray-green moss. A tiny pink mouth underscored features that at first seemed too smooth and delicate to be real, but then he realized just the opposite was true. She was as real as leaf or stream, a cloud in a blue sky.

When she collapsed, he and Lyssa caught her together. Her head fell on Lyssa's shoulder, while her hand remained locked in Jacob's sure grip.

"That's a crazy girl for sure," Pipe Guy affirmed. "Can't no one live in a tree. She crazier than Essie."

"HERE." Pete poked Jacob's shoulder. He was holding the long, tattered jacket he'd been wearing. "N-n-aked girl b-b-be cold out here. And attract b-b-b-bad things. Don't s-s-ssmell so clean, but it'll still w-w-w-work."

The two men worked in tandem to wrap the girl up in the coat and Lyssa helped fasten the buttons on the old duster. As she did, she noted that Jacob was sweating. The strain of staying out this close to dawn was starting to tell. They had about an hour before the sun's rays would spear through the city skyline, and by that time Jacob would be extremely uncomfortable.

Don't worry for me, my lady. I'm fine. Though she and Jacob both possessed more than enough strength to carry her, he was the one who lifted the dryad. A man his size carrying a female would attract less attention than a woman of her stature. Beyond that, the girl, even in her unconscious state, would draw a sense of safety from his embrace. Lyssa wasn't at all surprised that, while her touch had freed the girl, Jacob's had given her the bravery to reach out, accept the rescue. His effect on women, particularly damsels in distress, could by turns intensely irritate or quietly delight her. Today's response was mixed—she didn't want to see him turned to a pile of foolishly chivalrous ash by the rising sun.

As they moved away from the tree that had sheltered the Fae for so long, Lyssa sensed something amiss. Pausing at the entry point between the two buildings, she looked back. "Jacob."

At the same moment she spoke, Essie's cry of distress split the air.

Willow trees, with the long strands of leaves like thick tresses, and the trunk shape like the curving female form, had long been considered a sacred Goddess symbol. Now it was as if the Maiden aspect was becoming Crone, but not in the gradual way nature intended. The leaves were browning, dropping away, the trunk thickening and gnarling, hunching in on itself. The roots split the ground, as if the tree was going to pull itself out of the earth and fall over.

"Touch."

Even Jacob almost missed the whisper. Looking down, they saw the dryad's eyes were open. She reached out of the coat, her fingers trembling. "Touch."

Jacob glanced at Lyssa. *She's so weak she's shaking. Whatever she's planning to do, she doesn't have the strength to do it. She could go right back in there. Or die outright. We have to help her, my lady.*

Essie's mouth was crumpled in anguish. She'd scurried back to the tree and fallen to her knees inside its canopy. As she keened and rocked herself, her little dog whined at her side. The two men helplessly flanked her, looking up at the dying tree.

"Go . . . touch." The dryad's voice was weaker, but more plaintive. It was hurting her, seeing the tree suffering.

Lyssa frowned. *You're right. She doesn't have the strength to do it. Not alone. And I suppose you'll refuse to move until she's at ease. Stubborn ass. Come.*

As they ducked back under that curtain of leaves, Pete touched Essie's shoulder, drawing her attention to what they were doing, Thankfully, it reduced her wails to quiet whimpers. When they approached the trunk, the dryad reached out again. Her arm was quivering harder, but this time Lyssa clasped her hand, not allowing her to make direct contact with the trunk. Instead, she lifted her other palm and laid it there. "Use me," the vampire queen said.

At Mason's, Lyssa's groundswell of energy had been like the tremor of an earthquake. This was gentler, but no less powerful. The earth took a long breath and exhaled through her. As she flattened her hand on the tree's trunk, a flutter of blue and green light danced down the dryad's pale arm and floated over Lyssa's skin, glimmering down to the contact point beneath Lyssa's fingertips.

Everything stopped, every muscle locked as if time itself paused. Then Jacob smelled subterranean earth, green leaves and . . . flowers.

Time lurched back into motion. The trunk was straightening again, new leaf buds replacing those that had fallen. But more than the tree was changing. The brown scraps of leaves on the ground were being shifted aside by blades of grass poking through the earth and human debris. The garbage disappeared under a carpet of grass and a multihued tapestry of wildflowers, spiky, defiant oranges and red-browns. Plants that could survive adversity and look good while doing it.

Lyssa had a distant, unfocused expression as she tapped the well of magic and gave it free rein. He sensed her willing her consciousness out of the way so that the dryad and other forces could direct the power she yet understood so little. However, when she at last returned to herself and saw what the power had wrought, a rare look of complete serenity crossed her lovely features. Brief as it was, he thought of a baby connected to its umbilical cord, that maternal connection providing all the unspoken answers. Then she drew away from the tree.

As she met Jacob's eyes, he leaned forward and kissed her. He held it a long moment, the dryad between them. When he broke the contact between them at last, she still held the dryad's hand. Lyssa tucked the girl's cold fingers tenderly inside the coat.

Jacob had been the recipient of his lady's merciless side more than once, enough to never underestimate how brutal she could be. However, despite her earlier impatience on his behalf, he also knew she had a limitless compassion for those deserving of it. Though neither of them knew the motives of Keldwyn or the Fae queen regarding this dryad, it was clear to them both she was a young female in need of their help.

Lyssa cocked her head, picking up his thoughts. "You like my merciless side. You respond to it quite creatively."

He couldn't deny it, but decided he'd save that response for a more appropriate time. The dryad made a noise, drawing Lyssa's attention. Her body quivered in Jacob's arms.

"It will survive now," Lyssa assured her.

"Yes . . . It will thrive. For a while." There was curiosity in the dryad's gaze as she considered the vampire queen, but her weariness overcame her. Within a few seconds, she was limp and oblivious in Jacob's arms.

~

When they left Essie and her friends, Essie was cavorting among the flowers with her little dog, drawing the two nonplussed men into a playful circle dance with her, the woman no longer afraid of lingering here. Jacob gave them some money, hoping it would be used for food, despite the alcohol heavy on Pipe Guy's breath.

Though the damn approaching dawn was making him more unsettled by the minute, he paused at the top of the alley for one last glimpse of the tree. A dark, dank tunnel of death and violence, leading to light and life at the end of it. A lot of metaphors there, for certain.

It will thrive. For a while. He wondered if that would apply to more than the tree, thinking of Essie and her little dog living in her fantasy world under those sinuous strands of leaves. Jacob didn't blame her. In their absence, he'd ask Elijah to check on the tree and the homeless woman so childishly enchanted with it.

"I'll drive while you sit with her in the back seat."

He shook his head. "You should be with her, my lady. She was disoriented before. Waking up with a vampire in the backseat might be a bad thing."

"Trust me, Jacob. There isn't a female alive who'd feel fear in your arms." Unlike the heat burning his skin, the warmth her tone held was welcome. Lyssa opened the back door for him. "No time to argue."

Just as Keldwyn had implied, what little life the dryad had was drawn from her tree. At this point it was a toss-up between what the most urgent problem was, Jacob's reaction to dawn or the Fae's fading life spark.

There was no packing to do. Keldwyn had said the Fae queen would not allow anything to go through other than the clothes they wore against their skin and weapons they could find in the Fae world. Jacob assumed that meant his knives would make it through but the nine-millimeter wouldn't, so he shifted the dryad enough to pull the back holster out of his jeans, unloaded the gun and handed it up to Lyssa to store in the locked glovebox.

Keldwyn had also recommended garments of primarily natural

fibers. Apparently, the Fae queen was so offended by polyester she might deliver them through the portal as naked as the Terminator. Jacob's normal choice of jeans and T-shirt fortunately fit the bill. Lyssa had taken care to wear an organic cotton dress, a pretty, flowing garment that enhanced the Fae look of her vibrant green eyes and pale skin. She'd brought along a blue hooded cloak that swept around her ankles when she donned it against the evening chill. With a braided belt threaded with a carrying pouch, she reminded him of a medieval lady, one who should be standing beside a white charger draped with flowers instead of a shiny Mercedes.

"Charmer. Get in before I can roast marshmallows over you."

The car's windows had a protective coating that would shield him from the sun's rays if they experienced a delay. He wouldn't go up in flames, though he would feel like he was being eaten alive by fever.

While he wasn't far from that state now, his elevated temperature hadn't dulled his wits. He noted a heavy car blanket folded in the shadows of the passenger floor boards. As Lyssa took a seat behind the wheel, he met her gaze in the rearview mirror. Ever since the transfer of her vampire powers to him, she'd regained a reflection. While he of course had lost his, he knew his queen would feel the weight of his regard. "With respect, my lady, make haste. If you reach the Fae doorway at dawn, it won't stop me from following you across, even if I have to burn alive to do it."

As a human servant, he'd experienced firsthand the innate sense of superiority vampires possessed. It gave them complete confidence to override the free will of one in a weaker position than themselves. He admitted to a taste of it himself now and again since he'd grown fangs. So when her eyes narrowed with that frosty look he knew well, he held his ground.

"You won't leave me behind, my lady. Fate always puts me at your back whenever you have need of me. You should stop fighting it and save your energy for better things."

"Like flaying you alive for your eternal insolence," she noted in her cool tone. Turning over the engine, a soft purr, she added, "I know you as well as you like to think you know me, Sir Knight. I may have thought it, but I wasn't going to do it. However, for clarification, what you call Fate, I call your pigheaded stubbornness."

"Tomato, to-mah-to," he said, unruffled.

She put the car in gear with a petulant jerk, and he braced his feet on the floorboards. Her anger with him was genuine, and he had no doubt at some later time she'd make him pay for it, probably by strapping him to a rack and flogging him in truth. That, too, was part of her nature. But so was her bone-deep worry about what would happen to him when they tried to cross. Since they had to swallow the bitter pill of their conflicting desires to protect one another, they rode in silence. He did try to reassure her, though, showing her in his mind the contingency plan he'd considered.

Irish lore often suggested the Fae world was underground, the light a constant twilight or dusk. However, if the lore was wrong and it was sunny on the Fae side, no shelter nearby, he could burrow rapidly into the earth. It wasn't a pleasant idea, for he'd have to leave her alone for the hours until sundown. Plus, vampires had no more desire to be buried alive than humans did. But he would survive and it was a doable plan.

Unless we emerge into the Fae world on top of a mountain of solid rock.

He chose not to respond to that. For one thing, he had an unfortunate distraction. The dryad remained unconscious, but it wasn't peaceful. As they passed through the city streets, acres of asphalt and glass buildings separating them from a direct connection with the earth, he could feel the wasting weakness of her body increasing.

"Hurry, my lady."

They'd scoped out several area parks within distance of the downtown area they'd been canvassing. She accelerated, heading toward the closest one. While she zigzagged through the predawn traffic, Jacob fished out his cell and made a quick call to Elijah. He told him about Essie and where they were leaving the Mercedes so he could retrieve it, hopefully because both of them would have been transported into a whole different world.

~

The park was silent, of course, the main gate closed. When Lyssa opened the door, Jacob slid out of the seat, carrying the dryad. For a moment they considered one another. Despite his elevated temperature and the hammering at his temples, the pain warning him to get below ground, he leaned forward, adjusting his hold on the Fae girl to close the distance to his lady's lips. He gauged her mood enough not to make contact. Instead, he stopped just short of her mouth, teasing her with the proximity, earning a flash out of those mesmerizing jade eyes. "Let's just do it, my lady. Whatever happens, I love you."

"You are a pain in my ass. Always." Her jaw was tight, but the dark strands of her hair fell over her forehead, framing the mysterious power of those long-lashed eyes, tempting himto close the distance. She shut her eyes at the brush of his lips, then opened them when he drew back.

The next moment didn't require an exchange of thoughts, a mutual decision. Their hearts were shared, after all. Putting her hand on his face, she went to her toes. Reading her emotions, he bent his stance enough that they could press their foreheads together, even as he held the dryad between them. They both understood the need not to alarm their son, but as one, they briefly touched his subconscious once more, leaving a lingering feeling of love, acceptance and reassurance there.

She straightened, held his gaze one vital second. Then, giving him a nod, she turned. Together they walked around the main gate, which was designed only to keep cars out, and took the second walking trail identified by signs.

In her winged Fae form, Lyssa had visited many of the forested areas of Atlanta in the dark hours of night, even the more sparsely wooded ones. Now she guided him without hesitation toward a creek. It wasn't a large body of water, probably unknown to most people who didn't leave the walking trail. As they moved deeper into the woods, the canopy helped ease some of the scorching itch between Jacob's shoulder blades. He wondered if the faint smell of smoke was coming from his skin. There'd been recent heavy rains, and so they heard the creek's rushing, bubbling noise before they reached it. Jacob drew the cool smell gratefully into his nostrils.

The trees thinned, and there it was.

When Lyssa glanced at him, he saw her note his soaked T-shirt clinging to his body. The dryad's body pressed against his chest was an abrasive friction. Dawn was perhaps five minutes away. A vampire didn't have to breathe, but he was doing so, and the sound of it was labored. The dryad stirred, making an uncertain noise as if picking up on the disturbing changes happening to her cradle. Lyssa's brow creased, her lips thinning. Jacob shook his head, setting his teeth.

"Focus on the doorway, my lady."

If he couldn't cross over, he'd barely make it back to the car using vampire speed. Or he'd dig himself underground, as he'd indicated. There was no time for her to consider alternate possibilities. The fact that he was right didn't make her any happier about any of it. She set her jaw.

"Give her to me. If you don't cross over, I need to be the one holding her."

He gave her a look, but that same time constraint prevented any more discussion. As he shifted his burden, the dryad's gray-green eyes opened briefly. "We're taking you home, lass," he murmured. "Hang in there another couple minutes."

"You have great faith in my ability to open this portal," Lyssa said, worry making her tone sharp.

Jacob settled the Fae in his lady's arms. Lyssa held her capably even though it looked incongruous, the two females of like size. In fact, the dryad was slightly taller. Since he was already in trouble with his queen, her arms were occupied, and he might be dead or at least in excruciating pain in the next few moments, Jacob gave his lady a healthy pinch on her delectable ass, adding a squeeze that he couldn't help but make a caress. Her freezing glance became something else as she picked up on his shift in emotion. "You did say I was a pain in the ass, my lady. And I have total faith in you. Always."

It was the right combination, for it jabbed at her royal temper, even as it reassured. She stepped to the bank of the creek. Jacob stopped at her side. Closing her eyes, Lyssa breathed in, tuning everything out, the dryad's fading life spark, the fact Jacob could be incinerated in the next few moments. She made it all go still, reaching out for whatever it was her Fae blood could sense. It was close to the dividing line of night and dawn and they stood at a body of moving water in a park that had been here for many years. It had to work.

Jacob stayed still beside her, trying to hold his breath, trying not to sway on his feet as the flames of hell began to lick at the soles of his feet, sweeping upward. He wasn't bursting into flames, but he could feel it coming, any moment.

"Put your arms around both of us, Sir Vagabond," she said, in a frustrated tone. "I have no idea how this is going to go, but I can feel—Now. Put your arms around me *now*."

At the snap of the sudden command, he wrapped his arms around her. Their combined weight slid them off the bank, and she staggered, having to hold on to the dryad rather than use her arms to balance. The creek rocks stabbed through the thin slippers she wore. Jacob wore boots, but the rush of water soaking his jeans was bliss. He tightened his grip on both women, bracing himself to hold them steady. But he could only hold them steady against the things he knew.

He felt it then, too, what Lyssa had sensed. An energy rushing down upon them. And music. The melody was familiar, tugging at him like a mother's lullaby, calling him . . . somewhere. The doorway and the music were in that energy rush, forming a billowing mist as it rolled toward them.

It wasn't coming fast enough. Raising his head, Jacob saw the dawn light pierce through the trees, sucked in a breath as sunlight stabbed through his chest like a stake. Then that sunlight expanded outward, blinding him, and the water rushing over his feet became diamond shards, slashing his skin.

~

Once, when working at the Ren Faire, he'd been thrown from a horse. His foot had caught in the stirrup and the mare had panicked. As she bucked and twisted, her hooves hit him in the head and other far more tender parts. She'd dragged him a good pace before they'd been able to calm her and get him free. That was a fond memory next to this. The slam into hard ground, like a giant had picked him up and hurled him against a brick wall, made the rocky pasture ground he'd bounced across seem like a feather bed in comparison.

"Shit." He didn't use the word often, but the moment seemed to require it. He tried to move and none of his limbs responded. Panic sliced through him. Surely he hadn't arrived in the Fae world injured and unable to protect Lyssa, a complete liability to her. Of course, knowing his lady, she'd get tremendous female satisfaction from winning the coveted I-told-you-so laurel.

If you are able to be a wiseass, I'd say you are fine.

He'd located his lady in the first second, but was relieved to find the mind-to-mind connection was intact. In the next breath, he realized she was right. He was hurting too much to be paralyzed, an ironic relief. A shudder racked him down to his bones, making him bite down another heartfelt curse. He felt like throwing up, but managed to push that back as well.

Now she knelt, sliding his head into her lap. Her hair brushed his face before she gathered it up, pulled it away, though he liked the silk of it against his flesh. It distracted him from the fact he felt like ten pins scattered across a lane by a truck-sized bowling ball.

"Give yourself time, my love. Look at it all. Just look at it."

Hearing the solemn wonder and rarely used endearment, he took the time to do just that.

He pried open his eyes. She'd straightened so he was staring right up into the sky. He'd viewed many beautiful night skies, that tremendous expanse that made the soul feel inexplicably small and yet treasured at once, as if he were gazing into something far deeper than his eyes could see. This was as if that screen had been pulled back, so he could see why his soul felt that way. A carpet of stars spread out in random swirls against the deep purple expanse. The large yellow moon hung among them, tiny wisps of dark clouds making it look as if it was drifting, a ship at full sail. He wondered if Van Gogh had ever visited the Fae world in his madness.

Three shooting stars burned a path below the moon. Then he realized they weren't shooting stars at all.

Fireflies danced in the air above him, so bright they blended with the stars, except instead of clean white light, there was a touch of red flame in their afterburn. When one came in range, he was staring at a tiny fairy, no bigger than one of Lyssa's fingernails. A naked male with long silver hair and tiny black antennae protruding from it, just above his ears. He studied Jacob with insectlike green eyes. Instead of almond-shaped, they were perfect, pupil-less circles. The wings of the firefly Fae were like a hummingbird's, moving so fast they were invisible except for a telltale blur of motion. His skin abruptly glowed bright with that reddish light, then he zoomed back up to his fellows again.

With the pain receding enough for his nerves to register something other than agony, Jacob realized he was on a soft bed of green grass, his elbows tickled by nodding wildflowers. As he processed that, the dryad stepped into his line of sight.

She paid no attention to him. Her gaze was on the skies as well, the fireflies specifically. Though she was still obviously weak, she was standing on her own. The way she was breathing—deep, from the soles of her feet—it was obvious she was pulling in energy, holding herself up with it. When she reached up, the tiny creatures landed on her slender fingers. At the contact, her mouth tightened, making her thin face even more painfully drawn. Her gray-green eyes, like the bark of an ancient tree, overflowed with tears.

Lyssa laid her hand on Jacob's chest. He closed his fingers over hers.

Still holding the tiny creatures, the dryad shifted her attention from the skies to the green field that spread out to her right, populated by white flowers that glowed silver and gold in the moonlight. Jacob followed her gaze to the edge of the meadow. A thick forest marked the boundary, but beyond the forest there were four hills, so substantive they looked like the overlapping domes of four planets on the horizon. Even in the darkness, it wasn't hard to see their shape, because of their size and what was perched on the top of each one.

Four castles. Just like the stories he'd heard, each one represented an element. The Castle of Air looked like it was made of crystal, the moonlight making the facets glitter silver. It shimmered at its foundation, as if instead of a moat it was circled by a twisting, cycling wind.

The Castle of Water shone as well, but the gleam of its walls was obviously a complicated series of waterfalls, shaped and directed by the castle's angles and channel points. Even at this distance, the cascades reflected silver and blue. The top of the hill was a body of water, and the castle sat on it, instead of a land mass.

The Castle of Fire was unmistakable, a torchlike flame shooting up into the darkness, haloed with an aura of gemlike deep reds, purples and browns. Its moat was a flow of lava.

Since the Earth castle had less reflective surfaces, it was hard to determine its features, even with vampire sight. The grand silhouette was lit only by the lights of its inhabitants, but Jacob envisioned walls of clay, turrets covered with moss, trailing ivy and braided vines instead of drawbridge chains. Idly, he wondered if any of them had a dragon.

Silly knight. You didn't even bring a lance.

Lyssa's fingers whispered over his temples, helping him focus. The clean air had a sweet, wild taste. An indescribable world bursting with life energy, unfettered, brimming with magic. No wonder the dryad was so overcome. She'd spent two decades of her life without this . . . lifeblood. He'd detected a mere wisp of it when he'd held her in his arms. Her essence was intertwined with all the life here.

Magic existed in the human world, but it was an echo, a memory of what it had once been when their two worlds had been joined. Mere rivulets, trickling out the seams of the solid locked doors that divided them. A spark of it must survive in every soul, because Jacob felt a recognition now that brought a tangle of joy and sorrow together.

The dryad turned toward him, her small mouth pressed into a line, those tears running down her face still. She wore nothing, her long body a smooth sculpture, pale skin colored only by the soft pink of nipples and sex. She had a pendant around her neck. It had been dull stone when she'd stepped out of her tree, but now it glowed green and amber, a luster like the heat energy of a banked hearth fire. Keeping her gaze on them, she removed it, laying the object at Jacob's feet. Then, in a blink, she was gone, moving swiftly across the field. The wings that had been like crumpled paper against her spine now snapped out like a geisha's fans, a flash of green and gold color. She moved only a foot above the grasses, as Essie had described. The fireflies were a trail of glitter behind her, in close pursuit.

"Do you think she gave us that as proof that we brought her here?" Jacob mused.

"How would she know we freed her to prove something to the queen?" Lyssa responded. "Perhaps it was a way of offering thanks."

Jacob bit back a groan as he managed to sit up. As he did, he picked up the pendant, feeling its warmth. Sliding the chain through his fingers, he lifted it, threaded it over Lyssa's head and then situated it in the pleasing valley of her breasts. His fingers rested there, over her heartbeat.

"According to the old lore," he said, "the Fae believe saying thank you is an insult. Instead, you give gifts, tokens of appreciation. But it would have been helpful if she'd stuck around, at least until we meet the queen."

"If I'm right, and the queen put her there, then perhaps not having her with us is less confrontational."

She helped him stand, then surprised him by removing the necklace. As she went to her toes to put it around his neck, he bent his head obligingly, sliding his hands to her hips to steady them both, but said, "Isn't that your trophy to bring to the Fae queen?"

"Perhaps, but your newest female admirer laid it at your feet. Plus, as my servant, you're supposed to carry my things anyway, right?"

He considered the pendant where it lay against his T-shirt, amused when her fingertips stroked the hard cleft between his pectorals in imitation of his own sensual meanderings in her cleavage. "I guess this means at least one Fae likes me, even though I'm a nasty vampire."

"One and a half. If I count for anything in your little fan club." Lyssa sniffed. "Of course, my love is fickle. I wouldn't depend on it overmuch."

That made him smile outright. Fortunately his head didn't split open. He'd gotten too used to bouncing back instantly from injury. The Fae queen had let him come, but apparently wasn't entirely happy about it. Lyssa, on the other hand, seemed as energized as she'd been before she stepped across. Perhaps more so, because the magic in this world seemed to enhance her Fae side in a way that only magnified her captivating presence.

"You need blood," Lyssa said.

"Not yet." He shook his head. "I would never tell you what to do, my lady, but in this world I'd recommend treating me as you did when I first came into your service. Simply expect I'll be at your back and serve as you demand. Let me worry about the rest."

She gave him one of her impenetrable looks. "Seeing as you *are* my servant, and I value your services, if I see a need to protect you, I will. It's very hard to train a new servant. Some of them are impossible, though. It's best to simply dispose of them and start from scratch with a more docile model."

Despite his aching body, he flashed fangs at her. "I am ever at your disposal, my lady." He nodded toward the castles. "I expect we'll find the queen in one of those. Looks like we can make it to any one of them at an easy pace in a couple hours."

"Time and distance are probably more fluid here. Whichever one we head toward, I have a feeling we'll still end up at the one she wants us to visit." Lyssa lifted a shoulder. "Since Keldwyn said she'd expect us by the end of the full moon, and we're early, I don't see a need to rush, except to find you cover before dawn, which feels quite a few hours off. Apparently we arrived right after sunset."

Jacob frowned. Lyssa could sense the rising and setting cycles here, but he couldn't at all. He supposed he could have the vampire version of jet lag, but in the mortal world, he was as aware of the time as if he had an internal Greenwich clock. When he'd first become a vampire, he'd understood why vampires never had clocks in their homes, unless put there for the convenience of human staff. But here . . . nothing.

Like his fast healing, it was something he relied upon, not just as a convenience, but for survival. Regardless, he put his uneasiness aside and offered Lyssa his hand. It pleased him that she took it. They headed across the sloping field, through the silver and gold flowers, down toward the edge of the forest. Each step jarred him, but he set his teeth against it. It would get better, and as soon as they were someplace less open, he'd feed.

He considered the horizon. "So do you think the Castle of Air is transparent? We could sit on the front lawn and watch the lady Fae changing clothes."

"Leave it to the male mind to jump to the most important thing about a transparent castle." Lyssa pinched his arm. She swung around in front of him, holding both hands now and peddling backward. Her jade eyes sparkled, her mouth curving as she looked up at him.

"My lady?"

"It feels so . . . different here. So familiar . . ." She shook her head, but let go of him to turn a full circle, her arms outspread. "Did you notice, as weak as she was, how our dryad was walking, her eyes sparkling? There's a vitalizing force here for Fae blood. It's like coming to a place you've missed for a very long time, where you thought you'd never be welcome again."

Her lips curved. "It makes me want to dance. I have a great urge to . . . frolic."

"Many people would drop their jaws if they saw you frolic."

"But not you."

"I saw you dress up like a slutty teenager and go to the mall. My lady has given me the pleasure of seeing the girl inside the woman."

"And you will never let her live it down."

"Not even if I live beyond eternity."

She sobered. "I can't imagine what it must have done to her, being disconnected from this for so long."

"Our world had enough magic to shelter her. No matter Keldwyn's cynicism, the magic is still there, my lady. Just hidden deep where only the eyes that can see it will find it. Like Essie's."

"And yours." She slid under his arm, putting hers around his waist, so she gave him some reluctantly needed support as they made their way toward the forest edge. The dark gloom called to him, to what was in *his* blood. The vampire blood.

"You knew about the Fae propensity to give gifts, instead of thanks. How did you know that? Is it a class all Irishmen have to take?"

He snorted. "My parents were raised on the stories, and they passed them on to their sons. After they died, my aunt kept up with it, probably to remind us of our mother. I can't say for sure what parts are truth or fiction, but a lot of the ones we were told have been around a very long time. Maybe the telling of them feeds that thread between our worlds, even if the information isn't a hundred percent accurate. It's the spirit of the telling that matters, the desire to believe the tales." He didn't like how much he had to lean on her.

"Jacob."

"I know. When we get to the forest, I'll feed. I'm sorry, my lady."

"The only reason to apologize is for your ridiculous *need* to apologize. Tell me more of the stories you were told, the ones you think are true."

"Many are about impulsive lads or lasses who wandered too deep into the knolls and came upon a fairy ring. If they stepped inside it, they were in the Fae world, where time passes far differently. Though they knew to avoid the rings, a lad wouldn't be able to resist the pretty fairy he saw dancing there." He grunted as he stumbled over a root, and her arm tightened on him. "He'd be so wrapped up in her beauty, he would dance and dance and dance with her, until he wasted away. When the Fae night waned, she'd let him go, for to her he was only a dance partner. Thrust back into our world, he'd find centuries had passed, all he knew of his own world gone."

Tilting his head down to gaze into her beautiful face, he slid his hand along her fine jaw as he teased a lock of her hair. "But that didn't matter. What tore his heart out was losing the girl he'd danced with for centuries, though it only seemed a heartbeat of time."

She laid her hand over his. They'd stopped inside the boundary of the forest, the shadows now cloaking them. "I forget you used to tell stories on the Ren Faire circuit, Sir Vagabond. Sir Knight. You still have a good touch."

Before he could respond, a rustling in the grasses drew their attention back to the meadow. A blink later, a large bird with crimson feathers erupted out of the wheat-colored grass and spread his wings, dislodging a handful of petals from the gold and silver flowers as he soared into the purple starlit sky. Sparks showered off the wings as he took flight.

"A phoenix," Lyssa whispered. Her gaze moved westward, where the field folded downward into another shallow tier. "Jacob, look."

A pond of silver glass lay in that direction. Ripples coursed gently across it, the result of two unicorns foraging on water weeds in the shallows. Nearby, swans slept as they drifted, heads tucked under their wings. Perched on their backs in small circles, as if taking an evening tea, were more clusters of the firefly Fae.

While the two of them had discovered remarkable things together, Lyssa knew those things mostly involved the exploration of their own souls as they'd bonded. This was the first time in their relationship that they were seeing something new and unexpected for the both of them. She liked that. However, a blink later something disrupted that pleasure in his mind, an unsettled, scattered feeling entirely unlike Jacob.

Worried that his need for blood was becoming more critical, she looked up to gauge his pallor. He was still staring at the lagoon, but his gaze had shifted from the unicorns. On the far bank, there were more Fae, only not whimsical fireflies. They were human-sized females, with glossy ebony hair and skin like smooth dark chocolate. Perched on rocks, they brushed one another's hair and braided flowers into it. The wind rose as if a Goddess was breathing, and that breath brought their voices. They spoke in murmurs that floated across the consciousness like a pleasant dream.

Jacob shifted forward a step. Even at that distance, several turned their heads in his direction. One smiled, the face of desire, and a single, pure note of song broke from her moist lips, a greeting and invitation.

“Water nymphs,” he said hazily. “Like sirens. We should ask . . . they may know . . .”

Lyssa locked both arms around his waist and gave him her firmest, most not-to-be-messed-with queen’s voice. “Definitely not.”

Jacob shouldn’t be as susceptible as a mortal male to the allure of the creature, but the nymph had detected something vulnerable in him and capitalized on it. He was weak and needed blood. Lyssa tried to draw him deeper into the forest, away from the lagoon, but she was too late. He was already dragging his feet, glancing back at that pond with blind longing in his gaze. The singing was growing stronger, more enchanting. He was far too pale.

She slid her hand into his front pocket, closing her fingers on that same switchblade she’d borrowed from him earlier. Just as it had then, it allowed her a provocative tease of his upper thigh. Since his mind was already swimming in a lust as murky as that silvery lagoon, his confused attention turned her way.

Before he could dismiss her and focus on the sirens again, she opened the blade, brought it to her throat and jabbed her carotid with pinpoint accuracy. The blood flow was an immediate rush, one that could make *her* dizzy and wobbly.

The result was all she intended, however. Her servant’s full focus snapped to her. His lust had been coaxed to the forefront; now she brought bloodlust into the equation as well. Given how pale he was, she thought blood *need* was more accurate, an undeniable hunger.

Letting go of him, she backed into the forest, provoking the predator she knew lived within him, on several different levels. Her bare feet found a trail, perhaps used by deer or those unicorns. The wood closing around her was centuries-old, populated with trees perhaps even older than herself. The breath of ancients dwelled in their canopies. Power. It reminded her she had power of her own.

She stopped. She was aware of how she looked poised there, the sinuous line of hip and length of leg hinted at beneath the thin cloth of her dress. The upward tilt of her breasts as she cocked her hip. The pale fragility of her throat, marked by bright blood, was a contrast to the challenge in her green eyes and the curve of her moistened lips.

“You can have your sirens, Jacob, or your Mistress. Choose, and I may let you have what you really want.”

He was on her in a heartbeat, pushing her against the broad trunk of one of the trees, trapping her. His warrior instincts were intact, for his hand closed first over her wrist, fingers sliding along the sensitive Venus mound of her palm to take the knife from her. He caressed the erotic beat of her pulse. The weapon fell point first, sinking into the earth clear of their feet, but he didn't intend her throat to receive such a pardon. Sinking his fangs into the flesh at that nicked artery, he wasted no time with it, his hunger making him pull hard at the sustenance she offered.

The ever-present desire for him sprang to full, vibrant life, strengthened by the pulsing magic that existed here. She didn't resist the urge to rub against him, to make sounds of encouragement, tiny sensual noises that told him she wanted him inside her right at this moment, wanting to join in the celebration of that life force all around them.

Normally she would have been the aggressor, taking control despite his best alpha efforts to hold on to the reins, those efforts only arousing her more deeply. However, as he returned to himself, a growl rose in his throat. She felt his black anger that the nymphs had been able to distract him from his devotion to her for even a moment, a blink of time he could never get back.

It was overwhelming, feeling how furious that made him with himself. The depth of his devotion was breathtaking. For all the complexity of the love that had grown and spread between them, the root of it was so primal. She was his, the only one he wanted, and he would prove it right here.

Opening his jeans, he held her against the tree with a body that had become all hard, tense muscle. She moaned as he shoved into her without preamble, already knowing she was wet and ready for him. With no underwear beneath the skirt, he'd had to do no more than lift it, spread her thighs and wrap her legs around him.

Her breasts ached against his chest, and an odd yearning rose in her then, intertwined with the powerful desire coursing through her. Perhaps because she was both lover and mother to vampires, the sense of loss she had for their son, that she couldn't hold him, feed him, came to life now along with her need to nourish Jacob.

Jacob understood the melding of the two deepest cravings of her life. As he thrust into her, he left her throat and pulled her neckline down, off her shoulder so he exposed one breast. When he punctured her at Kane's favored nursing point, it made her cry out in throaty pleasure and pain at once, arching against him as he laved at the blood and her nipple, teasing her.

It was all animalistic, but as he drank, she sensed the keen, intelligent mind steadying. He would take this as a near-miss lesson. He wouldn't delay feeding out of pride again, not when her protection was at stake. Balance was needed, in body and soul, and the best way to achieve that between them was with a simultaneous blood and carnal connection.

As she pressed her skull back against the rough trunk, another guttural sound coming from her throat when he thrust deeper, she saw eyes peering at them through the branches. Animal and Fae eyes both. She sensed no harm from any of them, just curiosity at these new beings among them. Still, Jacob's whimsical, sad story held a warning. The Fae girl had meant no harm to the boy who wasted away dancing with her. *For her, it was simply one night.*

Jacob brought her nipple farther into his mouth, making her gasp at the searing pleasure that arrowed down into her pussy, intensified by the full penetration of his thick cock. He lashed at the taut peak. As she cried out again, he used his hips and callused palms to press her thighs back, widening her to an even more arousing angle. She caught her fingers in his hair, digging into his nape, and his arm banded around her middle. Taking her away from the tree, he laid her on the mossy carpet of the forest floor. As he did, his eyes met hers, and she felt the shift, knew there was a deeper component to it now. It had unsettled him, how quickly this strange new place could drive a wedge between them. He needed to grasp that connection between them, reassure himself of it.

She reared up against him, telling him what she wanted so that she was able to push him to his back and straddle him. Her hair tumbled forward over her shoulders, sliding along the still-damp blood staining her neck.

No reassurance needed, Jacob. The magic between us is uniquely ours. Long before I had faith in it, you believed it was so powerful that nothing could destroy it. And you were right. Have been right, every time.

Don't taunt Fate, my lady. His blue eyes were dark as midnight.

Trailing her fingers over his lips, she took away some of her blood and tasted it, winning a renewed flare of desire. His cock was hard inside her, but he held back now, letting her take the lead. His strength was returning exponentially, she could feel it. She would match that strength in him, play with it like her toy, as she was wont to do. Tightening her inner muscles on him, she gave him an arch look laced with arrogant challenge.

Water nymphs, Sir Vagabond? You've been collecting punishments all day. Her green eyes fastened on his. *I will take my climax, but you will hold yours, let your longing to spill your seed in my cunt grow until it rages.*

6

Since the growth of her Fae powers and Jacob's turning, she hadn't often exerted the sexual power of a Mistress over him. There'd been far greater concerns facing them. Plus, that theme ran through their relationship in many subtle ways, not always requiring the overt ones. However, something about this strange yet altogether familiar world, the way it made her feel recharged, like the queen she'd always been, activated it strongly, no matter the unusual timing or circumstances. She saw him register it, felt his thigh muscles tense beneath her, his beloved face settling into the expression she knew so well. His alpha nature resisted her dominance, but he would serve her, because that was what he'd pledged to her. Heart, soul and body.

Clamping down on his cock, a tight, wet fist, she began to move slowly, rising on her knees so that the head almost slid out of her opening. Then there was the excruciating stimulation of it coming back in again as she descended. His gaze drifted over her throat, to the naked breast, the stiff nipple, the two marks his fangs had made, the smear of blood there. His nostrils flared, showing how much he wanted to lick it off. She kept her hand pressed on his chest, his heart thundering under it as she rose and fell. As the desire to release built, she arched, tossing her hair back so it fell against the bare upper thighs.

Glorious pleasure, glorious power. And a glorious, magnificent man to share it with. It was his turn to rear up now, and he did, capturing her upper body, holding her as he licked away that blood on her breast. He also helped her move upon him, his expression a straining rictus, telling her how he was holding back, fighting his vampire nature as well as his male one. All for her.

Perhaps that capriciousness Keldwyn had warned her about was infecting her. Jacob would say it was simple female nature, but suddenly she didn't want him to hold back. She wanted him to release, wanted to face whatever they were about to face with the scent of his seed on her thighs.

Command me, my lady. Let me give you what you want.

Come for me. Come now.

You first.

They went together, as wild, feral creatures, his teeth scoring her throat again as her nails drew blood from his broad back. She shuddered, holding on as he finished just behind her, still pushing into her fast and desperate, his hands tight on her hips. She gripped his shoulders, rubbing her face in his hair, then up against his jaw like an animal in truth, liking the scent of him. He smiled at that thought, his lips pulling against her throat.

"We're not making much progress toward that castle," he said at last. "But you did say we had time."

"Hmm." When he adjusted so his back was comfortably braced against the tree, the shift of his cock still within her made her breath catch anew. She gestured toward a thin web of upper branches, through which they could distinguish the distant turrets of the Castle of Fire. "Notice anything?"

His brow creased. "It's moved. And it's farther away."

"Even though we moved closer." She shook her head. "I've been a queen for too long to tolerate games. I won't chase her down. If she wants me tonight, she'll come get me. For now . . ." She arched back, a lazy movement that trusted his hands to cup her lower back and hold her steady as she looked up into the canopies of the ancient oaks spread over them, then back out into the meadow, where the unicorns were now grazing. "I don't know what will happen once we get there, but this may be the only time we'll experience and enjoy this world at our leisure, without interruption."

She straightened. "This forest is ancient, and it provides dense cover from sunlight. The deeper you go in, the darker it gets. I've seen at least several trees that have above ground root systems we can turn into a protected alcove with more branches and foliage. We'll scout out a proper one for the morning sunrise. Tomorrow night, if she hasn't come to find us, we'll find her."

She wasn't one for idling. This was a strategy, and she could tell Jacob knew it. Beyond the message she was sending to the Fae queen, it would be a tactical advantage to understand this new world better. "And I want you to tell me more stories. While they may be embellished, some may be rooted in truth. I have a feeling I'll be able to tell the difference. There's usually a rhythm or pattern to every society's stories. It's a dialect you can use, so to speak, for anticipating behavior."

As she stroked his hair back from his neck, he pursed his lips. "Since we've no idea of the welcome we'll get from the queen, your plan seems as good as any." He glanced over at the nearest cove she'd indicated, its frame of heather and ferns. "And if my lady would pass some hours dreaming in my arms in such a place, it sounds too tempting to pass up."

"Ever the charmer. Come explore with me. Help me learn what is fantasy and fact."

"In this world, I don't think there is a difference, my lady."

~

She hadn't anticipated how right he was.

After a reluctant separation of their bodies, they left the shelter of the forest and chose a different hill and meadow to explore, one where the silver and gold flowers gave way to lovely, delicate lavender blooms that reminded her of tulips. As they moved through the field, she saw Fae only minimally larger than the firefly Fae, but not larger than the spread of her hand. They seemed to be hovering over the tulips like bees considering honey collection. However, when he recognized what they were doing, Jacob brought her to a halt. His hand closing over hers, he pulled them both into a careful, silent squat as he scrutinized the blossoms surrounding them.

He spoke in a whisper. "My aunt told me what—at the time—I

thought were silly, girlish stories about Fae mothers putting their babies to sleep inside flowers."

She followed the direction of his pointed gaze. Lyssa peered inside the cradle of a purple blossom, only to find a tiny bean-sized baby, sleeping deep. What she first thought was a baby blanket she realized was the baby's oversized wings, folded carefully around the small body. The babe was a little girl, whose cornsilk soft hair was a darker shade of purple than her cradle.

With a smile, Jacob brushed the stem of the flower, setting the bloom to nodding like a rocking cradle in truth. The babe cooed in her sleep, hands closing and opening near her face. At a warning noise, they looked up to see a Fae mother hovering just above eye level with her lavender wings. She also had purple hair, and snapping brown eyes. With her blue dress that fell in rounded layers around her bare feet, she looked like a flower turned upside down, but she buzzed in Lyssa's face like a very annoyed bee, her arms akimbo.

"Just got her to sleep, I did," she hissed, her voice like stabs at a tiny piano's keys.

"Our apologies," Lyssa responded in a whisper, giving Jacob a sidelong glance. The mother waved them off, putting an adamant finger to her lips. Jacob squeezed Lyssa's hand, leading her out of the field and back onto the forest paths. Once there, Lyssa's brow creased thoughtfully. "She wasn't the least bit afraid of us harming her baby, two total strangers. She was merely concerned we might wake her."

Jacob caught her elbow, bringing her up short as a troop of gnomes, the tallest one not past Jacob's knee, broke out of the brush. They were carrying a load of what looked like walnuts on a makeshift platform. The gnomes eyed them balefully, several of them grunting, but no other communication was encouraged. As they disappeared into the forest, they left behind a metronome movement of disturbed ferns.

"We've tried to engage several Fae in conversation tonight," Lyssa observed. "With the exception of the water nymphs, none of them seem to want to engage in conversation with us."

"Like the mountain pixies," Jacob recalled. When he and Lyssa had sought refuge in Keldwyn's territory in the mountains, a cadre of pixies had fixated on Lyssa. They'd sit upon her when she was in her winged Fae form, chattering, stroking her hair or skin, but they didn't want her to talk to them at all. The few times she tried, they paused, looked at her, then continued speaking among themselves as if she was an interrupting child, speaking gibberish.

"Around Keldwyn, they were very watchful, deferential." Jacob leaned against a tree, then shifted as the tree gave an irritated groan, the branches rustling overhead. "My apologies," he said courteously. "I should have asked your permission first. Good thing we had an accommodating tree earlier," he added to Lyssa, to her great amusement.

"Maybe the intuitive sense is far more developed here. If so, most of them should be able to tell if we mean harm or not, and since we don't, they're just ignoring us. Since I haven't been acknowledged by the queen, maybe they're not allowed to interact with me until that occurs. Which suggests they know who we are and why we're here."

"That could be disturbing or helpful."

They walked some more, saw another group of gnomes tending a small herd of goats in a rocky field. A female gnome with pretty white hair and lively dark eyes in her round potato-like face was seated on a rock, her short legs dangling as she brushed one goat's beard, tying ribbons into it. Like all the others, she ignored Jacob and Lyssa.

When Lyssa felt dawn approaching, they returned to the resting spot for Jacob they'd chosen, a shallow but well-protected alcove beneath one tree's half-exposed root system. They further reinforced and prepared it for the sunrise. Since the soil was soft, Jacob bade her wait while he took some fallen leaves and carpeted it, to keep her from getting the soil on her clothes. Then he settled in, putting his back against the wall of earth, and invited her to come into his shelter and take a position between his thighs and bent knees.

"How about another story?" she asked.

He tugged on her hair. "You're worse than Kane, figuring out ways to delay bedtime."

"He's only successful because his father spoils him."

"Me? You're throwing stones in a glass house." He snorted. "I'm surprised you don't know these stories, my lady. Was it painful for your mother to talk about your father and his world?"

"It was dangerous. We both know how vulnerable a vampire child is. My life, those first few years, depended on hiding behind the protection of the vampire world, when the Fae were trying to find and kill us. My father had agreed to his sentence as a condition of letting my mother escape the Fae world, but once she left and bore me, apparently the Fae felt killing us to reinforce the lesson about the two species breeding was more important than honoring my father's bargain. Eventually, something changed and we were no longer hunted, but not before they killed her servant, the one who posed as my stepfather in Japan. As you may remember."

He did. His first lifetime with her, a samurai guard to a young vampire girl child. The screaming and blood, his roaring command at her maidservant to grab her up and run . . . It was when Jacob died for her for the first time as well. She'd grown up under the shadow of possible assassination. It was no wonder she'd been mature far beyond her years, almost a queen from birth.

Lyssa's hands closed on his forearms, and she pressed her face into his neck. He could tell she was listening to his heart, that reassurance of life, and he laid his head down on hers as she spoke against his flesh. "They hunted us for decades after that. She couldn't risk any show of love for my father, even simple bedtime stories about his people. She was the one who taught me to hide any evidence of my Fae blood. It was to appease both races, and that saved my life. When they eventually stopped trying to murder us, the Council believed it was because their spies confirmed I wasn't demonstrating any Fae capabilities. I wasn't growing up as a stark example of a mutation between species."

She drew a breath. "It seems odd that it was so long ago, yet I can still feel the pain of that. Maybe all this has sharpened the edge of it again. Soon after the attempts stopped for good, my mother chose to meet the sun. I think the ultimate cause was grief. The loss of my father, the strain of protecting me, of having to be on her guard constantly. There was no one in her life she could ever trust, not truly. My father had the largest part of her heart, and his loss was a sorrow that always haunted her.

"For years I was viciously angry at how the Fae had treated her, though rationally I knew it was the Fae leadership of that time, not the entirety of the race." She gave a small, bitter half chuckle. "I was trained to be rational, no matter the emotions I felt. She taught me that, too.

However, my refusal to learn anything about the Fae, continuing long into my maturity, was my one small rebellion, and of course a foolish one, since it's best to know all one can about friends or enemies. Quite often during a thousand years, they swap sides."

She shrugged. "Time passes, and when I might have learned more, I was busy with other things with my own people. So that's why I don't know many stories."

"But she did tell you something, because you started growing roses."

"Yes. I'd see her sitting in her bedroom next to the rose he gave her, fingers whispering over the petals. It wasn't until later I learned his fate, and then I realized she was imagining it was him, her fingers touching the rose bush he'd become. One night, her loneliness and sadness must have overcome her, because she came to me in my bed. When she was wrapped around me, her mouth against my ear so no one else could possibly hear, she whispered that I should never doubt how very much my father had loved me."

He loved us more than his own life, his own happiness. And that is a very great love indeed.

She tilted her head back. "So I am no longer an angry child, Sir Vagabond. Tell me what I need to know. Tell me the things you think are more fact than stories."

Jacob lifted a shoulder. "Fae lore is so varied, my lady. There are commonalities among regions, of course. It's said the original Fae were like gods, with great powers. They worshipped the Goddess Danu, and were called the Tuatha de Danaan. Their king had an array of magical weapons that made him undefeatable. A spear and bow no enemy could survive, a cauldron that gave limitless amounts of food to a moving army. A harp that, when played, could drive a person to suicidal despair or euphoric happiness."

Jacob shifted her deeper into the vee between his thighs, his hands spanning her waist, stroking her hips. "As man and Fae drew apart, those Fae disappeared into the earth. Others say that the remaining Fae diminished in size, becoming smaller and smaller. Like the little mother and her baby. They rode on grasshopper or squirrel mounts. I think it's far more likely that they've always existed in a variety of shapes and sizes. At one time, almost any otherworldly creature was considered part of the Fae. Hobgoblins, giants, trolls, gnomes . . ."

"For a man who doesn't trust the Fae, you know a lot about them," she teased, caressing his jaw.

"It's the reason I don't trust them," he pointed out. "Just imagine the stories I heard about vampires."

She smiled at that. "Yet, *you* came looking for *me*."

"Well, Gideon did say I was the pretty brother, not the smart one."

"Only a smart-mouthed one." She tugged his hair, but settled down comfortably enough, stroking his knee. The sun was going to rise soon. She surveyed their surroundings carefully, gauging whether any of the sun beams could penetrate their position. He wasn't deep underground, but the forest was ancient and dense. He should be fine as long as the sun here followed a predictable east to west track. She felt his reluctance to close his eyes and leave her on guard duty.

"Sleep, Jacob," she said firmly. "It's no different than when we were in the mountains. One watches while the other sleeps, so we each get some rest."

"In which case, you sleep first, my lady. I'll need more sleep as the day moves toward noon. You sleep now, and I'll sleep from noon to dusk."

Despite her concern for him, it made sense. Plus the blood seemed to have restored him. Adjusting to slip her arms fully around him, she pillowed her cheek on his chest again. She sighed as he banded his arm more securely around her back, fingers stroking her hair along her spine. Then she started humming.

Jacob recognized one of the lullabies he used to lull Kane to sleep. Being young vampires, both he and his son had to go to sleep right before dawn, something she sometimes teased him about. However, it was one of the best times of day, for often he would cradle Kane in his arms as they lay in their wide bed. The babe would play with fingers and toes, his own and his father's, and sometimes Jacob let the little fangs pierce him at the wrist or throat, a small sip of his father's blood. While he held him, he'd hum the songs, rock him, eventually shift him full onto his chest so his heartbeat could help the child fall asleep.

Enjoying the feel of him there, Jacob would drift off that way as well, his arm tucked around him. He'd awake briefly when Lyssa came to put the babe into his crib. As she did, she'd press a maternal kiss to each of their brows. Sometimes he'd lift his head to meet her mouth for a far more suggestive mating, trying to coax her into the bed with him for a while. However, other times he let it be what it was, enjoying that tranquility.

Now he held her tighter, rocked her a little, because the hummed lullaby put them in the same place, reaching out to Kane with the shared memory of their evening ritual. It also helped soothe her, though he could tell from her mind she was already calm. Exceptionally so, but he knew this side of her, as he knew the matching side in himself. Calm and steady might not mean prepared, because it was difficult to prepare for the unknown, but it was the best way to meet it.

As her voice drifted off, he took up the song. Looking up, he saw a small group of Fae about the size of the irritated mother, as well as another handful of insect Fae, had lighted on a branch above them, listening. These insect Fae were like crickets, bearing fiddles. Delightfully, they began to accompany his lullaby in chirping notes. Thinking of the music he'd heard when they crossed the portal, Jacob recalled the Fae loved few things as much as music and dancing. Higher up, he saw other eyes. Birds here and there, roosting for the night. A long limbed mocha-skinned Fae who might be some form of goblin, clad in little more than a loincloth. He'd stretched out on a branch, the curves of his body molded to it like it was a hammock. He appeared to be listening to the lullaby as well, his lips split back from yellow sharp teeth in a disconcerting yet sleepy grin. Just above him, Jacob caught the quick movement of a squirrel, fluffing her tail and curling it around her nest of three squirrel pups.

Having so recently touched the dryad, Jacob also sensed the spirit of the tree tuning in to their energy, to all the life resting within and upon it. Remembering the young female's face, the tears that rolled down her cheeks, he wished her well, hoping no more ill befell her. He also wished they knew her name.

The dryad's situation, Lyssa's story about her mother, and the stories he knew were laced with as much danger as delightful enchantment. This wasn't Disney, no matter what it felt like. They wouldn't be coming to the queen's court to sing "Kumbaya" together.

Still, he'd learned never to waste the pleasure of holding his sleeping lady in his arms. Singing to her, knowing she trusted him enough to lose herself in dreams—that was enough for this moment.

~

When he woke her at noon, he noted the debilitating lethargy he typically experienced from the sun at its peak was absent. The Fae world might have a more energizing impact on him than expected, an uplifting thought.

Mindful of his need to stay sharp, he made himself shut his eyes and fall into a restorative slumber while the sun made its afternoon sojourn. Despite his faith in Lyssa's capabilities, his instincts didn't sleep. Which was why just past dusk, he surged up out of the shelter, pushing Lyssa away from the blade swinging toward them. Ducking the arc of the sword, he hit its wielder mid-body, rolling them away from his lady. Unfortunately, before he could scramble off their attacker, he was pulled off and flipped over, a boot planted in his chest. It held him against the fallen Fae, as another blade pointed at his throat.

He blinked up at a man with wide shoulders, and the unmistakable demeanor of a veteran soldier. While Jacob expected all high-court Fae to be specimens of physical perfection, like vampires, this one had a wide, jagged scar down the side of his face. A breath closer and it would have taken his eye. The Fae had steady steel gray eyes, a rugged, lined countenance. Silver strands shot through the long dark hair parted over the pointed ears. The tunic over his silver mail bore a white dragon on a blue field.

"Noric was intending to swat you awake with the flat of the blade, vampire, not cut you in half. But good reflexes for a parasite. Noric, you should have anticipated."

Shoving the blade away, Jacob rolled to his feet. "Where I come from, a simple good evening and a cup of coffee to wake me would have sufficed."

Lyssa stood with regal dignity at the opening to their shelter, studying the new arrivals with her usual inscrutable expression. Now the male addressed her as if Jacob had not spoken at all.

"I am Cayden, captain of the Queen's Guard. We are here to escort you to Her Majesty the Lady Rhoswen's court."

Three more Fae with matching tunics were a few paces away. Their mounts looked like the muscular Lipizann horses of Earth, except the white coats had an ethereal, hazy gleam, and their large eyes were violet blue, enhanced by purple flowers braided into their manes. Runelike symbols were painted on their coats. As he watched, Noric sprang to his feet and rejoined the others.

Jacob. Come stand behind me.

Though it took an effort, he schooled his face to bland acceptance, and stepped behind her. The captain followed his movements, waiting a beat before sheathing the sword with the practiced ease of familiar use.

"Your escort is appreciated, Captain." Lyssa nodded. "Do we walk or double your mounts?"

"I'll carry you in front of me. The vampire can wait here. None of our horses will tolerate his kind."

I don't need a horse to keep up, my lady. I'll follow.

"I'm surprised he came with you," Cayden added.

"He serves me. Where I go, he goes."

The captain shrugged. "That may be, but he'll likely lose his life here."

Jacob flashed fangs, shifting a step closer so his chest brushed his lady's back, her loose fall of hair. "Then I guess today will be a good day to die, right?"

The Fae's eyes flickered over him. Though his expression gave away nothing, Jacob got the impression he'd said something of interest to the male. Whether that was a good or bad thing remained to be seen. Cayden jerked his head toward the castle hills. "If you fall behind, we're headed for Caislean Uisce."

The Castle of Water. The Fae had picked up some Gaelic in their history. Lyssa gave him a nod, then moved forward at Cayden's brusque gesture, directing her to his mount. His white horse stood apart from the other four, no need for the reins to be held, the equine a well-trained soldier himself. The saddle was a cinched blanket, no stirrups. Cayden moved to the horse's head to steady him, but otherwise didn't offer her a hand up. Lyssa gave him a sidelong glance. "Courtesy to a lady does not exist in the Fae world?"

The cool jade stare was capable of making most men squirm. Cayden was no exception. However, though Jacob saw him shift uncomfortably, he didn't budge, which suggested he had higher orders not to treat the Lady Lyssa as an honored guest.

Jacob knew she was capable of swinging lithely onto an untacked horse of nearly any size, having been a capable rider for more than nine hundred years, but her dress had a long skirt. With a disgusted look at the captain he didn't bother to disguise, he stepped forward and lifted her.

She'd barely gotten her seat when the horse's head swung around, the stallion's ears laid back. Jacob slipped back quickly, but the creature still came away with a piece of T-shirt and an ill-tempered look, shifting under the captain's soothing hand on his muscular shoulder.

"As I said," he repeated evenly, his expression like stone. "They don't tolerate your kind."

Jacob ignored him. "My lady. I'll be right behind you."

She nodded as the captain came around the horse's head. Cayden gave him a warning look he answered with a blank stare. Lyssa said he sometimes channeled Gideon. However, while his brother had a penchant for scathing repartee during the times it was most likely to get him killed, Jacob had enough restraint to limit his response now to the garden variety eat-shit-and-die look.

Cayden swung up behind her. A soldier would not allow an unknown passenger to ride at his unprotected back, but it was obvious, as he gathered up the reins, that he found the more intimate body contact between them distasteful. It rankled Jacob to see anyone behave disrespectfully to his lady, but it also worried him. If this was the welcoming committee, it made the reception they would find at the castle far more uncertain.

One thing at a time, Jacob. He smells like . . . ice cream, oddly enough.

She sounded unaffected by the captain's posturing. Since riding a horse in that manner required intimate contact, Jacob wasn't unhappy about the captain's distaste. He hoped trying to stay so rigid made for an uncomfortable, spine-jarring ride for him. However, his lady had her own particular streak of devilry. She'd probably melt back into Cayden like molasses sliding down a particularly straight tree, just to be annoying. He pressed his lips in a grim smile and fell in behind them as the horses set off single file through the forest paths.

A couple miles later, when they broke out of the shelter of the wood, Cayden urged them to a canter. The horses were swift, but no swifter than those in their world, so with a vampire's speed Jacob had no problem keeping up. As the castle approached, however, he couldn't help slowing to get a better look.

The waterfalls covering the castle walls fell down into catch tracks shaped to move the water in multiple curved spirals. In contrast, straight, glittering sheets of water fell over window openings in place of glass. More than a year ago, he'd gone to a mall with his lady where she'd taken him into a large, decorative fountain, sliding behind a small waterfall into an alcove just big enough for two people to take their pleasure of each other. She took more than that, feeding from him and giving him the second mark. The rush of the water, the glittering, translucent curtain, had given them the sense of a private haven away from the world.

Would it feel like that, staying in one of those rooms curtained by a waterfall? As they approached the outer moat, which rivaled a Caribbean sea for blue color, tiny cat's paws of foam lapped up from its surface, touched by the playful breeze.

"I'd like to get down, Captain."

As the captain stopped to oblige her, relief evident in his features, Lyssa slid off the mount, bracing herself on his thigh as she did so. He didn't flinch, but it was a near thing, despite the fact it was purely functional, not the teasing caress Jacob knew she'd enjoy using if she was really trying to unsettle a male.

However, he was satisfied to see the captain had unbent enough to support her elbow as she dropped to her feet. Jacob came to her side, drawing her attention upward. On the highest tower, a large white and silver creature crouched, eyeing them with blue eyes. A moment later, it emitted a loud roar, the wings spreading out in magnificent, intimidating display. Along with the roar came a spout of flame.

"A dragon," Jacob said, with deep satisfaction. "A real fucking dragon. God, I wish Gideon were here."

Lyssa couldn't help but enjoy his reaction and entwine it with her own. Dragons perching on castle turrets, fairies putting their babies to bed in flower blooms and gnomes braiding ribbons into the beards of goats . . . Even surly Cayden, in his mail and gauntlets, hair rippling over his back as he rode his white charger. All of them were images captured in fantasy literature and art time and again by a world longing for the reality of their existence. And she and Jacob were here among them.

"We can't tarry," the impressive but irritable captain said. "Follow me now."

Lyssa sedately proceeded across the drawbridge, Jacob a pace behind. The mist from the myriad falls settled like tiny kisses on her face and hands. The two water channels that ran on either side of the drawbridge down into the moat sounded like chuckling laughter. She saw a school of rainbow colored fish swim beneath the bridge, joined by a pair of mermaids, one with golden hair and one with brown, the strands caressing their bare shoulders like silken seaweed. They swam hand in hand. As the mermaids registered the passing soldiers, they came to the top, their heads breaking the surface. They spoke in a language Lyssa didn't know, but it was obvious from the smiles exchanged that fielding the undines' flirtatious comments was a normal routine for the guard.

Cayden gave it a measured moment, then spoke a sharp word. The soldiers straightened, faced forward, and the mermaids dove back under the water, continuing their swim beneath the open drawbridge. Lyssa saw more than one soldier steal a glimpse as they came out the other side, the sweet curves of breast and hip, the pale white arms as the girls rolled and twined together, all playful, sensual innocence.

Cayden wasn't one of those soldiers, his scrutiny remaining on Jacob and Lyssa with occasional sweeps over the guards patrolling the walkways that passed in front of and behind the water falls. They were armed with bows, swords and spears. "Are you expecting some danger, Captain?" she asked.

Cayden glanced at her, then forward again. "A wise man always does."

He hadn't addressed her by an honorific or even her name, Jacob noticed, though Cayden obviously knew who she was. Whether it was the same disrespect he'd been commanded to display, or the fact that Fae rarely used names when addressing one another, Jacob didn't know. Cayden didn't give him much time to ponder it as he led them under the open portcullis and into the quadrangle. He dismissed his men there, dismounted. Out of habit, Jacob noted entrances and exits, and the makeup of the castle population.

Most seemed to be the staff one would expect in the household of medieval aristocracy—housekeeping, cooks, animal husbandry—as well as the armed guards to defend it. While the guards seemed to be of the same stamp as Cayden and his three, the staff were a variety of Fae species. Everything from tiny, airborn Fae like the mother they'd seen, to large, knobby-kneed trolls, lumbering across the main bailey carrying bundles of goods in cloth bags or pulling wagons with the help of shaggy ponies.

As they prepared to pass through the archway into the castle hall itself, Cayden came to an abrupt halt, necessary because Lyssa did. She'd tilted her gaze upward. Due to the variety of waterfalls along the exposed walls, rainbows had occurred, some combination of magic or scientific phenomenon resulting in a crisscrossing of three of them before the archway. When Lyssa extended her palms, molecules of color patterned them. From where Jacob stood, a few steps back, it was like the three rainbows sought to plunge into the reputed pot of gold. Beyond the archway was a large fountain with a bronze statue of a racing pair of gazelles. The fountain caught the rainbow's colors and sparkled with them, giving the gazelles' hooves a sense of flashing movement.

Lyssa rocked from one foot to the other experimentally, shifting between the bands of color, letting them turn her skin red, yellow, blue and green as she moved. Looking back at Jacob, she smiled, pure and sweet.

Kane would love this, Jacob.

Cayden looked as if he'd suddenly found himself saddled with a creature of questionable sanity. It almost made Jacob grin, watching the guard try to figure out how to deal with her. Lyssa lowered her hands, her haughty expression flipping back in place like a well-oiled drawbridge. "We may proceed now, Captain. Thank you for indulging me."

If they had penny nails here, the captain would have looked like he'd swallowed a fistful. She'd neatly projected the idea that he was her escort, not a guard detail, and there was no way to correct the impression that wouldn't make him look foolish. A dangerous game, but his lady rarely played it safe.

Cayden chose to resume their course without further comment. As they moved farther into the workings of the castle, Jacob noted a change in class. Clothes became more ornate, aristocratic trappings more distinct. These were all high court Fae, human in appearance except for their pointed ears and slender, elongated forms blessed with good looks. Rather than seeming entirely indifferent to their presence, the court

Fae stared at Jacob and Lyssa, openly curious. The calculation he detected in some expressions suggested that more than the queen had known of Lyssa's coming.

Whenever those same gazes fell on him, the reaction varied from mildly distasteful surprise to outright scorn. Big surprise there. *The vampire rabble is loose in the castle. Better call the exterminator.*

They reached a tall pair of doors, outlined in silver. The white dragon logo was stamped over the archway. Cayden nodded to Lyssa. "There appears to be a full court in session, in attendance on the queen. When you are so bid, approach her throne and stop within the circle marked on the floor. If you go past that circle, the protections around the queen will engage and it will be very unpleasant. If you try to withstand the pain to reach her, you will be killed."

"I am here at your queen's request, Captain," Lyssa said. "We have no plans to attack her. In fact, our hope, though I suspect it is a slim one, is to be back in our world in time for dinner."

"You have no desire to stay in your father's world?"

Lyssa turned her gaze fully upon him. Though Cayden's remained impassive, Jacob had the distinct impression the guard captain hadn't intended to ask such an intriguingly personal question.

"This is not my world. It never has been, and it never will be. Does that relieve or concern you, Captain?"

In answer, he pushed open the door, gesturing her and Jacob to precede him into the large chamber.

Based on what Cayden had said, Lyssa expected noise, some chatter among retainers when the door opened—at least the queen conversing with an advisor or supplicant while the others attentively listened. Instead, the door opened into a completely silent hall, as if everyone inside had been listening to *their* conversation.

There were perhaps two hundred Fae in the room, lined up on either wall, leaving an aisle to walk up the center toward the queen's throne. That aisle looked like a sheet of moving water. At sporadic points, tiny fingers of current licked outside the aisle's boundaries at the ice blue marble floor, making small ripples of sound, the only noise. The high walls of the hall were likewise covered by sheets of silently falling water that disappeared into a low rolling cushion of mist. It drifted across the floor, billowing around the feet of those in attendance on the queen.

Every eye had turned to Lyssa. The skill of viewing a crowd without making eye contact, while appearing confident and unconcerned by their regard, was second nature to her. While vampire beauty was consistently dangerous, earthy, blood-driven, she noted the beauty of high court Fae was like sculpted glass, all slim, flowing lines and cool expressions. Their fine clothing was inspired by their natural world. Leaflike shapes of fabric molded to the elongated bodies and they wore jewelry of uncut gems. Flower blooms and petals, forever preserved with magic, adorned hair, necklines, hems. Sparkling gems sewn into the fabrics reflected motes off the wall of water around them.

She saw the occasional ornamental dagger, but for the most part they were not visibly armed. Cayden had not checked either of them for weapons, an unusual thing for a captain of the guard, unless he was exceptionally careless or weapons had no power to harm his queen. Lyssa didn't think he was careless.

Agreed, my lady.

She pressed her lips into a tight smile. Of course Jacob had noted the same thing.

As she walked along that aisle of water, intrigued by how the water flowed over her slippers but did not wet them or the trailing hem of her dress, she was aware that the scrutiny of all those retainers was intensifying. Curiosity was the primary emotion she sensed, the kind that was unpleasant, tinged with resentful anger. There was impatience, a bitter half bark of laughter swallowed back too swiftly to know from whence it came, not that she sought the source.

She moved down the center aisle at a steady pace, not faltering or hurrying, her head up. Centuries of birthright and her own blood carried her, conveying the message she intended.

Yes, I am here to respect your authority, but I have authority in my own right. I'm not *here to cringe before you.*

There was no welcome here, but like Cayden's refusal to help her on the horse, she had to discern whether it was genuine or manufactured, a carefully prepared backdrop for whatever the queen wished to accomplish.

What Cayden had called a circle was a sphere rising out of the floor, forming a dome like the hill on which the castle sat. The water flowed upward, guiding her up the incline. When she put her foot on the edge, it shifted, a moving walkway, until she was standing on the top of the sphere. From this view, it looked like a glistening round stone, forever turning with the water's flow even as the person standing on it remained stationary.

Up until now, the end of the hall had been shrouded with mist. But now it parted as if blown away by the breath of a Goddess. As she lifted her gaze, she sensed the magical barrier humming ahead of her position, as Cayden had warned. However, when she saw Queen Rhoswen, she wondered why it was needed. She certainly understood why crude weapons were not a concern.

Ice blue eyes stared at Lyssa out of porcelain features and a frame of snow-colored silk hair that waved around her face and fell below her waist. Rhoswen's crown was an antlered headpiece, the antlers pressing close to either side of her skull, the points coming together at the back. Strands of diamonds draped from the antlers to twine in her hair. A white corset pulled in to show the nip of the waist and rise of generous breasts for her slender frame. While a silver velvet cloak covered her bare shoulders, the diamond choker enhanced the slim grace of her swan's throat. Her skirt was diaphanous silver, shot with blue threads and seeded with more diamonds. The skirt was slashed into strips that parted and gave glimpses of long, shapely legs. A silver anklet with beaded chains that hooked over her toes was her only footwear.

While the queen riveted primary attention, her throne came in a close second. It sat on the crest of a waterfall that split into four parts and splashed down onto an array of crystals in a pool below it. A narrow set of short steps that would require exceptional grace and balance to traverse was the only path of descent.

As Lyssa met the gaze of the potentate, she expected to feel the touch of strong magic and she did, like the prick of a hundred icicles along her skin. From their reception thus far, she hadn't expected the Fae queen to be overly friendly. However, whereas those gathered here radiated vapid curiosity for her and a more intense version of Cayden's practiced disdain for herself and Jacob, what came from the queen was different. It was real, not manufactured or commanded at all, which made it all the more dangerous.

It was pure, undiluted hostility.

Though the beautiful features were expressionless, Lyssa knew she wasn't wrong. She'd been a queen too long herself not to be able to read another one. Whatever the cause, it meant things were not likely to go well. And coming here had been a mistake, no matter how little choice they'd had.

This isn't a complaint, mind you, because she looks like a Victoria's Secret pinup, but why do powerful queens insist on wearing uncomfortable clothes? If I was queen, I'd wear jeans all the time. T-shirts with my favorite logo. Something like: "Fairies Rule, Vampires Drool."

Jacob's impertinent reminder of his presence at her back steadied her, much as it annoyed her to know she'd needed it. Goddess, had the past two years really robbed her of so much confidence?

You'd look better in that corset than your ratty T-shirt, she retorted.

You'd look edible in either one. Though black is your best color. You're more badass than angel, my lady.

That was why she loved the insolent, noble idiot. Sending him a quelling thought, she didn't even flinch when the double doors closed with a thud. Cayden placed himself ahead of and to the right of Lyssa. Despite the obvious impregnable barrier the magical protection provided, apparently Cayden preferred to reinforce that with more manual means if needed.

Queen Rhoswen's ice blue gaze shifted toward a new arrival that stepped through the wall of water on her left. Cayden's mouth tightened as if he disapproved of the unorthodox entry, but the queen's sharp eyes merely narrowed. Following her gaze, Lyssa saw Keldwn there.

The first time she'd seen Keldwyn, they'd been deep in ancient forest, and the Fae lord had not bothered to disguise himself. Most Fae were associated with one of the elements, and Keldwyn's was Earth. His cloak had been an unfamiliar fabric that reminded her of layered brown, gold and red leaves that drifted to the ground in autumn, the edges curled and colors muted. On the inside of the cloak was a delicate inner web of gold thread, like leaf veins. If he'd spread it out with his arms, a fanciful hiker might have thought the cloak was wings, their gaze confused and caught in that enchanted web. In truth, the cloak *was* wings, when it suited Keldwyn to have them. He'd worn glinting gold mail under his plain brown tunic.

At Mason's estate, he'd exercised his ability to pass as human—technically. He'd dressed in simple dark clothes, and his pointed ears lay flat against the sides of his head, almost lost in the tangle of a loose black mane. Tall and lean, the broad shoulders notwithstanding, his face elegant and chiseled, he'd actually reminded her somewhat of Mason and his patrician air, a comparison she was sure Mason would not have appreciated, but Jacob would.

However, pointed ears visible or not, he'd emanated Otherworld even then. In these surroundings, it was obvious that this was Keldwyn's world.

He was back in his Fae raiment, only here, the magic with which it was infused was even more apparent, the mail gleaming, the pommel of his sword a deep bronze hue.

"Why, Lord Keldwyn. How nice of you to grace us with your presence after your self-imposed . . . retreat." The frost in Rhoswen's cultured voice resonated through the hall like the rush of the water. It actually lowered the temperature in the room, a power she herself possessed, one of the first Fae skills she'd used in her role as a vampire monarch. It was a subtle ability that could easily be disguised as an emotional reaction to intimidation.

"I don't need to ask why we are so honored." Rhoswen's attention sliced back to Lyssa. "What did he tell you about freeing Catriona? Did he explain how she came to be trapped there?"

Just like that. No greeting, no preamble. So Lyssa responded in kind. "He said the girl had been trapped there by a cruel, capricious witch. One jealous of the warmth of the dryad's heart, her capacity to love."

His lady didn't wait for a fight to start. If she deemed it inevitable and politically advantageous, she'd draw first blood. Still, the lie startled Jacob. While Lyssa remained locked in her straight posture, Jacob risked a quick look at Keldwyn. Though shock flashed over the Fae Lord's face, it was followed by something as brief, but unmistakable. Deep, vengeful pleasure.

The queen held Lyssa's gaze an extra beat, a response as unsettling as Keldwyn's reaction. "As you may know, Fae do not lie, but we are not beholden to give truth to mortals, or half-blood Fae. We are masters at straddling the line between. Some of us more than others." The queen's chilling gaze swept over Keldwyn. The diamond trails in her hair sparkled, the wave of white hair framing her breathtaking face. "I have heard that since your illness passed and you lost your vampire abilities, your Fae blood is rising in you so strongly, it may be eclipsing the taint of the vampire. Let us see, shall we?"

How she'd known the debilitating result of Lyssa turning him, Jacob didn't know, for they hadn't told Keldwyn, either. Perhaps the Fae spies were better than the vampire ones. It was a point to ponder later, because before Lyssa could respond to the queen, Rhoswen had risen from her throne.

She extended her arm. It was a graceful movement, the sinuous shift of her body a distraction to any male with a pulse, but Jacob interpreted it for the attack it was. He was already in motion, but unfortunately Cayden anticipated him as well. Two more of his guard materialized out of the wall of water at his back, lunging forward to restrain him. Their speed was greater than his own, his attempts to twist free and land blows met with brutal force. They slammed him to his chest in the aisle, where he discovered there was indeed unyielding marble beneath the thin magic of that moving water. His nose and jaw bounced off it, blood exploding in his mouth as his fang pierced his lip. He struggled against them, snarling, but the stone shifted to mud beneath him, oozing over his forearms and calves and just as abruptly becoming solid, unbreakable stone again, holding him fast.

He jerked his head up to find the white, crackling energy that had leaped from Rhoswen's hand was a magical net. It had spun through the air and landed over Lyssa. At first glance, it seemed inert. Lyssa was still standing fast on the sphere, seemingly unaffected. Then her mind exploded in his with a sharp crack of sound, and she cried out. He felt a tearing in his chest, his limbs, as if he was being ripped apart. Though he'd never experienced it in such a direct way, he knew what was happening.

"Goddamn it," he spat. Cayden barely glanced at him. Like everyone else, his attention was fixed on what was unfolding before them. Lyssa dropped to the sphere's surface, convulsing. When done willingly, her Fae transition was a smooth, elegant process. Forced, it was this agonized contortion, as if his lady was becoming a monster. Long, backward-jointed legs emerged from beneath the skirt. Her arms, which bore a sharp curved hook at the elbow joint, the joining point for her wings, tore out of her dress. Her torso was attenuated like a sleek greyhound, the curve of rib cage, each individual bone, visible under the tattered remains of her dress.

She looked like a sensuous, dangerous gargoyle, poised over the stone archway of an ancient Goddess's temple. Silver gray skin, long pointed ears, a barbed tail, lethal talons for fingers. Long fangs curved out over her chin, accenting the slim neck. Her leanly muscled form, the body of an ascetic hunter, had small breasts. With her clothing torn mostly off, her bare sex was readily apparent, the petals of the labia that same smooth silver gray. His lady was not immodest, but this was different. This was forced exposure, and it increased his rage, seeing how the Fae stared at the graphic display with fascinated revulsion.

"Just as I'd heard. It's nothing like we've ever seen before." Rhoswen spoke thoughtfully. Lyssa had struggled to her feet, her large dark eyes snapping with wild temper. Her wings snagged in the net, creating sparks. With a negligent flick of her hand, the queen expanded it into a wider holding area, so Lyssa could straighten them fully, fold them along her back. "You are ugly and revolting enough to be one of the lowest ranks of Unseelie, those who delight in frightening human children."

Titters passed among the assembled, some unkind chuckles. When the stone shifted and freed Jacob, Cayden pulled him up by the collar, giving him a warning look and holding him firmly with his men flanking him. He would be allowed to stand but not to interfere. Jacob didn't know if that was worse than being irrevocably bound, but apparently the queen didn't want him to miss a single detail. She wanted to humiliate Lyssa in front of her vampire servant as well. Jacob bared his fangs at the males but held his ground, his eyes sparking blue fire.

Rhoswen continued speaking. "Of course, because of your special . . . circumstances, some of the inexplicable bits of power you've displayed, it might suit us to keep you close while we determine what you will become. We may assign you to a consort of my choosing."

"I can promise you that will not happen."

Her voice might rasp in this form, her vocal cords affected by the change, but the cool resolve he knew so well was in full force. In his peripheral vision, Jacob saw members of the court aping the way Lyssa spoke, using fingers to mock the fangs over her lips, or hunching over to imitate her back legs. Those backward facing knees made her a powerful predator, allowing her to launch from hiding in the trees and pounce on wild prey.

His lady acknowledged none of it. When he extended a tendril into her mind, he found a solid ice center to her thoughts, capable of competing with Rhoswen's frost. He didn't pry into it, not right now. That wasn't what she needed from him.

Rhoswen raised a brow at Lyssa's quiet declaration. "That net will keep you as I wish. You cannot change back into your humanoid form until I permit you to do so. I could touch your eye lids with one tiny drop of enchanted honey, and the first person I put before you would become your obsession, your heart's desire for all eternity. Arrdol, for instance."

She nodded toward a Fae at the front line of her retainers. He stepped forward, a tall, broad male dressed in black and silver. He possessed a foxlike countenance and glittering dark eyes. "He has a taste for the unusual. I could assign your vampire lover as a slave to Arrdol's household, and though he might be weeping and heartbroken right before you, you'd never again have a thought of him. Unless you needed your breakfast, or your chamber pot emptied. You would spread yourself for Arrdol whenever he deigned look your way, even if he openly despised you. And he would, because though he is intrigued by your uniqueness, he would spurn the heart of an aberration like you. Every member of my court would."

A dry, harsh chuckle echoed through the chamber. Lyssa spread out her taloned hands. She raked them across the net, sending out sparks. "If you are trying to frighten me, impress me with your cruelty, you might remember I've lived in the vampire world for more than a thousand years. In their version of your scenario, they wouldn't use enchanted honey. They'd want me to feel the weight of my captivity, my helplessness, and the tearing agony of watching my true love suffer. Perhaps it speaks well of you, that you're not as practiced in the sadistic arts. I believe you summoned me for a reason, and that reason isn't simply to humiliate me in front of your subjects. A queen of your stature has far more pressing duties than that. Or at least she should, if she is a queen of worth."

Rhoswen stared at her. The dense, high pressure that swept the chamber suggested to Jacob they might be on the cusp of annihilation, about to be frozen behind the watery walls as Rhoswen's personal trophies. He saw it in the tightening of the muscles between Cayden's wide shoulders. Then Rhoswen's expression became that thoughtful façade again. She directed her words to the assembled group.

"It's distracting, like hearing a pet talk. I keep expecting her to wag her tail and beg for a treat."

Though the assembled Fae laughed, there was a forced sound to it. Lyssa squatted on her haunches. Spreading her wings, she shook them out with a flutter of motion, and curved her tail up around her ankles. Jacob thought it was like watching two queens on a chessboard, though Rhoswen had a lot more pawns at her disposal.

That ominous pressure shuddered through the room again, touched with ice as Rhoswen's expression changed, her lip curling. "You may have Fae blood, but you are a mutation, a mistake. You cannot pretend Fae kinship. The fact you come here with a vampire beast as a lover merely confirms it."

"Though I do not choose his people as my own, I honor my father," Lyssa responded. Though he expected it was carefully calculated, Jacob had no doubt that what he heard in her voice was true anger. "He was a high-court Fae, and he chose a vampire lover. Perhaps he did not find what he sought among the females here."

"A petty insult doesn't disguise the fact he chose poorly." Rhoswen looked toward Jacob. He noted her sharp nails were moving in a pensive ripple along her thigh, teasing at the fabric of her skirt. "The pregnant vampire female fled, leaving him to meet his fate alone. Like this one would, if I did as I said and made him Arrdol's slave. Right, vampire? If I gave her mind and soul to Arrdol, you'd flee this world as soon as I gave you leave."

Jacob wiped the blood off his mouth with the back of his hand, then spat on the floor to get rid of the taste of it, close to Cayden's boots. "I think my Mistress is right. You don't know what love is. And though I don't have your powers, Your Majesty, a vampire's sense of smell is keen. You're afraid of something you don't understand."

The strike from Cayden was expected, but the magical power added behind it was not. When he hit him in the face with the hilt of his sword, Jacob heard the sickening crunch of his nose and cheekbone, an explosion of pain that blinded him. As he staggered back in reaction, Cayden followed. Jacob forced his eyes back open just as Cayden lunged forward and drove his blade into his unprotected abdomen.

A second later, all hell broke loose.

7

All the pressure that had been building between two irreconcilable forces detonated. Lyssa snarled like a savage animal, and that net of white fire exploded in a billow of orange flame. Even dropped to one knee, holding the blade in his gut, his vision blurry from his shattered nose, Jacob had the satisfaction of seeing the blast impact pick Cayden up and fling him into a cluster of retainers, toppling them like dominoes. Barely in time, Rhoswen threw up an additional protection over herself, a ripple of ice. The flame roared over it, billowed the few steps up to her throne and swallowed the white wood like a ravenous dragon.

The two guards close to Jacob had not been affected by the blast, evidence that Lyssa had enough control of her reaction to cast a protection on Jacob and his immediate surroundings. However, as they broke out of their shock to start toward her, the element of surprise was now in his camp. Pain didn't stop a vampire. Hell, it had rarely stopped him as a human third-mark, because his lady had taught him to embrace and use it in myriad ways.

Now he used the adrenaline and his rage to yank the sword from his midriff. Swinging the bloodstained blade, he tripped one guard with it and then flipped it to hit the other hard in the face with the pommel. He wished he was returning the favor to Cayden, rather than one of his men, but the crunch of bone was still satisfying. He stomped on the midriff of the tripped one to keep him incapacitated, and then braced himself, sword at the ready, as Cayden charged out of the tangle of fallen court members like an enraged bull. There was no hesitation in his forward charge, despite the fact he'd drawn a short knife and Jacob had his long blade. Jacob felt the sweet anticipation that came right before engaging an opponent as crazy with bloodlust as himself.

"Enough." Rhoswen's voice reverberated through the room. The shockwave from it rippled across the waterfalls and vibrated through the floor. Jacob held his position, unmoving, as Cayden came to a skidding halt right before the lifted blade. The point pressed into his broad chest, his face flushed with anger above it. The defiant glare the captain of the guard threw his queen was one Jacob knew all too well from situations where his lady had held him back from needed ass-kickings. He would have spared Cayden some empathy if he hadn't obliterated such tender feelings by driving his sword in Jacob's gut. A quick glance showed that Lyssa hadn't moved from the top of the sphere. She stood where the queen thought she'd trapped her, only now it was clear that remaining there had been Lyssa's choice.

Of course, that could be a bluff. She might not have had enough control of the power to call it until events provoked it from her, but as long as she acted like it had been her plan all along, she had the upper hand. At least for the moment.

His lady made a crooning noise through her fangs, a small hiss. Stretching her wings again, she descended to the floor in front of the sphere, her toes practically aligned with the magical barrier Cayden had said would incinerate her. Then she flicked out her talons in a roll of impressive movement and shimmered back into her human form. Though she was entirely naked except for the belt and small velvet pouch low on her hips, she showed no modesty about that, her hip-length hair simply enhancing the beauty of the curves and cream skin. Her calm manner showed she knew exactly how good she looked, an ebony and jade mirror of the queen's pale snow. A mutation, indeed.

The fallen retainers had gained their feet, but returned to that silence. All eyes were on the Fae queen, waiting on her next move. It seemed the two females were in a passive deadlock, nothing obvious from either expression. As a result, the sound of footsteps on the marble was loud. Jacob kept the sword raised and trained on Cayden, though the male had stepped back a grudging pace. However, they both glanced toward Keldwyn as he moved away from the front line of the audience, toward Lyssa. As he did, he shrugged his cloak off his shoulders, the rust brown and dark black fabric gleaming from the flames crackling over Rhoswen's throne. Lyssa didn't acknowledge him, but he slid his hand to her nape, courteously gathering up the fall of dark hair to clear the cloak before he settled it on her shoulders. Then he stepped back, standing no more than a pace or two to her right, which put him at a right angle to the triangle he formed between the two queens. Interestingly, his position put him over that magical barrier, but he seemed unaffected by it. Jacob wondered if it was spelled only for Lyssa and himself.

The queen stared at him, but spoke to Lyssa. "He is no friend to you, you know. That dryad was left trapped in your world by my decree. She was sentenced to the consequences of her actions for her fraternization with humans, her defiance when I told her to desist."

"She was a willful child, experiencing her first infatuation." Keldwyn's voice was flat. Jacob wondered if Keldwyn had learned impassivity so well his softer emotions were permanently locked away somewhere, so deep he might have lost the key. Or maybe he'd never had such emotions to hide.

"She is a child no more, is she? So both our problems are solved. Or yours may be just beginning." Rhoswen shifted her attention back to Lyssa. "The dryad is the child of a Fae he loved, a Fae murdered in your world. To watch over this impetuous child, the great Lord Keldwyn exiled himself from us, choosing to live in the dwindling old forests of the human world."

"We all make choices, Your Majesty. You choose to imprison yourself in this world, trapped by your hatred of the humans and vampires. Everything that is not pure Fae."

Rhoswen lashed out with those sparking fingertips again, too fast for Jacob to do anything more than tighten his grip on the sword hilt, but his lady was not the target. Slashes opened up across Keldwn's face, though the queen made no obvious physical contact. Blood seeped from the wounds as Jacob noted the glitter of ice crystals in the wound. She glowered at Keldwyn. "I can imprison you in that same tree, Kel."

The male had not moved from the blow, not even to flinch. "Yes, you can. It does not change truth. It never does."

Obviously, there was something happening here, another chapter in an ongoing story. Unfortunately, from the way Rhoswen's attention now lasered back in on Lyssa, Jacob suspected it was tangled with their presence here. The Fae queen lifted her opposite hand, only this time she was pointing toward her throne. A cold wind rose, swirled around the wood and vanquished the flames with frost. Though blackened in places by the smoke, the throne had otherwise not been affected.

"Do not be deceived," Rhoswen repeated. "Keldwyn is no friend."

Lyssa bared her canines in a sharp smile. "*Friend* does not mean what the storybooks say. It is simply someone whose needs align with your own for a certain period of time."

"Too true." Moving back to her throne, Rhoswen perched on the edge of it. Bringing one knee up, she curved her bare, bejeweled toes over the edge of the seat. In the glittering white outfit, the corset's hold shifting on her breasts and the skirt splitting to show more leg, it was a provocative picture. "This display of power tells me a few things, but raises far more questions. Is it the transfer of your vampire powers that initiated the expansion of your Fae ones? You still carry the blood of a vampire, but in terms of characteristics, you are perhaps now more Fae than the other species, no matter your classification among us."

It was as if the violent confrontation had never occurred, and Jacob wasn't holding a sword in an offensive position toward Cayden, his two men back on their feet and surrounding him. However, they stood at a cautious distance, waiting for direction from their captain or an indication from the queen.

That aside, Jacob knew the Fae queen wasn't the only one who'd mulled the unanswerable questions. Lyssa had sired a very small handful of vampires in her long life, but none had taken her powers from her as a result of the turning, the way it had happened with Jacob. Lord Brian had concluded that it might have been a combination of factors—the Delilah virus that was now wiped from her blood, the stress of that terrible moment, or the exceptional third-mark bond she and Jacob had. But his tests proved nothing conclusive.

"Fae blood does not mean you know what it is to be Fae," Rhoswen said. "You have no history with us, no understanding of our world."

"I know that my mother had to seek refuge with the Vampire Council to escape the Fae assassins sent to destroy her. As a result, for ten centuries, I've had no desire to be part of the Fae world. Until I showed myself capable of exercising Fae abilities, you were fine with that."

"I did not invite you to be a part of this world," Rhoswen said, her blue eyes chilling even further. "I summoned you to determine if I should destroy you, or if you have a value to this court."

Lyssa looked pointedly toward the throne, the blackened tile. "Which one have I proven?"

Rhoswen's lips curved, showing a grim appreciation of Lyssa's caustic tone. "You've proven that you have enough Fae power that I cannot allow you to leave my court. Despite your tantrum, you and I both know I have the ability to bind you as a consort to a Fae Lord of my choosing. You are outnumbered here, you cannot leave the Fae world without me opening a gateway for you, and there are other, quite politic ways of burning your bridges behind you."

Rhoswen shifted to cross her legs. "Thanks to carefully placed bits of information, the Vampire Council already suspects you only have Fae powers. That you are no longer a true vampire, according to their narrow standards. It matters not how powerful a Fae you are. Even if you could blow every one of their limited minds out of their skulls, they would not accept you."

"I think you underestimate the nature of the Council's narrow-mindedness, even with your adept spies," Lyssa responded. "Power is irresistible currency, regardless of its form. I will take my chances with them before I will submit to a consort of your choosing. I have chosen my consort, and will never choose another, not in your world or mine."

"A vampire." When Rhoswen's tone dripped with scorn, Lyssa responded with a harsh note of laughter.

"You style yourself so different from the vampires, Your Majesty, but in truth you share the same prejudices. Not too long ago, my world came apart and I faced my death. It was then I learned something very important, something I shall never forget, no matter what role I have to play in any intrigue concocted by you or the vampire world. When it comes to Jacob, I don't give a damn what any of you think."

Though emotion swelled in his chest as her declaration echoed off the walls, Jacob could tell things were taking a bad turn once more. It would be back to a physical contest of wills in no time. Queen Rhoswen vacillated so quickly between cold anger, outright violence and indifferent flippancy, it was impossible to form a stable impression of her at this point.

Cayden was another matter. Jacob had been keeping his attention on the male. His body language wasn't merely responding to Jacob's passive threat, but to his queen's words, telegraphing the direction her moods might go.

Jacob cleared his throat, drawing the male's gaze. Unfortunately, since it was silent again, the sound shifted everyone's attention to them. Regrettable, but he was committed now. Dropping the point of the blade, Jacob wiped the blood on it on his jeans' leg, then extended the weapon, pommel first, to the guard captain. When Cayden took it, giving him a measured glance, Jacob offered a nod and a gesture, advance warning of his intention to move back to the side of his lady. Once there, he dropped to one knee, bowing his head. "My lady . . . Your Majesty . . . may I have leave to speak?"

If I say no, will it matter?

Far more than if she denies me. He gave her a sense of what he intended in a flash of words and images. It surprised her, but she gave him tacit agreement in a spare nod.

"Speak, vampire," the Fae queen agreed. "If I tire of your voice, I will silence you."

Fair enough. Thanks to the considerable healing powers he'd inherited from Lyssa, his nose had already mended, the hole in his gut closed, but they were sore as hell. And damn it all, he'd need more of her blood to fortify him soon. But for now, he was holding.

"Your Majesty, my ancestors were from Hibernia, the wintry, green land. Ireland. You asked if my lady understood the Fae, knew their history. There is a story I beg your leave to share." Averting his gaze, he dipped his head, a deferential motion, one well-practiced from his time on the Faire circuit. It was one that intrigued the female visitors, old and young alike. He was not intending flirtation, but he was an experienced storyteller, and he wasn't opposed to using his full arsenal to intrigue the Fae queen. Particularly if it avoided another life or death situation.

"A long time ago, when there was more congress between our two worlds, a human prince met up with a Fae one. By accident, the human prince killed a stag meant for the Fae prince. As recompense, the Fae prince said that they would change places for a year. He would appear as the human prince in the prince's world, and the human prince would appear as the Fae one in the Fae world. The human prince was an honorable man, and so he agreed. The term was for a year and a day.

"While the human prince was not yet married, the Fae prince had a wife, a woman of great beauty, in spirit and physical form. She would be nigh irresistible to any man, as one would expect of Fae royalty."

A cold smile touched Rhoswen's lips, recognizing the charm. A similar flash of wry humor came from his Mistress, with a slight edge. *Don't tell your story too well, Sir Vagabond.*

He pressed on, noting that Keldwyn was also listening. "Each night, when the human prince came to the Fae princess, he would lie in their bed and hold her, but he would not claim her, even though the Fae prince had not denied him this. During the course of that year, the Fae princess of course grew very sad, thinking her husband's affections had left her. But after the year and a day was over, the two males traded places again.

"The human prince was surprised to find that the Fae prince had been a wise and generous ruler, and left his kingdom even more prosperous, taking no advantage of anything but the adventure of living as a human being. When the Fae prince came to his wife, and saw her great sadness, he revealed to her what had transpired. She told him how the human prince had honored her husband, and said that the Fae prince had indeed found a great and true friend. They remained so for many years after that, until of course time took its toll and the human prince passed from his mortal coil."

"A pretty tale, one I've heard," Rhoswen said at length. "But what is your purpose in telling it, vampire?"

"I value this story for two reasons. First, it underscores the honor and loyalty a man owes a lady." Jacob bowed toward both women. "It also reminds me of ancient times, when the Fae and human worlds were not so separate, and not always at odds."

Rhoswen looked down her straight nose at him. "The problem with ancient times is that memory romanticizes and fabricates. In truth, most of the stories were bard's tales enhanced by drink and wishful, naive hearts. Whereas acts of human and vampire betrayal are shameful history documented among our kind."

Jacob spread out his hands in a conciliatory motion. It brushed his fingertips over the cloak on his lady's body, and he had to resist the desire to touch the bare knee just beneath its cover, making that precious contact. "Perhaps, Your Majesty, all of us have learned to judge our respective species by the actions of a few. As my lady pointed out, this appears to be the nature not only of humans and vampires, but Fae as well. I offer the humble opinion that it's a weakness we all should overcome. If the Fae queen is the first to overcome it, that would underscore her superior wisdom, would it not?"

Keldwyn cleared his throat. Cayden shifted, and Jacob made a concerted effort not to look toward him, going on faith that he wasn't about to be skewered again. Rhoswen glanced at Lyssa. "I'm beginning to understand why you keep him around."

"He has his uses," Lyssa responded.

"I can see that." In a graceful move, the queen was back on her feet and moving from her throne. With a wave of her hand, the magical barrier dissipated, like the sudden absence of crackling static from a highly charged electric fence. Cayden made a brief note of protest in his throat, but Rhoswen flicked her gaze over him and he fell silent. Jacob picked up another clue from it, however. Cayden was concerned that Rhoswen was underestimating Lyssa's abilities, and still felt that way. Since he'd just seen Lyssa's abilities first hand, and of course he would know his queen's, that meant that the two were more closely matched than Rhoswen was revealing.

Well done, Sir Vagabond. As you said, the key to the queen is the consort. Or in this case, the captain. Mind that lesson yourself, with your poker face.

It was a wry joke, because she knew his expressions were far too transparent. As the queen strode up to him, Lyssa shifted in her direction, but Rhoswen merely laid her palm on the side of his face. Putting pressure on it, she made him avert his head so she could study his profile. It allowed him to rest his gaze on his lady, but Lyssa's attention was on Rhoswen, a female bird of prey eyeing an interloper to her nest.

Rhoswen's fingers were as cold as they appeared, and now that he saw them up close, he realized she had long black nails that didn't appear to be painted. Impressions of frost on them looked like tiny snowflakes. As she drew him to his feet, the frost became snow in truth, dusting his skin, creating gooseflesh. She was even more stunningly beautiful at this proximity, her silken hair inviting touch as it swung forward, brushing the knuckles of the hands he had at his sides. If he glanced down, he would be gazing full on that marvelous expanse of breasts, possibly getting a view of the nipples the corset barely contained. Out of a healthy sense of self-preservation, he kept his gaze on his lady.

If you truly cared about your well-being, you would hide such thoughts from your Mistress, despite your promise not to conceal things from me.

Perhaps I care more about honoring your claim on my mind than my own well-being. It's not my fault she has an incredible rack.

He'd been deliberately crude to defuse some of the tension he felt from his lady, and he succeeded, winning a flash of amusement from her. Then Rhoswen began to speak.

"There is another tradition, one that human and Fae courts shared in those ancient medieval times. It is one the Unseelie Court has retained." Rhoswen put her hand on Jacob's pectoral, those wicked nails whispering over the cotton of his T-shirt. "You are my subject, Lyssa. If I desire to lie with your consort, I have that right. I will take him to my bed tonight, and determine what it is about him that holds your loyalty so deeply."

"Vampires are not your equals, no more than beasts to you, but they're all right to fuck." Lyssa's response was as dry as brittle bones.

Rhoswen laughed, though her nails bit into Jacob's skin. "Nice attempt. You're very convincing. But I'm not stupid."

"You are if you go down this road."

Rhoswen pivoted to face her. Ice crystals formed on Jacob's skin, even as Cayden's sword pressed into his lower back again, warning him against trying anything while Rhoswen's back was turned to him.

Rhoswen moved toe-to-toe with Lyssa. She was a few inches taller than his lady, making her lift her chin to hold the queen's gaze, though that didn't seem to discomfit her as Rhoswen might have hoped. However the Fae queen's voice was treacherously reasonable. "Is your line in the sand so important to you that you'd risk him? Cayden has wooden knives as well, and many guards at his disposal. Though I admit I have even more difficulty understanding this territorial reaction than I do the fact you chose a vampire for your consort, you have to pay the price for exposing your weakness for him to me. A queen of worth should know better." Her eyes flashed as she gave back the insult. "After all, my using his body is little different than what he would experience at one of your vampire orgies."

When Lyssa still said nothing, Rhoswen reached out and curled a hand in her hair, twining an ebony lock around her fingers, her nails sliding along Lyssa's collar bone. The gesture was threatening and feral. Jacob shifted, and Cayden shifted with him, only instead of the expected jab of the sword, he felt the male's hand on his arm, a firm but not bruising grip.

"'Tis a catfight at this point. Let them show their claws."

Cayden spoke in a bare murmur, too soft to be heard by the otherwise occupied queens. Perhaps the captain was also trying to find a solution here that didn't involve bringing the room down around their ears.

Rhoswen leaned in, her lips brushing Lyssa's ear. "Remember what I told you, half-breed. The combined magical ability in this room subjugates you to my will, whatever that will is."

Lyssa turned her head so there were only inches between their intent faces. "You were sure your power alone was up to that challenge a moment ago. I'll be happy to test your theory against greater numbers."

"Your Majesty." Jacob knew he was stepping fully into the zone of his lady's displeasure by speaking out of turn this time, but he did it anyway, with another glance at Cayden. As the guard captain released him, Jacob dropped back down to one knee. "I will service you however you need. I only require my lady's permission, because I refuse no order from her lips." Lifting his gaze, he met Rhoswen's. "Anything I do for you will be because she commands it."

They kept putting the queen into positions where she had to save face. He knew Lyssa was as aware of that as he was, but he wondered why his lady was playing such a precarious game, straddling the line between courtesy and royal umbrage, offering no deference to the Fae queen at all before her subjects.

I can detect the presence of Fae somewhat the way I do vampires,

Jacob. Keldwyn, Rhoswen and her guardsmen are the only real beings in this room.

That was a disturbing revelation, given how much power it must take to make the courtiers corporeal, moving and responding as such, like when Cayden was bowled into their ranks. However, it explained a great deal about Rhoswen's mercurial behavior. She wasn't performing for an audience at all, but motives of her own.

"As you said, he has his uses." The Fae queen spoke again, responding to Jacob's courteous challenge. "Though I expect at times you have an equal desire to turn him into a frog."

"There are various punishments I have concocted for him," Lyssa said tonelessly. "While creative, that has not been one of them."

"Queen Rhoswen." Keldwyn spoke. Jacob had almost forgotten he was present. The Fae Lord stepped forward, sketching a bow to her.

"Notice it's not 'my lady' or 'your majesty,'" Rhoswen remarked acidly. "He does everything within the bounds of courtesy and etiquette, though his hatred of me rolls off in waves."

"You did bind his child in a prison for over two decades," Lyssa observed.

"She is not his child. She's the child of the woman he loved. And children are like acorns, scattered over the ground. Some will root and grow, some will be eaten, and some will simply rot, fallen into corners where they are forgotten. Until they become trees, they are not important."

"Yet without them, there are no trees," Keldwyn said. He met her gaze. "My queen, there is a way you can resolve the fate of Lady Lyssa and her consort without a battle of wills. The Quest Gauntlet."

He turned toward Lyssa, his tone polite. "In our world, three quests must be met to determine if a subject is worthy to have his or her opinion bear weight in an unresolved matter, even if that matter is with the royal court. How they comport themselves for those quests, the queen's decision and discretion concerning them, settles the issue. The queen has used this method before—"

"For full-blooded Fae who live in our world."

"Your Majesty, the Quest Gauntlet is well proven in its fairness toward High Court or lesser Fae. As our queen, you are guided by the magical energies that pervade our world to set the tasks. If you do that as ably as you have always done it in the past, justly testing the mettle of others, then you may resolve many of your concerns in this matter as well."

The queen's gaze sparked with true malevolence. But the exchange told Jacob something else important. There *were* rules here, and the queen was not disposed to ignore them.

"I would suggest," Keldwyn continued in the pregnant silence, "that, despite my duplicity, their successful ability to arrive here after freeing Catriona would qualify as the first quest. Under the old ways."

"So sure of that, are you?" The queen's voice was acid.

"If you agree," he said, keeping his tone deferential, "then whatever two additional quests that are set might need to be arranged in accordance with the missive I've brought from the Seelie Court. Since Lady Lyssa's coming has aligned with the annual Samhain Hunt, the Seelie king requires her attendance. He would very much like to meet the daughter of Lord Reghan."

Jacob was kneeling in the aisle between the retainers. At Keldwyn's words, the moving water became ice beneath his knees, so solid and clear that he found himself gazing down into the water foundation of the castle. More undines swam there, hazy outlines through the frosted surface. Mist shrouded the hall, and snow fell thickly, swirling like a mild blizzard, kissing the skin with prickling cold.

The tense moment proved Lyssa right. There were no retainers in the hall. The animated, colorful figures were gone, replaced by a far more sparse assembly of ice sculptures in various poses. Cloven-hooved satyrs, the elusive nixen with ropes of seaweed tangled hair, winged Fae. One of them, looking much like Catriona, balanced on one slender toe, turning slowly under the snow flakes like a music box dancer in a snow globe.

Despite that entrancing picture, his attention snapped from it as Rhoswen spoke three words, bullets capable of cracking the thick ice beneath them, threatening death in hypothermic waters.

"How dare you."

Keldwyn's gaze flickered. Cayden had lowered his sword, obviously no longer considering Jacob a threat. However, his jaw was tight as iron, suggesting he'd like to use the blade on the Fae Lord.

"I am merely delivering His Majesty's exact message," Keldwyn said, unconcerned. "I am a liaison between both courts, Your Majesty, as you well know. I paid my respects to the Seelie king before I came here. He asked me my business in returning to our world. The interest is purely his, no influence of mine. You assume far greater things of this humble Fae than I am capable."

"Oh, no doubt. One day, Keldwyn, you will cross the line, and the very laws you use will damn you. And then you will pay for your presumption, for as long as it gives me pleasure to exact it."

"Perhaps one day we will both see impossible dreams granted, Your Majesty."

Jacob waited for things to go very bad. Lyssa's hand, resting on his shoulder, tightened perceptibly, suggesting his lady was braced for the same. But then Rhoswen gave a bitter laugh. She tossed her hair back, dispelling a shower of snow flurries, and abruptly the room was no longer an ice garden. It was merely a hall of mirrors and falling water, reflecting each other in a never-ending cycle. Though Jacob didn't expect to see himself, he noted none of them reflected, so it was still impossible to see who stood inside the hall . . . or if they were in such a place at all. Reality was hard to pin down here.

"Very well. The Quest Gauntlet it is. You are permitted to choose a champion, Lady Lyssa, or accept the quests yourself."

"I'm her champion."

"I accept."

They spoke at once, though Lyssa gave Jacob a searing look. *You have learned to speak out of turn far too often, Sir Vagabond.*

I speak out of turn only for your protection, my lady. With respect, there's been great need of that of late.

"Well, that will make things interesting," Rhoswen said, those blue eyes measuring. "One for each of you, I think. The first will be delivered to you on the night of the Hunt, but in deference to your busy social schedule, that one will be your champion's quest, not yours."

Lyssa's jaw tightened. "He is my servant. He cannot accept a quest on my behalf if I wish to take it for myself."

"The queen's discretion, remember? This is the way it must happen. As Kel said, the powers that guide me in the Quest Gauntlet know best."

Interestingly, there was no sarcasm attending that statement, and when she turned to Cayden, all traces of anger had once again vanished.

She was as remote as any monarch dealing with matters of mundane consequence. "Provide them a suitable guest room. They may wander as they will in our world. Make sure they are brought to the Hunt site at the proper time."

Cayden gave a short bow, though Jacob noticed as the queen turned away, he looked at Keldwyn. If ever there was an I'm-so-going-to-kick-your-ass look, it was on the captain's face. Keldwyn arched an anytime-you-feel-lucky-son brow. Definitely so many things happening here above their heads, and it was not an easy feeling. Jacob's intuition was going off like a blaring fire alarm. Just like a Vampire Council session, the more inside intel they had on what all the political maneuvering was about, the more likely they'd survive. They needed a way to get more information.

I agree. And my servant needs a lesson in obedience. It seems we can handle two birds with one net.

"Queen Rhoswen?"

The queen had been striding toward the base of her throne, suggesting that behind the four-way waterfall was an exit to another location in the castle. Now she paused. In the beat of time before she turned her head toward Lyssa, Jacob wondered if she'd been wiping an expression from her face. Frustration, rage? Weariness?

"Your Majesty, you spoke of a desire to lie with my servant. Was that a true desire?"

Rhoswen pivoted, a slow movement that drew the eye to the tempting shape of her delineated by the corset. It was only enhanced as she swept her fall of hair from the left shoulder, making the silver cloak she wore ripple. "It was."

Jacob remembered what Rhoswen had said. A Fae would not lie, though they were masters of misdirection and misperception. So the simple answer was probably the truest thing they'd yet heard, whatever the motives behind the answer. However, those motives were now double-edged, and he was balanced on that blade.

Lyssa spread her hands. "You were correct. Similar things occur at vampire gatherings. However, the difference between them and the medieval tradition is that I share my servant only in my presence. Why would I deny myself the pleasure of seeing him perform or participating as well, even if I am sharing him with another? Can you accept my offer under those terms?"

"Give me a taste of what pleasure I may expect, if I do."

Lyssa glanced down at Jacob. "Rise. Remove your shirt for the queen."

Jacob complied, stripping off the T-shirt. He kept his eyes ahead, on the throne, not looking toward Keldwyn or Cayden. He'd learned to handle situations such as this, but he still wasn't comfortable in front of males, particularly adversaries, who got to stand fully clothed and watching. Even more, ones not bound to sexual submission as he was. What got him through each time was the knowledge it was about his lady's pleasure, not his pride. He reminded himself of that now.

As Queen Rhoswen approached once more, the thought helped him stand fast. Her gaze was traveling over his upper body, a slow, sultry scrutiny across his chest, his stomach, down to the waist of the jeans. They rode low enough the musculature of his lower abdomen and hip bones were visible. He saw her gaze linger on the pendant Catriona had given him. It had become a simple brown stone again, the green and amber glow obviously activated by magic unique to Catriona. However, the Fae queen obviously recognized it as something of her world, because her lips tightened at the sight of it. Her gaze traveled downward, pausing on the cross brand. Then, as she moved around him, it was the servant's mark and the faint lash scars layering it that drew her attention. Her hands were truly like ice, such that he had to steel himself not to flinch. Trailing them down to his waistband, she played with the hilt of the scabbarded knife she found there. As she hooked her finger alongside it, sharp nails scraped the rise of his buttock.

"You have whipped him."

"Yes, but not in that instance. They were administered by my former servant, as part of the oath Jacob took. The Ritual of Binding a full servant must make to a vampire queen."

"So you have learned the way to pleasure through pain, have you, vampire?"

"What pleasures my lady, pleases me, Your Majesty."

Rhoswen returned to his front. As she did, she tracked in front of Cayden. Jacob noted the guard captain's face was wooden. He seemed as thrilled about this little tableau as he would be about having his foot gnawed off by wild dogs. Considering his jaw and gut still ached from its contact with Cayden's sword, Jacob couldn't say it didn't give him some satisfaction, even though he empathized with the captain's reaction far too much.

"Hmm." The Fae queen tilted her gaze, slid it down. "I want to see the entire man, make sure he is not deformed in any way."

Jacob glanced toward Lyssa. She could tell him in her mind, but he wanted to make it clear who ordered him, which suited both their purposes. He did it with courtesy, though, knowing his lady didn't want the queen rankled overmuch. Lyssa gave him a nod, and he opened the jeans, shoving them down his thighs. It was not his favorite position, for it left his ankles tangled, but he already sensed the queen would have no patience for him to remove the boots. She made a growling purr in her throat.

At the first vampire dinner he'd ever attended, he'd had to publicly service two women at once in front of a party of vampires and his lady. Recalling the panic he'd felt then, he had to admit he'd come a long way. But it still gave him that locking anxiety high in his chest, even as his cock inexplicably got hard and his heart pounded with need, knowing that he was responding to his lady's commands.

What pleasures my lady pleases me . . . In far more direct terms, her commands made him hard, made him want to do anything to earn the right to bury his cock inside of her, let him service her with mouth, hands, whatever she needed. At the beginning, it had been just a vague compulsion, hard to understand. While he still didn't always understand it, the things he would do for her and why, the reason had become far less important over time. Like now. The result was all that mattered.

He drew in a breath as Rhoswen's cold fingers curved around his thick, steel length, and her tongue touched pink lips. With her breasts so close, pillowed and cinched up in that corset, the trim waist that begged a man's hands and the legs beneath that looked capable of locking around a man's hips and taking him deep, it wasn't difficult to maintain the reaction.

"It seems your cock does not wilt from the touch of ice. Can it stay that way, through the coldest storm? Can you pleasure me as I desire?"

"I can pleasure you however my lady wishes me to do so." Looking down, he saw Rhoswen's drifting touch had limned the muscled lines of his abdomen with frost. He briefly met the blue eyes that were studying him so intently, then returned his gaze to the floor behind her. She was taller than his lady, but not as tall as himself.

Her fingers caressed him a chilling moment more, then slipped away. "He's tediously honorable, but his other qualities may help us overlook that irritation. You may clothe yourself, vampire." As he reached down to draw up the jeans, Rhoswen turned toward Lyssa.

"Whatever game this is, I accept. There are still a few hours until dawn, when I will have other pressing duties. You have an hour in your rooms, and then my attendants will provide you a bath . . . and prepare him as I desire." She swept her gaze back over Jacob, a feral look suggesting a dangerous hunger, then she locked eyes with Lyssa once more. "You are no fool. You know I am not very happy with the results of this meeting. Your servant will be used hard, to express both my pleasure and displeasure. Expect me to be cruel."

Jacob looked between the two women, and saw his lady's eyes light in response to the challenge.

Great. Her kind of party.

When Cayden escorted them to their room, Jacob wouldn't have been surprised to find a dank cell far below the earth, with the Fae version of rats—perhaps rodents with wings—their only attendants. But the chamber into which they were shown was small but well appointed, with a bed swathed in a gauze canopy, and a window open to the outside fragrant air. From it they could see the Castle of Fire illuminating the darkness. A bronze-colored dragon with red swirls along his sides was coiled on the parapets of that structure, occasionally sending out a companionable spout of flame and roaring to a green dragon on the top of the Castle of Earth, who responded with a groaning snarl and another stream of fire. It was like watching a pair of birds calling to one another from different power lines.

Keldwyn had joined Cayden in escorting them to their rooms. Interestingly, when they'd prepared to leave the queen's hall, Keldwyn had stepped to Lyssa's side, sliding her hand into the crook of his elbow. Jacob had followed behind them. Cayden had taken his leave immediately upon dropping them here, but Keldwyn lingered, glancing about the accommodations. What he was seeking or verifying, Jacob didn't know, but as he wordlessly turned to follow in the captain's footsteps, Jacob stepped in his path.

"Making sure all the listening devices are in place?"

"Your privacy is assured here. If the queen wished to know what was in your minds, she has ways of extracting that, far more easily than vampire mind tricks." Keldwyn gave Lyssa a short nod, made to move forward.

"Anything else about your ongoing personal drama with Rhoswen we should know?"

That got a response, but not in the manner Jacob expected. Keldwyn's gaze hardened. "Her proper address is Her Majesty or Queen Rhoswen, vampire. Neither I nor anyone else will tolerate such disrespect. I have duties to attend."

When Jacob merely blocked him again, Keldwyn's dark eyes went flat and dangerous. Lyssa had moved to the window. Jacob knew she didn't have any objection to his interrogation, though he felt a touch of caution from her. *We need more information, Jacob, but as Gideon might say, don't piss kerosene on a fire unless you're prepared to get your dick burned.*

Hearing the rough metaphor come through his lady's cultured mind-voice was unexpected. She rarely even swore. But most of his attention was on that very fire, flaring up in front of him.

"You know," Keldwyn said, "the last vampire I saw annoy a Fae was turned into a merman. Ironically, he's still a vampire in appetites. I expect the reason the Fae felt it a just punishment was because that particular vampire disliked the sea. Now he has to settle for fish-flavored merblood to survive. One week out of the year, he can walk the earth again. I expect he spends the entire time gorging himself on blood that tastes nothing like fish."

"That's an amusing little story. You ever notice how much effort you spend convincing yourself humans and vampires are inferior? I think what irritates the crap out of you is that though you can crush me like a bug, you and I feel the same way about things. We care, we love, we want to protect what's important. Like a girl trapped in a tree. And it's those similarities that drive you crazy, because you can't reconcile it with our differences and your idea that you're a world apart from the rest of us."

A muscle twitched in Keldwyn's jaw, but Jacob continued. "You wanted us to rescue her because you love her. Because there's nothing you wouldn't risk for her. I feel the same way about my lady and our son." He flashed fang. "So you remember that, the next time you send her into danger without all the information she needs. Now, I repeat. Is there anything else we need to know?"

Keldwyn's lips pressed together. "I will say one thing to your lady, but I do not do so because I fear your threat, vampire."

Whatever helps you sleep at night, you big fairy.

He kept that little taunt to himself, and accepted the reproving look from Lyssa as his due. But he did shift out of the way, leaving the communication path clear between his lady and the Fae Lord.

Keldwyn nodded to Lyssa. "Remember that deep wounds never truly heal without a balm. They fester, infect the heart and soul. Rhoswen has been a good queen for many centuries. But she could be a great one. You are the key to that."

Then he was gone, so swiftly he could have dematerialized into mist. The solid oak door was now securely closed.

Jacob joined Lyssa at the window. She appeared to be studying the view, but he could tell she was thinking, so he gave her a few moments. Looking down, he saw into a side courtyard. Beyond that was a practice field for arms. Some of the Queen's Guard was doing drills upon it. At this late hour, they were more informal, bantering, combining their dedication with the camaraderie.

Cayden was striding out of the side courtyard and onto that field. Gauging his temper, Jacob expected he was probably going to pummel some recruit half to death. "Should have gone for the early bedtime, mates," he noted, not without some sympathy. Then he glanced at Lyssa.

"Keldwyn's consistently helpful," he ventured. "Yet another cryptic message that tells us nothing."

Lyssa didn't smile. Her fingers curled in the crushed rust-colored velvet of Keldwyn's borrowed cloak. "You said 'our son' that time."

"Well, I was pissed off." Reaching out, he stroked a lock of her hair behind her ear. When he sat down in the window seat, crooking his knee to lay an ankle over his thigh, she let him draw her closer, his hands on her elbows, until he settled her in his lap. He put his hands on her bare body underneath the rich fabric of Keldwyn's cloak, and felt the satisfying tremble, the little sigh his touch caused.

I don't particularly care for his scent being all over you like this.

She pressed her temple to his shoulder, so that her face was averted from him, positioned so she could still look out the window but he couldn't see her expression. She gripped his T-shirt in both hands, however, her breath soft on his shoulder. *You always have had an inappropriate sense of possessiveness for a servant.* Then she spoke aloud, in a near whisper. "Fix it, Jacob."

When he unhooked the clasp at her neck, the cloak pooled to the floor with a puff of air against their legs. He untied the velvet pouch at her waist, handled it gently as he set it aside. *I worry about you bringing your father's enchanted rose with you, my lady. I don't want you to lose it. Or have it taken from you.*

Something told me to bring it. I don't know why, but, like you, I often trust my intuition. She gave him a half smile, too touched with sadness for his liking. Taking off his T-shirt, he threaded it over her head, guiding her arms through. Then he curled her more fully in his lap, still facing the window. He didn't like the darkness he felt from her. She was dwelling on all that had happened in the hall. And in that quick, uninvited glimpse, he saw one reaction that had affected her unexpectedly, goading her frustration almost as much as the more serious aspects of it.

"Oh, my lady." He cupped her face, bending his head over hers. "Whether you are Fae or vampire, you're so beautiful it makes any man's heart break. Something else is going on here. She had other reasons for mocking you, trying to humiliate you."

"I know that. Which is why this makes me angry with myself. I don't remember ever being so . . . vulnerable, even if it is only you who sees it. Does my vanity have such power over me?" Her eyes were shards of brittle green glass.

"No," he said. "But even a beautiful, powerful vampire queen can get her feelings hurt. Even in front of a make-believe audience."

She sighed, gave a delicate snort. "It has been many, many years since I haven't been viewed . . . as someone to respect. I had forgotten how it feels not to have that. Perhaps it's worse than never having such power at all, because to be accustomed to it and then have it stripped away so suddenly . . ." She shook her head. "Before Cayden struck you, she *did* have the power to hold me. If I knew the magic better, I'm certain I could have stopped her from changing me. Some part of me knows all of it, like memories that only need to be recalled. It's coming to me in bits and pieces. But right then, I was helpless. It was how I felt that awful day in Council chambers when they took your life. That rage and fear . . ."

Her nails dug into his arm, as it was still not an easy memory for her, for either of them. "This was different, more selfish. I was a student in front of a classroom, being mocked by the teacher, and all I could think of was myself and the rage that I was being treated this way. For one, pitiful moment, without any other obvious choices, I wanted to disappear, just like a humiliated child. She made me feel hideous. I'm beyond angry at myself for giving her that power. I'm a thousand years old, and should be far past such things. Yet damn it, once again, these past couple years . . ."

Her voice lowered, and he heard the minute tremor. Pain like this was always wrested from so deep within her. It was something she had great difficulty even letting him hear, let alone herself. "Sometimes I think I will never find that strength, that calm center again."

"You're a thousand years old, my lady. That means you haven't been treated like a child for a very, very long time. You had a moment of vulnerability. It doesn't make you chronically vulnerable." Cupping her face, he let her see the truth of it in his gaze, as well as the firm belief in his wide open mind.

She traced his lips as he continued to speak, his sensuous Mistress who never tired of touching him, and he hoped to God she never would. "I've had the pleasure of putting my mouth on every inch of your Fae form, every sleek inch of silver skin. I've felt those deadly talons of yours rake my back to draw blood in your passion, your fangs sink into my flesh. I can tell you I get fucking lost, mesmerized by your magnificence, in whatever form you are." He lifted her hand then, nuzzled her palm and gave it a nip, his eyes glinting. "Even as I'm also very cognizant of the woman, her strengths and weaknesses. I love all of you, my lady. She's playing a game. We're playing along, trying to figure out the end goal. That's all. The rest is bullshit."

Lyssa frowned. "She's afraid of something about me and you. No. Not afraid. Angry. Defensive. Keldwyn directed her toward this gauntlet idea, but she wants me to fail whatever test she sets. And that's not just for the 'benefit of her people.' Whatever this is, it's personal. Keldwyn gave us another clue with what he said just now. This is about Rhoswen and me, not the Fae."

"Yeah. Heaven forbid he should spit it straight out rather than holding it all in. Constipated fairy."

"I wouldn't suggest calling him that," she said. "But in all fairness, it's obvious he walks a very thin line here. There are rules that we don't know, and I think there are things he can't tell us straight out." She paused then, teasing his mouth with her fingers. As she traced the bottom lip, she pressed her finger on his sharp fang, giving him a small taste of blood. He sucked her finger into his mouth, dipped his head as she stroked through his hair with the other hand. Leaning in, she let her lips cruise along his temple, her nose flaring to take in his male scent.

"What else is bothering you, my lady? Her forcing your change isn't the biggest thing on your mind."

"Yet you chose to address it first."

He shrugged. "The smallest problem is usually the one you place in the forefront, while you try to sort out the bigger things. I was giving you more elbow room."

"I don't know why I bother to tell you to stay out of my head. That intuition of yours already picks up enough to make it redundant." Her gaze darkened with a trace of sadness. "I don't regret what I've become with you, Jacob. But it has . . . weakened me, somehow. I'm afraid I don't have it in me anymore, to be as cruel and merciless as I need to be to fence with the Queen Rhoswens of the world."

He raised a brow. "My lady, if someone threatened me or Kane, you'd flay the skin from their bodies and let them beg for death. Then you'd rip their heads off. Literally."

"True." She nodded. "That does make me feel better."

"I thought it might."

It was simple accumulation, he knew. The constant vigilance, being away from home and Kane, what lay ahead of them. He could help her with that, by giving and taking at once.

Dropping his head, he kissed her collar bone, exposed by the stretched neckline of his shirt. He nuzzled her there, gave her the tip of his tongue, then the press of a fang. She made a quiet noise of assent, and her hands tightened on his biceps as he pierced the vein, taking a slow draw that he felt all the way down to his groin, particularly when her body responded as well, her hips shifting so her bare ass rubbed against him, and her nipple drew up hard and tight against his palm as he cupped her breast.

When she shifted, he accommodated her, moving together as she straddled him. He withdrew his mouth long enough to manage the switch, but then he sank back in, his bite penetrating deeper as she opened his jeans. The moment her fingers closed around him, it drove away the memory of Rhoswen's cold touch, though he remembered his lady's eyes, the way she watched with that Mistress's expression as another woman handled him. A look that said, *He's mine. You touch him only by my consent.*

Thinking of it, feeling her claim both mentally and physically, he hardened further, growing strong and thick, ready to serve her.

All mine.

All yours, my lady.

She was in no mood for foreplay. She pushed herself down on him, and he swallowed an oath with her blood at the tight, wet heat of her. Clamping her legs around his hips, she drove him in deeper. In response, he slid his hands under the T-shirt, kneaded her ass to rock her upon him, making sure he was giving her clit the rhythm it needed for the fast, intense climax she wanted.

You won't come, Jacob. I want you hard and wanting when you service me and Rhoswen later tonight. I want her to burn with jealousy at what belongs to me, what she cannot take, no matter how she tries.

A dangerous game, my lady. He answered it with danger of his own, a deeper thrust, a concentrated look as he pushed her up to that pinnacle. He let her feel how he could not only take her there, but, when circumstances were different, he could take the reins from her, push her over and set the pace. And give her mindless pleasure worth the surrender.

Her head dropped back on her shoulders as the climax rippled through her cunt. Jacob gritted his teeth, barely holding his resolve against the stroke of heaven-sent muscles around his cock. So slick and wet, such a fucking mindless friction. He knew she did it on purpose, making it as agonizing as possible, but he still exulted in her cries, the way her hands dug in, holding on to him. That sinful mass of black shining hair teased his thighs as she dropped her head back, exposing her throat even further, irresistible to a vampire, or even a human servant, so aware of the deep meaning to it. But he left her throat for a different feast, mouthing her nipple through the T-shirt and ratcheting her climax up another notch, from a yearning cry to an outright scream that was echoed by a nearby dragon's roar, the lowing call of a unicorn stallion.

When she finished, he was breathing hard, shallow. She had her arms clasped around his shoulders as she got her own breath back. Wrapping his hands tightly in all that hair, he took her mouth in a long, urgent kiss. Making a sound of pleasure in his mouth, she squeezed down on him so he groaned, enduring the torture, fighting his own desires.

"All mine," she whispered again, catching her hands in his hair as well to hold his face steady, stare at him.

"Forever, my lady."

The knock on the door disrupted them. The attendants, arriving with Lyssa's bath. Jacob remembered then that they also intended to "prepare him," whatever godforsaken thing that meant. All he knew was he was fiercely glad he'd been able to give her this, have her to himself, before all of it happened. Lyssa gave him a knowing look as he set her off him gently, helping her straighten the T-shirt before he rose. Refastening his jeans with careful precision, he strode, somewhat awkwardly, to the door.

Oh, hell no. Standing outside the door were two large Fae males, taller and broader than himself. They had the pointed ears and aristocratic looks of Fae court members, but they wore nothing more than a pair of short half tunics and steel collars emblazoned with the signet of the court. One had shining red hair, the other one jet-black. The jet-black one gave a half bow. "I am Patrick and this is Lorar. We are attendants for the Lady Lyssa's bath. We also have clothes for her."

Though he was tempted to snarl and close the door in their faces, Jacob stepped to the side so his lady could see them. As he did, the two shifted forward into her line of sight, revealing two even more brawny males behind them. One golden blond, one with platinum silver locks. They gave him a nod as well, though the platinum one's eyes were a little too appraising. "We are Arthmael and Cadr, here to make you ready for Queen Rhoswen's pleasure," he said. "You will come with us to the preparation chamber."

Jacob flashed his fangs. "I'm not leaving my lady unprotected."

Arthmael raised a challenging brow, displaying none of the guarded courtesy of the first two. "Think we can't make you do so, vampire?"

Jacob braced himself on the doorframe. "If your queen's preparations for me include leaving my bloody corpse on the floor in here, then let's get it over with."

Patrick gave Arthmael a quelling look that actually seemed to have an effect, suggesting he had the higher rank of the two. Making a polite gesture toward Lyssa, he spoke to her. "We are Her Majesty's personal attendants. She does you a great honor, offering you our services. You have my word our only charge is to help you with your bath, not to harm you." He glanced toward Arthmael and Cadr. "These two are general attendants for the castle, appropriate in rank to handle your servant's preparation."

Making it clear no honor was being done for him, and the guarantee of no harm wasn't on the table. It was the wrong tact. Lyssa's jade eyes cooled. "I believe you, Patrick," she said. "However, since it sounds like my consort is not afforded the same protection, he will stay here. He was well trained on how to prepare himself to serve my needs. I think he can manage well enough for your queen."

"But if you really feel like you need to hold up my dick while I wash it, you might be strong enough to handle that." Though Jacob slid an indifferent gaze over Arthmael, he did note the male's intimidating build. The guy could likely squash a dragon into a shoe box.

Patrick maintained a look of great patience on his well-sculpted face. "Madame, your consort is not being singled out. Queen Rhoswen is a creature of powerful high magic. Even when a Fae is chosen to share her bed, certain preparations must be made to protect that Fae, as well as to guide him to ensure her maximum pleasure. The chamber where they will take him is in a temple. Arthmael and Cadr are guardians and priests of that temple."

Apparently there weren't enough biker bars in the Fae world needing bouncers.

Lyssa gave him her usual mildly exasperated look, but then Patrick sealed the deal. "You can speak in the vampire's mind, and he in yours, correct?" At her nod, he gave her a half bow. "You will be able to maintain that communication throughout. You can witness his preparation through his mind. If he is your servant in all ways, I think experiencing that will please you."

It was already inevitable, but knowing the mind communication would stay intact pretty much cinched it. Jacob knew as well as his lady that the four servants provided another opportunity to gather information. He still hated it. It went against every warrior instinct he had, as well as that unfortunate possessiveness she chided him about. But he'd learned early in the vampire world that there was no way to adjust every situation to suit his preferences.

We have to take some risks, Sir Vagabond. If it was not for the fact you are worried about my well-being, you'd go with them without argument.

Oh, I wouldn't say that, my lady.

He noted that Lorar carried her change of clothes in his arms, a deep green and gold robe with sparkling embroidery that would enhance her already overwhelming beauty. He didn't see any clothes in *his* attendants' arms, an ominous portent.

Removing Catriona's pendant, he placed it in his lady's hand for safekeeping, knowing she'd put it away in their small bag of belongings. Then, before he turned himself over to the platinum and gold bouncer twins, he stepped toe-to-toe with Patrick. "You do not cause her a moment of distress," he ground out. "Not one, or I cut your fucking heart out."

The man had dark, dark eyes, with a frisson of silver in the sclera. He cocked his head, his lips curving with a trace of male malevolence. "Our only desire is to give her pleasure. Mindless pleasure," he added courteously.

Great. He calmed himself with a vivid imagining of tearing their arms off, but made a bow to his lady. *Call me if you have need.*

Leave your mind fully open, Sir Vagabond. Her gaze strayed over his two attendants, then back to his body. In her eyes, he saw remnants of the desire they'd enjoyed right before the group's arrival. *I might like to look in on those preparations.*

~

It was difficult to decide what irritated him more. Two muscle-bound Fae helping Lyssa with her bath, or the two helping him "prepare" himself. Despite their spirited exchange, once out of the room, Arthmael became far more businesslike.

"Queen Rhoswen is a creature of the water worlds, a being of ice," he said, leading Jacob into the main bailey. They were headed toward a stone structure on the western corner, perhaps the temple. Cadr had fallen in behind them. "We must coat most of her lovers in a warming oil to ensure they can perform and that they do not suffer permanent damage by contact with her. As a vampire, you do not have the same physical makeup as a human male. She is intrigued by that and wishes to test the limits of it."

"A queen who likes to test limits. Something new and different," Jacob noted dryly.

I heard that, Jacob. He tuned in to find Lyssa was in the bathing chamber adjoining their room. She was watching, intrigued, as Lorar—on his knees before her—slid his hands under the hem of the T-shirt. As he rose, he brought it over her head. He guided her hair so it tumbled down her back, caressing her hips, her pale, heart-shaped ass. Patrick took her hand, his other fingers brushing the small of her back as he guided her toward the tub.

His reaction was like having a fire set to his internal organs. Jacob rocked to an abrupt halt, his feet planted against the unexpected violent reaction of his vampire blood. Pure, possessive fury. His fangs shot out, and his fingers dug into the stone wall. He had a glimpse of Arthmael and Cadr's startled expressions before he closed eyes he knew were turning crimson. Bloodlust, strong and pulsing. The need to tear, rend flesh . . . she was *his*. In the vampire world, she might exercise her Mistress side on another male like this without actually being that male's Mistress. There was a difference between the two, an important one. However, the things he'd known as a human servant, that he'd accepted, meant nothing to his still young vampire blood, no matter the years of her accumulated power heaped on top of it. If anything, that made the moment even more dangerous.

Lyssa . . .

I am your queen, Jacob. Your Mistress. Her voice was sharp, urgent. Commanding. *My heart is yours. Remember that you serve me, and that all of this serves a purpose. You swore an oath to me, and I command you to control yourself, by virtue of my blood in your veins, my mark upon your back.*

He fought his reaction. Jacob had the ability to shut down the avenue between their minds, and he'd have to do it if the only alternative was unleashing his homicidal cravings on those around him. But failing to stay alert and present in her mind, failing to be there to protect her if she needed him, was a far worse issue than bloodlust, and that thought helped him find balance.

Jacob took some deep breaths. It was not the first time she'd had attendants, male or female, for her bath. It was just the first time in a while that attendant had not been *him*. She gave herself over to their hands, not as an invitation to seduction, but with the expectation they would perform at her will, as they'd been commanded. Whether or not the Fae queen's instructions had included that scope, it was difficult for any male not to respond to that regal authority Lyssa projected. Lorar had asked her permission to remove her clothing, and now, Patrick also asked before they moved to the next phase of the bath.

When she agreed, it was after a moment's pause, as she confirmed he'd brought himself under control. His fangs were receding, though his fists were still clenched, his body rocking on his toes like a tense wire. Regardless, he began moving forward stiffly with Cadr and Arthmael again. As he did, he watched Patrick bend and lift her in his arms like a doll. When he set her down in a tub full of fragrant water, Lorar picked up a pitcher. He began wetting her hair. As he did, Patrick started singing a ballad in an excellent tenor. Putting soap-slickened hands on her shoulders, he massaged the muscles there. She slid her palms beneath the flower petals in the bath, lifting them up so Jacob could see lavender, yellow and blue colors.

It wasn't as bad this time, but he still had to fight down another surge when she stood up so they could soap her body from throat to toes. Patrick casually unbuckled and set aside his tunic so he could step into the tub with her. Kneeling, he started with her calves, working his way up with the soap as Lorar worked down from the neck.

Both men were aroused as a side effect of touching a beautiful, wet, naked woman. His lady wouldn't deny herself the simple indulgence of enjoying the view, studying the thickness and weight of their cocks, the shift of powerful thighs as their palms slid over her throat and breasts, the nip of her waist and her hips. Jacob turned his gaze outward to his surroundings while she did that, to see that they were approaching the small stone structure that did look like a temple, with an archway carved with more runic symbols and a sense of the sacred hovering upon the curves of its architecture. He didn't close his internal ears, though in the next instance he wished he had.

"I can bring you to climax with my mouth, my lady, if you so desire it."

Jacob imagined Lyssa's eyes lingering over Patrick's broad shoulders, firm mouth and stiff cock as she responded. "How do you find your own climax?"

"The queen's personal attendants may only have relief at her command, and in the manner she directs. When and how is for her to say. May I pleasure you, my lady?"

Will it get you harder, to see him with his mouth on my cunt, Jacob? His tongue teasing more cries of pleasure from my throat? You're still hard, aren't you?

If a thought could have the sound of grinding teeth, it would have. *You know I am, my lady.* He ignored his attendants' curious looks at his stalking gait. It was all he could do to keep his body moving forward with them.

It provokes you, another male touching me, but it also makes you insane with lust, to see me aroused without being able to touch me yourself.

I know that arouses you further, my lady. Goading and denying your servant makes you wetter and hotter. Sometimes I think it turns you on above everything else, including my poor attempts with tongue, hands or cock.

She made a chiding sound. *Being a vampire has apparently made my servant believe he has the right to be resentful and petulant with his queen. I command you to watch, Jacob. Don't you dare close your mind to this.*

She glanced down at the man kneeling before her. "Yes. Proceed."

Lorar set aside the pitcher. As Patrick slid his hands up her slim thighs, the other attendant moved behind her, put an arm around her waist. In one synchronized movement, Lorar lifted her so she was braced comfortably against his chest, her head lying back on his shoulder. Patrick guided her legs over his shoulders, the two of them cradling her between them amid the misty swirls of bathwater.

"We are here," Arthmael said.

Jacob tuned in to find the interior of the temple was one circular stone chamber, not overly large. Through an opening in the ceiling, he could see the edge of the yellow moon, a sign that the Fae version of midnight had passed. A stone tablet was in the middle of the room.

"Take off the rest of your clothes," Arthmael instructed. "Or Cadr can assist you."

Jacob gave Cadr a look that said what he thought of that, but he took off the boots and jeans, tossed them to the Fae. He'd been to enough vampire dinners that he'd learned not to be modest anymore, even with a full erection like now. As a backdrop to the image physically before him, he saw Lyssa arched up against Lorar's hold, Patrick's jaw working between her legs, his skillful tongue lapping. Her arousal unfurled in his mind like heated red velvet and curled lower, tendrils tightening around the base of his cock.

"Stretch out on the table, facedown."

Not easy to lie on a stiff cock, but he managed it. He saw Cadr note the branded cross at his hip bone before it was concealed. When he turned his head, Arthmael was studying the third mark on his back and the remains of the fifty lashes.

Patrick was eating deep into her pussy now, making satisfying male noises as Lorar continued to hold her, moving with her sinuous rhythm while his companion fucked her with his tongue, teased her clit, licked and suckled that responsive part of her. Her nipples were hard and tight, begging for attention. If Jacob was there, he could suckle them, just like she liked, and send her over the edge.

He adjusted on the table with a muttered curse, but then he stilled as something changed in his lady's bath chamber. The mist from the hot bath water shifted, curled. Out of it, floating with easy grace, came two butterflies. Their wings were a striking mix of chartreuse and pink, the tip ends edged with silver. One alighted on her right nipple. At first, the contact was barely noticeable, but then the butterfly started slowly beating its wings, increasing the constriction of its thread-thin legs on her nipple. She arched up, a harder cry catching in her throat.

Whereas before she'd been taunting him, now she was in need. She reached for him with her mind. She was all female sensual power, loving having two males service her, but wanting that connection with Jacob for the actual moment she'd let a climax sweep her away. She wanted her servant watching her in her mind. Burning to be the one with his mouth on her pussy, or taking her lips in a kiss, cupping her breasts to squeeze and create a different sensation beneath the butterflies' attentions. Her servant, with his alpha nature raging, his blue eyes fierce, wanting them away from her, wanting to brand her skin with his hands, his mouth, remind her of the pleasure his cock could give her.

He had no clue what Arthmael and Cadr were doing right now. They could be getting ready to stake him, for all he knew. He managed to register that they'd guided his arms out to either edge of the tablet, as well as his legs. When Arthmael started chanting, he sensed what was about to come, but they'd anticipated him as well, holding him down the brief second needed as manacles of pure ice materialized and locked his arms down at four separate points, from wrist to biceps. The same process occurred at his ankles and legs, all the way to the upper thigh. The binding was so close to his crotch, frigid cold pressed against his balls.

The restraints weren't a real surprise, but then the stone shifted, his body sinking down into its embrace. Arthmael put his hands on Jacob's head, turning it so instead of resting on his cheek and jaw, he was staring straight down into stone that had become water. He fought, but he was in no position to resist now. Arthmael held his face in the water until stone became thick, impenetrable ice, molding to his features.

A collar of ice locked over the back of his neck, holding him fast. He couldn't breathe, the opaque ice a closed mask from his temples to his jaw. Only his hearing had been left unencumbered. His body had been locked into the ice in a similar fashion. If he'd been able to lift up onto his knees, he would have seen an imprint of his body like a child playing in snow. Only this was not so frivolous. Though the nerves in his skin couldn't be damaged by prolonged exposure to ice, it didn't make it comfortable. The direct contact was already starting to burn.

While the rest of his front was encapsulated, there was open air on his cock and balls. Before he could be too grateful for that, there was an alarming cinch around them, the ice closing around the base of his stiff cock and testicles, framing them as they hung free and way too vulnerable beneath the tablet. He let out an enraged noise when a mouth closed on them. Arthmael still had his hand on his nape, so the mouth he was feeling was Cadr's. A strong, suckling pull like a man would do, then blunt, strong fingers pinching his testicles, stroking the sac, making his ass tighten and his whole body shudder.

"Prepare yourself, vampire. This next part will be painful."

Having a guy suck his cock was more than painful enough, but when Arthmael began to chant again, he let out a startled grunt, nearly choking when fire burned like an arrow shot through his nipples. He strangled on the pain, since it required a breath he couldn't take in his airless, dark world.

"We've pierced you with a slender but unbreakable rod of ice through both your nipples. The rod curves around your back and will conform to your upper torso like a tight strap, a sealed circle." Jacob felt the pressure of the rod against his back, another icy touch, but it couldn't compete with the pain in his front. He managed to focus on Arthmael's next words. "This rod allows the queen the pleasure of using the bar as lock point for a tether if she wants to keep you on your hands and knees."

Sadistic bitch. The needlelike pain wouldn't relent, because none of his appendages would succumb to frostbite and drop off, the way they would for a lucky mortal.

Jacob?

I'm fine, my lady. She'd been gratifyingly alarmed when everything had gone dark in his mind from the deprivation, but he was able to project what was happening. He guessed he should be grateful for what he'd experienced at vampire gatherings and at the hands of his lady, because this was just a different level of creativity. She knew it as well. Reasonably assured of his safety, she was already speculating, in that diabolical way of hers, what that ice rod would look like. How he would react to gentle or less gentle tugs on it, distending his nipples, making them raw and more sensitive at once. And damn if her intrigue didn't make him willing to have Arthmael do his worst. And Cadr. At least her mind was on this, not so much on what Patrick was doing. If she came, Jacob wanted it to be because what they were doing to him was turning her on beyond all control, no matter how twisted that might be.

What was spurring her arousal now was Jacob's reluctant awareness of a heated male mouth pulling on his cock like a damn vacuum cleaner—Jesus God, Cadr had a mouth made for porn. But they were preparing him for another queen's pleasure, and she didn't like that as much. It was grimly satisfying, knowing they both had some territory issues.

He bit down on another cry in his suffocating darkness as something slick, big and torturously cold was lodged at his anus and then pushed in, no matter how hard he tried to clench against it. Straps were attached to it, and then he was turned over, the ice slab remolding itself to his shoulders, back and ass so he couldn't expel the invasion. His face tingled painfully at the release from the ice, frost becoming moisture, like perspiration over his skin. At least no one was sucking on his cock, though it was so steel-hard with need it was brushing his belly.

When Arthmael reached down, touched the bar of ice that ran between his pierced nipples, he cried out at the sensation, his cock jumping. Looking down, he saw a diamond crust of frost over the rod, which coated his nipples as well, tiny drops of blood caught in the design. Arthmael experimented with the bar, moving it back and forth, and Jacob growled against the sting, his whole body shuddering. The dildo in his ass joined the torturous composition of burning pain across his body. Yet when Cadr closed his hand around his cock, testing, it hadn't lost a bit of its arousal. In fact, Jacob couldn't stop his body from thrusting up into the fucking skillful touch as Cadr stroked him, confirming that he was aroused enough to hump his grip, no matter his desire not to do so.

"Amazing," Arthmael murmured. Cadr stepped back, wiped his mouth delicately, giving Jacob a wicked look.

"He knows the way of it, for certain. Her Majesty will be pleased."

Lifting a wide steel band then, the Fae unlatched it and slid it around Jacob's base. Thick as he was, it was an extremely tight fit, but he had the feeling that was the intent. Once it was on, the same phenomenon happened as had occurred with the rod. The steel became ice, and crystals ran in broken lines down his cock, spreading out into a web that encased the head. It was still cold as hell, but so thin, almost condom-like, allowing a view of the flesh beneath, and maintaining what little flexibility the blood-engorged shaft had. He swore, writhing, the burning of ice competing against the burning of lust, his blood goaded into savagery by the intensity of the sensations.

He'd been peripherally aware of his lady's attention and what was happening to her, but now he tried to obey her mandate, tune fully back into the view of her in the bath chamber. As he did, he felt her arousal, pushed up so high by what they were doing to him, by Patrick's mouth on her cunt, working her relentlessly, serving her to the end. The combined stimulation had her bucking up in their hold, her release sweeping over her. There was an answering spasm from Jacob's cock, bound and frozen as it was. Before his eyes, he was getting even larger and thicker. The ice cock ring was agonizing. All of it was agonizing, and yet riding it was the bloodlust and the trained physical lust of a servant responding to restraint and pain, at his Mistress's pleasure. He couldn't think, his mind caught in brutal desire, a mixture of crazed pain, raw rutting need, and pure instinct.

Arthmael took a container of oil from Cadr and poured it in the center of Jacob's chest. Warming oil, so warm it tingled, but didn't affect the ice. The two men rubbed it thoroughly into his flesh, making him slick from his throat to the bottoms of his feet. Further bracelets of ice were added to his wrists and ankles, turning his body into this chaotic mixture of hot and cold, ice and flame.

"Your comfort means nothing. The queen's comfort and pleasure is your only desire. Until she is satisfied, these enchantments will not release you, vampire. It is their nature. So serve her well."

So lost in the sensations, how they'd aroused him, he didn't know how well he pleased his own Mistress when he gave a jerk of his head and spoke hoarsely, without a single thought to who they actually meant.

"That's always been my only desire. To serve my lady."

LYSSA *was* pleased by Jacob, but the enchantment, evidence of Rhoswen's trickery, angered her. Still, Rhoswen seemed to have a good grasp of the balance between pain and pleasure when it came to preparing a servant. Of course, Lyssa found that somewhat odd, because despite the fact Rhoswen was a formidable queen, there was a difference between that and a sexual Mistress, the way there was a difference between a sexual Dominant and an alpha. They weren't necessarily the same thing. Though she herself was both, she hadn't felt from Rhoswen the Mistress vibe, as Jacob might say. But she couldn't deny the Fae queen's knowledge of the way of it.

When she was brought to see Jacob, she was wearing the gold and green dress, her hair arranged in rich ringlets down her back, her feet in slippers. Her body was in a lazy satiation from Patrick's skillful mouth, but it was already stirring to life, just feeling her servant's state of mind. When she saw him, that stirring became a boil.

Jacob was completely unclothed, so she could see the rod of ice that passed through both nipples and curved around his back. In the front, the rod formed a V at his sternum that traveled down to outline the ridges of his abdomen. Below that, it dropped down, coming together to form the manacle of ice that wrapped around the base of his genitals. And his cock . . .

She had to lick her lips, because though she'd heard that cold shrunk a man, apparently for a vampire like Jacob, or because of the nature of ice in the Fae world, that was not the case. He had an impressive cock at any time, but he was distended half again beyond that.

Wherever his muscles were not limned with ice, they were glossed with warming oil, so he was a feast from every angle. He walked stiffly, with great care, because of the dildo in his ass. However, as he reached her, it twisted her heart, how he knelt to her despite his vast discomfort, underscoring his obedience to her first.

He was well trained to manage pain and desire together. She was an experienced Mistress, monitoring his emotional and physical state closely while knowing how to ride that line for her ultimate pleasure, as well as his. But beyond the training, his responses were deeply intuitive, how he reacted to being under her command, and that only increased the intense joy of being his Mistress.

They had his arms bound behind his back, those steel bands of ice around his wrists locked together. When she put a hand to his slick, oil-warmed shoulder and brought him to his feet, his body shuddered at that mere contact. His blue eyes clung to her with such wild need. She followed the bar of ice from one nipple to the other, putting some pressure on it so he rocked forward into her touch. Then she dropped her hands to close them around that enormous organ. Below the thin ice coating, there was an extraordinary pumping heat.

"You're magnificent, Jacob," she said, giving him a short, regal nod. "You will please the queen well."

He bowed his head, a jerk as if his muscles were having difficulty obeying his agitated mind. When he lifted his gaze, those blue eyes held hers. *I want to please you. I want to fuck the touch of his mouth off of you. I want to mark your cunt, your mouth, your tits, all of it, as mine again. I want to kill him, wipe his memory off the planet.*

Yes, he was out of control, the bloodlust jumping on the end of a thin lead. But she knew the man beneath the beast, and she could handle both with what she knew of the darkest recesses of his soul.

"Please the Fae queen, and then we shall see. And remember that no seed of yours spurts until I will it."

The climax she'd experienced from Patrick's mouth had been intensely erotic, pleasurable, a good climax. Similar to a good meal, a delicious blood. But it had no emotional component, and she'd gotten used to the unrivaled treasure of that. Craved it. It was why she'd reached out to Jacob when she climaxed. No matter that he was irritated, that connection, whether it was anger, annoyance, love, lust—anything from Jacob was welcome.

The erotic artistry of his preparation had engaged her as a Mistress, because she was always interested in how a servant could be drawn to intense arousal in a new way. But seeing him standing in the hallway, so beautiful and virile, his barbarism warring with his intellect, she was reminded anew he had been prepared for another woman. She was giving all that to Rhoswen. Intentionally, willfully.

The despondency hit her without warning, much like Jacob's earlier bloodlust, and almost as debilitating. It was a game, a battle of wits with another queen, Jacob a vital pawn in those maneuvers. She found herself wishing she could go back to that moment, take it back.

Damn it, she'd told Jacob she'd feared this in herself. She'd never been given to fits of sentiment or self-pitying angst. She shoved it away now, viciously. It never ended. It was a rise and fall, a new challenge to face, a quiet moment to savor, bitter tears to shed, rage to expend in violence or retribution, passion to share . . . all that mattered was he was here, with her, and she with him.

Exactly, my lady.

She met his gaze then. Drawing closer, she laid her hand on his chest, over his heart. *I thought you weren't supposed to listen into my head uninvited.*

I needed you.

She pressed her open mouth to the base of his throat. He held still, the strength of his body against hers, a magnetic pull. She trailed her hands down his arms, slid to his waist and down low on his hips, pushing herself against his cock, and relished his fierce groan. He wanted her mouth, needed the intimacy of the kiss, but she denied him, turning her face away. Instead, she brushed her lips against the rounded steel of his biceps as he tested his restraints in frustration.

Then she stepped back, glanced toward Patrick, who stood at quiet attention behind her. "Are you waiting on us, or on your queen's summons?"

He gave her that courteous, bland bow. "The latter."

He'd had a tremendous erection when tasting her pussy, but he'd shown no more than physical passion for what he was doing, no opinion or preference. Her interactions with them, the nuances of their brief conversations during her preparations, had told her something, though. Rhoswen had their loyalty, particularly Cayden's. And men did not give their loyalty for no reason. Even Keldwyn. *She is a good queen, but she could be a great one . . .*

"Then we are ready when your queen is," she said formally. She glanced over at Arthmael. They'd brought her here, rather than Jacob being brought back to her room. Maybe Rhoswen thought Lyssa would be tempted to sample the results of Arthmael and Cadr's hard work before she had first opportunity. Lyssa's lips curved in a feral smile. She would have been right.

Arthmael stood on one side of the temple opening, Cadr the other, matched sphinxes. "Though I have no standing among you, my compliments on your preparation skills," she said. "I am pleased, as I am sure your queen will be."

Arthmael appeared somewhat surprised at the gracious comment, and sketched a tentative bow. "Lady."

"She's ready." Cayden spoke behind them. When Lyssa turned, she saw he'd changed out of his mail and heavy weaponry to a tunic and hose. He gave Jacob a short, appraising look. Usually in such a situation, Jacob would studiously avoid making eye contact with another male, but this time he locked gazes with the captain, his expression challenging. A muscle flexed in Cayden's jaw, then he nodded to Lyssa with stiff courtesy. "Follow me."

The courtyard was relatively quiet at the now late hour, apparently most Fae preferring a traditional sleep schedule, though they did pass a handful of graveyard shift staff. Brownies cleaning the light sconces, house elves polishing banisters or mopping floors, things best done during times of low foot traffic. The inevitable guards at each entry point. They saluted Cayden as he passed. She noted the reactions to Jacob's appearance varied from outright appraisal and curiosity—mostly from the household staff—to the same deliberate, studied dispassion reflected in the face of the guards.

The captain walked a pace or two abreast of Lyssa, which allowed him to keep Jacob, following just behind her, in his peripheral vision.

Lyssa glanced at him. "I asked you earlier why the castle was so heavily defended. After meeting her, I'm even more curious as to why the queen requires such a substantial guard. She seems more than capable of repelling any threat on her own merit."

"No one can remain vigilant at all times," Cayden said neutrally. "And I am not so gullible that I would tell you who the queen's enemies are."

"Do you view us as her enemies?"

"I do not view you as friends."

"A clever tongue," she mused. "Does Queen Rhoswen have any friends?"

"Does any queen?"

Lyssa lifted a brow. She knew that frustrated tone. It came forth when a man loved a difficult woman with all his heart and soul.

It might not be a romantic love, like Jacob bore her, but it didn't necessarily have to be. Love was complex and had many forms. During the age of chivalry, she'd known men who gave everything they were to their liege ladies, though they'd never touch her in lust, considering it an insult to the honor they bore her. The pure love, it had been called.

"Friends are rare," she agreed. "But I expect if your queen does have a true friend, I am speaking to him."

He paused, giving her a measured glance. They'd reached the opening to a tower, where a pulley lift was provided instead of stairs. "I leave you here," he said, though his grudging manner made it obvious how he felt about that. "The queen's chambers are at the top."

He turned to Jacob then. The way Cayden kept his gaze rigidly fixed on Jacob's face suggested Rhoswen's captain had no wish to acknowledge Jacob's general state of bound nakedness. Of course, he stepped forward to confront her servant, close enough Lyssa thought he might be reminded of it quite rudely if he wasn't careful.

"The threat you issued to Patrick? If you harm my queen, you will suffer the same."

"As long as your queen does nothing against my lady, I will not act against her. I don't harm women." Jacob's gaze was just as unflinching. "Ever."

Cayden nodded. "Make sure everything is tucked into the lift, vampire. It's a narrow space and something extraneous might get whacked off."

Jacob bared his fangs. "Your envy is showing, Captain."

Cayden snorted at that. Lyssa was surprised when the guard captain offered his hand to help her step up into the lift. A subtle gesture, but one suggesting his attitude might be easing toward them. Or perhaps his queen was no longer in such a petty mood as to deny her the basic courtesies that should be expected.

That could be a good sign, or simply a distraction for something far worse Rhoswen had planned.

There was no visible source of power to the lift, but then she looked up. She touched Jacob's shoulder, guiding his gaze upward. A trio of thick vines, populated with what reminded her of her moonflowers at home, was gathered and held in the mouth of a hippogriff. The creature with the body of a horse and head of a raptor had deep purple and black plumage. She surged off the platform with the help of her powerful wings, taking them up smoothly. When they saw the night sky, Jacob realized the lift silo was open to allow the hippogriff to come and go at her leisure, or at the queen's desire. When she reached the top, she settled on the stone ledge with a dainty clop of hooves, deftly dropping the vines into a catch hook that brought the lift to a slight thump of a halt.

As it opened, Jacob met Lyssa's gaze. *By your command, my queen.*

A bracing reminder that only one royal held his allegiance. Sliding her hand down to the small of his back, she caressed his servant's mark along the way. Giving him a teasing scrape of her nails over his bare ass, she stepped out of the lift ahead of him.

Jacob wasn't certain if this was the queen's private chamber or simply the place she chose to enjoy those she summoned to her. He suspected it was the latter, because though Lyssa had taken him in a lush bedroom his first night with her, he'd later learned she'd had a matching underground chamber. That was where she went to be herself, unguarded and relaxed. None but a precious few invaded that sanctum. Rhoswen struck him as the same.

This chamber was a display area for a queen's power and beauty, not a haven for her personal quiet time. A large bed was hung with more moonflower vines and strips of silk. The fireplace was roaring, firefly Fae cavorting in the flames. In the corner, teal yarn was strung on a large spinning wheel. Whoever operated it was creating a tapestry that looked like an ocean wave, the completed portion crumpled below the wheel on the floor.

Positioned before an open window was a standing frame like a doorway, only sculpted of smooth black stone. It looked similar to the Torii outside Shinto temples, gateways to havens for the divine, but he had a feeling that was not Rhoswen's purpose for it. Through the window, Jacob could see the torchlike Castle of Fire.

Now he followed his lady's attention to something else. Positioned next to the fire was a no less intricately carved but far smaller throne than what was in Rhoswen's main hall. A comfortable guest chair sat opposite from it, but between them was a small table with a child's tea set on it. A doll with porcelain face, long dark hair and long-lashed green eyes sat in the guest chair. Rhoswen sat in the throne, of course.

Lyssa moved toward her, bidding him stay where he was with another touch on his shoulder. Contemplating the two women together caused his ice encased cock to respond, which almost wrenched a groan from his throat. The gold and green garment was a robe. The dress his lady wore beneath it at Rhoswen's behest was a stretched sheath of dark cobwebs, every feature of her body visible and yet temptingly shadowed by the lace work. It made her raven darkness, her dangerous edge, even more irresistible.

Rhoswen was her ice counterpart, the vivid blue eyes molten and white hair touched with a gleam in the firelight. She wore a filmy bit of white silk that hugged her hips and draped low on her breasts, showing her nipples through the cloth, the long lines of her thighs. A cluster of fragrant flowers like tiny gardenias were caught in her long hair. Unlike Rhoswen's plunging neckline, Lyssa's was high on the throat, so it made the tight, revealing fit of the lace over her breasts even more noticeable, the nipples impossible for a man to ignore. Her feet were bare, as were Rhoswen's.

Rhoswen's outfit made her appear softer, more feminine, and so the whole picture was disarming, which made Jacob even more on his guard. What appeared to be bees were hovering around the flowers in Rhoswen's hair, more of the tiny insect Fae. While others might fear her wrath, apparently the smallest of her subjects felt comfortable being in her chambers.

Still, that tea set and doll bothered him.

Rhoswen nodded to Lyssa genially enough, gesturing her to the chair with the doll. Those tempting legs crossed as she turned her attention to Jacob. Starting at his feet, she worked her way up, inch by inch. As she covered the terrain, her lips parted, moistening. He was far too aroused to ignore the fact the pink frosted gloss on them made them all the more mesmerizing. He could imagine a wide variety of crude, wicked things she could do for him with those lips. She made it worse by becoming more stimulated during her appraisal. Her nipples drew tighter before his gaze, thighs sliding in a restless shift, a telling arousal. Her musk was flavored with those flowers, but his vampire senses knew female readiness, no matter the species or scent.

Lyssa took a seat, picking up the doll and setting her on the table next to the tea set. Rhoswen nodded to the stone archway. "Put yourself there, vampire. And take your time. I'd like to see you walk."

Walking fast with ice shoved up one's ass wasn't really possible, so he could accommodate that. But that erection was going to kill him, the heat and cold making every step pleasure and torment both. As she drank it in, he sensed his lady doing the same. No matter the situation, Lyssa's natural sensuality would kick in to enjoy him to the fullest. He could resist it all he wished, but he knew it was one of the things that kept him hard so often.

Rhoswen purred, no other word for it. "I'm going to love taking my pleasure of that, vampire or not. How do you ever let him get any rest?"

"Who says I do?" Lyssa returned, and won the queen's tight smile.

When he reached the archway, he saw imprints in the floor to place his feet. He figured he must be getting more used to the magic of the Fae world, for he barely flinched when talons emerged from the floor and circled his ankles above the ice manacles, though he bit back an oath as those talons pierced his skin, drawing blood. His wrist manacles released, but it was a temporary reprieve. Rhoswen gestured above his head. "There."

He glanced up, saw the hook. Shifting his attention to Lyssa, he waited for her nod before he lifted his arms. The hook distorted and split, becoming a two-headed silver snake that slithered down over his arms, holding him fast. It delivered a menacing hiss inches from his face before melding back into inanimate silver, tightening so his body was stretched taut between the frame above and the ankle restraints below. He felt the pull in his back and shoulder muscles, the thighs and groin. And particularly in the nipple area, that excruciating stimulation.

"A nice display." Rhoswen nodded to the tea set then. "Can I interest you in a cup of tea, Lady Lyssa?"

"My Irish servant has told me it's not wise to eat or drink of Fae fare. That it can bind you here forever, or make you forget things you don't wish to forget."

"That applies to humans, not to vampires and part Fae." Rhoswen shrugged. "And most human minds are filled with things they'd like to forget, or that are already so forgettable, our magic is almost unnecessary to drive it entirely from their minds."

"Hmm" was Lyssa's only comment. "What kind of tea?"

"It's from the honey of a flower here called a lilania. It ensures one's pleasure is endless, because after every climax, your stamina and desire are doubled. If we drank enough of it, and if he was human, we could literally couple with your servant until he died. We had a mortal steal some of it once, a long time ago. Not only did he rut on his female until he killed her, he devoured her afterward. Literally. A cautionary tale to humans, that Fae magic is dangerous to play with, and that our worlds should not cross paths."

"Yet there was a time they did, quite often."

"Yes. And the tragedies far outweighed anything else." Rhoswen extended the tea. "You said you wished to share your servant with me. Will you allow me to enhance that experience, Lyssa?"

"And it is the only thing this tea does, enhances sexual pleasure?"

"It is. You have my word."

Two women, completely comfortable with having a naked, aroused and restrained man awaiting their pleasure, overhearing how they intended to push him far beyond his limits. To all appearances, they were both indifferent to his reaction to that, though Jacob knew his lady was quite conscious of how the erotic apprehension would keep him in an excruciating state of want. He bit back another painful grunt. God, even at vampire hands, he'd never experienced an agony quite like this.

He wasn't sure if he could bear it, but that choice was beyond his grasp. In reaction to the tangle of physical and emotional strain, his hands quivered in the restraints. The shudder that started there rippled out through his body, despite his efforts to quell it. The movement caught their attention. When they turned toward him, tracking him with twin focus, they were perfectly synchronized.

Their body language, the tilt of their heads, the shape of their mouths—they were an unimistakable mirror of one another. For a moment, it was so unlikely he doubted himself. But then, replaying it in his mind, he was sure.

My lady . . . you share blood. You can see the family resemblance.

An aunt? Grandmother? It was impossible to tell Rhoswen's age, just as it was impossible to tell Lyssa's, unless one got lost in her jade eyes. Then the centuries of wisdom swept over one like a wave, awe-inspiring or deeply terrifying, depending on what mood she wanted to project.

This was one of the instances where that wisdom proved itself. Not by a twitch did she betray a reaction, and he knew she'd heard him. Releasing a thought inside her head had an intimacy to it, like touching her inner thigh, that silken skin sliding beneath his fingers as she opened herself to him.

Holy Mother of Christ, he needed to stay away from analogies like that, though it was kind of difficult to do so. Especially with him prepared like this, and the two of them looking so incredibly fuckable. Each incremental hardening of his cock inside that enchantment of ice and heat wrenched a higher pain and a more blatant level of lust out of him.

Lyssa sipped her tea, pressing her lips together over the taste. "Like lemon," she said. "A very mellow form of it. With a touch of vanilla."

"Yes," Rhoswen said. The Fae queen sat back in the throne. Whether or not she truly was, she appeared far more relaxed than she'd been in her great hall. "I've had some of your foods, you know. Chocolate."

"And what did you think?"

"That your foods and liquids are far more likely than ours to lead to dangerous, forgetful bliss. Our younger Fae can't resist your Starbucks."

"Their hot chocolate is ambrosia of the gods." Lyssa put down the tea. "You sound indulgent with them. Yet you locked Catriona in a tree for twenty years. Was the lesson for her, truly, or was it for Keldwyn?"

Her tone was merely curious. Showing the effects of the tea, she let her gaze wander over Jacob, lingering in places that made her moisten her lips and made him stifle another groan of need.

"Both," Rhoswen said, watching her. "Too many of our young Fae are overly curious about the human world. I control the gateways, but youth can be clever and foolish at once. One tragic, horrifying example such as hers helped reinforce the gates better than a hundred enchantments. There have been far fewer infractions since." Rhoswen put down her cup as well. "She was a lovely girl. It was regrettable, but necessary."

"The vampire world has lived in the shadows of the human one for a very long time. Why can't the Fae?"

"I think you already know the answer to that question." Rhoswen gestured to the open window, past Jacob's stretched form. She directed Lyssa's attention to the Castle of Fire, the green rolling hills beyond, a dragon soaring through the sky against the yellow moon. "How does all this fit into your concrete world? The earth, the source of magic and life, is desecrated with your asphalt and garbage, your greed and fear. You drown out everything but your own voices with your ceaseless noise. What kind of queen would I be if I threw open the gates, let youthful foolishness like Catriona's destroy the next generations of our Fae in that cacophony? Free will is earned, not by simple existence, but by maturity, wisdom."

"That sounds quite sensible," Lyssa noted. "But even if you are the wisest queen in the world, eventually the throne must pass to someone else. And what if the next one isn't so wise? What if it is someone who uses the restriction of free will not to teach and protect, but to increase their own power and abuse it? It's a very delicate line, and all leaders face it. A civilization governed by free will always teeters on the brink of self-destruction. That's part of its appeal and danger at once."

The Fae queen gave a delicate snort. "You are practiced in such conversations."

"Not so much. It's difficult to find someone who understands the unique issues a monarch faces."

The Fae queen rose abruptly, moved to a cabinet where she added what looked like more lemon to her tea. As she did, one of the bumblebee-like Fae left her hair and drifted over to Jacob. It was a female in bright yellow clothing, her feet enclosed in remarkably tiny slippers. When she hovered directly in front of his face, violet eyes staring at him out of a halo of brown curly hair, Jacob pursed his lips and blew gently. It sent her back in a lazy somersault. Immediately, she returned to the same position and four others zipped over from Rhoswen, wanting the same treatment.

The pixies they'd met in the mountains had been similar in their childlike delight with the simplest things, and Lyssa expected Jacob had acted on his memory of that. He took the time to blow each one back in the same manner, patiently giving them all a turn, though his body continued to quiver from the sensual abuse it was enduring. Her servant, nearly tormented to madness for their pleasure, at the same time indulging the whimsical play of the tiny creatures. He couldn't resist female demands, large or small.

You have a generous heart, my love.

And a cock so frozen it's going to snap off if you don't decide to do something to heat it up soon. With respect, my lady.

He bared his fangs, the reddish glint of his eyes telling her that, whimsical play or not, her servant's savage lust was still ready to be called at her will.

Rhoswen returned to the table, but not to take a seat. She took one more swallow out of the small teacup, spreading the lingering moisture over her lips to make them glisten. When Jacob's gaze focused on them, she gave a feline smile, glanced at Lyssa. "I tire of idle chatter."

Sliding her filmy garment off her shoulders, she let it drop. She wore nothing under it, but her body was marked with inked patterns like henna, intricate symbols and swirls that caught the eye, drew in the mind. The design curved over her shoulders, around her biceps and snaked down her back and upper abdomen, finishing in a single curl on her upper thigh. Butterflies, exotic flowers and dragons hid in the pattern. It was dizzying and titillating both, inviting touch.

Jacob looked, as he knew she wanted him to do. The round high breasts she'd displayed in the corset were just as appealing now, every man's fantasy in proportion with the curved hips and slim thighs.

When she pulled the jeweled clasp out of her hair, the pale silken skeins fell past her hips.

She turned to Lyssa then, a mute invitation. Lyssa rose, dropping the gold and green robe, but kept on the transparent black lace garment. She moved around the chair with that dark, dangerous sensuality she did so well. As she came closer to the queen, close enough to touch, Jacob thought that seeing them together was enough to tempt a man with all sorts of damnation.

"I think you rarely get the chance to have a conversation like this, either," Lyssa observed.

Rhoswen obviously hadn't expected Lyssa to move into her personal space so intimately or continue the conversation thread. Her face tightened, her body going rigid, but she held her ground. The corner of her mouth curled in scorn. "I do not feel any kinship with you. Your being a queen in your world means nothing here."

"I was told the Fae do not lie. We are not in front of your guard, or your imaginary retainers. It is just us. You invited me to have tea here with you, alone."

"You set the terms for this meeting."

"Yes. I offered to share my servant with you. If that was all you desired, we would have already been doing that. Instead, you invited me to tea, and you have a child's tea set, a doll that looks like me for some reason. I think you are not sure whether to hate me for who I am, or embrace me as the last remnant of what you have lost."

Lyssa held her gaze as she slowly reached out, slid her knuckles in a measured gesture along the woman's cheek. The queen quivered. In her eyes, there was something alive and almost too big for the room. Lyssa touched her still mouth with a thumb, a gentle caress.

"We are half sisters. Aren't we, Your Majesty?"

It was equally breathtaking and terrifying to watch his lady figure out the path into someone's soul. Thinking of her lack of confidence earlier, Jacob wondered that she couldn't see her aptitude for it. If she died and went to Hell, it would be not for her sins, but because the devil needed her skill in parsing souls.

If he went, it would be not only to follow her wherever she went, but because he was far past the point of selling his soul for some relief. Despite the serious nature of their conversation, or maybe because of it, he was about to howl like a wolf caged in a room full of females in heat. It wasn't far from the truth.

Lyssa stepped back, not letting her touch linger, which was a good call. The Fae queen now looked as remote as one of her ice statues, everything she was hidden behind that cold exterior.

"When I was young," Lyssa said, "I was told that Fae didn't feel sorrow. How could they? They weren't mortal, they didn't experience the wax and wane of aging, the sorrows and joys that could happen in the same finite lifetime. But vampires aren't mortal, either, and I found out that sorrow and joy are part of every life, no matter how long."

As she spoke, she moved across the room, glancing over her shoulder at Rhoswen. Reaching Jacob, she settled against him, rubbing her ass against his cock, pressing her shoulder blades to his chest and abdomen. His body reacted as if she'd impaled herself. He clenched his hands into fists, dropped his head enough to nuzzle at her ear. She let him tease her throat, but kept her eyes on Rhoswen. The queen watched them, motionless, expressionless.

"Earlier, I implied you don't know how it feels to love someone with your entire soul. You see it from a distance, like a treasure you want but that eludes you. It makes you angry, a child deprived of a shiny toy she really wants, so she's cruel to others who have it. Or you take the toy away and destroy it." She flicked her glance up at Jacob. "Or test its limits to the breaking point. But I think it's far more complicated than that, and far less trivial."

"I love no one with my entire soul. I don't have that luxury." When Rhoswen spoke, there was a hoarse, unsteady note to it, an uncontained wildness in her eyes.

Tread carefully, my lady. She's a rattlesnake, and the rattle is at full volume.

"I didn't think I had that luxury, either," Lyssa responded. Shifting so she was half facing Jacob, but where Rhoswen could see what she was doing, she slid a hand over his side, tracing the muscles stretched so tight in his restrained position. Leaning in, she curled her tongue, a delicate torture instrument, over the ice rod piercing his nipple. He made an animal noise of need. "But then I learned it wasn't a luxury at all. It was brutal, demanding that I tear myself open down to the soul and find out how strong I really was."

Her gaze met Jacob's. "When my life fell around me, and all was darkness, it was that which made me a strong queen. A better woman."

She had her palm on his heart now, the heel of her hand resting on the ice rod, giving him an erotic tease as she gave him that gesture of intimacy. "In hindsight, I think I used being a queen as an excuse. It was my fear that stopped me."

Rhoswen moved forward, the slide of her thighs framing her sex, the movement of her body making the tattoo writhe in a sinuous pattern on her skin. In some places, he thought he saw the dragons, butterflies and other life forms in the design glimmer, shift to new positions. When she reached them, she faced Lyssa, Jacob between them. He sucked in a breath as she drew sharp nails down his side, deep enough to leave rivulets in the valley between the ribs. They seeped small drops of blood. "You are no longer considered a queen by the vampires, and you are an outcast, a lower Fae at my mercy."

"I beg to differ, Your Majesty." Jacob managed to speak, though with a thick throat, his hands and forearms flexing under the silver manacles. "She's more queen now than she ever was. She doesn't need smoke and mirrors to validate it. It's obvious to all. Especially to you."

Now who's pulling the rattlesnake's tail? Lyssa gave him the gentle reproof as he grunted, the result of the Fae queen closing her hand on his cock cruelly tight. He was pretty certain they'd wrench a scream for mercy from him soon.

Fluid leaked from the tip of his organ, dissipating the light coating of frost over the head with the heat of his seed. Rhoswen swiped it with a finger and brought it to her lips, touching it to her tongue. "You already know it is very unlikely you will leave my world alive, vampire. But I can make it a painful end or a fast one."

"With respect, Your Majesty, my own lady has implied the same, many times."

Unexpectedly, Rhoswen laughed, a brittle sound. "I'm sure of that." Her grip eased, and now her nails stroked along his length. She lifted a brow toward Lyssa. "I am feeling the effects of the lilania. How about you . . . sister?" Her voice was mocking, neither denying nor confirming the truth that hung in the air between them.

~

Lyssa flattened her palm on his chest. She followed the same track, down to where Rhoswen's hand was, until both their fingers curved over him, Rhoswen adjusting to cup his testicle sac while Lyssa took over stroking the shaft.

Everything about Jacob—the straining muscles displayed so well by his restrained body, the enormous cock, his ass clenched tight and back muscles rippling, those hungry eyes and tempting mouth—Lyssa knew all those features, yet the tea was making them even more vivid to her. She thought of the beetles in her garden, the way they moved so slowly over the surface of a leaf, exploring and biting. She wanted to do that to him, wanted to tease and taste. She was wet, her thighs soaked with her fluid already, and he could smell it, those nostrils flared. Even though he registered the Fae queen was aroused, an additional stimulant for his carnal nature, he was keyed in to her unique aroma, his mate's scent.

"I want that delectable backside." Rhoswen's fingers trailed over his flesh. "You may have his front, and enjoy the special pleasure of a cock encased in ice magic. That also gives you the fang side of this beast. I have no desire to be bitten. When I was talking about the possibility of fucking him to death, it made him harder, did you notice? He's a twisted, dark creature."

"You ladies make it difficult to care about self-preservation." Jacob's voice was touched by his wry humor, mixed with courtier charm. However, it was also hoarse, his desperate need obvious, infused with heated lust. The vampire in him made that urgency a violent demand, though the servant in him was keeping it contained, barely. When Lyssa stepped in front of him again, the battle between the two was clear in the way his hungry blue gaze coursed over her, his fangs stabbing over his bottom lip.

Touch me. I need to feel your hands. Their heat.

He of course knew the demand would earn him nothing but cruel denial. He expected it, even as Lyssa knew the demand was made in earnest. In the end, it wasn't about games at all, but brutal honesty and need. Giving him a look so unmoved by his plea it made him bare his fangs in a savage grin, she instead inched the dress up to her hips. When Rhoswen slid around to his back, Lyssa bent over, exposing her ass and wet pussy to him. The broad head of his cock brushed her buttock. He tried to stab into the wet folds he wanted, but of course he didn't have that range of movement.

She spread her legs, reached through them and back, high enough to clasp him as Rhoswen had. She had to maneuver him to a downward angle, but as long and thick as he was right now, he was able to amply accommodate her. Closing her thighs over that icy coolness, she reveled in the unique feel of it, the coolness somehow meliorated by the furnace heat beneath, the pressure of seed boiling in his testicles, ready to spurt inside her. It made her shiver, remembering how that virility had put Kane inside of her, a rare vampire child, binding them in yet another forever way. She also felt vibration, shudders of reaction from the rest of his body translating to that steel bar between her legs. She played with him, taking her time, sliding herself over the broad head then several inches up his length. Then back down. Jacob yanked against his bindings so hard the frame quivered. "Fuck . . . my lady."

"Shhh," she murmured. She turned her head to see what the Fae queen was doing. Rhoswen had moved behind Jacob, but the queen was standing a pace back, still watching them. However, now that Lyssa's attention turned to her, Rhoswen withdrew the ice phallus from Jacob's rectum, earning a grunt from him, a tightening of his face against the searing feel of it. Discarding that into a basin on a table, she took what appeared to be a heavy crystal phallus from a side wardrobe.

Inside the facets of the object, spirals of lights played. She slid it into a harness made of sturdy cloth with a velvet overlay, a beautiful piece of embroidery that could have been the girdle of a medieval dress. Small, jewel-like bells were sewn into the design. As she tightened it on herself, they made a pleasant chiming noise. However, Lyssa's sharp eyes saw another embellishment to the girdle. Barbed prongs were worked into the fabric. As she pushed the phallus into Jacob, they would catch on his flesh, tear at it in tiny, savage bites. He would be goaded toward climax, but the pain would be the reins holding him back. At least in theory. She knew her servant well.

Lyssa rotated her hips on him, giving him a tempting view of her ass, and was fiercely delighted by the barrage of images that went through his head. Shoving her down to her knees, fucking her slick cunt, with all the brutal strength of a stallion at the end of his patience. Fuck, he couldn't wait much longer. She was dripping on him, and he wanted to lick all that cream away, then kiss her, let her taste herself on his mouth. He'd never been so hard in all his life. And yet he'd wait on her pleasure.

Only by my will, Sir Vagabond. Don't forget.

Yes, my lady. It was all he could manage, his mind caught in a maelstrom.

Straightening with calculated slowness, she slid off him and turned, just as Rhoswen positioned herself behind him. "Mount him," she told Lyssa. "I want to feel him inside you when I take him from behind. I want to feel the flex of his ass muscles over this crystal cock while he's pumping into you."

"Take time to enjoy the view," Lyssa advised, giving Rhoswen a look of sensual accord. "Seeing those cheeks flex when he takes a woman is worth an extra moment. But when you put the phallus in, know that he'll resist, making it an even tighter fit. He'll make it burn to punish himself, because he has a natural aversion to being fucked like a woman."

Though Lyssa had done it to him several times, she'd never allowed another woman to fuck him with a strap-on. She'd also never allowed him to be fucked by a male. She knew enough about him now, and he knew enough about himself, about his need to serve her, that he could come for her on command no matter the circumstances. But he was still a traditional straight male, her knight, and for her, for this servant, there was a code of honor she didn't violate on a whim. Closing slim fingers over him, she rubbed her thumb on that throbbing vein beneath the cock head in a devilishly knowledgeable way. He bucked in her hold, swearing even more colorfully.

"Hush. More of that, and you'll be gagged, Jacob."

Rhoswen didn't know, but by asking Lyssa to mount his cock she'd actually given him an out that Lyssa wouldn't have normally provided him. When he was inside Lyssa, he could bear anything. In trusted company, she would have refused him that comfort, because that was her nature, to make him surrender and prove it wasn't the circumstances that gave him sexual pleasure, but her will.

Her code aside, the more he resisted something, the more likely she would test that boundary. Like now, telling Rhoswen the way of it in front of him, just to see those blue eyes narrow, the tension in that delicious jaw. She wouldn't give Rhoswen all her secrets, though, particularly not those about Jacob. The possessive Mistress in her would hold on to the things that she knew led to a complete breakdown of Jacob's shields, bringing him to an earth-shattering, vulnerable release.

Rhoswen's brow rose at Lyssa's advice, her lips curving. Just as it had happened while they were drinking tea, discussing the proper way to rule, Lyssa saw that brief flash of synchronicity, a familiarity that warred with the animosity between them. Though that part was genuine, she wasn't certain if Rhoswen's arousal now was true or simply manipulated, a queen's objectives instead of a Mistress's nature calling the shots. Fortunately, from a thousand years in a vampire environment, Lyssa was more than capable of taking her pleasure *and* keeping her finger on the pulse of the current political environment. Maybe she could teach Rhoswen by example.

She slid her hands up to Jacob's broad shoulders. If his hands were free, he would have clasped her hips, helped hitch her up with a display of all that rippling strength, but she had the litheness and flexibility to manage it herself—taking advantage of his strength was an added indulgence. The tea truly was making every sensory detail even more stimulating. There were times she'd thought wanting Jacob would kill her, even without a pharmaceutical aid to enhance it, so this time it might be a real danger. She thought of the stories he'd told, of the lad getting trapped in a fairy circle and dancing away centuries with his love, then pining away for her. She related to that far too well.

Curving one leg high on his hip, she levered herself up so that she had the crease of her ass pressed down on his hard, cool length, and enjoyed another provocative rub there. Then, tightening her stomach muscles, she maneuvered outward and up to catch his broad head in the wet mouth of her sex. Rhoswen overlapped her hands, those long black nails gleaming over the horizon of his broad shoulders as the Fae queen positioned herself behind him. From Jacob's flinch, Lyssa knew she'd pushed the broad crystal head into the rectal opening, but she'd stopped just inside, holding until Lyssa finished her own pleasurable penetration.

She caught his mouth, sliding her lips over his, teasing his tongue as it lashed at hers. His ferocity made it a heated tangle. God, he had the most devil-blessed mouth, and the things his tongue could do . . . She groaned, a soft, deep noise, as she sank down on him, inch by inch.

He was so deliciously cold and hot at once. And so hard and thick . . . possibly larger than she'd ever experienced him, bless Fae magic, though it was so significant it was almost uncomfortable, particularly as his hips jerked, wanting to slam up inside her. His powerful thighs trembled beneath the clamp of her legs, a stallion that wanted to run wild. She made her way to the hilt, her buttocks resting on his swollen testicles. He was pushed up almost into her womb, but she'd been mingling pleasure with discomfort for a very long time. It was why she knew how to put her servant on the knife edge of it so well.

Rhoswen slid her hands away then, adjusting herself below. Jacob growled into Lyssa's mouth, blue eyes flashing as she pushed into him. Lyssa had taught him how to release the muscles by pushing back, but just as she'd warned, sometimes he was stubborn. Whether or not she enjoyed the act itself, it was obvious Rhoswen enjoyed the power of taking the choice from him. It was in the rasp of her breath, the brief glitter of her eyes. Jacob shuddered, making a labored grunt as she reached full penetration. Then she withdrew and slammed back in again. It rammed the glass phallus home, but more than that, he was stabbed by a full dozen of the barbs on those tiny bells, their sweet chime a contrast to the blood Lyssa smelled. In the next blink, she knew there were thin rivulets running over his buttocks and down his quivering thighs, those small bites taken out of his ass.

In response, his cock thickened inside of Lyssa, and his fangs scraped her, at their maximum extension. He wanted to feed, was ravenous for it, but still he held back. Considering the lust and violence roaring through him, she knew it was a monumental effort for a vampire still technically in fledgling stage.

Lyssa was not about to give up the opportunity of immersing herself in all the sensations her servant's surrender was providing, not with the lilania encouraging her to find an even more vibrant peak of sexual pleasure with him. Moving her grip from his shoulders to his biceps, she held on as she bucked her hips on him. She gave him all of her, teasing the limits of his restraints, knowing he couldn't thrust as fully as he wished.

Coolness slid over her hands. The serpentine binding around his arms had slithered down over his shoulders, over her hands, around his throat. It snaked down between them, splitting to curve over her thighs then double wrapped her waist, cinching her more tightly onto Jacob's loins, wrenching a cry from her throat.

Rhoswen laid her fingers over the silver collar binding him, drew back, then rammed back in again, letting them both feel the reverberation in cunt, cock, testicles and ass. Her mouth was wet, cheeks flushed, but the contrasting tightness to her face warned Lyssa, too late.

Jacob saw it first, and his body turned to iron, muscles bunching in protest. Tearing his mouth free of hers, he tried to twist to see the queen, shake the bindings.

"You bitch," he snarled. "Let her go."

SHE hadn't been mistaken. She'd seen brief flashes of longing in Rhoswen's face, a desire to somehow immerse herself in the pleasure she and Jacob were experiencing. As a result, Lyssa hadn't feared Rhoswen's magic, her desire to rope them together in that pretty silver binding. But the queen had another agenda. And the instrument for it had just entered the room.

The fox-faced Arrdol set aside his cloak, his gaze coursing over Lyssa's lace-covered back, her bare ass and thighs, clamped high on Jacob's hips.

My lady—

No. Her mind rejected it, too many dark things swirling up on top of the rudely interrupted coitus, disorienting her.

"You will feel such pleasure, having Arrdol inside of you." Rhoswen had the bloodcurdling hiss of a snake, hypnotizing prey. "Even without honey on her eyes, a woman can become addicted to his sensual ways."

Rhoswen taking her consort, one of her retainers taking Lyssa as the interloper, the two of them bound as unwilling prisoners between them, subjugated. They'd anticipated trickery, so Lyssa didn't know why she was having difficulty rallying. But as Arrdol came closer, those shadows were closing in on her mind. There was a coldness to her skin.

No. Don't touch me, don't touch me . . .

"*Don't* do this." Jacob was fighting the bindings like a beast in truth. However, as his efforts increased, muscles bunching impressively, the restraints on Lyssa began to tighten, particularly the one on her throat. She started to choke.

"Careful, vampire. That Fae blood that allows her to be in sunlight also requires her to breathe. A Fae may be immortal in terms of aging, but strangulation can kill us." Rhoswen adjusted herself, burrowing the dildo deeper in his ass as she leaned forward, pressing her breasts to his back and talking to Lyssa directly, staring into her green eyes. "If you try your little magic trick in those bindings as you did in my great hall, they will constrict further, and become so cold they will burn into your skin like fire, all the way to the bone. I can interfere with your accelerated healing, and make sure that it doesn't work. You will no longer be so pretty. Death, disfigurement, or pleasure, submitting to my will. An easy choice . . . sister."

Her blue eyes were like frozen ice. "You are no queen here. You will learn that whatever I tell you is what you must accept. Arrdol will have you, because I say he will."

Lyssa's hands convulsed on Jacob's neck. She was floundering, and he saw it, within and without. The pleasurable effects of the tea clung to her, but they were being twisted in a horrifying way into something uncontrolled and far more terrible. A nightmarish memory she carried and he alone knew, because everyone else who knew was dead.

When he'd come into her service, he'd thought he understood submission to a vampire mistress, a vampire queen. She'd challenged him, stripped him raw, taken away choices. But in the end, he realized she hadn't. That he'd been willingly hers from the beginning, and the choices she'd taken were shields she'd broken open to show the depths of what he would give her.

This was different. Rhoswen was no Mistress. She wasn't seeking submission, that pleasurable, ultimately willing surrender that Lyssa craved from Jacob. Rhoswen wanted to break her spirit, shatter the far-too-fragile thing Jacob knew existed deep inside his nearly invincible lady. Her pale face was paler, her jade eyes flaring with rage and something else . . . She didn't feel fear. This was dread, a spiraling feeling of tragedy that took her back to something that had wounded her so deeply she'd thought about walking into the sun rather than surviving it.

No. All his protective instincts, his fierce, unrelenting love for her, surged to the forefront. He unashamedly used that vampire mark to pour it into her, all the way down to the bottom of her soul, an abyss into which she was rapidly sinking. He found her there, pulled her gaze reluctantly to his with a wordless snarl before she could look away.

Even if it happens, it's just you and me. They're nothing. When I submit for your pleasure, to others, it is all about you, your pleasure. That's what makes all of it doable.

But that was him. She couldn't do this.

This wasn't jealousy, worrying about another man touching her. It was so much more than that. There were some things she couldn't handle. He knew it, because he was inside her soul. Despite his best attempts, her gaze was dulling. She was pulling away. Her skin was becoming ice cold, even more so than the frost rimming his stomach muscles or still imprisoning his cock, his charge to satisfy the Fae queen obviously not yet fulfilled.

"Don't do this, Your Majesty." He growled as Rhoswen responded with a punishing thrust. *Fucking bitch.*

Arrdol had set aside his sword belt, was moving forward, unlacing his breeks. Jacob heaved mightily, managed to turn his head enough to lock with the queen's gaze, no matter that the tendons in his neck popped. "This is the act of a fucking monster, not a queen. Don't do this to her, damn it. Not again. She won't survive it again."

Arrdol placed his hand on Lyssa's shoulder and Jacob whipped his head back around, hissing like a viper. "Get your fucking hands off her, or I swear to God, I will tear out your guts, you fucking bastard."

The silver bindings upon his arms and legs abruptly became so cold that fear stabbed his heart, remembering Rhoswen's threat to scar his lady. He fought past the pain of it, trying to focus on Lyssa as his body convulsed in agony. Then everything disappeared.

~

He was standing in a small field surrounded by thick forest. It was night, thankfully, the meadow illuminated by moonlight. Butterflies the color of gold dust gleamed in that light, floating up and down among flowers so iridescent in their mixed colors he could almost imagine that he was in one of those places deep under the sea, where all the creatures and plants were phosphorescent.

"This is one of many places in our world." Rhoswen stood several feet from him. She was clad in a cloak of starlight. Through it he could see her bare body, marked with that intricate tattoo. Her hair was down, that and her bare feet making her look deceptively vulnerable, all soft female.

In two steps, he was on her. Seizing her by the shoulders, he took her to the edge of the field and slammed her against the broad trunk of a tree. The oak made a deep growl of protest, the branches quivering in warning.

His reaction had startled her, he could tell by the quick flash of it on her face, but then she was gone. He howled as the tree staked him through the thigh, going through the bone. It snaked out the opposite side, ran diagonally up his bare body and pinioned him against the rough bark. She stood before him once again, her eyes flashing, teeth bared, but he was in no mood for her games or the venom she was prepared to spout.

"If you're going to have her raped, if I can't stop it, at least let me be there to help her get through it." He couldn't reach Lyssa's mind. He was trying desperately, and nothing was getting through. Where the hell were they? He leveled a look of pure malevolence on the Fae queen. "You might as well go ahead and honor that threat to kill me, Your Majesty. Because if you harm her like this, I will kill you. I'll rip your fucking heart out from behind those superior tits and turn you into vampire meat."

Rhoswen's elegant hands closed into fists. "I can easily kill you, vampire. And if you die, she dies."

"She'd rather die than go through this. So I'd rather you kill me than do this to her."

"You think she'd prefer death to some forced pleasuring by one of my court? The lilania will make sure it's pleasurable, no matter how she feels about him."

"So it's emotional as well as physical rape. Good to know you're as psychotic as any human or vampire you claim superiority over." Jacob spat in her face, earning a glorious rage in return. The tree speared him in both arms, the other leg, through the abdomen. He screamed at the agony of it, but he was still alive. She hadn't staked his heart yet, even though he was somewhat surprised that he didn't black out.

Then he realized it was because it wasn't real. She hadn't staked any of him.

He was on his knees on the forest floor, breathing hard. The Fae queen stood ten feet away, leaning against the same oak, its low branches rustling quietly in a tranquil wind. Reaching up, she played with a quivering cluster of leaves. Her expression was remote, the rage gone. Jacob decided she was the most schizoid female he'd ever had the displeasure of meeting.

"You cannot reach her because I stopped time," Rhoswen said casually. "Nothing is happening to your lady, Jacob, not yet. The same second is spiraling in that chamber, and will continue to do so, as long as I will it so."

He rose then, eyeing her. It took a few moments to wrap his mind around what she'd said and tamp down the warrior and vampire blood lust. Having felt Lyssa's state of mind in that last moment, he didn't like knowing that was what she was feeling, but at least his lady was not being raped as he stood here in this absurdly beautiful meadow with the Fae queen. "So what now, then? You were just in the mood for a private chat?"

"Your Irish comes out in your voice when you're truly angry," she noted. "It's appealing." Straightening, Rhoswen moved toward him, slipping the cloak off her shoulders so it became a bed of starlight behind her. "Lie with me, the way you lie with her. Let me feel what she feels."

"You want to take something from her that she considers hers exclusively. The way you think she took something of yours. Your father."

The starlight disappeared, the gentle breeze and the meadow. He stood in a desolate, frozen field, naked and shivering, despite the fact a healthy vampire typically didn't react to cold weather—not counting enchanted ice being shoved through his nipples or in his ass. He didn't see Rhoswen but he sighed, raised his voice. "I don't care to be on the same wavelength with that arrogant bastard, but Keldwyn's right. Being pissed about it doesn't change the truth. So what's the plan? I obey you or you let Arrdol rape her?"

"If you wish to call it that. I expected a vampire to understand such cold exchanges."

She reappeared before him, the starlight spinning around her, making it hard to read her face. When her fingers brushed him, he realized the ice was gone. All of it. His nipples throbbed like a son of a bitch, though, telling him all of that part had been real. His cock was still stiff, but it was the lingering effects of having his lady's cunt closed around him, not an erection forced by Fae ice magic.

He narrowed his eyes at Rhoswen. "Keldwyn was wrong. He said you were a good queen, one who could become a great one."

She stilled. "He said that?"

"Yeah. I thought he was smart. Apparently not." He swept his gaze over her, thorough, appraising, in a disdainful way that had her mouth tightening in anger. "I can fuck you. I'd fuck a pile of manure if that's what it took, and I'll make it seem like you're the only woman in the world, if you get off on forcing a man to tell you lies. But my soul belongs to my lady. Lust can be enchanted. Your honey-on-the-eyes trick is all about infatuation, that mistaken idea that lust is a soul-deep feeling. You could make it work for you, I'm sure. I'm not invincible. Eventually, every torturer finds a way to break her victim, because we aren't alive if we don't have vulnerabilities."

He took a steadying breath. "But it would still all be fake, because I love Lady Elyssa Amaterasu Yamato Wentworth, last Queen of the Far East Clan, with every cell of who I am. I was created, and have been reborn three times, to serve her. That gift comes from a power far greater than you, Your Majesty. If you act to destroy it, or mask it, or hide it, there are consequences. It tears a hole in the fabric of all our worlds. You live by rules, I can tell. And I'm believing what you're doing now is outside the boundaries of those rules. In fact, from what I've picked up from your captain of the guard, I think the way you've been acting all along toward my lady isn't the person you normally are."

He stopped, setting his jaw. She'd left him naked, the same as herself, as if they were Adam and Eve standing at odds in the middle of Eden, making a decision to decide their ultimate fate. He wasn't one to wait. Taking himself in hand, he gave himself a lewd stroke, cupping his balls. "So what'll it be, Your Majesty? What do you want to do?"

"You're impertinent," she said quietly.

Jacob gave a bitter half chuckle. Letting go of his cock, he shifted to a more aggressive stance before her, crossing his arms over his chest, unabashed by his nakedness. "I serve a true queen," he said. "That means I call it like I see it. She deserves nothing less from me."

"Then you will do as you said. If you will not love me as you love her, you will still lie with me, give me pleasure. And I will spare her Arrdol's attentions and release her."

Their surroundings had once again become the meadow, soft colors, fragrant smells, romantic atmosphere. The cloak was back on her body, veiling and revealing it at once. "No," he said. "Not here."

He studied her, the long fall of her blond hair, the mesmerizing eyes, the generous body beneath that shimmering cloth. Shifting forward, he moved into her until he was almost stepping on her toes. She tilted her head back, staring up into his face, a frozen ice princess. He thought princess instead of queen, because there was something younger, more inexperienced about her right now.

Lyssa had said he understood things intuitively, things that allowed him to get the measure of someone in a way others couldn't. And as Rhoswen stared up at him, he felt that click into place.

His Mistress had vulnerability, but she was a Mistress through and through. She let him take care of her, protect her, but there was a constant element of permission to it. It was why no physical or emotional circumstances had changed that relationship. She could be a mere human, and he the most powerful vampire or Fae, and he would be her servant. As her servant, he would do his level best to care for her however necessary, even if he had to override her will, but there were consequences to that, her will always part of the equation. In Rhoswen's face, in her words, in her actions, he sensed something different . . . conflicted.

He'd seen the question in his lady's mind as well, unable to determine what had driven Rhoswen in the chamber, if the Fae queen truly enjoyed the pleasure of restraining a man or if it was all about the politics, her warring feelings about Lyssa.

Now, with just the two of them here, despite all the other things roiling in his gut, he followed that intuition. Putting his hands on her shoulders, he dropped to her wrists, gripped them hard. When he pulled them behind her, he clasped them at the small of her back with one hand so he could jerk open the tie to the cloak, let it drop. Wrapping his hand in her hair, he made it tight, let her feel the pull. Her lips parted, a dangerous shimmer going through her. A tremble. Her eyes went opaque, and the emotional swirl that came from her was enough to send a cloud of disturbed butterflies surging up around her and fluttering away.

Son of a bitch. He stared down at her. Suddenly, it was as if she were ice in truth, the brittle, delicate kind that formed in the corners of windowpanes, or edged the slender branches of trees.

"If not here, then where?" Her voice was a whisper.

"Somewhere dark. A place of stone and steel."

A blink, and it was done. They were in an armory, surrounded by swords and crossbows, shields. Jacob had nursed the hope of a fully equipped dungeon where he could strap her down to a St. Andrew's cross and beat her within an inch of her life. However, since she had magical powers that could easily slip such bindings and malevolent vengeance, this would do.

Sweeping an array of helmets off a bench, he shoved her down on it, face forward. Her hair was a curtain around her body, but it parted like silk, showing him the pale buttocks, the pink sex. She was all cream. It was no wonder she drove Cayden to distraction. The Fae male exuded the dominant vibe as strong as any vampire master Jacob had met, no matter that he served as captain of the Queen's Guard. He'd probably endured the torment of it because he sensed this elusive trait in her, like a wolf on a hard-to-track but irresistible scent. Given Rhoswen's unpredictable nature, Jacob was sure he hadn't run her to ground yet.

He plucked a bridle off the wall, detached the reins. Pulling her wrists up to the top edge of the table, he tied them and wound the straps around the hook there. It stretched her upper torso along the table, her hips at the edge.

"Spread your legs," he ordered, his tone harsh. "Show me your cunt."

It was a weighted moment, but then she shifted, spread them farther. She was wet, heated. That shudder went through her again, punctuated by a tiny tremor. He remembered what Lyssa had said about Rhoswen's powers over the mind. She'd made time stop, so he expected it would be easy for her to wipe this from his memory afterward, keeping it all to herself. Was the queen figuring out how she wanted life to go, discarding the frames she didn't want, piecing together the history of her life, her kingdom? No. There had to be a thread of reality she couldn't alter, and a limit to her magic. There were rules, as Keldwyn had said.

"Fuck me," she demanded, her fingers twisting in the reins.

Jacob hefted a short sword and swung, the flat of the blade striking both buttocks with a smart slap that elicited a shocked yelp. She tossed her hair to the side, stared at him. He twirled the blade expertly over his wrist, cocked his brow. "Care to try that again?"

She could annihilate him with a blink. Instead, she moistened her lips. The blade had left a red stain over her white cheeks, and as he watched, more honey flowed from her pussy. "Please," she whispered. Tears gathered in her eyes, a flash before she turned her head swiftly away, spoke to the table. "Do it, or I'll release the time frame. He'll fuck her like a common whore and make her love it so much she'll never get over hating herself afterward."

He hit her again, and though he wanted to use the edge, he stayed with the flat, tossing it away with an oath. He was hard enough, because repulsed or not, his cock was going to respond to a restrained woman, wet from getting her fuckable ass spanked. Male and simple, after all. But still . . .

He'd taken women before, at vampire dinners. At Lyssa's command and direction. But this—a rival, one who was manipulating the stakes, and not even making all that clear what the ultimate stakes were—that was a different matter altogether.

The armory wall shimmered, and he had a window back into that upper chamber. Rhoswen had unfrozen the moment. Arrdol was stroking Lyssa's hair back from her shoulders, enjoying the weight and feel of it. She was alone there, bound to that frame as he'd been, while the Fae Lord bent to put his mouth on her flesh—her throat—goddamn it all. As he did, he was pressing a cock that looked like a fucking baseball bat under his tight hose up against her ass.

"Freeze it, now."

"Fuck me, now."

"Lady, you are one fucked-up piece of work." Fine. Goddamn it twice over. With a strangled oath, Jacob put his hands on her reddened ass, squeezed the cheeks hard enough to convey his displeasure, and slammed into her. Not her pussy. He went for her ass, and shoved in hard, despite the lack of lubrication. She cried out and he leaned over her, gripping her hair and pulling her head up so she could glare at him through those tears, though her breasts were heaving and the nipples tight from arousal.

"Bad girls get it up the ass, honey. You weren't specific about where you wanted to be fucked. Gentleman's choice."

"You're no . . . gentleman," she retorted.

"I'm vampire scum, beneath your notice, remember? But not too beneath you to fuck, as my lady said. Now hold on for the ride, because I'm hoping like hell it's going to hurt. Freeze the damn thing."

"Make me come first. I stop it when you make me come." She flashed him a look of triumph.

Snarling every curse he knew, Jacob pulled out of her, flipped her over and shoved back into her wet pussy, caring less about the usual hygienics. He hoped they had infections in the Fae world, and that he gave her one that made her itch like a dog infested by fleas. As he changed positions, he clamped a large hand around her slender throat. That restraint hit the right note. To a powerful woman who craved submission, a collaring, even if it was just a male's ruthless hand, was sometimes enough to accelerate her toward climax. He began to stroke into her, smooth and relentless, his other hand going to work on her clit. He made sure she saw the way his gaze devoured the provocative wobble of those magnificent breasts as he pounded into her, again and again.

Dragging her to the edge of the table so her ass hung over empty space, he smacked it hard as he pumped into her. The punishment made her gasp, her pussy clench over him. She was resisting him, trying to draw it out, knowing every moment it took would torment him, but she didn't know her opponent. If there was one thing Jacob knew, it was the intricacies of a woman's body, and what would send her up and over like a cannon. He wanted to put her through the wall.

He concentrated on that goal completely, refusing to look back at that window and see what was happening. Every second he wasted on that, Lyssa would be at the mercy of Arrdol and those nightmarish memories.

Rhoswen's eyes were widening, lips parting. He saw the surprise and frustration that he was driving her up to that pinnacle so quickly. Each time he spanked her in tandem with the powerful thrusting, a moan broke from her throat. He should tell Cayden his queen might drive him less crazy if he dragged her into his armory several times a month for discipline. Maybe they were here because she'd fantasized about such a thing. She was doing it with Jacob, forcing him to it, because she couldn't offer it to Cayden willingly.

A queen who never let down her guard could never be vulnerable. He knew the type all too well, though his lady had a straightforward honesty to her ruthlessness that seemed absent here.

A cry broke from Rhoswen's lips. Her fingers dug into the reins so hard he saw one of the nails break. She didn't notice, milking him fiercely with the force of the climax. She managed to spare him a glance out of glazed, glittering blue eyes, but he showed her his teeth. Even if he had to cut off his own cock to stop it from happening, she wasn't getting his release. He gave her the full measure of her own release though, thrusting into her just as powerfully through the full arc of her orgasm. She couldn't hold on to control any longer. Her cry turned into a long scream.

The violent way she writhed and convulsed, it was as if she hadn't experienced a climax in a long, long time. The straps dug hard into her wrists, so her fingers started turning blue. With a mental curse at himself for caring, Jacob stretched above her and loosened them with a quick jerk, so she was still restrained, but only because her fingers were tangled in the straps. As he maneuvered over her, he sank deeper, and he felt her mouth on his chest, teeth scraping and then biting down as the climax took her over yet another wave.

Her release went on for some time, and as he massaged her clit to the finish, he steeled himself to lift his gaze. Through that window, he saw Arrdol was gone. Lyssa was still bound to the archway, but alone, staring out the window at the fire castle, the flames reflected in her green eyes, white face. He'd bitten her, the bastard, left teeth prints in her shoulder. Jacob still couldn't reach her mind, couldn't tell her what was happening.

When Rhoswen let out a soft noise, signaling her repletion, Jacob would have pulled out of her, stepped back, but she locked her legs around his hips. The reins were gone and now, with a swirl of mist, a disorienting sense that had him bracing his hands back over her on the table, he found himself somewhere else, his palms pressed into the ground of that meadow, his fingers spread on either side of Rhoswen's lovely face. She was on her back, Jacob on top of her but unable to move, as if she held the weighted net of an enchantment upon him. Every hard line of him was pressed into every soft curve of her, her mound pressed to his stiff, unrelieved cock. Reaching up, she touched his face.

"I see why she keeps you," she said softly.

"I sincerely doubt that."

Her lips curved in a humorless smile. "A kiss, Jacob, and then your lady is safe, and all yours again. As much as she will ever be, since you are vampire and she is Fae, and your relationship is doomed."

"I'm not taking you as the world's best expert on lasting relationships."

"That is your last opportunity to treat me with insolence," she promised. Cupping the back of his head, she pulled him down to meet her mouth. Wet, heated, knowledgeable lips that parted his, her tongue sliding in to tease and seduce, keep him hard inside her. He felt dirty, wanted a shower more than anything except his lady. He'd never wanted to do permanent physical damage to a woman before, but this one might take him into that territory. Any one who harmed his lady, male or female, would get no mercy from him. Even so, Rhoswen's earlier tears bugged him, as well as his momentary carelessness that had led to the lack of circulation in her hands. Fucking Sir Galahad. That's what Gideon had called him.

Breathing a heavy sigh into her mouth, he settled onto his elbows and imagined it as his lady's mouth, that generous moist heat. Her hands stroking along his back, cupping his buttocks, keeping him inside her as he hardened anew so that he could satisfy her once again. Those jade eyes, so deep in color he'd get lost in them, knowing he'd do anything for her.

He wasn't too far gone in the fantasy, though. When one of Rhoswen's hands began to travel down his chest, to his abdomen, he caught her wrist before she could touch the cross branded over his hip. Opening his eyes, he stared into the queen's face. "No," he said. "That's not yours."

The clamp of his hand on her wrist brought a trace of that earlier look, what he'd discovered about her that had taken them to the armory. But there was more, too. She was a Fae queen. She knew the power of sacred rites and symbols, and things you didn't mess with. When he let her go, she moved her touch back to his biceps.

"Kiss me again."

That was easy enough, with his eyes closed. Leaning in, he pressed against her soft mouth, inhaling the scent that was different from his lady . . . or not. It *was* the same . . . only now he wasn't kissing the Fae queen's cool lips.

His gaze sprang open. The setting had changed once again. Lifting his head, he stared down into Lyssa's face. They were in their guest chamber, just the two of them.

The queen who trusts no one . . .

He started up, but he took Lyssa with him, his arm banded around her waist. He was balls-deep inside her wet cunt, and she trembled at the movement, framing his face with her deceptively small, elegant hands. "God." He put his forehead to hers. "Are you all right, my lady?" And of course at the same moment, he was unashamedly plundering her mind, making sure. She'd been deeply rattled, but she'd held, and Arrdol had only touched her throat, her back, leaving that mocking bite on her shoulder.

"I'll extract his teeth and you can wear them as a personal trophy," Jacob promised.

Her lips twisted in a small smile. "I prefer my emeralds and diamonds." Studying his face, the smile, faint as it was, went away. "Where did you go?"

"To Hell. That's what I call any place you aren't. But I'm back with you now."

"I'm all right," she said softly, registering the quiver in his muscles, the wildness in him.

"Good. I'm not." Withdrawing from her, he laid her down on the covers, asking her to wait there with a gentle squeeze of her arm, though he kept hold of her fingers until they reached the extension of their arms. Moving into the bath chamber, he found soap, a full cauldron of water and used both to scrub himself vigorously. To rinse, he poured the remaining contents of the cauldron over him, heedless of the floor. Tossing it aside, he came back to her dripping wet. Without preamble, he scooped her up off the bed, his arm around her back, palm on her buttock, and slid full force into her, so decidedly it pushed her against the headboard. She gasped, caught his biceps and arched into him.

All yours, my lady. This cock is all yours. Every part of me is yours.

I know. Her gaze held his, and she stopped him in mid-thrust by digging her nails into him, a Mistress's command. *Jacob, stop. Cease. Turn over.*

He rolled, letting her straddle him. Laying her hand on his heart, staying there for a full measure of beats until he was steadier and more in need at once, she held his gaze as she slid her hand up, up, collaring his throat. Just as he had with Rhoswen, only this was his Mistress. Her touch there sent a surge of blood into his cock. As she felt it, her eyes darkened. She began to rise and fall upon him, and he held still at that unspoken command, letting her set the pace, taking the pleasure she wished from him. He was her slave, to do with as she wished, and he wanted to immerse himself in that. Now he was trembling even harder, his hands flexing on her hips.

I don't know what's a dream and what's real here.

"This is," she responded. "We are."

He reared up then, tore the black lace from her body, shredded and got rid of the hated thing entirely. The clothes, Lyssa's darkness against Rhoswen's light, had been the Fae queen's attempt to make her half sister look like a mere shadow of herself. In his mind, just the opposite was true. Capturing her breasts in both hands, he suckled the nipples, until her cunt rippled on his cock and he sent her over. When she finally whispered a throaty, "Come for me," he gave her what he gave no other.

~

She could be nurturing, too, his lady. After their climax, she bade him lie still, and placed her mouth on him, tenderly sucking and laving his nipples, her sweet tongue soothing the ache there. Then, despite his halfhearted murmur of protest, she made her way down his body, licking and nipping, light kisses, and put her mouth full over him. As a vampire, he had a short recovery time, so he wasn't at all surprised to feel his cock rise in her mouth. But while she liked keeping him aroused and wanting her, that wasn't her intent this time. She was reasserting her claim, no different from any other primal creature, marking him with her mouth and touch. And it aroused him incredibly, watching her do it, knowing the purpose.

When she'd satisfied herself at last, she let out a small sigh and then curled between his splayed thighs, her head on his lower abdomen, lips nearly grazing his throbbing cock. Her fingertips traced the cross she'd branded into his flesh.

They hadn't spoken of any of it. Not right now. To help her deal with what had happened with Arrdol, he'd given her the control and climax she needed, the comfort of his surrender. She'd given him all of this to help with Rhoswen. Though he felt it festering in her mind as it was in his.

"What is this Hunt we're supposed to attend?" She tilted her head up to look at him, her eyes lingering on the terrain between, showing how pleasing she found it. It made his cock harden further under the press of her body. The wanting of her never stopped.

"And I hope it never will. I couldn't bear it." Her mouth quirked. "To handle the loss of your affections, I expect I'd have to kill you. Painfully and slowly."

"There's the gentle queen I know and love. I'd expect and deserve nothing less," he assured her.

She tilted her head to nuzzle his palm and bite, not so gently, winning a flicker from his eyes, a tightening of his hand in her hair, two predators in lazy love play. "So tell me about this Hunt, before I have to resort to torture."

"Torture is a tempting weapon in your hands, my lady." He gave a muffled curse as she scraped her nails across one still tender nipple. But he didn't stop her, didn't close his hand on her wrist. "You keep this up, I'll never tell you anything, just coax you underneath me"—he unfurled a very graphic image in his mind—"spread your legs and . . ."

"The Hunt," she declared, flexing her nails with ominous intent over the other nipple.

He relented with a tight smile. "Once a year, on Samhain, the Seelie court mounts up and rides through the mortal world at night. Since the Fae are descended from Danu, an earth goddess, their intention is to bless the crops and woods, to ensure a good harvest and fair hunting season to help people make it through the winter. It's an ancient, ancient tradition, my lady. The fact they still do it is . . . reassuring. It's the entirety of the High Court, dressed in their finest, the steeds painted and draped in silks and bells. Legend says if you see them that night, you shouldn't stare, because you could be struck blind, or pulled back into the Fae world in their wake, forever lost to the mortal world. Or, even worse, you could incite their anger if you don't offer the proper respect as they pass, since the Fae have capricious tempers."

"I hadn't noticed," she said.

"Hmm. Knowing you have half-Fae blood has explained a lot to me about *your* temperament, my lady."

"If I didn't have an annoying and insolent Irishman for a servant, I would be sweet and fair-tempered every day."

"Should we call Thomas back from his peaceful cell in Heaven and ask him about that?" Chuckling, he pulled her up his body. She wrestled with him, but she didn't put up too much of a fight, her gaze softening when he rolled them over so he was back between her legs. The minor angles and shifts to come together were almost instinctual now, following the desire to be joined. She bit her lip as he pushed in, flexed his thigh muscles to make her feel his demand, the thickness. In the semidarkness, her jade eyes glowed.

"As a boy," he continued in a husky voice, "I dreamed of seeing the Hunt, based on the stories my mother told me. Later, Gideon made them even more vivid, battles with other Fae and galloping charges through the woods, the Wild Hunt going to collect dead souls. A lot of magic happens on that night. Should you see a white hart, you're supposed to try to hunt it down, because if you strike the creature through the heart, it will turn into a princess of such beauty, it will make a man weep. And she will love that huntsman for the rest of his life, being his loving, sweet, gracious, faithful and obedient mate."

"That's a lot of adjectives for a teenage boy to string together."

Jacob grinned. "We liked that story. We were too young to know that a sweet and gracious female, let alone an obedient one, was indeed something only found in a fairy tale."

"Whereas *arrogant* and *male* go together so well for certain individuals, they might as well be the same word." Lyssa traced his lips with her fingers, her own parting as he closed the distance between them, pressed in for the kiss with her fingers still on his mouth. The way he smiled against her, she knew he didn't disagree. Or maybe it was the fact he no longer cared, his big male body strong and ready, his mind impatient to bring her pleasure again.

She was more than ready to accept the gift. Not only would it stave off the horrors of the night, but the homesickness she felt down to the depths of her soul. She hated it here. She wanted to go home. And the fact she felt it the way a child did, as an all-consuming longing, made her even more worried. She pushed it away. She didn't need a poisonous tea to help her get lost in the temporary balm of sensual oblivion. Just Jacob.

11

When sunrise came, though Jacob was reluctant to give himself to sleep, Lyssa insisted on it. Upon her request, the Fae household staff had provided heavy curtains for the open window. Just before darkening the room for dawn, she lingered there, watching a pair of phoenixes fly past, feathers catching an early glimmer of dawn's rays. Several fairies, trailing glittering dust, winged their way with erratic swiftness across the field. They were laughing and chasing one another. Though one could never tell with Fae, they acted like teenagers, rushing home before dawn's light and their parents' waking betrayed they'd been gone all night. She thought about what Rhoswen had said, wondered if they'd figured a way to slip out to spend the evening carousing in the mortal world.

It was odd, thinking of teenage rebellion in such a context. But there were far more similarities between the two worlds than Rhoswen wanted to accept. Fae, vampire, human . . . those were just the clothes for the souls trapped inside, all trying to find things that were remarkably the same.

Cayden was out early, doing sword drills by himself. He was stripped down to breeches and boots, and working up a fine sweat, his long hair tied back but sleek at his temples. She watched him for a few minutes, never averse to studying a fit man exercising the full range of his muscles in a half-naked fashion, then she let the curtain fall shut.

She could see in the dark, though at this point she couldn't say if that drew from her Fae abilities or her lingering vampire ones. Jacob was watching her. The blanket was pulled up to his hips, barely. With one arm over his head, fingers loosely grasping the carved wood spindles of the bed, the other lying loosely on his abdomen, he made a pleasurable picture. His gaze was serious however, concerned. That concern probed into the dark areas she'd experienced earlier in the evening, and she refused to go there. Not right now.

"I really don't want you wandering around without me," he said quietly.

"I know. But I need to see and be seen in this world. I need to understand it better, through my own eyes. And I want you to truly sleep," she added, with a reproving look. "Don't follow me around in your head, and don't worry. She hasn't killed me yet, which means there are reasons she needs me alive—either that, or killing me would cause her too many problems. That protects us both. She knows enough about vampire lore to know if she kills you, she kills me."

She didn't add whether the converse was true. She knew Jacob stayed away from that topic as well, neither of them able to confim if her original third marking of him still existed under the overlay of his. She didn't mind him staying away from it—it wasn't something she wanted to know had been lost, either. Unless it might save his life, though having been in his mind, she knew how he felt about living without her. She felt the same way about living without him.

Crossing the room, meeting those blue eyes that understood and saw so much, she bent and touched his forehead, following it up with a kiss. "So sleep, and sleep deeply. You have a Hunt coming up, after all. And perhaps a white hart to chase, though I wouldn't suggest you catch that princess, if you know what's good for you."

His fingers curled into her waist and he nudged her chin downward to give her a much deeper, more stirring kiss, one that dispelled any amusing images of her tucking him in for the day like a child. That thought summoned another feeling, though. Seeing it, he caressed her cheek. "He's probably driving Mason crazy as we speak. Your old friend will rethink any desire he's ever had for his own children."

She snorted. "He's not driving Mason crazy. All he has to do is thrust Kane at Jessica and he turns into the world's best baby. Your son is besotted with her."

"Not even a year old, and he has his first girlfriend. A much older woman at that. That's my boy."

Lyssa pinched his arm, hard, and slipped away when he made a grab at her. "Sleep. I'll bring back some of that honey to make you besotted with me, and then you'll be the perfect baby, too."

Some fairly heated images of retaliation filled her mind for that remark, images that warmed and bolstered her at once as she closed the heavy oak door behind her. Despite her confident words, once she sensed him settling down, she laid a hand on the door. She didn't know any protection spells that would stop a powerful Fae queen on her home turf, but she availed herself of a simple prayer charm to keep him safe. Whatever Rhoswen's agenda, the personal and royal motivations were mixed, and that could make an already unpredictable Fae even more so.

But it didn't change what she'd told Jacob. Though they had stayed away from a great deal of the more difficult things that had occurred last night, he'd told her of Rhoswen's ability to bend reality and time. Lyssa hovering over him in the room wouldn't be as useful as meeting other Fae in this world and seeing what resources and allies they might garner from that. And she needed some time to think. Not about Arrdol, his hands touching her, his dark eyes coming close, becoming someone else's eyes . . . She stopped, gave herself a vicious shake. She needed to focus on the fact she had a half sister and what that might mean. The rest was the past, gone and buried.

Traveling down the winding stairs to the main floor, she found her way to the courtyard. The castle was bustling with Samhain preparations. All manner of servants were employed in cleaning, cooking, decorating. Knowing Jacob was uneasily moving into sleep, she took a seat on an out-of-the-way bench for a few minutes and gave him the images as a bedtime story. Flocks of Fae girls with flowers in their hair and gauzy garments barely covering their nubile bodies flitted to high points in the cathedral ceiling of the great hall. They pinned streamers of autumn greenery and blossoms there that draped down so close to the floor in places that they brushed the shoulders of those coming and going. Flirtatious sensuality seemed to be a natural thing to Fae females, for like the undines under the drawbridge, the girls shamelessly teased the young guards or handsome court members that passed through, taking quick darts down to tug a lock of hair or steal a hat.

Though Cayden was a somber, steely-eyed type, with a veteran circle of the same around the queen, many of his guard appeared young. Regardless, none of those who came through were averse to bantering back and forth with the laughing girls, fueled perhaps by the festive holiday air.

A veritable army of brownies were cleaning every corner of the great hall. One even scooped up her feet with a surprisingly strong hand to sweep beneath them. He set her slippered feet back down as if she was a piece of furniture, with only an irritated grunt for acknowledgment. Other Fae polished the multitude of long tables that had been set up, another group coming in behind to put down the place settings. Intrigued, she noted the dinner plates ranged from the size of a turkey platter to a teaspoon. Doll-sized tables and chairs had been placed on the big table between normal or larger settings, and those received the tiny plates.

"The Unseelie tradition is to have several representatives from each Fae species join us to celebrate Last Night after we return from our own hunt. Or Haunt, as the case may be."

Keldwyn stood at her elbow. The Fae wore a plain brown tunic over hose and soft boots. His dagger belt was slung low on his hips, but overall it was a casual look for him, despite the unwavering aristocratic reserve. "You know," she mused, "I can't determine if you've appointed yourself my fatherly guardian, or if you're just guiding me down the path of good intentions toward Hell."

His lips curved, the smile not reaching those dark eyes. "While I am older than you, Lady Lyssa, you are not the type of woman to elicit paternal feelings from any male. Unless he is your father in truth."

"So Hell it is."

Lyssa knew Jacob had a great deal of distrust of the Fae lord, but her feelings were more mixed. In the beginning, Keldwyn had been nothing but indifferent to Lyssa, but unlike other forest Fae, he'd not gone out of his way to be unkind to her when she'd been on the run from the Vampire Council. During the weeks they stayed in his territory, sometimes he'd even visit their campsite at night. He'd take a lithe cross-legged seat on the ground and whittle new arrows for his bow, or idly carve some pine knot he'd found on the forest floor. He spoke little, neither encouraging nor responding to attempts to draw him into their conversations. Despite both of their sharpened senses, he always slipped away unnoticed. If he'd been carving, he'd leave behind whatever he'd created. A squirrel, a bear, a bat.

One night he carved a pixie, probably inspired by watching the creatures who liked to follow Lyssa around. When she was in her Fae form, they perched on her like tiny foraging birds on a gazelle in a *National Geographic* photo shoot. Of course, as soon as they discovered Keldwyn's creation in Jacob's pack, they took it. For the next few days they carried it about, twittering and excited. Dressing it up in various garments of leaves and flowers, they posed beside their likeness, giggling. When it finally disappeared, she expected they'd accidentally tossed it into a bear's mouth.

Lyssa kept the carved animals, though, tucking them away for their then unborn child. She still had them, intending to give them to Kane when he was old enough that he wouldn't turn them into gnawed corncobs. Jacob had suggested burning them instead.

The thought gave her a tight smile. Reaching out to touch her servant mentally, she was pleased to find he'd fallen into sleep at last. So now she turned her full attention to the Fae lord. "Did you know him? My father? You brought me the rose, but you've never said how well you knew one another, whether you were friends."

"No, I didn't."

"No, you didn't know him, or no, you never said, and you don't intend to do so?"

He shifted to study the decorations the Fae girls had put up, lingering on a cluster of nuts and berries twined with dark ribbons. Amused, Lyssa saw a small male Fae pluck one of the berries for a snack, only to be instantly pursued from all corners by the Fae girls. It looked like a flock of mockingbirds chasing a winged interloper on their nesting grounds. "You know," Keldwyn said, "the men in your world purportedly hunger for clever women, probably because there are so few of them. I, on the other hand, appreciate a world populated by female simpletons. Ones who do not try to dissect every word I say."

"Perhaps if you were less evasive, a clever woman wouldn't have to keep her radar so well honed around you. She could afford to be a little less clever."

"As you yourself have found, Lady Lyssa, the price of being less evasive is often too high a price to pay. May I offer to escort you around the grounds? Queen Rhoswen will not make an appearance for a while. She is holding court this morning, and then will have a full afternoon until the gathering tonight."

Lyssa rose, slid her fingers into the crook of his offered elbow. "What kind of court matters does she arbitrate?"

"Many. She of course has a Council that handles a great deal of them, but any Fae may appeal to speak his case before her if he is not satisfied. However, she is known to be far less lenient in her decision making, so it's best to be certain the principle is very important. For instance, if you'd been up earlier this morning, you would have seen a stampede of squirrels over the drawbridge. Every part of the forest has an earth Fae who cares for and rules over it, in a guardian capacity of sorts. Sometimes they misperceive their role and believe themselves a minor monarch with delusions of conquest. One of the area goblins had been infringing on the territory of another, taking his squirrels. So, to set him back on his heels, Queen Rhoswen told him he not only had to give back the squirrels he'd taken, but also all his own as well, for the next month and a day. Until then, he must pick up and store the autumn nuts himself as the squirrels would have done."

"Did he bring the squirrels with him?" Lyssa imagined the freed squirrels scampering across the drawbridge, headed back to their rightful territory.

"No. The decision gavel releases the magic to enact the queen's decree. The squirrels in question were summoned instantly for the beneficiary. He led them out of the castle, a chaotic sort of Pied Piper procession."

Lyssa noted other Fae glancing at them curiously as they passed, but they didn't engage the two as they headed for the open drawbridge.

A constant flow of Fae and equine traffic came and went, as well as other creatures. Centaurs, clopping along in twos and threes; a grumpy-looking griffin perched on top of a carriage driven by an ogre. Long lines of gnomes like ants, obviously bringing further foodstuffs for tonight's celebration.

Keldwyn guided her off to the side to keep her from getting tangled in the procession, a courteous hand placed at her lower back. Sometime in the night, the unobtrusive castle staff had left her a simple gown with high waist and square neck. The linen was a fine, pleasing cloth that molded her curves and flowed with the movement of her body. There was embroidery at the neckline and a lacing at the back to snug it in to her body, something Jacob had been more than happy to help her do.

"If you stay long enough, you might enjoy sitting in on the midnight court. It's arbitrated by Lady Gwyneth, a Fae sorceress who specializes in the sensual arts. The midnight court allows sexually dissatisfied wives to come and complain about the shortcomings of their husbands."

Lyssa slanted him a glance. "Have you ever been brought to task before them, my lord?"

"I have never been mated," he responded. His dark eyes flickered. "But, if I had a bride, I am fairly certain that would not be at the top of my list of shortcomings. Many others would take precedence."

"I can vouch for that," she agreed. "What did you mean by *Haunt*? So while the Seelie bless the crops and farmers, the Unseelie go out and . . . ?"

"Give your humans Halloween stories to remember. The blast of cold air for no reason, the spirits at the corners of their eyes. In the days before motorized transport, when a man was riding alone through the woods at night, the Lady in White could appear on the back of his horse. She'd wrap her cold arms around him and give him the fear of his own mortality as he tried to gallop away from her, outrunning his fear of death." Keldwyn lifted a shoulder. "It's a little more complicated now, given that fewer men are riding horses through the forest. But she finds she likes Harley Davidsons fairly well."

"So the headless horseman, covens of witches sacrificing a baby in the wood . . . all of it is Unseelie Fae practicing scare tactics?"

"Most of it," he agreed. "It's actually quite fun for them. Each year, they put even more effort into it. Many of them dress up in costume, much like the humans. They also compete to bring unique things back that Queen Rhoswen might allow past the portal. Something that intrigues or pleases her enough." He leaned in, spoke in a conspiratorial whisper. "Last year, she permitted a few birdhouses, because they made such enchanting houses for the smaller Fae."

"You are either feeding me a line of rotted mushrooms, or trying to disarm me with charm. Either way, my guard is still not relaxed, Lord Keldwyn."

"I doubt your guard has relaxed since you were a child and lost your samurai. If it has, I'll warrant it's only when you are alone in his company, restored to you twice now."

Before she could respond to that unexpected statement, a soldier reined up. Glancing at her, he nodded to Keldwyn, a half bow. "My lord, did you need a horse? Are they all taken this morning? You're welcome to my Fineas if you have need of him."

"No, Lygar, though you do me honor. I am purposefully strolling with the Lady Lyssa this morning, showing her the Samhain festivities. You need not worry for us."

With a touch to his forelock and murmured, "My lord," the guard continued on.

"They respect you. No matter Queen Rhoswen's contempt."

They'd reached the other end of the drawbridge, and he directed her past a fork in the two roads leading out from the castle, choosing the one she knew, from their bedroom window, rolled gently down to a village.

"Of all the treasures Queen Rhoswen has, the greatest one—and therefore the one she values the least—is her captain of the guard. Despite his reticence, Cayden understands many things. About his queen, about me, about this world and yours. And much like your servant, he serves them all far beyond what they deserve, far beyond the range of even his great heart. A leader influences his men, and as such, she has a Queen's Guard that any queen would envy. Their integrity, courage and courtesy, as well as their skill, are beyond reproach. And if ever they fall short, he's as uncompromising in that as he is fair about other things. A guard might trip up and get the sharp edge of the queen's tongue. However, if he fails in his duty, he fears Cayden's cold fury far more."

"Hmm." She returned to the words he'd spoken before Lygar intercepted them. "How long have you followed my life, Keldwyn? A clever woman would deduce my father meant a great deal to you, the way you've kept track of his daughter all these years."

"Perhaps I, like others, have merely been trying to unravel the mystery all these centuries. Why one of our most powerful Fae Lords defied every law of our world to cleave to a vampire woman, get her with child, and gave up his life for her."

"I don't think it's a mystery to you at all. To others, maybe. But you were willing to risk much the same for a child not your own. You may have given the appearance of throwing us to the wolves, but Rhoswen always knew you were behind it."

Keldwyn took her elbow, drawing her around a pile of manure left by one of the passing horses. "Her Majesty has never brought back anything from your world during the Haunt. However, for many years, before she became queen, I always brought her back some chocolate. I'd leave it where she could find it, but not know who brought it. I still do it. Last year it was Rolos. She likes them."

Lyssa remembered Rhoswen mentioning chocolate. Like Jacob, she wasn't entirely sure what was real or fantasy when it came to her half sister. While their familial connection was a striking fact in itself, it remained to be seen whether it would be a biological fact only, or something more significant to the two of them. She already knew it was inordinately significant to Rhoswen.

"What has changed for her, Lord Keldwyn?" she asked. "My Fae abilities might be the trigger that brought me here, but why am I such an issue for her? You say she is a good queen, but so far all I have seen is irrational anger, driven by pain that seems far too fresh to be connected to our father's death a thousand years ago."

Keldwyn showed no surprise that she'd figured out the blood link between them. "Rhoswen had to fight something very similar to your Territory Wars here. She became queen about three hundred years ago, after many battles between the four castles that had to do with centuries of poison seeded by her mother and descendants of King Dagda. Like your own Council, there were very different ideas of the role of the mortal world. Suffice it to say, in the end, Rhoswen sat on the Unseelie throne. Tabor, descendant of Dagda, now sits on the Seelie one, thank all the gods, and that poison has been eliminated. But in order to make that happen, Rhoswen had to take her mother's life. Tabor killed two of his brothers."

As Lyssa's brow creased, he nodded. "It resulted in years of instability, fear and quick, brutal justice for any uprisings supporting the old factions. That was when Rhoswen completely shut down the doors to the mortal world. Human crossings have been rare, exceptional circumstances only these past few decades. It was not only to protect the Fae. After the wars, our numbers had dwindled. Fae were stealing children, bringing them here. Once the children ate or drank in our world, they could never be returned, parents left bereft with no knowledge of what had happened to their offspring."

Lyssa could imagine something like that only too well. It must have reflected on her face, because Keldwyn's expression for once showed genuine emotion, a deep chagrin.

"As I said, it was a horrific time. But the Fae numbers still haven't recovered, because our birthrate has slowed to an alarming rate. Some believe it is because we have cut ourselves off from the lifeblood of the mortal world, that there is an essential lifeline between our worlds that helps feed balance, fertility. Rhoswen herself may even have begun to believe that, but she will be cautious, because she's seen the abuses that happen on both sides."

Lyssa considered that. "All right. But that still doesn't explain why she wants to hate me so much."

"Because your father was high on the list to be chosen for the Unseelie throne." Keldwyn turned to face her, coming to a halt. "When he was executed by virtue of Tabor's brother and Rhoswen's mother, that cloud of suspicion and anger hung over Rhoswen's head for many centuries. But now, it is well past time to name a successor. She has discretion to choose, but it must be sanctioned by her Council and the Fae themselves. And thanks to court gossip, not from me"—he gave her a straight, stern look that said it was the truth—"the rumor has spread that there is another daughter of Reghan, one with a child."

"Kane is a vampire." Lyssa's gaze snapped to Keldwyn's face.

"Yes. One with Fae blood. Not just yours, but that of your father. My lady, you came from vampire *and* Fae royal lines. Your servant has reincarnated three times to be at your side, and was turned into a vampire of inexplicable power *by accident*. I think it's safe to say that your son will be far more than a mere vampire."

The music coming from the village was getting louder, an irresistible melody that called the feet to dance. While Lyssa tried to quell her reaction to his words, Keldwyn took her arm, resumed walking. "And that is all I will be saying today, Lady Lyssa. You are intelligent enough to figure out the rest, when Fate chooses to unfold the other pieces before you."

She knew not to waste effort persuading him otherwise, but she wasn't going to let him off the hook that easily. "Have you seen Catriona yet? Is she well?"

It was the most personal question she'd ever asked him. Though she looked for some change in his face, she saw none. However, she noted that he paused before he answered.

"When a Fae is freed after such a long time, there is a period of adjustment. She is here, in our world, but she has gone to ground, to heal. I am respecting that, for now."

She thought there was more to it than that, but she left it alone. The music was swirling around her in earnest, demanding that she notice the sun touching her hair and warming her dress, the fact that they were coming into a village filled with laughter, excited cries and wonderful food smells. "Where are you taking me?"

"This is the merchant pavilion area for the Samhain celebration. I assume all women like to shop."

"I have no currency here."

"I'm sure I can cover any purchases you wish to make."

Lyssa's first thought was she wished Jacob could see it, because it was a snapshot from a Tolkien novel. Pennants and pavilions in multiple colors stretched out through the streets of the village, filling every corner. The crowds checking out the wares were an astonishing array. She saw small gnomes stumping out of the way of lumbering giants. A woman passed them with a small pet dragon on her shoulder, the tail curled around her upper arm. As she moved, she phased in and out of the colors of the pavilions, a rainbow chameleon, the creature cheeping softly on her shoulder, changing colors with her. Handsome men in tunics wore short daggers and soft, thigh high boots, escorting lovely women in dresses like hers, only trimmed in more jewels.

The air was full of flying Fae of various sizes, cutting above the crowd in aerial acrobatics, and amusing themselves by occasionally tossing out small projectiles. They would explode in the air, raining everything from glitter dust, flower petals or the occasional shower of acorns or pebbles on the shoulders and heads of the earth-bound, resulting in laughter or good-natured threats.

In this world, all these mysterious, remarkable creatures were not remarkable to one another at all. They hawked and bargained, flirted and scowled. They sat down to scratch their backs against a tent pole, or drank a tankard, legs stretched out, relaxing as they appraised those who passed.

"Care for a mask to scare the mortals?" Keldwyn inquired, stopping at one stall and lifting it for her inspection. It appeared to be a scrap of bark with eyeholes, but when he lifted it up to his face and let it go, it hovered there. Now he had a monstrous visage that enhanced his natural features, the eyes large, dark pits of hellfire, mouth stretched with sharp teeth, pointed ears swept downward and back for a more menacing, animal-like form of aggression.

"Impressive," Lyssa said, reaching up to touch it. It still felt like the bark, though her fingers phased through the magical energy.

"From what I hear, she already scares the kiddies with her looks." That remark came from a crone sitting in the booth, working another scrap in her hands with a knife and what looked like a scraper for skinning. "But if you want to make yourself even more frightening, miss, you can have that for a bargain."

"A *Fae bargain*. Two words fraught with peril." Keldwyn snorted. Ignoring the woman's rude gesture, he lay the mask down and took Lyssa's elbow again. "Pay them no mind," he murmured, moving her away from the booth.

"You thought as much yourself when you saw me. It's to be expected." She was resolved that no one but Jacob would ever know she was vain enough to be hurt by it.

Keldwyn made a warning noise, just as she was brought up short by a tug at her elbow. Looking down, she then had to look up, following the small Fae as she moved from Lyssa's elbow up to the level of her face. The fairy was the size of a doll, but obviously a young adult, like those Lyssa had seen flitting across the meadows this morning. It was in the curious, open eyes, the set of the mouth, the somewhat cocky-yet-not-quite-confident demeanor. That, and the small cluster of similar-looking Fae males and females hovering nearby, suggested it. Despite the dwindling numbers of offspring, young Fae still ran in packs like any other teenagers.

"Will you show us what you look like, as a Fae? They said it's like nothing no one has ever seen. Do you fly? Will you fly with us?"

Lyssa glanced at Keldwyn and he shrugged, though she thought there was an indulgent look hovering around his eyes. The male definitely had a soft spot for children. Despite that, she noted the young Fae kept her between herself and Keldwyn, obviously finding the High Court liaison far more intimidating than Lyssa.

Why not? She could tell other adult Fae were listening, watching. Jacob wasn't the only one with intuition. In this world of unknown rules and unpredictable responses, this felt right.

"Certainly," she said. However, while she wasn't modest, there was something about disrobing in the midst of such a public crowd that felt inappropriate. As she glanced around, Keldwyn read her intent and gestured her toward the narrow channel between two of the tents. As she moved into that opening, she found the tents were angled so the back corners came together in a closed vee, forming a private area. Keldwyn positioned himself in front of her. Like all high-court Fae, he was more tall than broad, but she was petite and it was cover enough.

Slipping off her ankle boots and the high-waisted dress, she laid the garment over his shoulder and tucked the shoes into his curled hand for safekeeping. They didn't really believe in undergarments here, so that was all it took. She shifted into the Fae form, a much smoother process when it wasn't forced by Rhoswen's magic. She had to remember to keep her wings tucked in so the tough, leathery substance of them didn't cut through the silken fabric of the pavilion tents.

She hesitated, but then that hesitation snapped her spine straight. She was a queen, not a teenage girl. She didn't allow self-consciousness to dictate her actions. Instead of stepping out in front of gawking eyes, she gathered herself and shot straight up, executing a dramatic roll and swoop that took her over a cluster of Fae browsing. The unexpected aerial maneuver dropped several of them to the ground in reaction, to the delight of the teens and her own personal satisfaction. Lifting herself back up on a nice twist of air currents, she met the eyes of the young Fae girl, hovering a few feet below her, her dark eyes wide and round. "Coming?" Lyssa rasped over her curved fangs.

They launched themselves after her, colorful figures with flowing hair, dancing eyes and slender bodies. Keldwyn gave her a wave to catch her attention and raised his voice. "Meet me at the field just below the village. I'll join you there."

~

It only took a moment, but she was surprised to see him already there, and that he'd procured his own method of flight. He sat comfortably on the back of a female black dragon, one leg bent and heel propped on the creature's muscular neck, the other dangling in a relaxed manner. The dragon was so large she could have curled Lyssa under her wing span like an egg. As they passed over Keldwyn and his impressive mount, he adjusted to a straddle, speaking a quiet word. The dragon launched into the air, integrating into their flight pattern gracefully. As the teens maneuvered around her like sparrows around a pterodactyl, Lyssa took the wing position, staying within the dragon's peripheral vision. Violet eyes shot with yellow pupils considered her as the female gave a deep-throated acknowledgment.

"You do like the dramatic, Lord Keldwyn." With effort, Lyssa managed to conceal how impressed she was at the lithe and sinuous way the male moved with the dragon's shifting flight. It reminded her of how effortlessly Jacob sat a horse. At Mason's estate, he and Jessica had ridden Mason's Arabians a couple times, and it had been well worth watching.

"I might say the same. That was quite a take off. Enjoy yourself with your new friends, Lady Lyssa. I will stay above you, but in range." With another Fae word spoken to the dragon, Keldwyn ascended gently, so the backwash from the dragon's giant wings didn't take Lyssa for an unintentional somersault. As she watched him go, a thoughtful frown creased her brow. Lord Keldwyn was definitely not a predictable male, but despite Jacob's suspicions and Rhoswen's outright denigration, he was the closest thing they had to an ally in this world.

Now that Keldwyn had moved out of range, the young Fae became far more assertive, closing in around her, studying the movement of her wings, the way her tail moved like a serpent in the air, helping her balance. After a barrage of questions, they moved into more competitive territory.

"Can you do this?" Allandra, the one who'd bravely approached her, now did a triple somersault, so close in front of Lyssa she executed a sharp banking maneuver to avoid running over the girl. But Allandra was more lithe than expected, moving back proportionately with the rotations. Then she hovered, staring at Lyssa expectantly.

She'd told Jacob it had been a long time since she'd been treated the way Rhoswen had treated her in front of her mock court. It had also been a long, long, *long* time since she'd been viewed as a potential new playmate. It was not a bad feeling.

She could do a triple somersault and did, even catching one of the male Fae within the coils of her tail and taking him along for the ride. He whooped with the pleasure of it. When she released him with a spin of motion and took off at full speed, she set off an impromptu game of tag. In the populated and suspicious human world, she had to fly at night, in hiding. Even at Mason's estate, surrounded by beach and rain forest, she had to be careful. Not here. She was different here, yes, but it wasn't a difference that had to be hidden.

All creatures of flight were bonded by the exultance of soaring through the clouds, even if such an emotional connection couldn't survive on the ground. In the Appalachians, she'd discovered it with the pixies. Now she experienced it more fully, the Fae young delighted in what she could do and showing off their own reckless talents. As they did, they came close enough to brush their delicate, translucent wings against her. Sometimes they were overconfident, and she was able to balance them, keep them from taking a nosedive. The way they moved, straight sprints and quick lifts, drops and hovers, as they kept pace with her more batlike darting flight pattern, reminded her of dragonflies.

When she at last perched on a tree, they lined up on either side of her. Once she gave them permission, they touched her back, wings and tail, testing the texture of her skin. Jacob had said it was like a thin layer of velvet over a sleekly muscled seal. Her eyes in this form were widely spaced, allowing her far greater coverage of her surroundings for the purposes of tracking, hunting and anticipating ambush. As a result, when one young Fae male tried to move in close enough to touch objects of a more prurient interest, she smacked him off the branch with an artful snap of her barbed tail. It made the others laugh. Even he grinned, after he recovered just short of hitting the ground. He floated back up, making a cocky somersault in the air.

"Can't blame a bloke for trying."

Allandra rolled her eyes. "You try with everything, Tael. It's why you don't get none with anyone."

"Queen's party," one of the others hissed abruptly.

In a blink, they'd all disappeared up into the tree's thick canopy above her head. Intrigued, Lyssa looked down. A few blinks later, Rhoswen and an escort of her guard passed along the forest trail beneath the tree. Apparently, morning court was over and they'd been off on another errand. Whatever it was, they were on their way back, since they were headed toward the castle, not away from it.

The guards were dressed in what looked like full honor regalia, silver mail glittering at a high shine beneath blue and white dragon tunics. Unlike the bows and daggers she'd seen them don earlier, today they wore long swords with ornate jeweled hilts, and carried painted shields with a different crest, a red rose twined around a silver sword hilt against a black field. Rhoswen wore her antlered crown, this time with a fall of sapphires dressing her hair. Her dress was white silk, overlaid with blue velvet. She and the dozen in her entourage were moving at a silent, sedate pace, as if in a parade ceremony. The only noise came from small chimes on the chin pieces of the horses' bridles.

As she focused on the queen, the curiosity Lyssa felt about the procession and its purpose became something else. She should have expected the reaction, seeing as it had been roiling in her gut since last night, but she hadn't expected the sight of Rhoswen to trigger it so strongly.

Feral rage.

When Rhoswen and Jacob had vanished from the upper room,

Lyssa had gone numb inside, so that Arrdol's touch felt unreal, distant. Inside, everything had become cold and hard. Silent. Whatever happened next, she could withdraw into that dark, stone place, even knowing it was the type of place that could trap a person there, the haven becoming a prison. Particularly if it was built of memories that clawed and demanded she stay there.

Then she had opened her eyes at a familiar touch and found herself in bed with Jacob, joined to her, everything as it should be. But the way he'd trembled, the wild aggression and anguish in his eyes, told her that Rhoswen had made him believe she would hurt Lyssa. She'd used that to force him to do her will, do things that made him feel unclean for her, less deserving.

Last night, they'd focused only on the fact they'd survived. But now, looking down at the silver and blue figure coming through the woods, Lyssa had room for something else. She might have given most of her vampire powers to Jacob, but it didn't mean she couldn't feel savage bloodlust, particularly when goaded to it.

Rhoswen must have picked up on some change in the air, because she reined in her horse, glanced around, then up, to meet Lyssa's dark gaze. Lyssa registered a moment of surprise in the Fae queen's eyes, but then it was gone, as if Rhoswen had expected to meet Lyssa all along.

"Sister." That mocking tone again. "Are you sure it's safe to leave your vampire pet alone?"

"He's as safe as I am, right?" Lyssa dropped down to a lower branch, coiling her tail around it. It brought her closer, but she was still above Rhoswen. Cayden was keeping his sharp eye on her, and in this instance, Lyssa knew he was wise to do so. Rhoswen's horse sidled at her unfamiliar form, but Rhoswen calmed him with a touch. There was no tack on the stallion, Lyssa noted, though he was richly turned out with jewels in his mane and tail, an embroidered blanket with the royal signet spread over his haunches. "Will you be with the Haunt tonight?"

"We meet up with the Seelie Hunt first. Then I lead the Unseelie procession through the portal to start the Haunt. The two Fae courts don't wander too far apart. They're like a tangled pair of vines, unable to tear free of one another." Rhoswen gave a brittle smile. "Though I prefer our method of celebration to theirs. It's far more suited to the human world."

"Yes. I can see how you would feel that way. A crop blessing isn't nearly as enjoyable as violence and fear. Like blackmailing my servant into fucking you so I wouldn't be violated."

Cayden toed his horse so he was even with Rhoswen's mount. He stared up at Lyssa, his mouth a hard line. "You will show the Fae queen respect."

"When she deserves it, I'll be the first."

She was always more uninhibited, closer to animal instinct, when she was in her Fae form. Was it that, plus being in the Fae world itself, a place of ancient earth spirits, that made her that much more intolerant of anything but the bold truth? Or maybe her protective instincts surpassed even Jacob's, when goaded past a certain point.

Of course, because she was stirring a hornet's nest, she'd woken her servant. She felt his touch, knew he was picking up the dangerous waves she was sending out.

"Bring me the spear," Rhoswen spoke to Cayden, her mouth tight.

"Your Majesty?"

"You heard me clearly enough."

Power lanced out with the words. Cayden's horse threw up his head as several lines of blood appeared on the captain's face. While the queen did not turn her attention to him, Lyssa saw the flash of cold anger before Cayden's face went blank. His mask to hide murderous rage, she assumed.

Backing the horse, he called out in the Fae language. One of his men dismounted, moved to a packhorse and unlaced a long, slender item wrapped in black cloth. When he carried it to Cayden with obvious reverence and care, the captain of the guard took it, wheeled the horse and came back to Rhoswen, who hadn't removed her frigid stare from Lyssa throughout.

"Your Majesty—" He stifled a curse as another rivulet opened on the opposite side of his face. Rhoswen's blue eyes glittered upon Lyssa's.

"You may do as you wish to me, my lady," Cayden said through clenched teeth. "But think this through. This is not who you are."

"No. But a debt is owed to who I once was." She extended her hand. "Give it to me, Cayden. And do not make me ask you once more. Would you shame your oath to me by making your queen beg?"

He placed it in her hand. Lyssa noted that Keldwyn had chosen one of his typically fortuitous moments to be absent. *Fine.* She held her position, knowing she was faster in Fae form if she had to dodge.

My lady?

All is well, Jacob. She could tell him to mind his own business and stay out of her mind. He would honor that—except when he knew she was in danger. Then she might as well toss the command out into the wind over sea-pummeled cliffs. *Just a female version of a pissing contest.*

Neither of you are well equipped for that, my lady. I would suggest diplomacy instead. Or a retreat.

I'll make you pay for that remark later, Sir Vagabond.

"This is the spear of Dagda, the original King of the Danu, the King of the Fae." Rhoswen considered it as she balanced it in one palm. "This is one of the reasons Dagda was never defeated by an enemy. It never misses its target."

Lyssa cocked her head. "It's said that one of the archangels, Raphael, has a spear that never misses, no matter how far it has to travel. It also comes back to him like a boomerang after passing through his opponent. It sounds like Dagda's spear is in need of an upgrade."

"You dare insult our holy relics?"

Instead of the Fae queen's usual capricious venom, Lyssa was surprised to see a truly offended expression. "This item is sacred. Its meaning is central to who and what we are, what we have come from. We bring the spear forth only at Samhain. King Tabor carries it with full ceremony on the Hunt. It is our way of remembering."

Lyssa dropped to the ground a few feet in front of Rhoswen's horse. In a blink, she'd shifted back to human form. Despite her pale nakedness, she offered a slight bow, her hair falling forward over her shoulder. "I intend no offense to your history. Your moods are somewhat difficult to anticipate . . ."

She paused, somewhat distracted by a flicker in Cayden's expression that Jacob would have interpreted as *you don't know the half of it*. Clearing her throat, she continued. "But the tension between you and me has nothing to do with the respect due to such items. Please accept my apologies on their behalf."

Rhoswen stared at her. However, at length, she opened the wrap, revealing a spear with a silver tip that shone with a liquid light. The shaft was carved with letters Lyssa didn't know, possibly Gaelic or the Fae tongue. It was also inlaid with more silver. As the queen hefted it, Cayden slid the wrapping away and draped the cloth over his horse's neck. "This represents what is pure about our people," Rhoswen said. "It goes back to the beginning, like Excalibur and all the ancient enchanted treasures."

She changed her grip on it, lifting it out to her side, her elbow bent close to her body. "It would be most fitting to run you through with it. If you died on its shaft, it could be my blood offering this night to those ancestors, a reminder that their current queen remembers and knows what being Fae means." She lifted her gaze to the trees. "No obsession with things of other worlds. Fly away, little butterflies. Go find Catriona, and see if she has learned the lesson you still refuse to learn."

There was a rush of wings as the teens fled, a flutter of leaves. Lyssa noted then how still the surrounding forest had gone. Either the Fae and animal life were watching in careful silence, or they'd all moved out of the queen's sphere of power and influence, rightfully perceiving here was not a wise place to be. She remembered then how the tiny Fae playing in Rhoswen's hair so trustingly had vanished when the tone of the evening had changed.

"Your Majesty." Keldwyn stepped out of the forest.

Rhoswen's lips twisted. "Of course. He always shows up when least wanted or needed."

The Fae lord spread out his hands, expression as bland as ever. "Not wanted, perhaps. But needed, more than you wish to acknowledge. I did not anticipate the Lady Lyssa crossing your path as you returned from the Lake of Memory. You know that the power of the old ones there can distort your view and emotions for a certain time. It is why no magic is allowed to be practiced for a proscribed period after the visit."

"Lord Keldwyn, if there is one thing I have *never* known you to do, it's fail to anticipate."

The blue in Rhoswen's eyes all but disappeared, the pupils large and dark. Lyssa saw the distortion that Keldwyn had intimated, but she wasn't sure if a lake had anything to do with it.

The queen's caustic tone elicited nothing but silence from Keldwyn, and she turned her ire to Lyssa. "I keep warning you, and you continue to treat him as an ally. Your servant claims I am not a better queen than you, but I think this illustrates differently."

"From where I stand, Lord Keldwyn is not the one threatening me with a spear."

"I never claimed to be your ally."

Jacob's tension was growing, but the sun was bright in the sky. Lyssa could feel the heat of it bearing down on her skin, because the tree cover was thin here. Even if he could emerge now, he was too far away to do anything for her. His frustration was tipping up his bloodlust. She hoped an innocent maid didn't come through to fluff the bedding.

Jacob, I'm all right. Let me focus.

He reined himself back, with an abrupt effort that almost made her dizzy. But she steadied herself, met Rhoswen's gaze.

"Fine, then. You say Samhain requires a blood sacrifice to honor the purity of the Fae blood. So here it is." Lyssa spread her arms out wide, took a step back to better align herself with the line of that spear tip. "If you don't think it will sully the wood to plunge it through my black heart, the blood sacrifice is yours. Do it, Your Majesty. Salve the bitterness in your heart, whatever its source. If hurling that spear will bring you satisfaction, do it. But if you miss"—Lyssa bared her fangs—"You get your ice princess ass down off that horse and fight me, power against power, or hand to hand. It doesn't matter to me. Let's just put an end to this."

"Lady Lyssa." Keldwyn stepped forward, but Lyssa warded him off with a sharp slicing motion of her hand.

"Stay back. If you set this in motion, deal with the consequences."

Lyssa stared at her rival, ice blue eyes to jade. "I've met plenty of your kind in my life, Your Majesty. Those who want to be powerful, but aren't willing to accept the wisdom and humility to truly *be* powerful. So, impale me on your very special, very pure spear, and see if that brings you the satisfaction—"

Lyssa. Jacob's roar of rage and helplessness cut through her mind as Keldwyn started forward. Surprisingly, Cayden shouted Rhoswen's name with the same urgency. He even put his heels to his horse, as if he would join the Fae lord in trying to head off the inevitable. But they were too late. Rhoswen had hefted the spear and hurled it.

With metal and wood crafting the shaft, and metal at the substantial, sharp tip, it would kill vampire or servant, and of course she was both. As Fae, she wasn't entirely sure what would kill her, but if the spear was designed to fight Fae, she expected it covered that as well. She refused to close her eyes, refused to move. Though her heart accelerated like a galloping horse, everything slowed down as that spear came toward her. She had a glimpse of Rhoswen's eyes, torn between longing and hatred. Old pain struggling beneath a mask.

The spear hit her square in the chest, the force making her stagger back. She'd been wounded often enough that she could track the damage as it punched through her body, tearing heart muscle, bringing nerves to screaming life. She blacked out for a whirling second, though she was still swaying on her feet. Then the spear passed all the way through, such was the force of Rhoswen's throw. As it left her, she dropped to one knee. Vaguely, she heard a thunk of impact, a clatter of metal as it bounced off a tree. Her body had slowed its momentum, such that it couldn't embed itself into the trunk. Or perhaps it didn't embed itself in the tree for the same reason it passed all the way through her, leaving her in pain, gasping for breath . . . but very much alive and intact.

Keldwyn had his cloak wrapped over her, his large palm pressed to her chest, over her breast where the spear had entered. Her blood soaked his hand, but when he shifted his touch, Lyssa knew he saw the entry point closing, knitting before his eyes even as it pumped out more blood through the shrinking opening. "My lady," he said, the words caught in his throat.

He was so astounded that when Lyssa struggled to get up, he forgot his courtier's manners. Then he recovered and helped her to her feet. She had to lean on him for balance, the shock of the penetration and the swift blood loss making her a little shaky. Still, she faced Rhoswen.

"My servant told me that the spear of Dagda would strike down any enemy of the Fae. Which, by deduction, means that a friend would not be harmed by it. At least not permanently." She coughed, spat blood onto the ground between them. "Get down off that horse. I want to put my impure foot up your pure white backside."

Rhoswen's face was three shades paler than normal, making her ethereal beauty seem fragile. One of Cayden's men had retrieved the spear. Giving Lyssa and Keldwyn a wide berth, he brought it back to the captain. Cayden took it, studying the tip. He used his own cloak to clean off Lyssa's blood, then resecured the weapon in its wrappings, leaving it balanced on his pommel rather than returning it to the honor guard or his queen. Seeing Rhoswen still staring at Lyssa, he touched the rein on her horse, drawing her attention. "Your Majesty, the crowd waits at the village to see the Sacred Procession."

He had to repeat it, touch her leg instead of the horse. When he did, she jerked, seeming to come out of a trance. Rhoswen looked at the blood on the cloak and Keldwyn's hands. "Another time, Lady Lyssa," she said at last, her voice strained. "After all, the deal only applied if I missed. And I didn't."

She pressed her horse into a canter from a standstill, the steed prettily lifting his feet off the ground before he lunged forward, narrowly missing Lyssa. She refused to move, even though the fabric of the queen's skirts lashed against her as she passed, grazing Keldwyn's knuckles where they were curved on the outside of the cloak he had wrapped around her. Cayden gave Keldwyn a nod, then followed in her wake, the others falling into ranks. Lyssa didn't turn to watch them go, though she was aware every one of the honor guard gave her a second look as they passed her. Once she heard the sound of their horses fade, she sank back to the ground in Keldwyn's grasp. "What can I do?" he asked.

Come to me, Lyssa. I'm here.

"Get me back to the castle. I'm a third-marked . . . servant. Jacob's blood will restore me. I'm all right. It's the pain and blood loss, not an injury."

And that pain was fierce on a couple levels. The spear hadn't killed her, but her heart had been punctured by Rhoswen's venom. Her half sister wanted her dead. Which was a ridiculous thing to care about, because they shared blood and nothing else. Sharing a father didn't make them family.

"Get me to Jacob," she repeated, realizing her voice was fainter, more breathy.

Keldwyn nodded, swung her up in his arms. The dragon's approach was a darkness over the sunny sky, and then Keldwyn was settling her in the dip of the creature's neck, directly before him.

"You bastard," she murmured. "She was right, wasn't she? You planned this."

"I thought it might be good for the two of you to have a more private confrontation. I thought you might prove something to her. You did. Something vital."

"Remind me to put my foot up *your* backside, when I feel more up to it."

12

THE urgency Jacob felt was as potent as a dragon's fire by the time Keldwyn reached their guestroom. Lyssa had lost consciousness on the flight back, but she was alive. He knew the lack of consciousness helped her conserve strength. The wound wasn't mortal of course, but she was severely weakened, and that was never a good condition for a Fae or vampire, particularly when they were surrounded by few, if any, friends.

On that note, he barely managed to keep from snarling at Keldwyn like an enraged bear when he came into the chamber. As the Fae lord laid Lyssa on the bed, Jacob brushed him aside and slid his arm beneath her. He reached for his knife, but a blade appeared before him. Glancing up at Keldwyn, he nodded and averted his head, letting the Fae make a deft slice at Jacob's carotid. The blood welled up fast and thick as Jacob brought Lyssa up to that flow, letting it meet her lips.

Instinct could be blessing or curse. Fortunately, this time it was a blessing. Her body knew what it needed, even passed out; she latched on and began to drink. As Jacob held her even closer, he spoke, not looking at the Fae lord. "I think it's best if you leave. Because when she gets done, I won't have the control to keep from tearing out your throat."

Keldwyn flipped the knife over deftly, shoving it back into his scabbard. It was an arrogant response, one he followed up with a short, impersonal bow. "I'll see you both at dusk. A servant will bring you appropriate riding attire."

He stopped at the doorway. "Be warned. Earlier this morning, Queen Rhoswen informed me that she has divined your quest. You will be provided a special mount for tonight."

As usual, the bastard didn't give him anything useful. Just an ominous portent of more trouble to come. Of course, right now Jacob didn't really give a Fae or rat's ass about what the night would bring. Stroking Lyssa's hair, he worked to get his pulse to stop racing. A rapid bloodflow might choke her. He kept seeing that throw, the spear shooting through the air and thudding into her chest, knocking her slight body back.

His hands had added to the blood on her, because he'd torn his palms, the result of hitting the rough textured walls in frustration during those interminable moments. He'd had enough rational thought left to stay put, knowing he'd be no help to her if he burned himself to a crisp trying to rush to her side. Of course, if Rhoswen's spear had taken her life, he would have done it without hesitation, hoping to at least make it to her side before sunlight turned him to ash. If it had, he'd will the wind to carry that ash to her, damn it.

Jacob's binding to Lyssa had been willing from the beginning, so it hadn't mattered to him one bit that Lord Brian wasn't able to confirm the elements of Lyssa's original third-marking were still upon him, beyond the serpentine mark. She'd had the ability to speak in his mind in the months before he found her in the mountains and gave her the third mark to protect her and their unborn child. However, he knew she wasn't able to plumb his mind to the soul-deep level that Jacob could hers.

Brian hadn't had the chance to examine them until after Jacob had marked her, and therefore couldn't determine what residual elements of her third-marking existed under the shadow of his. A fledgling's mark shouldn't be able to conceal a much stronger vampire's, but in this case, Lyssa was no longer a much stronger vampire—she'd given that strength to Jacob. As Lyssa herself had noted earlier, if Jacob was killed, she would likely die, the proof of his third-mark soul bond upon her. But they had no proof that was a two-way street. At the time, Brian had been willing to try further tests to confirm her original markings, but Jacob met with him privately while Lyssa was occupied with other matters and refused. In those days during her pregnancy, when she was coping with everything that had changed about herself, he'd rather have the uncertain possibility that the bond she'd given him was still there than confirm it was gone.

He knew—from both sides of the coin now—how vital that bond was, how much it meant to his queen, the emotional value of it. He didn't care about science or the gods, not when it came to this. Whether or not the lingering effects of her original third-marking on him would make his death inevitable from hers, his heart made it inevitable. That was all that mattered.

His threat against Keldwyn wasn't an idle one. The Fae Lord might wipe up the floor with Jacob. But if will alone would take the fight, it would be Keldwyn reduced to a pile of bones, the truncated wings perched pertly on top.

Shhh . . . It was her voice, her hands touching him, stroking his shoulders, as she recovered her energy. *It's all right.*

Palming her delicate skull, his fingers tight in her hair, he pressed her mouth closer to his throat, feeling that physical proof of life. "You took a huge risk, interpreting the lore that way. What if I'd embellished the story, merely to entertain you?"

"Then I would have been extremely miffed with you." She dropped her head back, rubbing her lips together to take away the excess blood. Her color was better, and he could feel the strength in her grip on his arms. "You wouldn't embellish, because you knew I was seeking facts from the stories you were telling me."

"What if my mother, who told me that story, was embellishing?"

"Then we'd blame your mother." Lyssa gave him a smile. "I've been told that's what all children do, as long as she's around to blame. If not, they go for the father."

She trailed off then. "It's likely as simple as all that, isn't it? For Rhoswen. Though not in her behavior toward us, I see the elements of a fair, strong queen in the way her people react to her. They've shown a patience and loyalty that doesn't happen if it's not deserved. She obviously has her people's devotion, though they've learned to be careful of her temper."

"Not unlike someone else I know." Jacob straightened to a sitting position on the bed, one foot on the floor as he shifted her into the cradle of his thighs. He wasn't ready to let her go yet. "You've opened an old wound, one she's been carrying around for a thousand years, a new personal record for how long a woman can hold a grudge. I'm guessing that when you were just a lowly vampire, she could justify hating you from afar, ignoring you. But now that your Fae blood is developing, it's reopened the wound. It was a slap in the face, hearing what your capabilities are, then seeing them up close and personal. He not only gave his love to a vampire; he also gave his blood and some of his abilities—actually, it's starting to appear like quite a bit of his abilities—to the daughter she bore him."

"There's more to it as well." She told him what Keldwyn had said about Rhoswen. "I'm still missing some pieces, but it does explain why, after all these years, it's a sore point to her. As you said, an old wound that's been reopened."

"God save us from girls with daddy issues." Jacob dodged her swat, catching her wrist and placing a kiss on her palm to mollify her, though he eased his grip as she pushed against it to stroke her hand through his hair, touch the side of his neck. "No wonder Cayden has been walking around with that permanent, 'oh shit, what is she going to do next?' expression."

She sobered. "I don't like Keldwyn's veiled warning about your mount. She's shifting her temper from me to you tonight."

"Which is where I prefer it to be." At her warning look, he sighed, gave her an admonishing squeeze. "She knows it's all the same, my lady. She's trying to find the weakness that will bring us both down."

He knew Lyssa couldn't argue that one, and so they sat silently for a moment. She played with the hair at his nape, then spoke. "I know you're not disposed to think kindly of Keldwyn, but in some confused way, he may be trying to help her as well. I believe Cayden knows that, though he gets on the guard captain's nerves almost as much as he does yours."

"Good. Something else for the two of us to bond over."

"Hmm. My mother never spoke of another child, or another woman who held my father's heart." Lyssa frowned. "I wouldn't like to think of my father being deceitful in his love, either to my mother or another, but of course it's possible. I never had the chance to know him, and it is easy for a child to romanticize a dead father."

"Maybe it's time to ask Keldwyn a direct question. And if you want me to pull off any of his appendages to get answers, just say the word."

~

Riding clothes for Lyssa meant a beautiful high-waisted dress with embroidery at the block neck, and point sleeves that had a long drape at the elbows to match a flowing train. Rhoswen had sent attendants to help Lyssa once again, only this time it was waiflike Fae women with long thin arms and quiet, shadowlike movements. The one in charge had suggested, in a rasping voice, that Lyssa allow her to pull her ebony locks up enough to keep them out of her face, yet let the bulk of it trail down her back in a thick mass. They'd produced different accessories, a necklace of jade stones, matching ear bobs, lavender flowers for her hair that matched the dress. There was silver thread edging at the hems of the sleeves. Along the back of the train was a more elaborate, Celtic-style embroidered design.

When she asked who was supplying the clothing, she was told it was at the discretion of the queen. Despite the fact Rhoswen had done her best to kill her this afternoon, she wanted Lyssa to be suitably dressed for the Hunt. Perhaps it had to do with her meeting the Seelie king, and not wanting to appear petty.

Jacob had donned Catriona's stone pendant, and it complemented the short tunic, boots and hose that suited him so well. From the first moment she'd seen him at the Eldar, the spa where he'd come to "audition" for the role of her servant, he'd reminded her of the knight he'd once been, long ago, the one with whom she'd spent one memorable night during the Crusades. He hadn't remembered that right off, nor had she connected the two so intimately, but as their bond had deepened, she had become certain he and that knight were the same soul. As time passed, Fate had been kind, giving him the memory she had of that night in bits and pieces.

What he didn't remember from that time, but learned from her in their present day relationship, was that she'd conceived a child that fateful night. The babe had been stillborn. She vividly remembered that pale and fragile little daughter she'd buried alone. Her knight, the Jacob of that time period, had died three days after the night of conception. If the babe had lived, if Jacob had survived to return to her in his incarnation as the knight, she was sure that little girl would have been adored and cherished by her father all his life.

Girls with daddy issues. She wondered again at the nature of her father, what he'd thought of Rhoswen and her mother. It was a dull twinge, thinking he might have turned his back on them.

They were prepared to their attendants' satisfaction, and it was time to go. Taking Jacob's offered arm, she let him lead her from the room, the two of them moving down the winding staircase. Though she was aware of his quiet scrutiny, she couldn't push the memories back.

From the first, she'd known Kane wasn't the incarnation of her daughter. The near-term fetus had been delicate and soft, so feminine and sensitive. For all that he was an infant, Kane was a bowling ball of testosterone. But she'd wondered if Kane, when in the Hall of Souls, had touched her little hand.

Of course such thoughts were fanciful and maudlin, for the soul of that long ago baby had certainly gone into the body of some other fetus, hopefully to be born in better times. Born to a mother who'd gotten to hold her, live, hale and hearty, with kicking feet and a scrunched-up face, squalling irritation at being so rudely born. Not still, like a little ghost in the womb.

She'd stopped on the stairs, was staring vacantly out an open window on the staircase. As she focused, she saw an array of luminaires had been strung along the drawbridge. Similar decorations outlined all the castles, with the exception of the Castle of Fire, of course, though she noted the fire had myriad colors tonight and the flame was more animated, jumping high and swirling out wide in fanciful shapes, like a light show.

"My lady." Jacob slid his arm around her, picking up the tone of her thoughts.

I'm all right. She nodded, acknowledging the comfort. Those who lived much shorter lifespans assumed the past grew dim after a while. That memories didn't have as much power to hurt. That was true, somewhere in the middle of one's life. But as the years accumulated, they came back with a renewed power. Though they didn't hurt the same way, poignant regret was there, more sharp. The desire to reach back and change things increased.

Giving her a look of quiet understanding, he offered his raised hand, in true courtier fashion. She laid hers upon it, tightening her fingers on his knuckles, and let him lead her down the staircase to the main hall. The tables were set, the decorations a profusion of autumn color. Ice sculptures that looked like Fae maidens, undines, satyrs and other dancing creatures glistened, thanks to the gentle light of the three candelabras hung from stout chain. Hawthorne, ash and rowan branches were woven into the black wood frames, dotted with the gold, red and brown colors of flowers appropriate to the season.

As they moved out into the courtyard, they found the Queen's Guard had dressed for this event as well. Jacob drew her to the wall so they could safely survey all the activity. They were meeting up with the main Unseelie host out on the front field before the castle, but well over a hundred of the males were getting mounted up here and it was a sight not to be missed.

The guards were all on black horses tonight, painted with white, skeleton-like slashes along the flanks and neck. Through some magic, the horses' hooves appeared to be wreathed with flame, though the creatures seemed unconcerned by what would spook a normal animal. Their riders were dressed all in black, with long cloaks and silver painted faces, which made their expressions seem remote and eerie.

In the center of that formation, she saw a handful of younger Fae, perhaps the ages of her earlier group. They were dressed in a variety of masks and scary costumes like she'd seen sold at the pavilions. When she and Jacob arrived, they were cavorting about the courtyard, laughing and loud, but at a sharp word from Cayden's lieutenant, they settled into an open carriage. A pair of black centaurs took up the yoke, bearing breastplates with the queen's dragon insignia. Apparently, this small group of young had been awarded the privilege of accompanying the Haunt, but only with close supervision.

Lyssa saw Keldwyn, striding out of another corridor. He was also all in black, but wore an elaborate mask of layered feathers that fanned out in rust and gold colors, accentuating the stern lips and firm chin. His dark hair was clasped at his nape and, as he turned his head, she saw the clasp was a silver skull.

She didn't see Cayden, which was surprising, since Rhoswen made her appearance next. She rode out of the stables on a white charger painted in black slashes, the mirror opposite of her escort. When her eyes settled on the Fae young, her expression cool, they immediately became even more somber and well behaved.

"The Lady in White," Jacob murmured, his hand tightening on Lyssa's. "Jesus."

The queen of the Unseelie was garbed in a creation of white silk that turned her into a ghost with her pale face. Her long skeins of white hair were unbound so the ends spread over the blanket on the rump of her charger. She had those sparkles of snow and starlight upon her skin, as did her antlered headdress.

A belt made of heavy chain rested low on her hips, the excess of it running up to a set of loose manacles she bore on her wrists. She looked ready to drag some unsuspecting mortal back to the Fae world against his will, pulled behind her horse in those chains.

She made her way past the assembled guard. They sat straight and expressionless as her gaze passed over them, assessing. When at last she reached the lieutenant, she nodded. Though his expression didn't change, it was obvious the minimalist praise was the equivalent of a roaring accolade to him.

As she continued toward the drawbridge, the guard fell in line behind her, the center carriage with them. Seeing several others of the high court on foot, walking out behind the formation, Jacob and Lyssa accompanied them, moving to the drawbridge and beyond to join the main host of the Unseelie entourage. The high court members drifted over toward outfitted horses being held patiently by castle stablehands, but Lyssa and Jacob were caught by the spectacle of the waiting cavalcade—and the sudden sharp screeches that split the darkening night.

Lyssa found the banshees, long, thin-bodied creatures draped on the shoulders of several giants in the procession. The banshees looked much like normal men or women, though their eyes were luminous gold, and they all seemed to have burnished red hair.

Harpies winged swiftly up and back, reminding her of her own bat-like way of flying as they took teasing passes over the heads of the others. They looked much like the stories, with skeletal faces, burning dark eyes and long, grasping fingers, their gray hair streaming out behind them as they turned and rolled in the air, impressive aerial maneuvers in a sky already populated by hippogriffs, griffins, dragons and phoenixes.

Interestingly, there was also a large murder of crows. The black, glossy-feathered creatures collected on the branches of nearby trees, making a substantial cacophony when not taking flight in sudden explosions of synchronized movement around the other flying folk.

Beneath the spreading branches of the oaks the crows seemed to favor, Lyssa saw a woman even more pale skinned and white haired than Rhoswen. She was in a silver sleigh drawn by a foursome of horses. The sleigh seemed to be made entirely of ice.

"The Snow Queen," Jacob murmured. "She coaxes a child into the sleigh with her, and then takes him to her castle of ice. To make him her own child, she erases the memory of the parents from his mind."

"Remind me to never let Kane go out in the snow," she responded.

The trolls and ogres were banded together in a tight group. Viewing their round, glittering eyes and broad faces, Lyssa realized a happy-looking ogre was downright disturbing. Yips and bays announced the arrival of the hell hounds. Their handlers were a satyr and a centaur. Instead of straddling the centaur, the satyr squatted on his back on shaggy haunches and cloven hoofs. Though he had a steadying hand tented on the centaur's withers, it was obvious they were companions, not mount and rider. The satyr made a short, musical trill on his pipe, bringing the hounds back to mill around them. Before that, they'd been running about, slathering on any person who let them jump up on them. Their red eyes glowed, long, curved fangs glistening with drool. It made Lyssa miss Bran and his siblings.

It was awe-inspiring, magnificent, macabre. As several shadowlike creatures passed them, she drew in a quick breath at a blast of icy wind. An overwhelming sense of desolation came with it. Jacob drew her close, giving her his warmth. "The Gaoth Shee," he said. "Sometimes, when you pass over a fairy line in the mortal world, you'll feel their touch. And when you do, the lore is you suffer a malady soon thereafter, like a stroke. I assume we're immune."

"Let's hope." It reminded Lyssa that, despite the festive air tonight, there were other, far darker things happening. When she studied her half sister's serious face, her intent scrutiny of everyone in the procession, she realized Rhoswen didn't consider this a night of mirth at all. She wanted to terrify the mortal world. She wanted them scurrying back into the safety of their homes, not venturing into dark, old sections of forests and other places where they might find their way into her world. Tonight had a deadly, determined purpose.

As such, when Rhoswen raised her hand, Lyssa wasn't at all surprised that the assembled fell silent within seconds, all their playful antics vanishing. They were about to become the creatures of the night, the vengeful spirits that humans feared, the things that exploited a mortal's deepest terrors. It was the Ichabod Crane legends coming to life. And afterward, they would come back here to feast and play, their hard work done.

Rhoswen met her gaze, gave her a slight, impartial nod. Her horse bent his noble head restlessly, shaking the snow out of his mane, nostrils flaring with mist from the frost that emanated from his Mistress. When Rhoswen spoke, she raised her voice, making it clear her address was for a public audience.

"Our visitor will need a proper mount to ride with the Seelie king tonight."

A lovely palfrey was led from a pavilion on the lawn. The mare was decorated with ropes of greenery and lavender flowers in her dapple gray mane. Lavender embroidered silk was cinched with braided ribbon over a saddle pad. The reins were likewise tangled with a trail of lavender and green ribbon.

"Thank you, Your Majesty." Lyssa nodded to her. "A lovely mare. I hope my servant's mount is not as gentle, however. He is quite a horseman, and likes to be challenged."

Apparently enough was known of the queen's intentions for the second quest that Lyssa's words surprised a chuckle out of a member or two of the Guard. The lieutenant's sharp glance brought them in line.

"It is our pleasure to accommodate him." Rhoswen's voice had that silver, brittle sound that resonated off the trees, off the silence of the listening Fae. Not even a horse shifted with restless impatience. "Like a faithful hound, he goes whither you goest, right?"

An outraged whinny came from the pavilion, a thud of hooved feet. The side of the pavilion shuddered, as if a support had been kicked, and then Cayden was leading out Jacob's mount, using all of his strength to control the creature.

The massive black stallion was built like a draft horse, with powerful withers and thick neck. Glowing red eyes glared at the gathering. The high court, whom Lyssa assumed contained many Fae of considerable power, drew back apprehensively as the horse surged forward and then was forced by Cayden's quickness to swing his haunches around in a circle. He kicked, causing the nearer Fae to draw back farther.

Lyssa's brow rose as the horse snorted, producing two short gouts of flame that dissipated with wisps of smoke, like a dragon. This horse had no tack except a bridle and cinch. Instead of flowers or strands of jewels in his long mane, he had tangles of seaweed and shells. As he swung around, Lyssa smelled the ocean coming off his damp, heated skin. The steed's front legs were hobbled, forcing the horse to move at an awkward, hopping gait. When she saw Jacob looking at the headpiece, his expression darkening, she realized a bearing rein was holding the horse's head at a painful upright angle. The discomfort and restraint prevented him from dropping and bucking.

Jacob had been the master of horse at the Ren Faire, and she knew well how he felt about seeing one mistreated.

Easy, Jacob. There's more here than meets the eye.

"A water horse is a very difficult horse to catch. Impossible to ride, unless you wish to ride to your death."

At the sound of Rhoswen's voice, the horse let out another shrill, bloodcurdling cry. Cayden shifted with the stallion once more, narrowly avoiding having his skull crushed with a swing of the massive head.

Oh, lovely fucking Christ. A kelpie.

Lyssa glanced at Jacob. From the set of his jaw, it appeared the situation was far beyond optimal. Perhaps even in the realm of hopeless impossibility.

Ah, my lady, there is no such thing as hopeless around you. Impossible, yes; hopeless, no. He gave her that warm look he did so well, though it was laced with tension.

"Mortal legend claims a waterhorse coaxes children onto his back," Rhoswen said. "Then he races away, plunges into a loch and drowns them. It is believed he has a strong binding magic to keep them on his back until the last breath leaves them."

The Fae queen considered the creature, the brutal effort he was expending, trying to stomp her guard captain into the ground. "Since the bodies were rarely found, it was also suggested that the horse took them to the Fae world. Or ate them, once he had them below the surface of the water." She shrugged. "Only the waterhorses know for sure. Even the Fae are wary of them, as you can see. The Irish called them kelpie. Right, Irishman?"

"Aye. And the Scottish called them *each uisge*." When Jacob looked toward the queen, Lyssa saw his blue eyes were almost as cold as Rhoswen's. "To be feared . . . and respected."

"Supposedly, if you have the kelpie's halter or bridle, he has to obey your will." Rhoswen gave Jacob a tight smile. "As far as we know, Firewind has no such weakness. He despises most Fae, let alone humans. He won't tolerate a vampire on his back at all. Perhaps because he feeds on blood and doesn't like the competition. However, if you do manage to get on his back, be careful of the unique trait he inherited from his sire, Firebreather."

She lifted her hand toward the horse, gave a sharp command that was reinforced by a flicker of magical energy. Jacob started forward, but Lyssa caught his arm. Firewind's head snapped around, long ears pinning back as his malevolent expression intensified. A wreath of flame erupted from his withers and, in a dramatic sweep, encased him from neck to tail, the long black strands like a flame-covered flogger as he lashed them over his haunches. Cayden had his hand on the bridle's cheek piece, avoiding the fire. Then the flame vanished and Firewind made another valiant attempt to get his hooves off the ground.

"Ride him in the Hunt," Rhoswen said, fixing her eyes back on Jacob. "That is the second quest. If you do not succeed, or if you don't dare to try, your lady has failed the Gauntlet, per your failure as her champion, and her fate rests wholly in my hands. Since I know you are as full of pointless nobility as Firewind is of flame, I expect you will immolate yourself. But try not to singe your fine backside, vampire. Some things should remain sacred."

Rhoswen turned her attention to Lyssa. "You will ride with me at the head of the procession. We proceed to the rendezvous point with the Seelie court. Your servant will join us, or not."

The stablehand holding Lyssa's palfrey moved forward, presenting a hand to help her on the steed. Lyssa turned her gaze to Jacob. *Sir Vagabond?*

"I'll catch up," Jacob told her. He gave her a wink, though there was no such affability in his gaze. His mind was already concentrated on the task ahead because, of course, it wouldn't occur to him to do anything but try, just as Rhoswen said.

Lyssa nodded. She accepted the stablehand's help onto the mount with the brief press of hands on her waist, since mounting with a dress train was not an easy task for any species, Fae or vampire. She caught a brief flash of surprise on Rhoswen's face at her detachment, but she couldn't feel any smug satisfaction. For one thing, looking serene and unconcerned was taking all her effort. As she bent her knee over her mare's withers in a sidesaddle position, she saw Jacob take two steps toward Cayden.

"Looks like you're a little out of your depth, Captain. Ready to turn him over to me?"

~

For Jacob's thirtieth birthday, she'd surprised him with a visit to the particular Ren Faire that had been his home for a couple years. They'd invited him to rejoin the jousting that night. Vividly, she remembered how he'd swung up on the back of a horse, no stirrups, just holding a handful of mane. The moment his fine ass had touched the horse's back—she and Rhoswen at least agreed on that—he'd become part of that horse's body.

The horse he'd ridden that night, Boudiceaa, had been a badly abused mare who'd become the Faire's top attraction because he'd taught her to trust again.

She held on to that memory to reassure herself as she calmed her own mount. Firewind had managed to agitate most of the horses in the procession. It gave her an extra moment to linger, watch Jacob move toward that monster. As he did, he was loosening his shoulders, his gait. He tilted his head, cracking his neck with an audible pop that made several of the Fae flinch in surprise.

When he was four steps away from the kelpie, he nodded to Cayden. "Let him go."

She had accelerated senses, but the ability was not the same for all Fae. Some seemed surprised to see Jacob standing where Cayden had been a moment before. As the captain moved out of range, the kelpie screamed his rage and twisted around, pivoting with over a thousand pounds of muscle at his disposal to crush whoever was offending him. Though the creature was moving even more swiftly than he had with Cayden, his frustration mounting to berserker level, her servant was staying a step or two ahead of the horse. He made the rapid turns with him, an odd merry-go-round of twisting, dangerous movement.

"Mount up," Cayden called out as if nothing dramatic was occurring. "The queen is departing."

Lyssa started as a guardsman's hand landed on her bridle and led her horse toward the front of the procession. From that vantage point, she couldn't keep her eyes on Jacob unless she twisted around in her saddle. Rhoswen wanted her to appear agitated and concerned, she knew. While she could be in Jacob's mind—in fact, she was in it now, amazed by the instinctual flow of counterreaction toward the horse, as natural as a swift river current—it was not the same as being able to watch him. She needed to withdraw from his head, because if he did get in a difficult position, an agitated reaction on her part, even internally, would be a distraction he could ill afford. *Damn it.*

That, too, was part of the test Rhoswen was executing, wasn't it? Settling her seat further, Lyssa made an impatient noise, collecting her reins and pulling her mount away from the guardsman. Moving the palfrey into a pretty trot, she came to Rhoswen's left side as Cayden swung up on his own horse on the queen's right. As they moved away from the field, every squeal that split the air, the sound of earth thudding beneath hooves—hopefully it was earth, and not bones—was a hammer at her consciousness, screaming at her to jump into his mind again.

She ignored it, keeping her hands loose on the reins, her shoulders relaxed, even as her heart and gut were tight as two tangled fists. If Rhoswen got him killed, it didn't matter if it killed Lyssa as well. She'd come back and haunt her bitch sister for all eternity.

~

As Jacob kept up his dance with the horse, he started crooning in Gaelic. Calming words, a singsong chant he'd used with fractious and mistrustful mounts in the past. Whether or not it would have any effect on a kelpie, he knew nothing was going to get better until that bearing rein was released. It had been misused to deliberately goad the horse, the way cinching a strap over the testicles of a bull was done at rodeos to make them buck more ferociously. It proved Rhoswen as a hypocrite in her scorn toward humans. She was treating one of the creatures of her own world abysmally to serve her own purposes.

He put aside the anger, because the horse would pick up any negative feeling and feed off it. Plus, he was handling a creature that was not exactly a horse. Every time those nostrils flared and expelled a billow of flame, he had to stay clear, though more than once the heat seared his skin. He could smell the fibers of his tunic smoldering from proximity alone.

Vaguely, he was aware the Unseelie procession was filing down the hillside. They'd meet the colorful Seelie train at Caislean Talamh, the Castle of Earth, and that route would be lined with more Fae, celebrating and encouraging the riders. He would have liked to see all that. If he survived this, maybe he could.

"Another minute," he gritted, to both of them. He needed the procession to be clear of the castle, giving him room to do what he needed to do.

The horse squealed, baring yellow teeth the size of his thumb knuckles. "I got it, you're pissed." Jacob grunted with the effort to hold fast to the bridle. He flexed his other hand, ready to go for his knife. It might not be wise to cut off the only thing controlling the horse, but he followed his instincts, as he always had. Gideon had often said there was a reason the words *instinct* and *insanity* differed by only two letters.

With two quick movements, he sliced through the bridle and cinch, and tore it all free. Catching a handful of mane, he twisted himself up onto the horse's back, clamping down with knees and thighs, both hands buried in that long, long mane.

He'd expected the flame. It swarmed up over his hands, exploded and covered the stallion's body, the heat searing through his clothing, hungry for his flesh. Firewind was in motion, galloping pell mell up the hill toward the castle. Those who'd gathered for the procession and lingered to watch his match with the kelpie now scrambled to get out of the way. Firewind moved in an erratic zigzag, so they had to be very quick, using wings as well as feet. Some only had time to throw their bodies out of the horse's path as he clattered onto the drawbridge, a streaming ball of rust and black flame with enraged crimson eyes.

Hold on . . . Jacob hammered himself with the mantra, his jaw clenched, a strangled cry in his throat as the fire licked at his skin. The excruciating pain would shortly become lethal, the fire burning him to ash. If Rhoswen was right and a kelpie wouldn't release its prey until it was drowned, then Firewind had to choose to let him off. It didn't matter. Jacob wasn't getting off until he'd accomplished the quest. Instead, he trusted the horse's nature, which wouldn't care whether or not he was carrying an undrownable vampire. As a result, with an abrupt left turn, one that would have jerked his shoulder out of its socket if he hadn't anticipated it, the horse gathered himself and leaped off the drawbridge.

Plunging into the moat below, Firewind scattered a pod of selkies. Jacob bounced down hard, gritting his teeth at the less-than-kind slam of the horse's solid body against his testicles. The dousing of the fire was pure bliss, though. He suffered the abrasion of the water against the burns, but knew those would heal in a reasonably swift manner. Swimming strongly, the horse descended. The moat was so deep, he couldn't see the bottom, which made him wonder if there was a bottom at all. The waters were populated by unusual fish, selkies, curious merfolk and even a pair of sea serpents of intimidating size. They eyed Jacob with obvious relish. If the current predator got tired of him, he suspected they were ready to finish the job.

Jacob ripped his tunic at the neckline and managed to pull it all the way off, securing his hold on it and the mane a blink before the horse rolled. Though Firewind did it several times, twisting and bucking in the water, Jacob kept his eyes closed, following the horse's movement by instinct, knees and elbows in tight.

The kelpie made an underwater cry that reminded Jacob of an angry killer whale. The powerful body shuddered, rocked and convulsed, and abruptly his swimming became rocket charged. Glancing back, Jacob saw Firewind had shifted the back legs into a powerful tail, the front legs churning to help with the movement. His neck and head were extended like a thoroughbred in the final stretch.

Jacob moved with him, thrusting his body out over that elongated neck. He brought the wet tunic down over the waterhorse's eyes and moved fast, tying it beneath the jawline, thank all the gods for vampire speed. Firewind screamed and rolled again, but Jacob pulled in the slack and shoved himself back down the neck to grapple the mane and hold tight with his knees once more. On his way there, Firewind's head snaked around. The kelpie bit his shoulder, sending a trail of blood inking away from them. Jacob wrenched free, got himself out of range. He held both ends of the tied and ripped tunic like reins now, his palms clenched hard in the cloth to hold it fast on the animal's eyes.

The horse swung around so fast Jacob didn't see the wall of rock until it was too late. The crushing impact knocked his left hand loose, though the right held, tangled with mane as well as cloth. A strangled cry wrenched from his throat as ribs cracked, his left knee was pummeled into several pieces and his shoulder dislocated. The horse screeched his frustration, as loud as a banshee, even under water.

This was no horse. This was a creature of the night, a child's nightmare, an equine version of the Hounds of Hell, its only intent to kill him.

Oh, bollocks on that. Boudiceaa had been the most ill-tempered hellion of a horse he'd ever known, with a true desire to murder anyone on her back. This horse was male, which meant he should be far more reasonable.

Despite the blindfold, Firewind was headed back up to the top. He was probably going to burst into flame again. And whereas he'd been happy to try and dislodge Jacob under the water and crush him like a mallet shattered an oyster shell, aboveground he'd likely bind him to his back until he was a tiny pile of ash that Firewind released to the wind, along with the remains of the tunic blindfold.

As the kelpie broke the surface of the water, Jacob fumbled in the pouch that had been belted beneath his tunic, hoping the only thing he'd brought in anticipation of Keldwyn's warning was still intact. It was.

There were gray spots in his vision. Unfortunately, vampires could pass out, if the stress on the body was too great and there was no ready blood supply on hand. Usually, he only needed to draw from his lady once every several days. It was becoming a daily occurrence here.

Don't pass out. You'll be eaten by sea snakes, and Lyssa will be seriously pissed at you.

The kelpie was tossing his head about, thrashing in the water. Firewind hadn't counted on being too disoriented to find the bank right away, though he should manage it soon enough by smell, if he calmed down. Otherwise, he'd dive again. Jacob made his decision. He became

Firewind's eyes, soothing him in Gaelic, using hand and knee signals and the horsemanship of a lifetime to convince the horse to follow his direction. The horse didn't trust him right away, but then the wind shifted and he realized Jacob was taking him toward the bank. Jacob expected something smug went through the horse's mind like, *What a dumbass*. He wasn't sure he didn't agree.

They were a quarter mile from the rear wall of the castle, no longer part of the circular moat, but in one of the feeder tributaries. As the horse gained the solid ground, shifting back to four legs, he shook off like a dog, making the seaweed and shells in his mane slap Jacob's hands. Then he gave a quick squeal, a bone-jarring hop that almost dislodged Jacob.

The good news was he wasn't using the reputed Super Glue abilities to lock Jacob on his back, maybe because it only worked in the water, to make sure his passenger drowned, a moot point with a vampire. He also didn't appear to be able to use his fire right away when he emerged from the water. A small but vital blessing.

So Firewind went for the nasty trick that the most temperamental and intelligent horses knew. He buckled, headed for the ground roll to flatten Jacob like a pancake.

Jacob threw himself clear with a pained cry, right before the hooves would have kicked out on the turn and caved in the side of his skull.

As Firewind scrambled back to his feet, Jacob wrapped the hand of his dislocated arm in the trailing tail of the tunic. He let out an agonized grunt as he used the force of Firewind's yank against it to pop the shoulder back in place. Using his other hand, he pulled the item out of the pouch belted on his bare waist. It wouldn't have worked underwater, because the scent might have been masked. Firewind had been too agitated when he was guiding him to shore, but now was the time to give it a try. His window of opportunity was the size of a postage stamp.

He'd asked the kitchen staff for the apples earlier in the evening, and they hadn't been too grudging about it, though the narrow-eyed fairy cook made sure he didn't take more than two. He'd made idle cuts in the apple with his knife as he talked to her about the proper way to marinate squash. Afterward, he discreetly dropped the apples in a bin of sugar, coating the fruit and then wrapping them up in a scrap of waterproof skin he'd found at the stables. He'd learned to be prepared for almost any contingency, and the waterproofing would help seal in the flavor. A sugar apple had been one of Bou's favorite treats at the Ren Faire, sure to mellow her up when she regressed into foul temper and fear.

Keeping his arm up so the horse could scent the apple was an exercise in torment, since his ribs were broken and the shoulder hurt like a son of a bitch. It was amazing, what kind of pain a man could overcome when he knew it couldn't actually kill him.

That great head turned toward him, those eyes drawing closer. *Jesus.* The blindfold had dropped so one eye was visible. The other crimson orb had enough heat and fire that the glow was faintly visible through the thick covering of the folded tunic. So either this would work, or he would draw back a stump.

As he expected, the horse wasn't too careful about missing his hand with teeth, but at least they only sank into his palm and missed taking off some fingers. Vampires could survive amputation, but often the limbs or digits didn't regenerate. Firewind didn't keep gnawing on him, though. He drew back, apple in his mouth.

"You're smart, strong and fast." Jacob grunted. "But you like sugar and apples, and you won't move without direction if you're blindfolded. You're still a horse. Easy, there . . ." He fumbled for the second sugar-coated apple. The horse shifted, showed his teeth, shook his head again and backed against Jacob's hold, pulling him a few inches across the ground. He stopped, gave a snort. Jacob could almost hear the click of connection in the horse's diabolical brain. Lying there on his back, hand clutching the tunic, Jacob could be dragged. Firewind's ears perked up.

"Oh, no, you don't," Jacob groaned. Those damn broken ribs would keep him from moving swiftly enough to shoot back to his feet and mount the horse again. If Firewind chose to drag him pell-mell through the country side, stomping on him until he was pulp inside a battered skin, there was little he was going to be able to do except let go, something he wouldn't do.

Then he heard it. That haunting song, a sigh of sound that stirred a man's heart and groin at once. Turning his head, blinking blearily, he saw a trio of the sirens emerging from the depths of the loch. *Great.* Instead of being dragged to his death by a waterhorse, he'd meet his end at the hands of three incredibly beautiful naked women who were already turning his mind into a lust-fogged soup, no matter his battered physical state. Given the two choices, they'd be his preference, except his lady would be far nicer to him in the afterlife if the horse killed him.

Firewind whinnied, shifted. He pulled against the fabric, eliciting a pained grunt from Jacob. But the horse's ears pricked forward, a universally affable equine expression. With a whuff of sound that sounded like the horse version of a pleased purr, he folded his back legs beneath him, the rest of him following, thudding into a resting pose beside Jacob. He put his head down. His heavy sigh blew sugary apple bits over Jacob, nostrils flaring wide.

"You are foolish."

The voice didn't come from the sirens. Though it was a lovely female voice, like the sound of wind through the trees, he couldn't turn his gaze from the sirens. He tried hard, knowing that he *really* needed to get back up on Firewind, get him moving away from here. But his injuries had taken a toll on his will, and it seemed as if the singing was making it worse and better at once.

The sirens drew closer, covered only by their sleek ropes of hair and glossy bits of seaweed and shell adornments in their hair, much like the kelpie himself. They moved to Firewind, surrounding him, petting him, putting tiny white lotus flowers into his mane. The horse made a low, groaning noise in his chest, tossed his head, but submitted to the treatment. Jacob hadn't realized a kelpie could be entranced by sirens as well. While Firewind didn't seem as helpless to their song as he did, the horse was definitely being calmed and charmed by the music.

A small, slim hand cradled his face then, trying to pull it away from the mesmerizing women who were smiling at him. They had sharp, pointed teeth much like his own vampire ones. Curious. Also a little creepy, but those voices made everything okay.

The hand on his face tightened, then rudely yanked it to the left so he wasn't looking at the sirens anymore. He was looking up at a different face, but a familiar one. Catriona. And looking up at her, the sirens' call was still difficult, but he could resist. Barely.

"Keep looking at me," she said in that breathy voice. "It will keep you from being completely entranced."

As helpful as that was, she didn't look pleased with him. Her mouth tightened into a thin line. "A waterhorse is not a horse of your world. Lord Firewind is a member of the Unseelie court, one of the peers of his kind. Restraint and disrespect, such as what the queen did, drove him mad with rage. He and his family line have been the helpmeet of kings. The siren song is soothing him now, for he is fond of them and their song is telling him you are not an enemy. However, when it stops, it is likely his anger will return and he will take it out on anyone foolish enough to try and ride him. You," she added, as if she thought he was too addled to figure out who she meant.

"It's the queen's quest. I have to do it or my lady suffers."

Those large gray-green eyes blinked. Before being locked in her tree, he wondered if she'd ever been seen in his world and mistaken for a space alien, with her slim body and those enormous eyes, the fey features. He realized he might not be thinking quite clearly at the moment, but she was quite lovely. Always before, he'd thought those UFO pictures made aliens look like oversized bugs lacking antenna.

"Vampire . . ." She was tapping his cheeks with gentle fingers to bring his focus back. Finding her hand, he closed his own over the thin wrist.

"Jacob," he corrected. "My name is Jacob."

She lifted her other arm, showing a halter with reins attached to it. As she slid it off her shoulder, he noted it was made of braided hair, hair that was a match for Firewind's dark mane and tail. Behind her, he saw a groomswoman from Rhoswen's stables. She was eyeing all of them warily as Catriona rose and moved toward the kelpie.

Jacob tried to struggle to his elbows, concerned for the diminutive dryad as she approached the horse's massive shoulder. However, she crooned to him, and the sirens increased their song. *Oh, crap.* He'd forgotten and taken his eyes off Catriona, such that it made his head spin. He wanted to drag his body over to them and grovel at their feet. He wanted to immerse himself in their scent, those beautiful, fathomless eyes, the soft, willing flesh. It was appalling, to be standing in his own head, seeing himself react this way. One part of him wanted to resist with everything he had, while every other part wanted to go over and drool at their feet like a happy dog. If Lyssa was here, she'd just give him a good, sharp kick in the ribs.

What did it say about him, that he kind of wished for that at the moment?

When the groomswoman squatted next to Jacob, he barely paid her any attention. But she pinched his arm, hard, drawing his impatient attention. She held up two balls of what looked like softened candle-wax. With a faint smile of amusement, she tucked them into his ears. Once she was done, the sirens' song was a very faint, pleasant, yearning dream, allowing his will to return. Mostly.

Catriona had gone to her knees and bowed to Firewind. She was speaking to him as she removed Jacob's tattered tunic from his head. When she was done, she held out the halter, bowing once again. Firewind tossed his powerful head, which probably weighed twice as much as Catriona, but she took it as assent. Fitting the halter over him, she adjusted the reins on his neck, confirming the halter was an exact match for the blackness of his hair. The horse grumbled, but made no other protest.

Jacob gave the groomswoman a short nod of thanks. She was a wiry, pixie figure dressed in the court colors, the brief tunic and hose style suited to working with the mounts. Her eyes were a strong, mint leaf green, her short hair a glossy chestnut. When she offered him a hand up, he shook his head, patting his ribs, indicating he needed to figure out the getting up part on his own. He expected it would involve something pathetic, like rolling over to his stomach and pushing himself up on his hands and knees to crawl a few undignified paces. Firewind would probably enjoy watching him fall on his face before trampling him.

Catriona handed off the braided-hair reins to the groomswoman and came to Jacob's side. "Aren't you healing?" she asked. "I thought vampires healed themselves."

"We do. It's just a bit slow right now." As he managed to push himself up to his knees, the slim girl gently laid her hands on his chest and back, providing a surprising amount of support for his ribs. He shamefully had to use her strength to get to his feet. Once there, he swayed a moment, then took a couple steps forward, toward Firewind. She stayed close at his side, steadying him.

"If you are determined to do this, you must touch the halter first." When he took the wax out, keeping his gaze on her face with effort, she repeated it. "I have spoken to him. He will determine, by your touch, if you are worthy. If you had the power of magic to hold him, as the queen did, his approval would be irrelevant, but it is not the right way to do it."

"No, it's not," Jacob agreed. "Did the groom . . . Will she be in trouble for providing the halter?"

"No. She is an old friend, and the halter was not in the queen's keeping. Yeshi simply knew where it could be found."

He looked down at her. Her hair was spider-web soft against his bare upper body, her profile determined but so incredibly delicate it would stir the protective instincts of a stump, let alone him. "Are you doing okay? Since you got back?"

She glanced up at him, a flash of surprise in her gaze. But then it was gone and she nodded, her small mouth pursed. "It is . . . an adjustment."

Her gaze focused on the pendant. It seemed to please her that he was wearing it, and yet he sensed a wistfulness in her gaze. Clearing his throat, he untied it from his neck, offered it to her. "Since you just helped me, as much or even more than I've helped you, will you allow me to offer it back, as my gift of thanks to you?"

She glanced up at him, measuring. With a slow nod, she took it back, put it on her neck again, giving him that flash of vibrant green and amber light in the heart of the stone before it settled back into the polished earth color. "You are very kind," she said.

Turning to the sirens, she spoke in a musical language. They nodded, gave him a detailed appraisal and several very come-hither, incredibly hard-to-resist smiles before they glided back toward the water, generous hips swaying. The cleft of their bottoms were framed and enhanced by the twists of seaweed and shells in their long hair. The breasts he'd seen before they turned had been full and ripe, sitting up high, the nipples pink and erect.

Puzzled, he looked down to find Catriona braced full against him, her wings pumping hard to hold him in place as he strained forward. "Put the wax back in your ears," she said breathlessly. "Then touch the halter."

He gazed at her, muddled by pain and blood loss, and a discordant surge of heated lust. Her mouth formed a wordless oath. Letting go of him with one hand, she snatched the wax balls out of his palm with the other and put them back in his ears. Then, one hand still braced on his chest, she tugged on his other arm, lifting it toward Firewind, a few paces away. The horse eyed him balefully. His upper lip lifted, showing teeth, the ears sweeping back.

"Wait." Jacob shook his head, his other hand falling on her hip to hold himself steady. It was then he realized the inevitable result of the three sirens—he was heavily aroused. In the snug, very thin hose, that part of his anatomy was pushed rather solidly into Catriona's flat stomach. "Oh, Jesus. Sorry." He tried to back away, swayed, and she caught him, continuing to hold him with the additional propulsion of her wings and firm grip.

"It's all right. You can't help it." He was able to make out those words easily enough. Her pointed ears were tinged pink and she kept her gaze on his chest, though.

He cleared his throat, tried to set her somewhat to the side so he could turn, place his hand on her shoulder for balance, instead of the more intimate pose. It also allowed him to face Firewind squarely. Bowing his head, Jacob bent his knee, gritting his teeth at a searing, mind blackening cloud of pain as he made the respectful obeisance.

"Forgive me," he said. "Forgive my ignorance, my lord."

The waterhorse snorted. He felt the vibration of hooves clomping through the grass toward him, fortunately at a more sedate pace. When he looked up, Firewind stood right over him, gazing down at him disdainfully. The halter, however, was within reach of his hand.

Jacob took it, closing his hand on the strap, but then, with another murmur of thanks and apology, he also braced himself on the massive shoulder to bring himself all the way upright. Since Firewind didn't whack his head off his shoulders like a T-ball, he assumed he'd been found worthy, or at least tolerable.

Catriona reached up, plucked the wax back out of Jacob's ears. "The sirens are gone," she explained. "He liked the apples. He wants more. But he says it's time to catch up to the Hunt. You've wasted enough time."

"You understand him?"

She shrugged. "Of course. He is Fae. Sometimes he is horse . . . sometimes other. He says he will bear you for this night, for you are worthy. However, at dawn's light, he will tolerate no more and you must take off the halter made of his hair. He requires that you return it to me, or to Keldwyn, but not to the queen, even if she commands it. Will you risk her wrath?"

"I think we're already deep in wrath territory when it comes to Rhoswen, so sure. I'll be happy to give it to anyone he wants."

Catriona turned to Firewind. Though there was no spoken communication, it was clear Firewind found those terms acceptable, for she turned back to Jacob and asked, "Do you need help getting on him?"

"Male pride is a terrible thing. Not sure I can make myself say yes to that, no matter how true an answer it is."

Firewind blew out a snort. This time, instead of fire, Jacob was surprised to find himself sprayed with a light mist of salt water, perhaps from their swim in the moat. Stretching out his forelegs in an attitude of total imposed-upon suffering, the waterhorse went to one knee and Catriona helped him mount. Jacob managed it without staggering or uttering vile curses not appropriate to utter before a Fae lord or a female dryad, but it was a near thing. Once he was seated, she handed him the reins. "Good hunting," she said simply.

"Where are you—"

"Back to the forests. I have been watching you, these past few days. The timing today was fortunate."

"Yes, it was." He'd automatically shifted to a proper seat, the boon of long experience. Things were getting less painful, though, the bones and wounds healing, but he felt weak as a newborn and knew he had to be far too pale. "Have you been watching Keldwyn, too?"

"Yes. I am not ready for him to see me yet, though." Her voice softened, and her eyes had a glimmer of tears. "Go with the Goddess's blessing, vampire."

"Jacob," he reminded her. But she was gone, with several nimble strides that launched her a few feet in the air, skimming over the tributary. As she crossed it, she did a pretty twirl, her feet kicking up the water, and the sirens emerged to wave. A selkie leaped into her path, a sleek shine of moonlight across his skin, and her fingers trailed his flank playfully before she cleared him, and was past the water, headed back to her beloved forest. She also got a wave from Yeshi, walking up the hill toward the stables.

Jacob looked at Firewind as the waterhorse turned his head, met his gaze. "Do I just tell you where I'd like to go? I get that I shouldn't use heels or tugs on the reins, but I can't promise about the knees and thighs. That's second nature to me."

The horse shook his whole head and neck, a shudder that went through the withers, which Jacob interpreted as a shrug. "Is it too much to hope that we don't have to go there at a gallop?"

At the horse's look, he sighed, took a firm hold of reins. "Yeah, I know. We're already late. Let's go, then. Do you want the wax?" He opened his palm to show the two balls Catriona had tucked there. "So you don't have to hear my screams of pain?"

The horse laid back his ears and blew a small spout of flame out of his nose. "Wax gone," Jacob said, tossing it. "At your pleasure, my lord."

13

FORTUNATELY, the bones had knitted enough that the furious gallop was uncomfortable, not excruciating. It didn't take very long for Jacob to see the tail end of the procession, but it was good that Firewind had run, because they weren't far from the glittering train of horses that had to be the Seelie host.

He cantered along the line, his knees holding him on the horse, one hand wrapped loosely in the mane and braided reins. He'd recovered enough to hold a good seat, and kept his attitude casual, as if it was nothing to ride up on a waterhorse that could burst into flame at a moment's notice. He saw his lady riding with Rhoswen. It had been a curious honor, given Rhoswen's attitude toward Lyssa, but he expected since Lyssa's attendance had been specifically requested by the Seelie king, Rhoswen was playing politics, making it appear as if she was treating Lyssa as an honored guest. Or it could be more of the schizoid love-hate behavior she'd been demonstrating to her half sister throughout their compelled visit.

As they approached, he noted the palfrey was little more than half Firewind's size, but given his lady's petite stature, they were a proportionate match. With Lyssa sidesaddle, the skirt of her dress spread out on the horse's haunches, and the palfrey's arched head and flowing mane, they made a beautiful, feminine picture. It didn't matter to Jacob who led the procession. She was the one who stood out, who riveted his attention.

Based on that, he couldn't blame Firewind for trying to steal a playful nip of the mare's neck. He had a similar urge toward her rider. The stallion won an offended whinny, a sidling dance on four dainty hooves. It was instinct to control his mount with a quick whistle of breath, a hiss of admonishment. Before he could think *oh, crap*, regretting his faux pas with the prickly equine Fae lord, Firewind's feet left the ground, but only a few inches. It was a retort, yes, but it was just as much a cocky, handsome display to the mare. Then he settled to his version of a sedate pace, which meant a menacing stalk.

"Manners. Be a gentleman, you big lout," Jacob muttered.

Of course, he was one to talk. Wearing only the indecently snug hose, holes burned through them in a couple spots, he was well aware he was nowhere suitably dressed for this entourage, but Rhoswen had set the terms. She could explain his appearance to the Seelie king. At least his boots had held up well.

Lyssa's green eyes revealed nothing. However, he knew she saw the strain of the trek through water, would feel the weakness the burns and injuries had left him. Though she'd been worried, he could also tell she was proud of him, pleased he'd achieved Rhoswen's quest.

It was an age-old feeling, the sense that he'd done something worthy of his lady's favor. That he'd won her heart anew, the true prize for a quest performed well. That, and the pleasure of her body later, when she'd offer herself generously as a further reward.

Oh, really? I expected you here at least ten minutes ago. I think you're losing your touch.

As she looked him over, he saw her remember the first time she'd met him, how he'd been wearing an outfit remarkably similar to this one.

Though that one didn't have the added benefit of being glued to your body with water, Sir Vagabond. Her gaze lifted to his face. She knew he needed blood, but she didn't ask or coddle, knowing this was not the time. And it was not her way, regardless. One of the many things he appreciated about her.

Rhoswen glanced back, as expressionless as his lady, underscoring the family resemblance once again. He didn't think it would be politic to grin about that, no matter how giddy or slightly unstable he was feeling at the moment.

"So you figured out the secret to riding a waterhorse, vampire. You look a little . . . overcome by the experience. And far underdressed."

Jacob inclined his head. "If my appearance pleases my lady, then that is enough. And yes, I did figure out the secret. Treat him as he deserves to be treated."

"Under that maxim, I was overly merciful with the bearing rein. He should count himself fortunate." After that cryptic comment, Rhoswen turned her attention to Lyssa, dismissing him and Firewind. "When we reach the Seelie host, I will introduce you to King Tabor and turn you over to him. But remember what we spoke about." She met Lyssa's glance. "A day from now, at dawn, the herald will come."

Jacob gave Lyssa a quizzical look, but she made a neutral gesture, putting him off.

Later, Sir Vagabond. It concerns the last quest.

Hellfire, Rhoswen didn't waste any time. Given that they'd had the conversation before he arrived, it suggested Rhoswen had possessed more confidence about his success than expected. Or that she had spies who reported to her the moment he'd succeeded. He'd vote for the latter, but it didn't really matter. He'd overcome the second quest and lived to tell the tale.

Yes, and don't waste this moment on worry of what may come. I know how much you've longed to see the Seelie Hunt. Let's enjoy it together.

She truly was remarkable. He found himself wanting to touch his lady, feel her body close to his. Offering a rakish smile, he held out a hand, leaning down. "Would you like to ride together, my lady?"

He wasn't sure if she would agree, but there was an intriguing sparkle in those green eyes. So intriguing he couldn't help touching her mind, curious.

She loved seeing him on a horse. When his body became one with the creature, moving together in sinuous strength and grace, she fantasized about having her own body pressed against his, feeling it. She'd wanted that experience—riding a horse with him—for a long time.

You should have told me that at Mason's, my lady. I would have been happy to ride on the beach with you and given you all you desired. He could fulfill one of his lady's personal fantasies here and now. The evening was getting better by the minute, no matter that he looked like a drowned rat and felt like he'd been beaten half to death.

You are incorrigible. But her eyes said she wanted him no other way.

"Lord Firewind." He twitched a rein, gaining the horse's attention, which was probably a good thing, since it looked like he was trying to stare fiery holes into Rhoswen's back. "May my lady join me? I value her safety far beyond my own, so if she will not be welcome, I need to know that."

In response, the horse did a pretty leg change, damn near a prance, shaking out his abundant mane. He earned a more considering eye from the mare and a small smile from Lyssa.

"I believe that's a yes," Jacob said dryly.

Turning her mount's reins over to one of the guards, she lifted her arms. Leaning down, Jacob slid his arm around her waist and brought her over to Firewind's back. Despite the complaints from his abused body, he made it appear an effortless move. He settled her in his lap, holding her before him sidesaddle as she tucked in the excess train of her dress. Relaxing into his embrace with a small, relieved sigh, she laid her hand over his on the reins, a brief squeeze. Then she slipped her fingers over the horse's mane, the greenery and white shells threaded there. "Seaweed?"

Jacob nodded. "In water, he has a tail, a great powerful thing"—*boy howdy*—"as green as your eyes, with gold edges on the tail and scales."

"Hmm." She touched the horse's neck to get his attention. "Lord Firewind, can you sidle to the left of the Unseelie entourage without appearing . . . rude?"

The horse responded instantly, as if he was more than happy to put some distance between himself and the queen. "Do you really kill children?" she queried softly. "Drown them?"

The horse whuffed, a glint to his eye that wasn't really an answer. However, remarkably, through Lyssa's mind, Jacob could make out fragments of the waterhorse's response, reflecting Lyssa's limited understanding of the Fae language.

"Truth is always . . . complicated," she repeated for Jacob's benefit. "Yes," she agreed. "It is."

She asked nothing further. Like his lady, he'd like to know more about the complex and dark beast carrying them, but sensed that was all they'd get right now. Plus she had other agendas to pursue. Leaning against his chest, she put a hand on his face. As she did, she tilted her head back onto his shoulder, exposing her throat, the tempting line that drew his eyes to the swell of her breasts, the way the train of her skirt outlined her thighs. "Drink from me, my vampire," she murmured. "Replenish your strength for the night ahead."

He hesitated, aware of eyes on them. Her nails dug into his flesh—that Mistress's warning. She locked gazes with him. *I don't care what they think, Jacob. Their ridiculous notions of hierarchy and superiority mean as little to me as the Vampire Council's. You are my servant, but I am also yours, in this regard. Use me to strengthen yourself, so I know I have your full abilities to serve and protect me tonight.*

She always knew the right combination of words to compel him, but in truth the pounding of her blood, so close, already had his fangs lengthening. He covered her hand against his face gently with his own, an acknowledgment. Then he bent his head to that artery and sank his fangs into willing flesh. Firewind shifted, alarming him a moment, remembering what Rhoswen had said about blood, but Lyssa's mind touched them both.

He says you won't stir his hunger with the smell of my blood, for I'm not human. He only drinks human blood. In copious amounts, and he has already fed this day.

Jacob decided that was a thought best not pursued. Conscious of the host they were approaching, he drank swiftly. As she reached behind her back, he closed his eyes when she found him, stroking his cock where it nestled against her hip and buttock, an idle pleasure that strained the hose further. As long as she kept herself pressed up against him like this, it would be disguised. As well as stay painfully hard.

The way I most like you, Sir Vagabond.

The blood nourished, while the knitting of his bones strengthened. As vitality returned to his limbs, they climbed the slope to a portal, a large black wooden frame shrouded in mist, reminding him of the stories that warned travelers to stay away from a fog, because it made it too easy to wander into the Fae world. The night sky had darkened further over it, stray bits of green lighting striking and reflecting off the glossy wood.

What else awaited them upon that hill made an equally absorbing impression. The Unseelie were the dark side of the Fae world, more malevolent in their intentions, whereas the Seelie, while quick to anger or exact retribution for insult, essentially had motives for good. He wasn't entirely sure of that assessment, for all Fae tales warned against congress with them. However, he couldn't deny sheer power came from the knot of royals at the head of the Seelie train, even more overwhelming than what Rhoswen had displayed thus far.

Keldwyn was part of that group. He sat upon a dappled gray stallion, relaxed and as dispassionate as ever. If Jacob ever needed money, he knew who he'd be taking to the poker tables in Vegas.

Not me?

Having been in your mind, I'm too familiar with your moods. I would give them away with my poker face.

Anyone who ventured into Keldwyn's mind might be forever lost there. I wouldn't take the gamble.

True. He might eat their brains like a zombie, only from the inside out.

She cleared her throat over a chuckle. Jacob took the opportunity to press his mouth to the juncture of her throat and shoulder. Reaching up, she rubbed her thumb over his lips, cleaning the last of the blood away. In his current attire, he was tempted to paint some of it on his chest and come off as a wild Celt. They seemed to expect nothing less of a vampire.

His attention returned to the Seelie entourage. King Tabor was easy enough to pick out, since he was at the head of the triangular formation. His long gold hair was plaited with ropes of earth-colored gemstones down his back. Most Fae males had strong faces with remarkable, ageless beauty. Cayden's scar had been the exception. However, Tabor's face had a lined rugged quality that suggested maturation, like the cycles of the earth itself. His eyes were leonine amber. The way he sat his steed showed a fit male who'd known battle. A glance at the male's eyes told Jacob that Tabor might be the oldest of all of them, Rhoswen and Lyssa included. It might explain the lines on his face, but Jacob suspected there were other causal factors. He had a steady center that Rhoswen lacked, as if he'd faced his deepest self and accepted what he'd seen there.

Had Tabor and Rhoswen grown up together? It was an odd thought, considering both would be well over a millennium. He wondered at what age a Fae was no longer considered a juvenile. Vampires didn't really consider one of their kind mature until they passed the first century mark, and then they were still the equivalent of a twentysomething adult.

"King Tabor." Rhoswen nodded. "May I present Lady Lyssa, daughter of Lord Reghan." Her pause before giving Lyssa the title was audible, showing she didn't particularly care for assigning the honorific. It wasn't a surprise she felt that way, but it was telling that she did it now, before him.

Tabor's gaze swept Lyssa from head to toe. Unlike most males who appraised her, Tabor didn't display the covetousness or lust, just an unexpected intensity. The Seelie king drank in her appearance as if seeking familiar landmarks, like old friends meeting after many years. Only Jacob realized it wasn't Lyssa who was the old friend.

Rhoswen sat motionless. Perhaps because she had a different purpose tonight, she wasn't emanating her usual frosty reaction, but Jacob thought he saw something more vulnerable lurking in her gaze. Cayden had unobtrusively moved his mount closer, so his leg brushed the flank of the horse Rhoswen rode.

Just as she'd done with Rhoswen, Lyssa inclined her head. The short courtesy that wasn't an act of obeisance, but one royal acknowledging another.

"Thank you for accepting our invitation to join us, Lady Lyssa." Tabor's deep timbre was like quiet thunder rolling behind the hills before a summer rain. Rhoswen was powerful, no doubt, but this one . . . If he wanted everyone around them to burst into pixie dust, this male had the ability to do it. Jacob was pretty sure of it. It was disturbing and riveting at once, similar to the effect of the sirens on his senses, minus the lust, thank the gods.

The fingers that loosely held his steed's reins were marked with intricate tattoos that circled the base of the fore and ring fingers, then banded his wrists and disappeared up the cuffs of his earth-and-gold-colored tunic. The gold circlet on his head had similar markings. "Your father was a particular friend. It has been our pleasure to see his blood take precedence in you. We are glad to have the long overdue honor of welcoming another of his line back to our world." He glanced at Rhoswen. "Though I see our dark queen has not yet decided it is an honor."

"You may make your own determinations for your own interests, my lord Tabor," Rhoswen said stiffly. "My interests lie elsewhere tonight, if you give me leave to go pursue them. I look forward to our paths crossing later in the evening."

Tabor bent from his saddle in gracious courtesy to his female counterpart, though his eyes held hers steadily. "You have our leave. Good hunting, beautiful queen. Embrace the pleasures of the Samhain hours."

"Always." She glanced at Lyssa. "Good riding. May you know no fear of the night."

As she turned away, Cayden gave them a nod and followed her. Tabor watched them return to the head of the Unseelie procession and begin to lead the macabre spectacle of the Haunt past the Seelie train, toward the portal.

"Each year, we play a game." Tabor directed his words to Lyssa. "Much like your football games, we toss a coin to see which side enters the portal first. She won this year, so we shall wait for her to go through with her people, if you do not mind the wait. Our sorcerers configure a different entry point, because our quests are different, and do not mesh so well together. At least not until the end, when we come back together. Then we reach out to those who've passed out of our world, celebrate endings and beginnings, and hope that all our worlds benefit from abundance in the coming year. At least, that is what *I* hope."

The king swept a glance over Jacob. While he suffered a moment of discomfiture, thinking his battered appearance might seem disrespectful to the Seelie king, Tabor didn't display the dismissive edge of contempt he'd begun to expect from most Fae.

The Seelie king returned his attention to Lyssa. "You've had an interesting first visit to our world thus far, I think."

"Being part of the vampire world for centuries has been good preparation for the challenges of the Fae one, Your Majesty. We do not regret our visit."

"Well spoken." As he looked toward the portal, Jacob noticed that Keldwyn stood somewhat apart from the three retainers closest to the king. One was a silent woman with skin black as onyx and topaz blue eyes. In black tight breeks and vest, armed with a variety of blades, she had the look of both bodyguard and assassin. The other two were armed, but they had the demeanor of friends, those who'd been the king's comrade-in-arms in the past, and served as advisors in peacetime.

Like Rhoswen, the king appeared more than capable of protecting himself. But Jacob knew the guard for a capable leader was often there as a buffer, to give him time to rally if there was a surprise attack. His Aussie friend and fellow servant, Dev, had said as much once about his Mistress, the Lady Daniela. If his skill gave her a few extra seconds to survive before he was taken off the grid, then he'd done his duty. Jacob didn't disagree, and for that reason felt an affinity for those in the same role. Even when they treated him like a distasteful bug under a microscope, like Cayden or the ebony woman now.

Nearly a third of the Unseelie train had disappeared through the portal. As they passed, the green lightning crackled, and waves of magical energy wafted down the hill in heated winds. The slope on which they waited looked across at all four castles. Though Jacob had heard there'd be major light shows later in the evening, when the Hunt and Haunt returned, there were minor explosions of fireworks going on now, practice runs of aerial shows by different groups of the flighted Fae, everything from traditional fairies to dragons, griffins and others.

"It's a display worth seeing," Tabor commented. "There is no night quite as special to us as Samhain."

"I thought Beltane would be more significant," Lyssa responded, with a slight smile. "The celebration of life and fertility. Growth."

"Insightful. It's perhaps like comparing Christmas to Easter in your world. One is for celebration; one is for remembrance. And though celebration is needed, remembrance is vital." He gave her that intent scrutiny again.

"You have his eyes," he said, his voice lowering. "And I do not mean the color. There was something . . . fathomless in Lord Reghan's eyes. For a Fae, that is saying something. He was unique in our world, so it comes as no surprise that you are as well."

Keldwyn shifted on his horse, ostensibly to look at the fireworks. Because of the play of dark and light, Jacob thought he saw sadness in the male's eyes. Then it was gone.

"Not so much to the untrained senses, but to the ancients, like myself, Seelie and Unseelie abilities are very distinct," Tabor continued. "With one breath, I can tell if you are Seelie or Unseelie. Like him, you are both, a rare thing. But you are even more, because your Fae form suggests the Solitary folk, our Fae who are not of the high court. You bring all of them together, an unclassifiable and therefore unknown quantity."

The ebony woman shifted closer to Tabor's side, the way Cayden had done when Rhoswen had to introduce Lyssa as Reghan's daughter. However, this time it was Tabor who offered reassurance in his glance, the nod of his head. Then he looked back at Lyssa, his attention sharpening upon her.

"Your power is strong, wild. Your years of discipline as a vampire queen have given you an instinctive rein on it, even without training, but the savage side of that blood will unleash it in defense of those you care about. He, too, had that quality."

"So why did you sentence him to death?" Lyssa asked evenly.

The ebony woman's face hardened. A percussion wave of energy pushed over them, an unpleasantly claustrophobic feeling.

"Dahlia, enough." Tabor said. When Dahlia shifted irritably on her horse, the feeling eased back. "Aidan, Leigh, leave us. All of you," he added, looking pointedly at Dahlia. "I would speak to Lady Lyssa alone."

There was a brief silence, a battle of wills. The king scowled at Dahlia. She jerked her horse's head around, followed by the two males. Though high court Fae weren't inclined to open mirth, Jacob noticed the men had something close to grins playing around their mouths, as if they would tease her about her overprotective nature.

The king sighed. "He was executed because our species is not exempt from being reactionary, particularly when our world is in an uncertain state. Your father's actions—cleaving to a vampire, getting her with child—came at a time when things were going badly between the Fae and human world. Superstition was closing in. Many unpleasant incidents occurred . . ."

Tabor closed his eyes, shook his head. "*Unpleasant*. The wrong word for so many horrific acts. Only the distance of centuries would permit it, to make those times sound even more distant, when we all know an act of barbarism is usually as close as the nearest fear, whatever that fear may be. It is not an excuse, because I was hardly more enlightened at that time, but I will tell you I was not king then. My brother was."

Peripherally, Jacob was aware of the procession of Unseelie continuing to file through the portal, the murmur of conversation and movement along the Seelie train, but like his lady, his attention was captured by the king's words, the import of them and his steady glance. "I can tell you that many of the years where we shut ourselves off from your world have been violent, terrible ones. For all of us. It is why I cannot always blame Rhoswen for the way she feels about things. Killing a brother is a terrible thing"—shadows crossed his visage—"but to kill a mother is to kill the root of your self. Though it has been several centuries since it occurred, it is a wound that perhaps never heals."

He glanced at the ebony-skinned woman, whose horse stood apart from the others as she continued to stare fixedly at him, even from a distance. "As you can tell, Dahlia is my version of your vampire. Though the other two are my men-at-arms, my personal guard, she is my true protection, an incomparable sorceress as well as a good friend. She is, however, singular in her defense of me, brooking no disobedience or insolence from anyone." He smiled faintly. "It's perhaps good that I am king and not her, for your question was a fair one. You deserve an answer, after so many years."

He shrugged. "Each year we celebrate Samhain in this way. We go to places where there is still belief, where there is less technology and the agriculture practiced is still the way of the earth. And sometimes, in the reflection of those who catch a glimpse of us that night, I still see who and what we were when we were allies, human and Fae."

There was a squeal, a thunderous clatter. Firewind shifted restlessly, but as Jacob steadied him, he saw the Unseelie ranks part for a male in a chariot. His team of frothing, bloodcolored horses barreled toward the portal. Thick mist followed in his wake, but then Jacob saw it wasn't mist at all, but a cavalcade of twisting wraith spirits, with dark eyes and skeletal faces. The chariot wheels were pale flame, and rattled with a dragging train of human bones. He sincerely hoped it was an embellishment from the pavilions. The chariot plunged through the portal, its passage illuminated with a billow of white light and blood colored smoke, as well as an extra explosion of fireworks above it. Appreciative cries erupted at the display.

Tabor shook his head. "Gwyn ap Nudd, as the Welsh call him. The king of the Underworld. He goes to collect the souls due to the afterlife this night. As frightening as it looks, it's actually an honor to die on Samhain. The Veil is thin. It's a good night to pass, with many helping hands to take a new soul through the gate. The ride in the chariot will take the souls through the seven levels of Heaven and many other remarkable places before the night is done."

A group of harpies flew through then. Not to be outdone by their flamboyant predecessor, they conducted an impressive midair choreography before the portal. It reminded Lyssa of a parade, with Rhoswen as the parade master. She stood by the portal entrance, evaluating each group's ability to strike terror into human hearts.

Following her gaze, Tabor nodded. "To know about your father, you need to know about the women in his life. Rhoswen's mother was young, opportunistic, spoiled and ultimately corrupt. Because of her youth, and because there was in fact something quite unique about her—a shining gem, much like her daughter, though with much less heart—she was able to turn his head for a short time. Long enough to get with child, which of course does not take very long. But she couldn't disguise her true nature, and he would not cleave to her. He did acknowledge the child, cared for her with a true fondness."

"He loved her." Lyssa stared at Tabor.

"Most decidedly. He was a very big part of Rhoswen's life until . . ." Tabor shook his head. "It enraged Magwel that he would not give her the regard he gave the daughter she bore him, so she thwarted him from seeing Rhoswen. I suspect she poisoned Rhoswen's mind against him as well, making her believe that he didn't care for her, even though he continued to try and reach out to her. In later years, I was able to reveal this to Rhoswen, but by then, your mother had happened, and it became more complicated."

Lyssa shifted against Jacob's body, her eyes darkening as she remembered Rhoswen's bitter words. *Children are like acorns. Some are left to rot . . .*

"When he fell in love with your mother, it was not a love we as Fae could understand. But I have eyes, and I knew it was true. Rhoswen's mother was close to the Unseelie queen. It took time, but eventually the unthinkable was done. Your father, one of our strongest, was sentenced to death.

"He could have fought my brother and the others who spoke against him, and the loss of life would have been grievious, because the Fae courts were very divided on the issue. However, he agreed to accept the sentence if my brother agreed the Fae court would not seek retaliation against his vampire mate. The Seelie court abided by that. The Unseelie didn't. I do not hold the Seelie court blameless, however, because my brother did nothing to stop the Unseelie court. He felt that our honoring the agreement was all that was required. Even though he was lovers with the woman who sent the assassins. Rhoswen's mother."

Earlier, she'd told Jacob that something that happened a thousand years ago shouldn't have such a hold on her now. Yet getting the answers she'd always lacked was more overwhelming than she'd expected. Tabor had paused, was studying her face. Jacob's mind touched her in warm reassurance as he picked up on her uncertain spiral of emotions.

"My apologies, Lady Lyssa. I did not adequately prepare you for the import of what I intended to tell you. I felt it was significant to meet you tonight, to tell you these things on the night of endings and beginnings. However, perhaps I set too much store by symbolism. We can wait until—"

"No." Lyssa shook her head firmly. "There may not be another time, Your Majesty. I welcome anything you can say that might help me understand the confusion of my childhood."

"No child should have to deal with what you and your mother faced. Fortunately, the vampire world resorted to the talents of a mortal sorcerer to stop the assassination attempts. Unfortunately, on this side of things, it was not over so quickly. I could no longer in good conscience support my brothers, so our world divided into factions. We suffered through on-and-off armed conflicts, no sense of cohesion, for centuries. When I killed both of my brothers in battle, Rhoswen's mother, now Unseelie Queen, became my bitter enemy, and things became far worse. Until Rhoswen took her mother's life and called for a truce."

He looked back at the portal as a group of sinuous women, dressed in elaborate wrapped cloths, like Indian women in saris, proceeded toward it. One transformed while they watched, her brown skin becoming overlapped with scales, her eyes large and unblinking with the slitted pupils of a snake. Flicking a long, forked tongue at the other women, she amused them as her legs disappeared and were replaced instead by a long snake's tail that propelled her even more quickly to the portal. They shifted to catch up, laughing as they did so.

Lamias, Jacob supplied. *It's said they trap faithless men in their coils with seduction and then strangle them to death.*

Well, they seem in a cheerful mood for it. Lyssa closed her eyes. Hearing what Rhoswen had done to end the civil war in her country, she'd found a common link, an empathy she wasn't sure she wanted.

"There's much I do not know about the relationship between Rhoswen and her mother," Tabor said, "or what made her decide to do it, after she'd stood behind her through so many battles. However, after the truce, Lady Rhoswen mourned in seclusion for five years, during which Keldwyn stood as her regent. When she came back, he stepped aside and became liaison for both courts."

His mouth tightened. "Since, as you say, we may not have an opportunity like this again, I will say the most important thing. I owe a debt to your father. Though Queen Rhoswen and I act as equals on most things, I have the power to overrule her court decisions. It is a power I try to use rarely, because I understand the danger of undermining her authority, given the beings that reside in her portion of our world. Do you understand?"

He held her gaze a long moment, until she nodded. "I do."

"Good." He shifted his attention back to the portal. "She is a mixture of contradictions, the worst of her mother and the best of her father always warring within her. Her Fae respect her, but she won't let them love her. Being barren does not help matters, for we have never had a barren Unseelie queen. Her mother cursed her with barrenness when Rhoswen killed her."

Reghan has another daughter. A daughter with a child . . .

Some wounds couldn't heal, even over a thousand years. Particularly when every day was a reminder of the past.

A troop of hobgoblins marched through the gate, naked, short and long-limbed, bearing an array of noisemakers that created a din that vibrated through the ground as they tested them out. Rhoswen managed an approving look, though Lyssa imagined she wanted to rub her temples to stave off the headache they were probably seeding. Though they didn't need masks to be scary to human perception, many had purchased from the vendor Lyssa remembered anyway.

Masks. How many masks had she worn in her life? How many had Rhoswen worn? Maybe that was why masked costume events had never appealed to her.

The enticing trill of a lute brought her attention back to the next person in the elaborate parade. She'd seen satyrs around the castle and in the village, but this one had the same look that Firewind had about him, as if he was a leader among his kind. His bare upper body was broad and muscular, and though his lower half was like the haunches and cloven hooves of a goat, the legs were strong and reminiscent enough of a human male it wasn't as offputting as she would expect. His long curling red hair and trimmed beard looked like touchable silk. A dozen female Fae trailed in his wake, dancing, laughing, wearing flowers and very little else, long hair flowing over bare skin and fluttering wings.

His absorbing blue eyes turned to her as if he felt her regard specifically. Lifting a lute to his firm lips, he trilled her another provocative tune, as if he were inviting her to dance, or more. Despite the seriousness of her discussion with Tabor, she felt the sun break through those clouds, give her the desire to smile. Perhaps even to laugh, take his hands and join him in that dance. Unlike the dangerous lure of the sirens, in this instance his attraction felt almost compassionate, as if he was picking up on the weight of her heart as easily as Jacob did. On top of that, the way he gazed at her was intent, sexual and quite pleasurable. What intrigued her even more was he included Jacob in that frank assessment, making it clear the invitation was open to both.

Jacob's wry chuckle whispered across her ear, making her shiver. "I'm going to guess that's Robin Goodfellow, also known as Puck. He's reputed to be the Jester of the Fae and loves to cause confusion among mortals and Faes alike. It's said he sends travelers in the wrong direction, pinches lazy servants, and pulls chairs out from beneath people who are malicious gossips. Should I hold you tighter, my lady, to keep you from flying to his side?"

She pressed her lips against a smile, laid her hand on his thigh. *I was thinking I'd have him come over here and give my lazy servant a pinch.*

Since he made you smile, I'm going to pretend to ignore that comment.

She looked toward Tabor then, steadier. "Why a rose bush?"

Tabor shook his head, his mouth hard. "Magwel recommended the method of his death. Your mother loved our roses. As you already know, Reghan gave her a plant, allowed her to take it into your world. That was another crime, though creating a child with her was considered the worst. As you've no doubt realized, at that time we had stringent rules to keep our two species apart. It wasn't long after that the portals were closed completely and the Separation Edict set into place, by mutual agreement. There is a great deal of wisdom to it I support, but not for the same reasons as Rhoswen. Many of the Edict's principles hold today, except on a night like this. The Veil is thin, not just between our worlds, but between the here and now and the afterlife, and that must be honored, no matter our rules and laws."

As the last of her people passed through it, Rhoswen was positioning herself to take the Queen's Guard through the gate. "On this night, the queen does all she can to keep the two worlds far apart, and we go to bless it. We hope that one day things will be different, whereas she fervently prays they never will. She is certain that inviting mortal congress will bring us to true destruction, not just self-imposed exile from the earth. And she could well be right. I cannot see the future. That's not a gift given me. But there are certain ways I do not wish to live."

He met Lyssa's gaze. "The last day I saw your father, the proudest, noblest man I've ever known got on his knees with tears in his eyes. He pleaded with my brother to honor his promise, to spare you and your mother. However, I remember he had his gaze fixed on Rhoswen's mother, because that was who he truly needed to convince. The hopelessness in his eyes said he already knew it would come to naught. After I killed my brothers, I knew what that hopelessness felt like, despairing at what we had come to be . . . I don't want that kind of world. We are better being dust and the stuff of wishful dreams than that."

His expression intensified. "Which is why I have asked Rhoswen to consider sending you back to your world as a liaison between our two courts and the Vampire Council."

~

It took Lyssa a moment to digest it, not sure at first she'd heard what she'd heard. She could sense Jacob's similar reaction, and was glad again for the solid warmth of his body behind her. Up until now, he'd remained silent, an innocuous servant. Tabor had not once addressed him, but it was obvious the king was very aware of his presence, of the connection between them. His eyes had swept over the mark of Jacob's fangs at her neck, along with the intimate rest of his hands on Lyssa's hips, her leg over his calf, his thigh alongside her hip.

"The Vampire Council is as prejudiced against the Fae as your people are against them." She kept her tone politely incredulous. "How do you propose to compel them to accept a liaison?"

"I am not without my spies in your world, Lady Lyssa." Tabor gave her a tight smile. "Their ploy to take your child is an attempt to reclaim your advisory capabilities without according you status among them." He quirked a brow. "And if you need more intel than that, I have overestimated your abilities as a queen."

The amber eyes were suddenly far more regal, distant. "Our conversation has had a note of sentiment that could be misleading. I may seem far more accepting than my lady Rhoswen, but I am no less ruthless in the defense of our world. The boundaries between worlds grow thinner every year. Our young Fae know there are other worlds, other dimensions, and they want to explore them. The tighter we rein them in, the more those reins chafe. It's taken me quite a few centuries, but I am beginning to think there are better ways than the Separation Edict. We grow weaker and fewer, not stronger. Rhoswen and I look at the same problem in a very different way. Perhaps opening communication in a limited way between our worlds will help us all. At least I'm hoping to help her understand that."

Good luck with that, Jacob thought. Lyssa was inclined to agree.

A rocket went off. They looked up to see a spiral of silver and gold color explode across the sky. As it fell toward the portal archway, it formed the Unseelie crest briefly before it disappeared into the darkness. A cold blast of air shuddered past them, making Firewind lift his hooves off the ground. Jacob held on to him with mane and knees, cradling Lyssa against him as the horse came back to ground. "The Gaoth Shee are always the last to pass through," Tabor noted. "They will catch up to Gwyn ap Nudd once they've had their fun terrifying the lone travelers this evening."

The ebony woman and the two companions for the king were returning, the procession behind them shifting, ready to depart. Tabor held out his hand and Lyssa placed hers in it. He passed his gloved fingers over her pale, slim ones, studying them. "I would enjoy a less strategic conversation with you, Lady Lyssa. I could teach you *juste*, the Fae version of chess. Reghan used to play it with me, and I think you would excel at it. Perhaps we will have that opportunity sometime in the future. Until then, be thinking of what I said. You are welcome to ride close at our side, or drop back to visit with any in our procession. You'll find many are interested in meeting Reghan's daughter."

Moving his horse into a proud trot, he headed for the portal. Dahlia urged her mare into a canter to bring her back to her liege's side, and the two personal guards followed. As Firewind pawed the ground, Lyssa murmured, "Let's wait a moment."

Jacob understood and agreed. Because of all that Tabor had given her to think about, she wanted to sit here, still her mind and watch for a moment. Beneath a sky alight with more stars than they'd ever seen in the skies of the mortal world, that procession of stately figures headed for the portal. Dressed in silks and jewels, unearthly in their beauty, they were illuminated by orbs slowly oscillating around them or mounted on staffs. Some of the luminaries were fairies, perched on the shoulders of the human-sized Fae. The mounts were all combed out to glossy sheens and decorated with flowers, jewels and silks. They saw Fae in carriages, and not just large ones drawn by eight outfitted horses. There were ones enchantingly smaller than shoeboxes, rolling along precariously beneath, but with just as much grandeur as their larger counterparts.

Though she'd seen banshees, dragons, hippogriffs and griffins go through with the Unseelie, this made her think of a royal procession from medieval times, only with an ethereal beauty and synchronized movement that suggested there was a higher level of communication between them than first apparent.

Glancing up at his face, Lyssa saw Jacob was as enraptured as she was. She wondered if even Tabor, who seemed far more sympathetic to their world, realized how it affected them. Did he know how many mortal childhoods had nursed dreams of magic and fantasy? In the stories they read, the creatures and beings they met there, so many children had just *known*, deep in their bones, that they had to be real somewhere. And it wasn't a child's whim, lost to adulthood. It still dwelled deep inside so many of them, the belief that the magic they saw hidden in all the natural things of their world—the spider spinning a web jeweled with dew, a rainbow after a rainstorm, a field of wildflowers so diverse and unplanned in the richness of color—those things were proof that magic like this still existed. The imprint was still there, a bean-shaped baby waiting to be discovered in a flower bud one day.

Could the two worlds ever be brought together again, fulfilling the dreams and curiosities of both without irreparable harm? The young Fae liked the human world, because it was new and different, and they were amazed by the gizmos humans had learned to create in lieu of magic. Whereas, the humans were in awe of the things that came so naturally for the Fae. The ability to fly, to transform into a tree, to ride a waterhorse and discover the beast was more than a myth.

And that he likes sugar-coated apples.

She'd seen that in his mind, as well a lot of other very harrowing things when he'd reappeared. "All right," she said at last. "We'd better fall in toward the back."

She realized then her voice was a bit strained. Jacob's arm was around her waist and she was gripping his forearm hard. Pressing a kiss to her temple, he gave Firewind a slight press with his knees. The horse, though used to going everywhere at the speed of a battlefield charge, reflected the tone of the procession. He stepped sedately into the flow. As he did, Lyssa saw a pair of Fae women lean out of the carriage parallel to them. The male Fae on top also leaned down to look at her, but not with unpleasant curiosity. They looked interested in talking, as Tabor had warned.

Or perhaps they were just enjoying the indecent cling of Jacob's hose on his very fine, very tight ass and hoping to catch a frontal view, which she was keeping all to herself, that impressive package nested up against her buttock and hip.

He scored her ear with his fang, making her smile. It helped loosen things up inside of her. Not bad things, but something . . . poignant, like a long ago loss that might still be found within range of the fingertips, if one knew which direction to reach.

Like toward a liaisonship that would bring the two worlds together.

14

They didn't go to simply one destination. Throughout the nighttime hours, the Fae procession phased in and out of the mist, appearing in various places. Corn fields in the rural Midwest, sugar cane in South America and rice fields in Cambodia. Thick forests, where local peoples still relied on hunting for food, not soulless sport. Some of the places through which they traveled were so untouched by the industrial world that Lyssa felt she'd seen the same tableau hundreds of years ago. Either because the magic portals allowed for time adjustments or because the time zones themselves aligned with the nighttime of the Fae world, all their destinations were quiet and dark, between the midnight to three a.m. hours. At each field or forest, the Fae walking on the outskirts of the procession, usually women or young girls, scattered what looked like seed from large baskets. The seeds floated outward and then down, coated in a soft glow. Once they settled on the earth they disappeared, seeding the earth with good tidings for plenty and abundance.

Though the sorcerers had set them in different paths, there were a few times they did see evidence of the Haunt's presence, at a distance. Sirens on mooring buoys in a river, calling to young men sitting on the docks drinking beer. Male fairies dancing among enchanted red and white mushroom circles, coaxing young women to join them. They passed through blasts of air from the Gaoth Shee, heard the baying of the hell hounds. She saw humans who had strayed from the populated areas, casting fearful looks into the darkness, sensing the Unseelie eyes watching them, calculating the mischief they would do to the loner. They didn't see the opulent reassurance of the Fae procession, passing just outside the range of their vision. Tabor's mouth would tighten, but he did not interfere, the two factions continuing their parallel courses.

For the most part, the Seelie entourage set a sedate pace. However, when they reached a wide-open pastureland for sheep, dotted with low fences underneath the glowing moon, there was a cry from a section of the procession. King Tabor grinned as Aidan and Leigh pointed out the white hart, lithely prancing on the field several slopes down, cutting coquettish circles. "Shall we have ourselves a little harmless sport?" he queried. "My lady, will you join us?"

She could feel Jacob's eagerness, muscles quivering behind her back, amusingly reminding her of Bran being held back from a treat. She shook her head at the palfrey being led forward and instead, in a lithe move, helped by Jacob's strength and her own, she shifted herself quickly around his body and adjusted her skirt so she straddled Firewind behind him, setting her hands securely around his waist. "Let's go," she said.

"Well done," Aidan praised her, giving her a handsome smile. "She's mine this year, mates."

"Not if I get there first," Tabor laughed, flashing white teeth. Though Dahlia stopped just short of rolling her eyes at Lyssa in female commiseration, it was a near thing.

"I have the help of Lord Firewind and the favor of my lady," Jacob pointed out. "You might as well give up now. Ha!"

They tossed back a wealth of deprecating comments, but in the next breath, they'd all taken off. Firewind had a forward charge like an airplane taking off. It took him a length ahead, a competitive snort from his velvety nostrils resulting in a short spout of flame wafting by Lyssa.

She couldn't see the hart, but she didn't have to do so. This was what she'd dreamed about. Jacob hadn't had to tell her what to do. She molded herself to his back, her legs close along the outside of his hips so she felt every flex of his thighs and wonderful backside, the ripple of strength along his back, under her cheek as he and Firewind truly became one. The horse had accepted him as worthy for the moment, but when Jacob truly demonstrated his natural skill, she thought the kelpie felt almost as she did. They were meshed as one, no conflict between them, blood, bone and organs all synchronized together. Jacob's heart thundered so she felt its reverberation even where her hands clasped his waist.

First fence, my lady. Just stay in my mind.

They soared, there was no other word for it. She moved with Jacob's body as he leaned forward to take the fence, and Firewind came down on the opposite side with a joyous, bloodcurdling whinny, sparks flying off his hooves. Exultation moved through her, a rare, wonderful experience, feeling the strength and grace of man and horse together, the power of the incomparable male to whom she'd given her heart.

Firewind dodged as they came close to Tabor's mount. Two other Seelie Fae were on their right as they took the next fence, all close together, the pursuers shouting, encouraging and insulting in the way that men did. She caught a glimpse of Dahlia, who she expected had joined to stay close to the king, but even the ebony woman looked as if she were enjoying herself. She was also a tremendous horsewoman.

The horses veered as one, and she saw the hart cut back, a lovely ghostlike creature with luminous eyes and gleaming horns. The tail was a taunting flag as the magical beast bounded up the next hill, cut right and soared over the bank of a wide creek the sheep probably used for water.

Firewind cut on the same path, and she saw quite a few Fae rein back, realizing the jump was more than they or their mounts could handle. Tabor was still with them, however, as well as his companions and one or two others. While the others shortened their strides, Jacob leaned forward more, and Firewind responded, lengthening his gait.

Lyssa closed her eyes on a smile, tightening her arms on Jacob as the horse gathered and leaped over the creek, his fiery hooves hitting the far bank with an explosion of flame and a foot to spare. The wind streamed through Lyssa's hair, her skirt rippling over Firewind's haunches.

Then she heard Tabor's laughter, his friendly curse, and Firewind was slowing. Jacob eased him down, despite the horse's snort and shuddering response that suggested he wanted to continue to chase. Lifting her head, she saw the hart bounding away into the thick wood on the edge of the pastureland.

"She's not ours tonight, lads," Tabor said. "But she gave us a merry chase for sure."

"The best ones always do," Leigh offered with a chuckle. His brown eyes glinted and he gave Lyssa a half bow before he turned back to his king. "One of these days I'll catch her, you wait."

"Aye, and one of these days, you'll be prettier," Aidan teased.

Tabor nodded to Jacob. "You are a fine rider. You do your lady credit. Lord Firewind agrees, I think. It is hard to win his approval."

The kelpie snorted, but Lyssa noted he bowed the great head briefly, shaking his mane in deference to the king, a willing gesture he'd not given Rhoswen.

"My lady inspires me to great things," Jacob returned. "Her favor makes me capable of anything."

"Also something the best ones do," Tabor agreed. He lifted his voice. "It grows late. We must rejoin the Hunt, and meet back with the Haunt." He glanced toward the forest, and out over the pastureland, a trace of regret in his eyes. "It is time to leave this world for another year."

~

Though their travails had been from midnight to the three a.m. hours, they'd covered far more ground than those mortal hours would normally have permitted, thanks to the influence of the magical night and Fae time. And it wasn't over yet. When they returned to the Fae world, Samhain night would go on even longer. "The sun doesn't rise until the Ending Ritual," the Fae ladies riding in the carriage told them gaily. "We'll feast, dance, sing and celebrate until then."

Lyssa had returned to her sidesaddle seat in front of Jacob. He stroked back her windblown hair, helping her put it back in presentable fashion, that handsome curve to his lips as he replaced combs and ribbons. She touched his mouth with her fingers while he did, and when their eyes met, she saw the excitement he'd enjoyed in the Hunt still lingering, and wondered if it reflected her pleasure in it as well. Since he kissed those fingers, giving her a tiny, secret touch of his tongue to tease her on the pads, she suspected it did.

I love you, my lady. My heart is bursting with it.

If they weren't in formal procession, she knew she would have slid both arms around him, put her head back on his chest, felt him dip his head over hers as he did in that position, his own arms strong around her. But since she had to appear as a queen now—albeit a windblown one—she settled for stretching up and pressing a kiss on that beloved mouth, cupping her hands around the back of his skull to draw his head down and kiss each eye, the bridge of his nose.

I find you mildly tolerable, Sir Knight.

He grinned at her. Then his glance shifted and she followed it, since the procession was filing to a halt. Or rather, fanning out in a crescent to form a half ring around what appeared to be a human cemetery.

It was on the outskirts of a lonely swamp, the night air filled with the eerie calls of frogs. Jacob moved Firewind up closer to the king when he silently gestured for Lyssa to approach. The watchful Dahlia and two guardsmen gave him room to take up a position next to the king, where Lyssa could now see who else was in the cemetery.

Despite the graveyard hour—ironic, considering—a man was here. Elderly and wizened, bent by perhaps eighty or more years, he was nevertheless kneeling before a tombstone. Dozens of flowers of myriad varieties had made a carpet over the grave. His hands were still stained by the juices of the stems.

Though he thought himself alone, the man's sobbing was silent, but fierce, wracking the thin frame. When he shifted, Lyssa saw the name Rose Lanyon on the stone. It was a wide marker, intended for two. The name etched next to Rose's, Arthur Lanyon, had no year of death yet.

"*Arthur* means *bear* in Celtic. She used to call him her bear, because his hair was brown, like his eyes. And he was rounder, many years ago."

Lyssa glanced left and found Rhoswen there, sitting on her horse. In the shifting darkness on the other side of the cemetery, as the mist cleared, now she saw the outline of the guard and many of the Unseelie procession, arranged in a facing crescent to the Seelie host. The queen looked toward Tabor. She nodded, and he acknowledged the gesture, a decision made together. She swung down from her horse.

As Cayden began to follow her, she shook her head, touching his booted calf with a light hand. She gave him a rare smile, one that didn't hold malice or deception. It was simply a sad, sweet gesture that managed to tug Lyssa's heart as the Fae queen moved across the graveyard toward the sobbing man. She'd shed the chains she'd worn earlier.

When Tabor and Rhoswen had said the two groups would rendezvous, Lyssa assumed it would be back in the Fae world, not here. It was clear this moment had importance to both, for all were watching, a motionless silence. Though he was circled by hundreds of Fae, the man didn't appear to see any of them.

When Rhoswen reached him, she sat down on a cracked and weathered stone bench, one he'd probably placed there years ago. According to the stone, Rose had died thirty years before, perhaps from cancer or some accident that could take a loved one far too young.

Reaching out, the queen laid her hand on his shoulder. His head rose and he stared up into her face. Then his gaze drifted right. Now he saw all the Fae, fanned out in an array of multicolored lights and glittering youth. A crooked smile bent his tear-laced countenance, then it crumpled again as he buried his face in Rhoswen's lap. She cupped her palm over his skull, stroking and murmuring.

As she comforted him, Robin Goodfellow moved out of the entourage to stand behind her. Instead of the pipe, he bore a harp in his hand. As all of the assembled stilled further, he began to strum the strings.

"Dagda's harp," Jacob murmured in Lyssa's ear. "Capable of taking a man to utter despair, or offering him comfort in his darkest moment."

In this case, it was the latter. As the music unfurled, poignant, sweet, it took the sorrow and turned it into bearable memory, hope and something indefinable, something that gripped all of them. It made Lyssa twine her fingers with Jacob's.

In her mind, Jacob saw she was in Kane's nursery, pulling the covers up around his little shoulders. She looked around the room at the things they'd bought to delight his eye, as well as things she'd placed there from her extensive travels. He was there as well, coming into the nursery to slip his arms around her waist as they gazed down at their son. The night of this particular memory, she'd lain down on the soft carpet and he'd made love to her there. They'd slept beneath that crib, listening to the sound of Kane's dreams, the innocent baby noises, as they spooned on the floor near him, too content where they were to contemplate leaving him.

"There have always been special stories about Samhain night. That those who are torn apart by grief, or regret, or the need for forgiveness, might go to a sacred place, like a burial site. There they might be found by the queen of the Fae. As she holds their heads in her lap, she gives them forgiveness, comfort . . . release."

This came from Tabor in a reverent, rumbling murmur, though his eyes did not leave the sight before them. They did not look away, either. Witnessing was quite obviously an important part of the ritual. As the man's sobs eased, that combined focus brought something else. A sense of expectancy. A gathering energy began to grow among the ranks of the Fae, magic spreading out over the cemetery. Firewind's skin heated, and Jacob held Lyssa closer. The wind stilled, then slowly began to build again, a quiet, mournful voice accompanying the harp. It was a song of loss, of endings and beginnings, a reflection of Samhain night. Jacob felt it in the heart and soul, the lowest well of the belly, a yearning and utter stillness at once, and every face he saw, including his lady's, reflected the same feeling.

The man rose then. He swayed, staring at the Fae queen, his face wreathed with all those emotions and more. Then he collapsed at her feet. Jacob started to dismount to help, but Tabor made a quelling noise in his throat. Dahlia put up a hand, shaking her head, her blue eyes fastened on the scene.

Lyssa swallowed. The man rose from a body that had simply crumpled into the dried leaves, becoming decay and ash. He was a young man, as young and fresh as any of the Fae faces around them, yet with the same wisdom of age in his eyes.

Rhoswen turned his attention toward another figure, coming across the cemetery.

A young woman, her hands outstretched, those same years of wisdom and loss in her eyes. Past regrets and hurts gone, because now they were pure spirit, everything open to one another. The desire for such soul deep honesty, the effort toward it in their mortal lives, had won them the reward of sharing the gift of it in an immortal one.

Lyssa shifted her gaze to Rhoswen. The queen was watching them, tears on her cheeks. As she rose, all that power coalesced around her, and the music became a concentrated hum, all organic energy focusing in on her slim white form. Lifting her hands, she appeared to be gathering it in both palms, kneading it, spinning it out from the powerful anchoring energy of that couple. Lyssa remembered the wheel in the upper chamber. As the queen's hands moved, the sense of expectancy grew. The two groups of Fae had shifted forward, a solid wall around the cemetery, touching elbow to elbow. Shadows started to shift over the cemetery as the wind picked up.

Jacob?

I don't know. Maybe—

Lyssa dug her nails into his palm as the world exploded, like a giant god throwing open a portal. It blinded them all, so that she turned her face instinctively into Jacob's chest. He covered her eyes with his hand, bending his head over hers. But then she sensed an ebbing, a dispersal of that light, and her gaze lifted again.

Throughout the cemetery and beyond, floating free of the swamp, coming from the trees, she saw spirits. *The Veil is thin, not just between our worlds, but between the here and now and the afterlife . . .* She remembered Tabor's words as she recognized most of the spirits were Fae, reflecting the many species that traveled with the Unseelie and Seelie processions. Within the sacred space that Rhoswen had spun, the Fae of the living world now moved forward, reaching out so the corporeal and incorporeal touched. Lyssa saw one of the young Fae who'd been allowed to come in the carriage, reach out toward the spirit of what was obviously a father and mother she'd lost. Their expressions of joy and grief were so closely mingled, Lyssa couldn't hold back the tears that spilled from her eyes, already gathered and waiting there from watching Rose and Arthur reunited. She looked to King Tabor, and he nodded. He'd wanted her to see, because they all shared this. Mortals and immortals both understood the loss of loved ones.

"Lyssa." Jacob's whisper pulled her attention away, as did the shock that filled him to the depth of his soul, overflowing to her. When she followed his gaze, more tears ached in her throat, a sob and a cry tangling there.

Three people stood at the side of the cemetery, watching them. As Jacob slid off Firewind, he held up his arms to bring her down, but neither one of them tore their gazes from those three, as if they might disappear if they looked away. When they moved toward the spirits, they held on to each other, not queen or servant in this moment, but two lovers needing the reassurance and support of the other.

The man and woman stepped forward first. In their faces, Lyssa saw separate and shared elements of Jacob's physical appearance and character. When the man reached out and touched Jacob, a blue light flared at the contact. Jacob's knees gave out. The man and woman caught him together. They held him the way they would have held him as a child, instead of the much larger man he was now. The woman reached out to Lyssa to bring her to them as well, her touch cool and reassuring at once. She was glad Lyssa had brought him to them, that the path of his life had led to this. Lyssa didn't know if Jacob's mother knew the other things this path had brought him, but that didn't matter, did it? She let herself be drawn into that circle, a part of that family.

We love you, we love you, we love you . . . tell Gideon.

It was simple, short, forever, all at once. No other words needed, just that essential touch, that contact between worlds. Feelings were all that mattered in the afterlife.

Perhaps a breath passed, perhaps an hour. Either way, the magic knew when it needed to end. As they faded, Jacob's mother left a last whispering kiss on his mouth, her eyes so full of love. *We're happy, we're safe. We watch over and love you both . . . tell Gideon.*

When they disappeared, Jacob was still on his knees. Lyssa knelt beside him, her hand on his shoulder, her lips pressed to it as her tears wet his bare skin. As he kept his head bowed, a new hand came to rest upon it, a tactile blessing. "Turns out that you were far more appropriate for her than ever I imagined."

Lyssa looked up to see the familiar, dear spectacled face of her former servant. In a heartbeat, she was on her feet and had jumped on him, as driven by emotion as a young girl. Her arms locked around his shoulders, holding Thomas in the tightest grip possible, no thought of queenly reserve in her mind. More tears spilled forth to wet his monk's cassock while his always surprisingly strong arms closed around her.

I've missed you, my lady. Has this young miscreant been treating you properly?

Had he known how it would feel, to have his beloved voice in her mind once more? That it would make it almost impossible for her to speak either way for a few moments?

"Not at all," she whispered at last. "He's impossibly insolent and disobedient. I think it has to do with his teacher."

Thomas pressed his face into her hair, his mouth against her temple, as much a blessing as his hand on Jacob's head had been. "You may be right."

When he let her feet touch, she still kept a close hold on him, staring up at his face. "I'm so very sorry."

"There are no sorries to be said. Not in this place." His eyes were swimming, and it was an amazing thing, to think there were tears where he dwelled, but these were tears of joy and love mixed with the regret. "You are speaking to my soul, just as Jacob was speaking to his parents' souls. A lingering part of our unconscious, because of course in the years that have passed, they have transitioned to other lives, other roles. But the soul is eternal, multifaceted, capable of reaching out through time and dimensions separate from where our physical bodies are now, from the lives we're leading now.

"One day, when we are all together again, these memories, these moments, will return to the forefront of the soul, and we will remember. The past and present will come back together. Right now, it will enrich our unconscious selves, wherever they are, offering an unmistakable sense of comfort and joy." He met Lyssa's gaze. "There are those who have much atonement to do, so much that they could not be here tonight. But he thinks of you, my lady, and he weeps."

Lyssa trembled in his grasp, another sob fair choking her. Jacob had come back to his feet now. Putting one hand on Thomas's shoulder, he laid his other on Lyssa's waist, connecting them, strengthening her. Thomas turned his gaze up to him fondly, since Jacob was several inches taller. "I see things took some unexpected turns."

"It's to be expected, with a Mistress like this." Jacob managed the spirited reply, though his voice was thick. "It's so good to see you." The fervency to his words belied their simplicity, and Thomas gripped his forearm, nodding.

"My time is short. This night only allows a glimpse, a moment, for to risk more than that is to unwisely draw the living too much into the embrace of the dead. But there is one more I brought you to meet." Turning away, he beckoned with a gentle motion. Out of the mist that still swirled through the cemetery, hiding as well as revealing, a toddler came. A tiny, doll-like child, her thumb in her mouth. She had eyes as blue as Jacob's. Hair as dark as Lyssa's fell in fine silk to her shoulders. Thomas squeezed both of their hands, a mute regret to let go of them, before he picked her up, cradling her on his hip. She studied them both with curious, big eyes.

"This is another soul who has gone on to other lives, quite a few of them in fact. She's become a remarkable person. However, this is the child she would have been in her first life, as beautiful a spirit as the two who created her, with the help of a loving God."

A sweet smile curved the child's lips when she looked toward Jacob. When she reached toward him, he took her, but let her lower body slide into Lyssa's arms so they were both holding her. The child laughed, putting her palms on each of their faces.

"She recognized Jacob first, because the knight did take care of her in the afterlife, my lady. Just as you hoped."

Lyssa nodded, letting her daughter press her little fingertips to the tears on her face. The toddler made soft, childish noises, too young for words, but no words were needed. Jacob put his mouth to her forehead, as Lyssa's hand slipped to his nape, her other holding her daughter. Hers. Her family. Almost all of them. She ached for Kane, so hard it was a contraction in her womb, a painful memory of birth. Feeling it, Jacob held her closer, held them both closer. "He's here," he murmured. "Just as Thomas says. Some part of his soul is here, with us, feeling this. And we'll tell him all about it."

"God be with you both." Thomas put his hands on them once again. In that instant, Jacob felt the sweet weight of memory binding them, a link that would never be broken. Then the monk slowly faded and the child with him, a slip of her laughter left behind, making the leaves swirl around their feet.

All about them, the mist was lifting, showing the scenes like theirs drawing to a close. For a few precious seconds, they'd all been caught in a joyous and sorrowful paradise. He saw the same types of tears, smiles and pensive looks he and Lyssa had shared. For some Fae, their tears sparkled on their cheeks like the dust that came from their wings.

When he looked at his lady, Jacob saw her looking toward the cemetery's edge. Sitting apart from everyone else, Rhoswen squatted on her heels on the top of a large tombstone, her fingers resting on the stone's edge as if she were a white angel sculpted there. Energy still pulsed around her, her concentration obvious as she held open the Veil. However, as the last spirits faded, her eyes cleared, shoulders easing. Jacob started forward, but Cayden and Tabor already anticipated, catching her as the strength left her body and she slid off the tombstone into their ready grasp. There was a murmur of conversation between them, and then Cayden ceded her to Tabor with obvious reluctance. The Fae king lifted and carried her to a covered carrying chair. Tabor had given his horse's reins to Dahlia. It appeared the four chair supports were to be carried by himself, Aidan, Leigh and Keldwyn.

Lyssa moved in that direction. Jacob followed, feeling how fragile she was right now, how fragile they both were. While the cemetery was no longer utterly silent, conversations were quiet, a somberness that fit the moment, punctuated by the music of bells as the horses shook their manes, or the Fae expressed their feelings through their love of music, with lute, pipe and muted drum beats. Many Unseelie still wore the monstrous guises they'd donned, but now, as they perched in trees or on tombstones in their trappings, they had a sad, macabre look. They sat in contemplation or comforted companions overwhelmed by the experience.

He noticed the group of young Fae formed a center cluster, holding on to one another in silence, rocking as Robin Goodfellow, balanced on a nearby marker, played a song to make them smile through their tears.

When Lyssa stopped beside the carrying chair, Jacob reached tentative fingers into her mind to find she was dwelling on how Rhoswen had given them this. Yet the Fae queen had stood apart, taking no comfort from any past loved one herself. As if there was no loved one in her past she would be willing to see . . . or who would step forward to see her.

The curtains around the chair had not been lowered, Tabor and his honor guard standing at a respectful distance. Cayden stood next to them, holding his horse and Rhoswen's. Lyssa nodded to them all, then knelt at the side of the Fae queen. While she didn't take the woman's hand, she did touch the pillow near her head, so Rhoswen turned toward her.

"Thank you," Lyssa said quietly. "You gave me a gift without measure. All of us."

Rhoswen closed her eyes, her face weary. "Fae don't like to be thanked. We consider it insulting, empty platitudes. You thank with gifts, trinkets."

"Since the only thing I have of value is something I'm not likely to offer twice, you'll have to make do with a simple, sincere thank-you." Lyssa's tone was mild, however, a gentle note in it.

"Selfish bitch." The queen's lips twisted, but there was no heat to the words. Jacob sensed she actually appreciated the goading more than the hovering, concerned presence of the males.

"So I've been told." When Lyssa touched the pillow again, her fingers settled on a lock of Rhoswen's hair, a stroke. "Rhoswen, we are the only close blood family we each have left. Aren't we?"

"We are related by blood. That does not make us family or close." Rhoswen opened her eyes again, stared at her. "While I don't know all the spirits that press through the Veil on Samhain night, some of them I anticipate ahead of time, because their desire to come through, their anticipation of the night, is so strong. That is why the young Fae who have lost parents in the last year attend with us. They are given an opportunity to see them once more before the children must move on, go on living. This is our gift of comfort, to them and their parents."

She put her hand up between them then, pressing against Lyssa's forearm to push her touch away. "He was there, on the other side of the Veil. I could have allowed him to step past it, Lyssa. He has never waited there before, not for the many years I have done this. But he knew you were coming. I could have let him through, but I didn't. Because if he stepped out of that Veil with her at his side, your mother . . . If he stepped out and the first person he looked for was you, which is of course what he would do . . ."

Her gaze became hard and empty. "Then, queen or not, whatever I am supposed to be, it would not matter. I would have to kill you, because I could not bear that pain. I'm sorry."

15

AT her imperious motion, Cayden stepped forward and drew the curtains around the chair. Lyssa knelt there an extra moment, making him work around her, until Tabor came to her side, slipped a hand under her elbow and helped her up, Jacob on the other side. The procession was mounting up again. Jacob took her to Firewind, helped her onto his back. When he put his arms around her to take up the reins, he noticed she was cold.

As they moved away from the cemetery and reentered the mist that would take them back to the Fae world, the mood shifted with that fog. Conversation turned into ripples of laughter, then a more festive song trilled from a pipe. As they emerged into the Fae world, that current rose even higher, responding to the lights and music spread out below them, each castle trying to outdo the display of its neighbor. Fireworks were happening, triggered by their return, those aerial displays of Fae, dragons and other flying beasts interspersed with explosions of lights in the sky.

The joy of seeing loved ones was transitioning into the meaning of the holiday itself. A day of endings, a day of beginnings, of hope for the future and laying the past to rest.

His lady remained silent. Jacob kept her cradled in his arms, giving her his strength and warmth. She laid her head on his shoulder, alarming him not so much with her quiet, but her lack of care of what others thought, seeing her weariness. Looking ahead at the queen in the lead, curtains still drawn, he wondered what Rhoswen was doing behind that thick fabric. Noting Cayden's serious expression, also unaffected by the rising joviality of the group, he wondered if the two of them were having similar concerns about their respective ladies.

Lyssa slid her arms around his bare waist, her fingers hooked in the waist band of the snug hose, thumb tracing the upper rise of his buttock. He tightened his arm around her. *My lady? You are well?*

Just weary, Jacob. Just so weary of it all. Of what comes tomorrow, and the day after, and the day after.

"Sleep, my lady. I have you. I'll take you to our room when we get back to the castle, and you can rest."

She subsided. Firewind was once again riding some paces away from the rest of the host, the waterhorse not particularly the social type. Jacob wasn't surprised when Keldwyn relinquished his spot carrying the chair to Cayden and fell back on his own mount to keep pace with the waterhorse. Facing away from him in her sidesaddle position, Lyssa didn't stir at his presence. When Keldwyn glanced at her, Jacob had the odd feeling the Fae Lord wanted to reach out and touch Lyssa's head to offer comfort.

"The first time one experiences it, it is overwhelming," he observed.

It was one of the few times Keldwyn had initiated conversation with him. Then again, maybe not. Perhaps he was well aware that Lyssa was awake. "It is hard to know how to feel. On one hand, it is a deep celebration, to know that life goes on, to see those who have passed before. On the other, it is a reexperience of their loss, of the things said and unsaid. It is not unexpected to feel somewhat low in the aftermath, adjusting to it."

Jacob made a noncommittal noise. Keldwyn pressed his lips together, jaw tightening. "Is she all right?"

Jacob raised a brow. Lyssa was in her own thoughts, of course aware of Keldwyn's question, but unconcerned with whatever response he provided, trusting Jacob to offer an appropriate one. Though she'd correctly guessed he bore no love for Keldwyn, the concern in the Fae Lord's eyes was sincere.

"She misses our son," he said. "Lady Lyssa is not young, but she is a young mother, a mother who was still nursing her child. Tonight's events . . . they make one want to be with those you love most. And they make her weary of the bullshit."

If he was surprised by the frank speech, he of course didn't show it. Keldwyn nodded, his gaze coursing over the position of Lyssa's body, curved so closely into Jacob's. "I can see that. Perhaps there is something we can do, to bring the child here, if—"

Lyssa straightened with the swift grace of a bobcat, twisting around and leveling her jade stare at the Fae Lord. "No one from this world will go near our son. You think I would allow my child, a baby, to be brought here and mocked, treated the way I have been treated, the way Jacob has been treated?"

Keldwyn gave her a straightforward look. "If you fail the third quest, Queen Rhoswen will not allow you to leave this world. Your son will *have* to be brought to you."

The energy that sparked off her was enough to send an unsettling ripple not only through Firewind and Keldwyn's mount, but the other horses close enough to be affected by it. Though their riders couldn't hear the conversation, they sent wary looks toward Lyssa. "He has been left with those who will see to his care and raising, if it is needed," she said. "So that is not your concern. I do not know or understand all the intricacies of your mind, Lord Keldwyn, what your intent is with respect to me. I accept that, for I've spent my life in a maze of politics and schemes. But you heed me. You bring my son into it, in any way, and you will discover that I can be so ruthless and cruel, your Queen Rhoswen will look like a pixie fairy in comparison. I will not hesitate to wreak devastation on anything or anyone standing between me and my son's well-being."

On this point, he and his lady were in complete agreement. Jacob was sure his own gaze had gone harsh and uncompromising, his body warrior straight and alert, every muscle prepared for battle. After a long, tense moment, Keldwyn tilted his head toward the front of the line, toward Cayden and the curtained chair. "I understand the third and final quest will be delivered to you at dawn. I wish you luck, Lady Lyssa."

"Good or bad? Which will suit your purposes best?"

He lifted a shoulder. "Both have their advantages. Though I would not say I am your friend, and would hesitate over ally, I am not your enemy, Lady Lyssa. I think you know that."

"Mind if we go get that spear to test out the theory?" Jacob asked.

He gave Jacob a tight fuck-you smile. Reaching into his shirt, he tossed him a small sack. "Hold on to that. It can hold blood, preserving it for several days. You may find a use for it soon."

On that cryptic note, he turned his horse away, returning to the Seelie entourage, now moving in a parallel track with the Unseelie one. There was some fraternization, Jacob saw, but for the most part the two courts seemed to stand apart, a good indication that the leadership of them did.

"You are terrifying, my lady."

"Good, that was my intent." She shook her head. "I don't want to be with the court tonight. We'll go for a walk on our own. Enjoy this world on our own terms, not theirs."

Jacob made a noise of assent. "You have friends here, my lady. King Tabor as much as told you so. We will find a way out, even if the queen tries to prevent us."

"I know."

Still, feeling the chaos the evening had evoked, he knew whatever occurred at that dawn hour, she needed to be at a better mental place for it than she was currently. So if she wanted to walk, that was what they would do.

~

The celebration around the outside of the Caislean Uisce was an awe-inspiring circus of players, acrobats and magical displays based on the castle's favored element. Elaborate creative fountains were illuminated in myriad colors; a lake of ice was populated with animated ice sculptures; the games were everything from dunking to a form of curling using disks of ice.

The Seelie procession had turned off at the Caislean Talamh, and the Unseelie procession disbanded here. The royal entourage had already disappeared, so little attention was paid to them as Jacob stopped Firewind at the bottom of the castle hill, a distance from the revels. He helped his lady slide off.

Lyssa turned to lay her hand on Firewind's shoulder, looking into the large dark eye of the enormous stallion as Jacob removed the halter and gave the steed a slight bow. "Since Fae prefer thanks in the form of a gift, I'll give Keldwyn a basket of the apples along with your halter."

The horse snorted. His eyes gleamed, Jacob assumed at the promise of those sugar apples. Waterhorses might live on blood, but this one had a sweet tooth.

Jacob bowed more deeply, hiding his amusement. "It was an honor, Lord Firewind."

Shifting forward, the horse gave Jacob a shove in his chest that knocked him on his backside. Then he rubbed his very large and quite lethal head gently against Lyssa's shoulder, the velvet lips nibbling her face and neck, a horse's form of kiss. She stayed still, a small smile on her face as he moved back, made that pretty leg. Then, with a snort of fire that blasted the grass at Jacob's feet, the horse was in motion.

The Fae in his path swept back with warning cries as he charged full tilt toward the moat around the castle, the flames from his hoofs leaving small fires in the grasses. Gathering his haunches, he leaped into the air. He transformed in the air against all the glittering fireworks, the rear legs becoming the lustrous and powerful curved tail that helped him dive deep into the moat and disappear.

"Show off," Jacob observed, getting back to his feet and rubbing his still tender ribs. "Big flirt."

"Well, since he started out the evening trying to kill you—and almost succeeded, I might add—I think it's an improvement in your relationship."

"Hmm." Jacob looked down as she linked her hand with his, their fingers intertwining as she gestured toward the moonlit fields and forests that rolled away from the castle walls.

"Shall we go that way?"

She didn't want to go into the castle, even for a change of clothes. He was comfortable in what little he was wearing, so he had no objections to that.

It was rare that she chose to walk hand-in-hand. When she did so, it always underscored how petite she was, the top of her head barely reaching his shoulder. When they'd put her hair in order after the white hart chase, he'd wrapped it in a silver braided cord so it fell down her back, a compliment to the dress. She kicked off the shoes to walk barefoot, absorbing the feel of the earth through her soles. "There's a lot more to him than meets the eye," she remarked. "Firewind."

"Well, there's more than one legend about the waterhorse."

"There always is."

Jacob grinned, then sobered. "One story says a kelpie can also take the form of a seductive male who coaxes women to accompany him into secluded places. There he'd take their lives, drink their blood."

"Like a vampire. Do you think Firewind can shapeshift to a human form?"

Jacob snorted. "That last little maneuver, nibbling on your neck, makes me wonder. And during our struggle . . . some of it was man against beast, but there were moments it felt almost . . . warrior to warrior. But regardless, there's something very sinister below the surface on that one. Intriguing, but sinister."

"Again, much like vampires." Her fingers tightened on his.

"True. Though now that you're hanging with the Fae, you'll probably want to associate as little as possible with that fanged rabble."

She gave him a small smile, that sensual curve of her lips that made him imagine all the things she could do with her mouth. Though they were setting a casual pace, the castle had already dropped out of sight behind them as they followed the rise and fall of the hills before them. The firefly Fae were out in clouds tonight, buzzing around them in greeting, then flitting on about their business. Circles of dancing Fae dotted the hillside with glowing bonfires, the tunes of many different musical instruments wafting across the hills. The Fae musicians used the sounds of nature as their inspiration, so it wasn't surprising that they made a harmonious and appealing composition. Jacob wondered if any of the circles contained euphoric humans who had stumbled into them tonight to dance until dawn.

"Do you think Keldwyn misses our mountains the way we do?" Lyssa asked unexpectedly.

"I think it's hard to get into that old bastard's mind. But yes, I think he does." He looked down at her, leaning against his shoulder as they walked.

"I've often thought that's a measure of what a person truly is. If some part of them yearns for quiet and peace, for places of solitude, then no matter what else they seem to be, that's the window into their soul, into who they really are. Or want to be."

"So what about Rhoswen?"

"I think she's a powerful sorceress and queen who's had to build a lot of layers inside herself to be who she is. So she's afraid of those quiet places. Of the things that will be said to her soul there, buried under those layers."

"Hmm." Jacob watched a group of Fae fly across the field, several of them doing somersaults to avoid the chase of the others. "When I was preparing to be your servant, Thomas had me do a lot of sitting by myself in the chapel. He said that we have to be brave enough to face the stillness inside ourselves. He said Purgatory is like a monk's cell. The stillness will either drive you mad enough to tear the brain out of your own head to silence whatever voices rise out of it, or you'll find acceptance and true quiet, a peace that might make you wish you never had to leave that cell."

"Or the mountains, in our case or Keldwyn's." She slanted him a glance. "Then there are those whose heads are already filled with silence, because of all the empty space there."

She shoved him off balance, caught the hem of her skirt and was gone, running across the field. He watched her go, grinning, giving her a headstart mainly because he liked watching her run, the attractive movement of her breasts as she turned, the quiver of the small curves, the brush of her hair against her delectable ass. When she startled a covey of birds that looked like doves, their white wings gleaming against the moonlight, she laughed, turning among them, raising her arms as if she could fly as well.

He took off after her then. She bounded through the grasses as if she might transform into a slim-legged black hart herself, with shiny hooves and sharp horns, deceptively delicate-looking. Unlike the white hart earlier, he was pretty sure he could catch this one—and that his lady would approve of him doing so. He caught her at the forest edge, clamping an arm around her waist and swinging her into him, but she ducked under his hold and took off again. This time she shed the dress as she moved, flinging it away and transforming in one swift movement into her Fae form, launching herself on the leathery wings. He cut left, using his momentum to push off against the trunk of the nearest solid tree and leap through the air. When he snagged one slim leg before she could get above the tree line, she twisted with him, her hands sliding intimately over his chest and hip as she wrestled with him. He made sure they landed safely, though her wings slapped him, none-too-gently.

With a chuckle and an oath, he gave her sleek gray flank a healthy smack that won him an indignant shriek and a nip from the sharp teeth. Her talons scraped his flesh as she rolled.

The key was controlling her wings, so he made sure he had her pinned beneath him in short order, her wrists above her head, body pressed on her stomach into the forest floor. As she struggled, he knew she was fully aware of how that would rouse his predator instinct, make him harder. Reaching beneath her, he ran his hand down her firm belly, finding the bare mound there, teasing her. Her body transformed then, back to the pale flesh of his vampire queen. He could sense she had more mischief planned, and braced himself to be turned into a tree, his cock a branch protruding at just the right angle.

"It had better be a very smooth branch," she said, with a tiny sound that might have been a giggle. He smiled, pressed his face to her neck.

"I'm glad to hear your laughter, my lady. I worry about you. The moods you've been feeling tonight."

A sigh pressed them both more deeply into the earth. Lyssa embraced that cool cradle, with his welcome heat against her back, all around her. "You're right. I've never resented my responsibilities. I embrace them, because it's what I am born to be. But when I saw the hate in her face, I felt so . . . tired. Tonight, I crave something that will renew my spirit. I hunger for it. I am ashamed to say this to you, when your life is so young, and you have given me so much . . ."

He turned her. "My lady, I am in your mind, and you are in mine. You've no reason to apologize. I understand. I wish I'd been at your side all these years. Perhaps, if I had been, I wouldn't be so greedy for more." His lips curved. "Though in fairness, I doubt I'd feel any differently if I'd been with you all thousand of those years. No amount of time with you will ever be enough. Let's walk. You know walking helps you."

Recovering her dress, he helped her slide it over her head. As he did, he freed her hair, bent and kissed the hollow of her throat. Lyssa tilted her cheek against his hand. Before her eyes closed, she saw a trio of griffins fly across the face of the moon.

As they strolled onward, they found various Fae celebrations in the woods, tiny circles or larger ones, with copious amounts of singing, dancing and feasting. One of the smallest circles, where the participants looked no bigger than the tiny army men Jacob had possessed as a child, noticed them passing. A cadre of the small Fae flew over to capture strands of Lyssa's hair, lifting them in the air to try and tug her over. They did the same to Jacob, though since his hair was shorter and he was wearing much less, he was pinched in a variety of improper places by impish female Fae.

"What does the lore say about going into a Fae circle?" she asked, laughing, as they moved toward the circle, which was the size of a manhole cover.

"It's a danger if you're in the mortal world. While you think no time is passing, it might be centuries. I think we can trust it on this side of things, however, given that you're already Fae. I assume you'll protect me."

She offered an unreassuring snort at that. When they stopped at the boundary of the circle, the tiny Fae squeaked at them. "Come, come! Join our feast."

Jacob clasped her hand, gave her a wink, and they both stepped one foot gingerly into the circle, trying not to put toes in the feast table.

Instantly, the table was before them. Lyssa saw all the tiny Fae were their size, surrounding them in the ongoing revels. They had a large clearing to dance, and a troupe of musicians were vigorously sawing out tunes on their instruments.

No, my lady. They didn't get larger. We are now the same size as them, as long as we're in their circle.

Their hands were seized, Lyssa by male Fae, Jacob by females, and they were pulled into a chain of dancers. It twisted and turned, the required steps causing a change of partners that broke and came back together, swinging one another around. Jacob saw Lyssa laughing again, being passed from partner to partner, just as he did the same. It was a combination of mad whirling Irish jigs and contra dancing. The caller, a long-faced Fae with fingers the length of breadsticks, perched high on a tree branch and called out each change in a thunderous baritone over the cries and laughter.

The twisting and turning turned into a closed circle, one couple trapped in the center. When they tried to force their way out, they were good-naturedly contained as the circle moved forward and back, pushing them into each other. "A kiss, a kiss . . ." came the cry. "Make time stop with a kiss . . ."

A shy look exchanged between the two suggested an attraction existed, but hadn't been acted upon before now. Apparently their friends were taking advantage of the night to force the issue.

The girl, a pretty creature with curly red hair, pointed ears and brown eyes, was the one who made the first move. With a smile of joyous abandon, she leaped upon the slender Fae male. Wrapping her arms around his neck and her legs around his hips, she put her mouth to his, burying her hands in his long hair. He staggered back, to the roaring jeers of his friends, but then he quickly recovered, holding her tight and drawing out the kiss, making it deeper. As he did, and gained more confidence, he added a flare. He began to turn, continuing the steps of the dance to loud approval.

When she broke the kiss, she dropped her head and upper body back, trusting him to hold her in that position as they spun. Her friends reached out and brushed her outstretched fingertips, holding them briefly as she turned.

As he let her down on her feet, they continued the dance, moving into the flow once again, their cheeks flushed and eyes sparkling, absorbed in each other as the twisting and turning began anew.

The game was repeated with several more couples. Each time they were maneuvered inside the temporary prison, Jacob noted the demands became more bawdy. One husband was required to give his wife a smart spanking with the flat of his hand for her reputed sharp tongue, and then follow that up with an apologetic kiss on the offended part of her anatomy. For the next couple, they required the male to unlace the female's corset with his teeth, his hands held behind his back. When it loosened enough that it dropped lower on her waist, revealing pert nipples beneath a thin shift, he was rewarded with a kiss in the tender cleft, the girl holding his head there with a broad smile as they began to spin together again.

In the turning and twisting, hands were becoming far more familiar, particularly toward whomever each Fae regarded as his or her intended for the evening. Fun and frivolity were turning to greater acts of lust and desire as the night deepened. Then Jacob made a misstep and found himself in the circle, Lyssa thrust in on the other side.

One woman tossed a tree branch into the center of the ring, a thick stick perhaps three inches in diameter. Jacob didn't want to even consider the purpose, alarmed by what Lyssa had mentioned about smooth bark. But then a stout matron hollered out the terms.

"Gotta get him as thick as that, lovey. Won't get out of there until you do!"

"And if he's got a small 'un, guess you'll just have to use the stick to beat on it until it's swollen up from bruises." That came from a ruddy-faced faun, but the stout woman retorted, quick enough.

"We can see him well enough in those hose. Unless he's got himself a loaf of bread in there, he'll do."

More laughter. When Jacob tried a mock escape, there were shrieks and giggles, a lot of very intimate groping that sent him scampering without a great deal of dignity back to the center. Lyssa was considering him, a very unsettling smile on her face. Whatever else it was accomplishing, it was getting her mind off her earlier shadows, or at least pushing them to the back.

"Take the hose down, Jacob," she said, meeting his gaze. "I want to watch your cock respond to me without it in the way."

That brought a pause to the watching group. Though there was an escalating sexual dynamic, these were country Fae, so to speak. While Rhoswen knew the subtleties of a relationship like theirs, it wasn't so much a formal practice, even at the high-court level. So this was a show they weren't used to seeing. With that one command, she managed to inject the clearing with that sexual tension she'd always done so well. A tension that had his cock answering, no matter what the rest of him thought, being ogled by so many females, perilously close.

Meeting her gaze, a rueful smile on his lips, he hooked the hose, skinned them down his legs, took them off with his boots and put it all aside, bracing his feet to stand before her completely bare of everything except the cross brand, the lashes on his back, and that third servant mark. He knew it always did something to her, seeing him stripped of everything but those three things. Her servant. Her slave. Her lover, bound to her for eternity.

It made him hard, too, seeing the way it affected her. There were prurient titters, and a wash of good-natured heckling as it was clear he was already getting aroused. He'd attended vampire dinners full of malevolence, the intent to degrade and humiliate while sending a servant into an orgasm with blackout intensity. This was different. This night was about pleasure and remembrance, a loss of inhibitions, letting everything go. Their audience was aroused, delighted, wanting to see what would happen next. When he was a teenager, this was the bacchanalia he and Gideon had read about as they pored surreptitiously through their mother's books. Pan coming to the circle with his aroused member and his pipe to inspire dancing, coupling. He himself would couple with woman after woman, ensuring fertility, celebrating pleasure and life.

Lyssa began to dance, in a way he'd never seen her dance before. Her hips lifted, fell, moved in a figure eight like an exotic belly dancer as she turned. As part of the dance movement, she removed her dress entirely, so now he could see exactly how she was moving, the way her naked hips did the maneuver, how her back arched and her arms reached, tilting her breasts up toward him.

He couldn't help a possessive glance toward the males in the audience. Finding them all riveted, he pushed down his desire to snatch the nearest cloak and cover her. His old-fashioned ideas always asserted themselves at the most inconvenient circumstance. Still, he wished she was doing this for him in her bedroom back in Atlanta.

Focus on me, Jacob. This is all for you, and your cock.

He doubted he could make himself look away again, anyway. She undulated into a back bend, bringing her feet over her head in a slow, sensual flow of motion, winning an *ooh* from the audience, who usually accomplished such a movement with wings. Then she was reaching toward him as if in supplication, swaying on her knees like a flower on its stem, her hair falling down her bare back, her hand and arm motions a twisting ballet. Everything her body was doing suggested how it would writhe under or over his. As she spun to her feet, her pace quickening, her buttocks quivering with the motion of her hips, she took her hands down her torso, cupping her breasts and then sliding lower. When some of the flowers were tossed to her, she caught them, crushed the petals over her breasts, slid the silken feathers of them down to her sex.

As her hands slid upward once more, her gaze locked with his, that challenge and invitation at once as she reached her throat and collared herself with her left hand, the other sweeping back down, planting a clear image in his mind of the times he'd knelt over her, holding her on her back like that. The vampire dominance had taken over as he collared her throat with one hand, fingered her clit with the other until she came. She'd strain against his hold, letting him take her surrender, even as her green eyes glowed with a Mistress's sure knowledge that she could bring him to his knees, make him her slave whenever she chose. Whenever she ordered him.

"I think he's making that branch look like a twig, Maggie," one of the males crowed. "Course, I think she's giving us all stout branches of our own. Perhaps we should take them out, let her have her pick?"

"You pull anything out of those trousers, Homer, I *will* whack it with that stick."

Somewhere during her performance, the musicians had started playing, an erotic woodwinds melody that picked up her movements. When Lyssa at last brought her dance to a conclusion right before him, the music faded away. Keeping her eyes on his, she reached down, picked up the branch in question. A smile was on her lips, but the intensity in her eyes was what absorbed him as she laid the branch alongside his cock, let him feel the rough bark on his sensitive skin. Her fingertips brushed him, making the organ jump. He was wet at the slit.

"Almost," she murmured. "Maybe a mouth would help. Hands behind your neck, my handsome servant. Eyes closed."

He swallowed. "My lady, don't . . ."

Obey me.

He did, every muscle quivering in resistance as he heard the crowd respond with a sensual wave of approbation as her knees touched his insoles and her heated mouth closed over him. He steeled his resolve, tried to remember every reason not to come, the most important one being that she hadn't given him permission. He didn't like her on her knees before him like this, in front of them, and she knew it. Which was why she did it, to prove that she could do whatever she liked, if it gave her pleasure.

I may be on my knees, but you know how helpless you are to me right now, Jacob. It is not the position that proves power. You and I both understand that.

She suckled him hard, teased him beneath and he bit back an oath.

"He's going to lose it, darling. Best not push him too hard. Check the branch."

She withdrew from him, and he felt the branch push against him again, followed by a chorus of cheers. Thank God, mission accomplished. She rose, sliding her bare body up his, letting that wet tip kiss her abdomen. Then there was a whirl of motion as the dance was in play again. Maggie tossed her dress back to her. However, they were not the only ones underdressed now. Many of the Fae shed tunics or corsets to press bare skin against soft, thin fabrics. Jacob managed to get his hose and boots back on, despite having to be fairly agile and tolerant of the female hands that inhibited him, as well as dealing with an enormous erection to fit back under snug hose.

He noted that Lyssa was treated far more respectfully, other women forming a circle around her until she'd replaced the dress and could take their hands to start the turning, winding line of dancing again. However, this time, as she and Jacob came back together, they were maneuvered to the boundary of the dance area. With a smile and a blown kiss from the Fae couple nearest them, they were pushed over that line.

Suddenly, they were alone in the forest again. Or not entirely. Jacob looked down and saw the circle they'd left. As the tiny figures continued to dance, several hands raised in affable farewell.

16

"I'LL be damned."

Jacob looked up at his lady. She was breathing hard, and so was he, though he didn't need to breathe. Her eyes were alive, that deep jade color that told him she was wildly aroused. He was more than willing to accommodate her, what with his tree branch erection and all.

"There'll be no living with that first chap," he said casually. "Now that he proved he could kiss his girl in a way that stops time for her and all the other lasses."

"I think she was the one who kissed him. Do you wish you could stop time for those other lasses?"

"The only one I've ever wanted to stop time for was you, my lady." Reaching out, he caught her fingertips. She drew close enough to pluck the petals off his shoulder that had fallen there during the dancing. It was a distraction that allowed her to brush her body against him.

"You are a magnet for female trouble," she informed him.

Jacob lifted his brow, raked her with a suggestive gaze. "Like you don't attract your fair share of overly zealous male attention."

"Not so much here. Except for the likes of Arrdol." She couldn't help the shudder, and his gaze darkened, his hand tightening on hers. "It bothers me that memory has such a hold on me," she added. "A memory that is gone and done. It makes me angry that I froze like that. I should have done something."

"I expect she had her chambers heavily enchanted to prevent you. It might not have stopped you, but it would have drained your strength considerably."

"But I would have tried," she said, and there was an edge to her voice. "That means something. I froze like a victim. And I will not ever be that."

"No, you won't. You aren't."

"Yet I seem to be fighting that feeling all too often these days."

He squeezed her hands. "Over two years, you lost your husband and your former servant. Your husband betrayed you, violated you with his best friend." He paused, wishing he didn't have to bring that one up, knowing that Arrdol had done that recently enough. "The Council betrayed your loyalty, you were a fugitive in the mountains for months. You had a child and lost your vampire powers. You've only recently had any time to feel the impact of all that, my lady. You need time. That's all."

She sighed. "Time is something we rarely have, Jacob."

As they walked onward, the forest ended. They were in a clearing with a lush lagoon. Coming to the steep bank, they looked down on the water, where lotus blossoms floated across the mirrored expanse and the branch tips of willow trees drifted in the current created by the breeze. They made him think of tree dryads, materializing enough to trail their fingers through the water to create ripples. Or dipping their hands in to pour the water along the smooth bark of their trunks, which would shimmer into sleek female bodies and back to trunks again. The magic of the place was heavy in the air, but there was a potency to it that warned Jacob. He laid his hand on Lyssa's arm, instinctively shifting in front of her, watchful.

Then he heard that whisper of song, and knew the danger of the place was not to her. *Damn it.* Sirens again. However, that whisper didn't have the same pull on him as before, perhaps because it was the first time he wasn't weak from blood loss. But it had a different note to it. It was a sigh of true pleasure, not one intended to ensorcel a man's mind. At least, no more than any woman's sigh of pleasure could grip a man's attention.

Lyssa caught his arm, drawing him down to a seated position on the bank, their presence concealed by the foliage there. She nodded to the far end of the lagoon that the willow trees had hidden from their view.

There were seven water nymphs, all long limbs and beautiful bodies in various shades of color . . . milky cream, chocolate brown, Dahlia's deep ebony, golden . . . they had lotus blossoms in their hair, twined around their limbs and throat, mixing with intricate silver tattoos that curved around their arms, their upper bodies, their hips. As he watched them, Jacob was sure his lady's gaze was as wide as his own. Not because of the nymphs, who were of course remarkable, but because of who was with them.

Angels. A good dozen of them. They looked like soldiers of some sort, because those that were still clothed wore the same uniform. A red belted half kilt, the buckle scrolled with what looked like a military designation. They'd been well armed, though their weaponry was currently laid aside. Knives, bows and arrows, long, gleaming swords. Even though the immortals Jacob had met—Fae and vampire—never suffered from soft bodies, these men were every inch warriors, a trained hardness to the muscles Jacob knew well. Some bore scars to underscore it.

The wing color varied as much as the sirens' smooth skin. White, ebony, brown like a hawk. One had an arbitrary scattering of crimson feathers among the white. Folded against their backs, the wings were like impressive cloaks, the tips crossing at their ankles, brushing the ground.

They didn't seem ensorcelled by the sirens. Instead, it was a mutual pleasure taking, a variety of intimate pairings and ménages. He saw one siren in between two of the angels, her hand gripping the battle kilt of the one behind her as he obviously rocked her on him, while the other entered her from the front, his wings spreading in impressive display to balance him, give their penetration a smooth, rolling rhythm that had her moaning. Her head fell back on the shoulder of the one behind, her other hand fastened on the belted strap across the front angel's chest.

There was some wooing going on as well. Or perhaps that was merely the aftermath, before the angels and sirens in question began again. Lyssa gripped his hand. Since they were sitting in the grass, he pulled her between his legs, cinching her up against his still erect cock.

Would you have me take you like this, my lady, while you watch?

Yes. But I want to be in the water, among them.

He would have advised her to be more cautious, but for two reasons. One, it wasn't the first time he and his lady had dealt with angels. Intertwined with the heated sensuality was a familiar and undeniable . . . rightness, for lack of a better word. While their previous exposure with the beings had been brief, then as now, he knew in his gut these males weren't a threat to his lady.

Pressing a kiss to her hand, he rose, guiding her down the bank to the farther end of the lagoon. When they reached the edge, she dropped the dress to the side, and cut into the water. Her purr of approval told him the water was a good temperature for her, which typically meant it would be too hot for him. It was also shallow, almost to her chin, which was good, since vampires had no buoyancy. When he followed her, he found whatever enchantment existed upon the water, it matched his temperature preference as well. She moved into his arms, melting easily into a heated kiss, a continuation of the desire ignited in the Fae circle. They turned together, a slower form of that Fae dance, sinking even further into that meeting of mouths, the meshing of bodies. He reflected such a kiss did in fact slow time.

It brings it to a complete, blissful stop.

As he tightened his arms upon her, creatures moved past his legs with nibbling mouths and slippery fins, but they meant no harm. The lotus blossoms floated around them, brushing against Lyssa's bare back and collecting in that shallow valley, her hair tangling with the flowers. An occasional feather drifted past, dislodged from what was happening around the bend of the lagoon. They could see the angels and nymphs, could hear the sounds of their pleasure, but at the moment, they were lost in one another.

Jacob took them both under, so when they emerged her wet lashes were thick around her green eyes, her hair slicked back on her delicate skull. She wanted to renew that kiss, and climbed up his body to do so, holding him fast, his cock brushing the base of her buttocks as she sucked on his mouth, taking the sweet taste of the water away. When she nipped at him, she earned a growl from the animal in him as well. Skin to skin, bone to bone. He could feel every rib under his fingertips, the beat of her heart, rapid against his. Her legs constricted around him, muscles straining to hold him even closer. All that glorious wet hair, his fingers buried into it.

"Easy, my lady," he murmured. "No rush. Just this, all night long." A night prolonged by Fae magic. He could feel her need to move past the earlier melancholy, giving her desire a sharp edge. He soothed it, with mouth and hands. As he worked his way down, he coaxed her to lie back, stare up at the night sky as he gripped her waist, holding her level on the water's surface.

When a wingtip touched the water to his left, he raised his head. No more than an arm's length away, an angel was in the water with them. He had a handsome, intent expression, framed by golden brown hair. His wings were folded close on his back, so mostly Jacob saw broad shoulders. His eyes had no whites, all solid dark pupil, so it was impossible to read his expression, except that Jacob felt no threat from him.

His lady's gaze shifted to the winged male. As she did, the angel reached out, twined fingers in her dark hair, working his way from there to support the back of her neck with one hand, holding her level for Jacob.

"It's easier this way, no?" he said. His voice was as compelling as the sirens, only without the destructive grip of obsession. It evoked trust, desire and command all at once. "I am Raphael, my lady. And it seems you might have need of one more to help your servant give you pleasure."

Lyssa shifted her gaze to Jacob. Interestingly, her servant waited to see what her will would be, with no undercurrent of possessiveness or resentment. But then he knew her so well, saw the way she reacted to having the both of them so close, so willing to meet her needs. And his intuition reached even deeper than that.

A while back, Jacob and his brother Gideon had shared Lyssa, at her invitation. It had been the polar opposite of the nightmare Arrdol had resurrected within her. She was ready to banish the latter, wanted to enjoy being enveloped in male attention. More than that, she wanted the feelings that came with it. The neediness, the greed for life, to take more than the usual offering. She needed that tonight. If she could grasp that elusive feeling, she'd have the strength to tell the Rhoswens and Vampire Councils of the world they could kiss her regal ass. They had no hold on who and what she was.

Jacob's lips curved, and he sunk lower, taking himself to the water line. Levering himself between her knees, he spread them with wet hands sliding along her thighs. Raphael moved to stand just above her head, his hand still beneath her neck, but he flattened his other palm on her sternum, spreading his fingers so they followed the rise of her breasts in ten distinct lines of sensation. None of them made contact with the nipples, but from the caress and kneading of just that much of the small curves, the nipples became more erect under his and Jacob's intent gazes. Jacob put his mouth between her legs then. In his mind, she saw his enjoyment of the mix of the water with her slippery heat. Incredibly responsive to having a mouth on her cunt, particularly Jacob's, she arched up like a mermaid, making the water ripple out from her body. Raphael slid his hands under her shoulders and dropped lower in the water himself, leaning back so she was braced on his chest, but at an angle where she could see his large hands on her breasts, Jacob feasting on her with his mouth.

Jacob curled his tongue over her clit, licked, slid slow and deep into the channel beneath, then came back out again, teasing the labia with lashes of his tongue and pressure that had her working herself against his mouth, a reaction always sure to make him hard as a brick wall. Raphael gripped her breasts together, then gave the nipples one hard flick with his thumbs that had her crying out. Her mind was being taken over by swirling reds, no words. But Jacob knew what she wanted. After the Fae circle, she was close, so close, but she wanted nothing less than him inside her.

Inside me . . .

Raphael lifted her and Jacob accepted the gift, curving his arms around her back and hips to bring her close. As he did, Raphael moved in behind her. His wings spread out, brushing the skin with a shivery, tingling sensuality as they curved forward and shadowed her on either side. They brushed Jacob's shoulders. The angel pushed her hair to one side and placed a single kiss on her throat, as if he knew the significance of such an erogenous place for a vampire, full powered or not. Lyssa shuddered in Jacob's arms, held him tighter, her eyes closing. Her mind was that maelstrom again, hard to decipher, but he held her low on her hips, watched Raphael put a kiss lower, along her spinal column. She trembled.

Jacob tipped her face up and kissed her again, long and deep, using his tongue to tease her mouth. Raphael slid his hands along her waist as Jacob gripped her hips, curving over her bottom. The water was slippery, a natural lubricant with all the plant life and its oils spilling into the water, though her pussy didn't need it. As she adjusted, she inadvertently captured his cock head. It lodged in that opening, and he pressed his hand against her cheek, making her eyes open, stare into his.

"What do you want, my lady? Do you want us both inside of you?"

"Yes." Her voice was throaty, eyes intent on his. "I want that." She bit her lip as Raphael shifted his grip so it overlapped Jacob's on her hips.

"A slow slide down," the angel murmured in her ear. His wings folded fully around them now, enclosing them in a wall of feathers that brushed the skin and made the moment even more magical and unexpected. Any other male touching his lady usually raised Jacob's ire. Whether or not it was because this male was a heavenly host, Jacob could sense how his lady, so blessed with natural sensuality, wanted them both; how much she wanted this moment. He could deny her nothing. There were perhaps thousands of angels named Raphael in honor of the archangel, but if it was him, Raphael was gifted with the power of healing. And Jacob knew Lyssa could use a touch of healing tonight. Perhaps they both could.

The love he bore her, and she for him, was so clear. The angel was a carnal male, capable of being aroused by a woman like Lyssa, wanting to fuck her like any other male, but there was a broad love and acceptance in him as well that reinforced Jacob and Lyssa's love for one another.

Lyssa made a pleasurable noise as Raphael put his fingers inside her tight rear entrance. When he seated her more deeply on Jacob, he was pushing her down further on his fingers as well, preparing her.

"Relax and surrender to males who love you, sweet queen. It's not a matter of giving up, giving in to your exhaustion. It's a matter of letting it go. Let it all go. Experience this moment, every moment, in its shining clarity. Let the healing power of it inside of you."

He arched her back then, those soft, mesmerizing words replaced by something more urgent as Jacob bent and captured her breast in his mouth. Raphael nipped her throat, his hair brushing over Jacob's head.

She let out a small cry as Raphael replaced his fingers with himself, and began to enter her, sharing the limited space the two channels had, one of them already occupied by Jacob. Her fingers bit into Jacob's shoulder and he increased the suckling at her nipples, even as he adjusted himself inside of her, ready to stroke when Raphael was positioned.

Now they weren't alone in the water. The sirens and the angels had gravitated toward them, the various groupings swimming, kissing, twined around one another.

"Do not worry. I can neutralize the effect of the sirens on you, Jacob." Raphael lifted his head to give him that one reassurance, those dark eyes flickering. It was timely, because one siren brushed Jacob's back, then slid beneath the water. He made a noise in his throat, his mouth still on his lady as the siren's hands spread his legs so she could suck one of his testicles into the teasing heat of her mouth. Her fingers played between his buttocks, a brief tempting stimulation before she emerged and turned herself against his back, her generous buttocks braced on the upper rise of his as an angel apparently lifted and reentered her, using Jacob's anchored stance as a brace.

It pushed him farther into Lyssa, and of course Raphael responded in kind. Another angel had done the same with his siren, bracing her against Raphael, so now the angel turned his head to kiss that female as well, taking advantage of her lips as his hands stroked down Lyssa's arms, gripped her slender biceps, and he rocked forward into her.

Lyssa cried out, and Jacob stared into her eyes as he pushed in from the other direction, taking her up high, not quite letting her go over the edge, just building her with all the heated stimulation around them, knowing she needed it to go on as long as possible. The brush of feathers against their skin, the vivid reality of flesh meeting flesh in urgent need . . . Soft singing was going on somewhere on the bank, that ethereal beauty of the siren's song that he could now hear with a clear mind. It was yearning, desire, the ultimate search for ecstasy and peace at once.

He and Raphael could give her that, leaving her no fear or uncertainty, only pleasure. She'd learned a long time ago that full control wasn't always possible. But lack of control didn't mean loss of control. It was that which had plagued her since her transition, and the situation with Arrdol had underscored it. Tonight, though, only pleasure was ruling her.

Lyssa raked her nails down Jacob's chest as the sensation built. The siren was undulating hard against his back, responding enthusiastically to what the angel was doing to her, which felt like a great deal of powerful thrusting.

It was spiritual, visceral, primal, everything. She was lost in it, spinning almost like she'd been during the dance. Raphael's gaze was on her face, those solid black eyes like gemstones as he tipped her head back. "There is nothing to fear," he said. "You've always known that. Endings always come back to beginnings, and you will always find the one you need there."

The siren and angel behind Jacob shifted away, so now he pulled out of her and dropped under the waterline. Clasping her white thighs, he found the treasure of her heat once again. She was convulsing on the emptiness as if his cock was still there, but he could feel the reverberation of Raphael stroking into her ass as Jacob suckled her clit in his mouth, made it more prominent, her thighs trembling under his hands.

She thrashed, but in pleasure, and he held on, using his strength to take her even higher. He could tell Raphael was doing the same, holding her biceps so that they were essentially restraining her, but not in a way that reminded her of Arrdol or Carnal, the source of her dark nightmares. In her mind he saw she was immersed in the pleasure they were giving her. She'd discarded those fears and reached out to embrace that magnificent well of inner strength he'd never known to fail her. No fear would rule her pleasure, her happiness. Her savoring of every moment. Not his Mistress.

He teased her clit, plunged his tongue inside of her, until he knew she was hovering on that edge, then he pulled out and sank his fangs into her thigh, tasting the rich femoral blood. It nearly pushed her over, only the pain balancing her on that precipice.

On such a magical night, in a world where the exercise of magic was celebrated, it shouldn't have surprised him that along with unleashing her desire, loosening her hold on her fears, she also let her own special talents out to play. When he broke the surface of the water, he felt the power emanating from her, saw it sparking along her white skin. The lotus blossoms and water lilies now had company. Roses as large as his lady's hand had appeared on empty pads or joined the water lilies, making clusters of two to three blooms, in deep pinks, traditional rose, and all shades in between. He saw Raphael smile as his lady's magic expanded into a shower of rose petals, fluttering through the air like a gentle rain. They caught in the angel's wings and landed in the water, becoming spinning small boats for the delighted firefly Fae. More roses were climbing the banks as well, twining along the willow trunks, the air filling with their fragrance.

Jacob slid back into her again, moving in close so he and Raphael could synchronize their movements. She kissed Jacob, her mouth eager and hot, and he clasped her skull, tangling his fingers in her hair. He thrust back into her hard, into that tight channel made even more constricted by Raphael's presence. She moaned at the sensation, her legs locking hard on his hips.

"Come for us now, my lady. Share your magic with us."

Her jade eyes opened to stare into his, the pupil expanding to take over the green as he and Raphael stroked her, a relentless rhythm, no pause in the sensation and arousal. Raphael had spread his wings again, so that he provided an additional force and source of control to create an excruciating rhythm for them all. Even as that climax began to grip them, Jacob both despaired and delighted at that Mistress glint in her eyes.

Not . . . until . . . I . . . go.

He shook his head, acknowledging her. He always obeyed such a command, but fuck, the tightening of her muscles on him, on them both, made it difficult. Then Raphael pushed the issue by releasing, giving her that searing explosion of sensation along all the sensitive nerve endings in her rectum. She clamped down on Jacob like a vise, rubbing slick muscle against him, pumping hard, fast. The smell of roses grew stronger, and the blooms pressed against his body.

She gave a long, fierce, triumphant cry, like a warrior queen throwing out a challenge as she embraced the pleasure, let go of the fear, of whatever might have plagued her. She defied it and fully embraced that magical energy to find renewal in his arms. The arms of her soul mate, her beloved.

They were fragments of feelings, so strong they became disjointed thoughts, but he caught each one as treasure. When her eyes met his, her lips trembling on the consent, he gave her his seed, releasing hard and strong. He held nothing back as well, both of them trusting an angel's wings to keep them steady and on course as the wildness took them.

~

When they all slowly came down, Lyssa rested her head on Jacob's shoulder, making a quiet murmur as Raphael withdrew from her. He wrapped a wing around them, gave both a kiss, though Lyssa noticed he kissed Jacob on the forehead while he tipped up her chin for a lingering, memorable kiss on the lips. Breaking the contact, the angel gave Jacob a broad wink and Lyssa a smile before he retreated.

The other angels were preparing to leave, their pleasure sated as well. When Raphael moved in that direction, he bestowed similarly appreciative kisses on the several sirens who stopped him for that purpose. He was an obvious favorite with them. Generously, he didn't cut short a single embrace, and was lavish with his skilled caresses.

Though it amused Lyssa, she sensed the sirens were drawn to the same thing that had led her and Jacob to trust him for the remarkable interlude. There was a healing power not only in his touch, but his very presence. The flashes of gentle humor in his expression didn't make light of the world. Instead they conveyed he knew how very terrible the world could be. The weapons they picked up off the bank looked entirely too well used, including the spear and sword he hefted for himself. A spear that could return like a boomerang . . .

Watching him, she realized that, for Raphael, there were no significant walls between Fae, vampire or humans. This being was top of the food chain, but he accepted all life as precious and natural. Feeling that emanation as he joined them in shared sensual pleasure offered the hope that other powerful beings, such as Fae and vampire, could reach the same point.

Despite the darkness of the world surely an angel would know, he'd obviously preserved a well of joy in himself. Tonight he'd shared a glimpse of that with Lyssa, giving her a sense of perspective she'd been lacking. Jacob bent, kissed her hand, holding it in wet fingers, giving her the warmth of his mouth and his feelings, responding to hers.

Raphael donned his kilt when they drew closer to the bank, and now he sketched a bow in their direction. "Thank you, my lady." He nodded at all the roses. While the gnomes were carting some off in their wheelbarrows, the sirens were gathering them up, putting them in their hair. The firefly Fae spun with the petals, holding them over their heads like umbrella coverings. "For what you have given us tonight, I would grant you a favor of your choosing."

At his words, the other angels turned. The not-so-dormant power that pulsed around them was unnerving, a reminder that they saw the world from an entirely different view—the heavens.

"You are the one who gave me a gift tonight, my lord." Despite being naked, Lyssa knelt in the shallows. It was the first time Jacob had ever seen her do that, but she did it with grace and obvious reverence. "It is more than enough," she added.

"It was an equal exchange. No argument. Give me the wish of your heart."

She looked at Jacob, and he tightened his hand on hers, in perfect accord. In fact, Jacob was sure Raphael anticipated them, because his gaze had softened in approval before she spoke.

"Kane," she said. "No matter what happens to us, please protect him. Watch over him."

Raphael glanced at the assembled males behind him, arrayed in a variety of lethal weaponry. He met the gaze of the angel who seemed to be at the front of the phalanx. Serious dark eyes flickered, his chin dipping in a slight nod. "Done," Raphael said. "We will protect your child, Lady Lyssa. Have no fear of that."

Then, with one more of those smiles that seemed capable of making the worst nightmares into a distant memory, he was aloft, the others joining him. As they winged up high and fast into the sky, the sirens lifted their hands in farewell. They laughed as an angel with brown feathers swooped down to steal one last kiss, a lingering touch. As he rejoined the group, there was a flash of blue sparks, and they were gone.

~

Once they were dry, Jacob and Lyssa donned their clothes and left the lagoon. They strolled hand in hand, quiet in one another's minds. After a time, Lyssa moved in closer, slid her arms around Jacob's waist. He wrapped his around her shoulders, holding her as they walked that way, viewing the various wondrous magical sights that crossed their path during the long night. It was Lyssa who finally sensed that dawn would be approaching soon, turning their feet back to the castle.

Well before they emerged from the forest, they heard the drumbeat. A primal melody, reverberating through the ground. The many celebratory circles in the forest were gone, the smell of extinguished bonfires lingering. As they came out of the forest, they saw a great gathering covering the slopes leading up to Caislean Uisce and Caislean Talamh.

"This must be Ending Ritual," Lyssa murmured. "I didn't think to ask, because I thought it was what happened at the cemetery. But with dawn approaching, this makes more sense."

Jacob nodded. They moved along the outskirts of the gathered assembly to find a better view of what was happening in that valley between the two castles. When they reached a copse of trees, Jacob helped her up into the crook of one and then leaned against it beside her, his greater height giving him the same view.

In the center of an open circle, a large stone tablet had been erected. Thirteen cloaked Fae, six men and seven women, were grouped around it. They were hooded, their faces hidden, though Lyssa saw pale hands gesturing in graceful cohesion as they chanted along with the drums. The drums and distance would have muted the sound, except the front rows of watching Fae had picked up the chant and it was sweeping through the full crowd, the volume of voices and drumbeats growing. The power of it moved through the tree, vibrating in her chest. While she picked up pieces of the language, it was not enough to give the sense of the ritual. However, what was occurring in the center of the circle did.

Rhoswen was stretched naked upon the tablet, her hands bound in sashes of autumnal colors. Her hair was fanned out beneath her, a pale white-silver cloak. Tabor, likewise naked, lay upon her, thrusting into her body, his powerful shoulders flexing. He had his gaze locked with hers, and though Lyssa would say they were aware of each other, as Rhoswen and Tabor, something else had them as well, a wreath of magical energy capturing their faces and bodies, conduits for the power rolling out from the circle.

The Great Rite. The bringing together of male and female energy, representing God and Goddess, yin and yang, the fusion of balance. She'd seen it done several times during her long history, but the timing of it, the significance of Samhain, meant there might be more to it. Anxiety unfolded inside her, even as she knew there was nothing she could or would do to interfere in a sacred ritual like this. Jacob glanced up at her, picking up her agitation, but she shook her head, kept her eyes on what was happening in the circle.

They came to pinnacle together, both testament to the magic between them and Tabor's skill as a lover. Rhoswen came just before him, their cries joining together to blend in with the drums. As they climaxed, all the assembled cried out with them, a dark, sensual celebration of voices lifting to the night sky.

Tabor slowed his thrusts gradually, that aura of magical energy still wreathing his skin, glimmering like mist over the stone and the ground beneath their feet. When the drums at last receded to a steady heartbeat rhythm, two of the circle stepped forward and untied Rhoswen's hands. She wrapped them around his shoulders. For several long moments, they held each other like that, intimate, their heads pressed close. Lyssa wondered what they might be saying to one another, or if they were silent but connected, two such different souls.

At length, Tabor withdrew, rising onto his knees above her. He gave Rhoswen a nod that might have been confirmation or reassurance. The head priestess moved into the circle, wearing an antlered headdress similar to the one Rhoswen normally wore. With ritual formality, she handed Rhoswen a stone knife. Her voice rose, a trained priestess used to speaking above a crowd, though this one was now hushed, the drums silent.

"The Father, the Lord, the Protector, our King. We praise him for his sacrifice, knowing his life must end for the winter to begin, for the promise of spring to be seeded. May his life be released by the hand of the Maiden, the Mother and Crone. And by the Lover, Our Queen, the Renewer of Life."

Her words echoed in the hills and up against the walls of the four castles, which seemed to have drawn closer during the ritual. Lyssa saw people standing in the windows of all of the structures, joining the watching audience. She'd never felt such singular concentration. With the drums beating, the magic had possessed movement, like the strength of a powerful wind. Now there was utter stillness and, as Thomas had told Jacob, that was where the deepest power lay.

The priestess was joined by a young Fae girl, just past puberty, and a woman whose disproportionately swollen breasts suggested she was still nursing a child. They all bore stone knives like Rhoswen did. Lyssa tensed. "Jacob . . ."

The drums exploded into sound again, increasing to a fever pitch. All of the assembled Fae, even those in the windows, lifted their voices in one long cry. A battle cry, a cry of triumph, a savage cry. In the same moment, all four women plunged the knives into Tabor.

He stiffened, a strangled sound coming from his throat. Rhoswen had plunged her dagger into his heart and now she had her hand pressed against his chest beside the blade's entry point. The other three had pierced his back. When blood ran from the wounds, the other priests and priestesses moved forward, catching it in three chalices. As Tabor slumped, it was Rhoswen that caught him in her arms. Lyssa noted they'd known how to make the kill quick, for life was quickly dying out of his gaze, his soul already departing.

Rhoswen held him close, almost as she had just a moment before, then she turned him so he was the one lying on the stone tablet. Crossing his arms over his chest, closing his now lifeless eyes, she knelt at his feet, pressed her mouth to his arch, her hand gripping his ankle. Then she rose, several priestesses approaching to swathe her in white veils. She took the first sip from the chalice of blood the priestess offered her, before it was passed to the circle of thirteen, as well as the Maid and Mother.

"The Lady accepts the blood of the Lord," the head priestess said. "May we meditate on our gifts and lives during the dark winter months, and celebrate the coming of spring, when He is reborn, and reunited with both the Mother, the Maid and the Lover once again."

~

"You two are white as sheets. Which, given you're vampires, is saying something."

Jacob looked left to see a small gnome sitting on a cart. He was handing a squirrel almost as tall as himself pieces of an apple he was cutting into slices with a pocket knife. The squirrel moved around him in random movements, chittering, touching him with clawed feet, even as he kept waving her off. "Impatient creature. I'm cutting, I'm cutting. Hold your horses." He nodded at the tablet. "The king ain't dead. Not technically. He's immortal. He'll be dead for three days, thanks to the magic with which the knives are doused, then he wakes up, the land's renewed, et cetera, et cetera. He's done it every year since he became king, and he'll do it for five hundred years."

"What happens after the five hundredth time?" Lyssa asked. During Tabor's ritual death, she'd reached down from the tree, covering Jacob's hand with her own. Now she kept it there, though she eased her white-knuckled grip.

"He really does die. His blood and bones are given to the land. It's a special year, more powerful than all the others combined. Don't worry, though. He's got plenty more before we all have to say good-bye to him. Hopefully he'll have offspring by then as good as he is."

Jacob nodded. Of course, now that his heart rate had slowed, there was another problem closer to home to consider. For the next three days, their most powerful ally against Rhoswen would be "technically" dead. While Lyssa's raw power was a match for Rhoswen's, the Fae queen had far more years of skill and experience in using hers, and that—as well as all the Fae Guard at her disposal—gave her a deadly advantage.

Jacob thought of the way Rhoswen had knelt at Tabor's feet and kissed one. The tears shining on her face had been as genuine as any he'd seen. A complicated woman. From Lyssa's thoughtful expression, he knew she was in his head. "You think she planned it that way?" he asked. "Issuing the final quest while he's out of the picture?"

His own complicated Mistress gave him a look, a grim smile. "Absolutely."

17

THE herald came just before dawn, soon after they arrived back in their rooms. While Jacob went to answer the door, Lyssa stayed in the arched window, looking out. Many of the Fae had chosen to bed down on the slopes around the castles, falling asleep next to the smoldering remains of the bonfires. Rhoswen had disappeared into the Castle of Earth, escorted by the thirteen priests and priestesses. She wouldn't emerge for three days, sitting vigil by Tabor's side during his three-day terminal sleep.

The proximity to dawn didn't bother Jacob as much here, so he took advantage of the remaining few minutes of darkness to hand her the scroll unopened and shift into the window sill opposite her, drawing his knees up and linking his hands around them. His bare toes touched the hem of her dress.

When she opened it, a handful of rose petals fell out, their normal fragrance tangled with a scent Jacob recognized as water from the lagoon. Lyssa's gaze flicked up to him.

A queen must always have her spies.

As she began to read, her brow drew down, lips tightening. Jacob waited through what appeared to be three full readings before she handed it over to him. Rising, she moved to the wardrobe, began to leaf through the handful of clothing that had appeared in there for her over the past couple days.

Jacob looked down at the scroll.

You found your way to our world. Your servant rode a waterhorse. You survived the spear of Dagda. All admirable in their own way, but to have the right to leave or stay, you will perform one quest at my bidding, not at the fortune of circumstances or through your servant's cleverness.

As you know, Lord Reghan's punishment was to be turned into a rose bush and left in the desert to die. This bush was placed in a desert accessible through our portals, an enchanted place, a prison for those who commit crimes against the Fae.

Lord Reghan was a Fae of great power. Though he did in fact die in the desert, the rose bush has remained, a skeletal, dried up thing in the sand, refusing to be reduced to dust. When a Fae of his power dies, his soul, his essence, becomes a gemstone. That gemstone is beneath the dried rosebush, still feeding it through its power. I want the gemstone. I want the essence of my father's soul.

You will don the clothing in your wardrobe. Do not bother wearing anything else or try to put additional supplies in the pack I've provided you. They will not go through the portal. You have three days to find the rosebush. Though it takes a very, very long time for a Fae to die of starvation or thirst, there are other predators in the desert that will take advantage of your weakness as you feel those effects.

As always, you have a choice. You may go with the consort I've assigned you and stay in this world at my pleasure, or fulfill this quest. I would wish you good luck, sister, but though I wish you success, we both know I care little if I end up prying his soul essence from your lifeless fingers.

Jacob lifted his gaze back to his lady. "So much for sisterly love. She's full of shit and you know it."

"It doesn't change the fact that this is the last hurdle, the one that gives us freedom to go or stay." She'd donned leggings, a tunic and boots. He noted there was no cloak, nothing to protect her face from a desert sun.

"In three days, we could petition for that from Tabor, regardless."

"No. While he wants me to serve as liaison, he needs Rhoswen's agreement on it. He told me he was ruthless for a reason. It was a reminder. He doesn't interfere with the business of the Unseelie world except in an extraordinary circumstance, like calling off the assassination attempts on my mother. I doubt my discomfort at having to stay here as someone's consort would qualify as anything so drastic."

Not sure he agreed, but not having Tabor present to argue the point, Jacob considered the parchment, sifting through various options in his head. "Any chance you've ever grilled Mason on how he survived three hundred years in the Sahara?"

"I spent some time with him there. Not that it will be much help. This won't adhere to the usual rules of a desert."

"Was that where you learned the belly dancing?" He lifted his gaze to hers, things far different from her dance skills in his intent expression. Though she saw it, she kept her tone light.

"He taught me the steps, on a few very long nights. Did you like it?"

"I think you know the answer to that. Though I don't like to think about the ways he might have taught you."

"Possessive servant."

"Damn straight." He sobered. "This says you have to leave within the hour."

"This is my quest, Jacob. You can't go on this one, and we both know it." She nodded to the window. "Dawn will come in minutes. It's a desert. No cover, blazing hot sun. You won't survive it. I need you here, for when I come back."

The pack in the wardrobe contained a full water skin, a couple dense pieces of bread and meat, a wide brimmed hat and what appeared to be a small pruning knife. There was also a lined pouch, perhaps for carrying the gemstone. When she lifted it out and turned around, she wasn't surprised to find Jacob planted in front of her. He caught her hands and tossed the pack to the side. "How many times do we have to go through this, my lady? Where you go, I follow."

"And how do you propose to do that, Jacob?" Her temper flared as she yanked her hands back. "She's given me three days. I'm to leave in the next hour, or I forfeit the quest. She's deliberately designed this one so I have to do it alone."

"Which is why you shouldn't."

"I'll be all right. I can stay in mind contact."

"Unless that portal to the desert shuts down the mind link between us. She would have thought about that as well. I think you should call her bluff. I don't think she'll kill either one of us outright if you refuse. Tabor is now aware of your existence. If you refuse to choose either option, she might make us miserable for several days, but I don't think she'd be so ballsy she'd do something that can't be undone."

"I think she's determined to prove her autonomy at every turn. We've seen her wrath against me is quite personal and not always rational. Though our deaths might earn his great displeasure, she would weather it. In the end, she is a queen of the Unseelie. He can't unseat her without tearing Seelie and Unseelie apart, and they've both been down that road. "

"What if she thinks of another reason to keep us here, after you go through this, making it all mean nothing?"

"There are rules here, as Keldwyn said. This will be what earns me standing in her court, and that's a foundation on which everything else can be built, both here and in our own world." Lyssa gave him a sharp look. "You know all this."

He took two steps away and swore viciously, kicking the wardrobe hard enough the door slammed closed and a crack appeared in the dark wood. "My place is by your side, Lyssa, and you damn well know it."

When he turned back to her, furious, dangerous, those red sparks in his eyes, she reached up, laid her hands on his cheeks. It wasn't unexpected when he gripped her wrists, tightening in demand against her will, but she held his gaze, refused to back down.

"Your place is where I tell you to be. You are my servant, are you not? I am your Mistress."

Though he set his jaw stubbornly, she detected the first shard of helpless fury lancing through him. He knew she was going to win this one. A long time ago, she'd wondered why she accepted a difficult, alpha Irishman as a servant, instead of a more docile and accepting beta. There were many answers to that question. Now that she had him, she'd never long for such a beta instead of Jacob, but if he could occasionally revert to a more docile alterego, it would certainly make moments like this go more smoothly.

"This time, I have to go alone. You have to obey me, stay here and stay safe. I know it goes against every instinct you have in that great, noble heart of yours, but it's the way it must be. There is no other option, except failure and its consequences, and we cannot risk Rhoswen's consequences. *I* will not risk them. But beyond that, this is a quest I must follow. Not because of Rhoswen's demands or motives, not because I fear her. No matter Keldwyn's motives, or Tabor's purported alliance with me, I have to take command of my own destiny.

"Plus," she added, "I want what she wants. I want to put my hands on that rose bush. I want to hold his soul in my hand, the closest I've ever been to him. She denied me the chance to see him at the cemetery, and she has denied him. With that soul in my hand, I might at least be able to give him some peace, let him see who I've become."

Though she'd thought of her father often over the centuries, he'd been a symbol, a concept, an inspiration. Last night's events in the cemetery had made him real. She wanted to hold that true sense of him, feel his presence, let him feel hers.

He pulled back from her. "This isn't just my stubbornness, my lady, I swear. Everything in me says I'm not supposed to let you do this alone, no matter how that sounds. You've always relied on my gut before."

"But your gut is wrapped up in your feelings for me, you impossible man." She shook her head at him, wanting to smile, but things were too tight in her chest to allow that. "Remember the night I told you about my mother? About her dying of grief? I wasn't aware of it then, but the impact that left with me is part of what gave you access to my heart, Jacob. When death comes, I will meet it as a queen should, without flinching. That is my hope. But I refuse to die of loneliness, that isolation of the heart and soul never given fully to another. Because I have you, I won't. And that eases me, more than you can ever know. I can face whatever this is, because even when you are not physically at my side, you are there. Do you understand?"

As he stood, unresponsive, she stroked his face. She shut her eyes as he tightened his grip once more, but this time he pressed his lips into her palm.

"You have ever known what to say to humble me, my lady. But this tears me apart inside, you know that. I can bear anything in this world except being away from you when you might have need of me."

"Well, just think how much more appreciative I'll be of your services when I get back."

His lips tugged up in that wry smile she loved so well. "Yes. I'm certain that will be the case."

"I sense sarcasm, Sir Vagabond. Maybe you can work on that insolence problem while I'm away. Though I'm sure it would take far more than three days to resolve it. I would likely have to be involved, with a barbed whip to help inspire you."

"This flesh, heart and soul is yours to flay anytime, my lady," he assured her. He narrowed his gaze at the pack. "She's not letting you bring much."

"No." She hefted the bag. "Knowing Rhoswen's capriciousness, it's even possible this won't go through with me."

He pursed his lips, then left her to go to the nighttable. He lifted the sack Keldwyn had given him. "I'm betting this will. Wily bastard."

Retrieving his knife, he nicked his wrist, a deep gouge. Quickly pushing the narrow mouth of the sack against the wound, he let the stream of blood flow into it.

"If you get injured, this will keep you for a little while. And when I'm done here, you'll drink your fill from me, to add to it." He paused. "Or rather, I ask my lady to please take advantage of what her servant has to offer, to bolster your strength."

"You do remember how to ask permission. I was beginning to wonder. You forget your courtly demeanor when you're in a foul temper." She took over the steadying hold on the neck of the sack. "You forget you're my servant."

With the freed hand, he cupped her face, fingers wrapping around her nape. "I never forget that, my lady." She held his gaze, neither of them speaking, his blood flowing between them. When it was nearly full, she put her slim, feminine fingers around the thick wrist to bring it to her mouth. Fastening her lips over that cut, she drew deep. He muttered another oath, pulled her closer.

She at least accepted this part of his counsel, taking as much as she could without feeling overfed, enough that he looked somewhat pale when she finished. She didn't like doing that, but it would reassure him that he'd done what he could. And it wasn't patronizing him to think of it that way, because he was right. The extra blood would help if she was wounded or needed an abundance of strength.

Still, as he brought her over to the bed and stretched out on it, drawing her down upon him, she traced his mouth, brought her own to it, let him taste his blood there. "What about you? How will you feed to replenish yourself?"

"I'll figure out something. How are you going to find the rose bush?"

"The same." She gave him her mysterious smile, but also showed him an indication of what she was thinking. With Rhoswen's spies about, she wasn't going to voice it. He nodded thoughtfully.

"That might work. Of course, maybe one day our Fae friends will start giving straight answers to simple questions."

"Peace and love will overflow in our world before such an unlikely thing happens."

"I can see the Vampire Council sharing a group hug now."

"I'd kill all of them out of sheer horror. Mason would help."

The skin around his blue eyes creased, appreciating her, but then they held gazes for another long moment. Standing up on the bed, she slid off her leggings, accepting his hands on her calves to steady her. "Take off the hose."

He complied, and he was swelling for her, ready. She came down on him, slowly, letting him penetrate deep. "Your hands above your head, love," she whispered. "Give yourself to me, utterly."

He wanted to touch, hold, but he did it, his jaw working as she seated herself fully with a soft sigh. Her nipples were taut, straining against the snug fit of her tunic as she arched back, her hands reaching behind her to course up his inner thighs, run her nails over the sensitive flesh there.

She loved the way he felt inside of her. The first time she'd taken him this way, restrained merely by her command, was in her pool at the Atlanta estate. She'd fed from him and taken her own pleasure, but had not given herself the gift of intimacy with him. She regretted that now. Regretted every moment she spent holding herself away from him. The relationship had become so much more, once she learned to trust him as much as she demanded that he trust her. Bending down, she teased his throat with her tongue and teeth, moved down to lick at his nipple as she tightened her muscles on him, sliding down, then back up.

"Fuck, you're wet," he managed. "Let me touch you."

She shook her head. It was easier here, to pull magic from the energy between them, from the earth itself. His gaze snapped up as the posts of the bed became thick, rootlike branches that curved around his wrists, his forearms, reminiscent of what she'd done to him at the trellis at Mason's home. Only this time her magic was even stronger. The roots held him fast no matter how his biceps bunched, straining against them. The growth continued, over his chest, under, arching him up off the bed so when she came back down, scored his nipple with sharp teeth, drawing a tiny drop of blood, he let out a strangled sound, fingers flexing.

Behind her, the posts at the end of the bed were sprouting roots as well, roots that wound around his bare legs, then up and up, until she felt the rough texture of them slide against her inner thighs. He made a startled noise as one of those roots snaked underneath his testicles, putting pressure there as it insinuated itself between his buttocks, stopping as it reached the small of his back. Then it swelled to a thickness that parted the cheeks, held him open so that his jerks against the stimulation only increased its friction against his anus.

The only area left unbound was where she was mounted upon him. Bending forward, she let her hair trail over his bare skin in that way she knew he loved, that made him want her more. Wherever bare skin showed, she teased him with mouth, tongue, teeth and fingers, until he was surging up against her as much as he was able, fighting to fuck her with the full passion she was unleashing in him. Like his blood, this had a power and energy all its own. She was safe from his bite, because no matter how savage that desire became, he wouldn't take blood from her now, nothing to drain her energy. Leaning down, she nipped his lips, even as he growled against her.

"Bring your pussy up to my mouth. Let me taste you, eat your cream. Let me pleasure you."

She allowed that, straddling his head. A guttural sound of contented lust vibrated in her throat as he used that knowledgeable tongue, the delicate play of fangs and teeth, to work her clit, to emulate the act of fucking her, to make up for the temporary loss of his cock. "Love eating your pussy . . . making me so fucking hard . . ."

The words of raw male want, an additional stimulation, made her tremble. She wanted to come that way, and she did, stiffening and arching up, crying out the pleasure as he kept up the fast thrust of his tongue, the worrying of her clit in the firm press of his lips, the slide of his jaw along the inside of her thighs. His voice was in her mind, fully focused.

Come for me . . . give me your come, let me have the taste of you on my mouth, inside of me. Fuck me, my lady. Fuck me now while your cunt is still quivering. Let me feel it.

She wanted that, too. Pulling away from his mouth, she shifted down and slammed onto his cock with force, giving herself the excruciating pleasure of his enormous thickness shoving deep into her. The nearly unbearable aftershocks mounted as she pumped him, gripping him, rising and falling along his length. She watched all those delicious muscles constrict against the torment she was inflicting upon him. He was exercising his full strength against the enchantment, and that was what she wanted. She wanted it tested. She reinforced several places when she saw movement in the bindings, though the focus it required was astronomical, her body still captured in the grip of the pleasure he'd given it.

"Come for me, Jacob. Come for your Mistress."

He let go, her muscles milking him, giving him no choice in the matter whatsoever. He groaned out the release, called out to her. Bending down, she fastened her lips over his in a desperate, needy, everything-she-felt kiss. He answered the hunger and need, everything in his response a demand to her to release him, to let him hold her.

But she couldn't do that. As he finished, she kept riding him until he was jerking at the sensitivity. It made her lips curve in that feline smile that exasperated him, her delight in torturing him. When she at last lifted off of him, it was with reluctance. Time was passing, though, the parameter Rhoswen had set.

She didn't clean herself. She wanted his seed inside of her, wanted his scent on her body. So she put the leggings back on, slid the strap of the pack on her shoulder, making sure the waterproof flask with the blood was placed carefully in it. Then she moved to the window, making sure the curtain was secure to protect him from the sun that had crested the horizon in early morning mellow pinks and yellows. Turning, she gazed at him through the sudden darkness. His eyes glowed at her.

"Having you bound won't make it easier, but I know you won't fight and lose against your fledgling bloodlust to follow me, despite the sunlight. At nightfall, the enchantment will fade, and you'll be able to move. Be here for me, Jacob. Be here for me when I come back."

"I will always be here for you, my lady." His voice was hoarse, his body still tight, the muscles tense. It would have been a tempting display, if not for the sense of parting. "You will do it. I know you will. If anyone can do this, it's you."

Moving back to his side, she feathered his hair from his forehead. "I love you," she said.

Then, steeling herself from giving him anything further, from relenting to all the things she could see fighting within him, she moved to the doorway, let herself out. She wasn't surprised to see the herald waiting, a few discreet steps from their door. His job was to lead her to the proper portal. At least Rhoswen had given her that, though she was sure it was not a favor.

As she followed him down the winding stairs, the compulsion of a knight, the savagery of a vampire, kicked in, just as she knew it would. She heard the banging, the foot rests of the heavy bed shifting, slamming down on the stone floor as he tried to get free. The animal roar of rage and frustration came on its heels, driving her to move even faster around that winding staircase, so her heart wouldn't break for his pain.

As she'd said, she didn't accept that being a queen meant being lonely. However, some things a queen had to do alone. Else she wasn't a queen at all.

~

The place the herald took her wasn't far. She rode the same gentle palfrey, but when they ducked into the forest, she noticed the mare started to act nervous. This was a dark portion of the wood, and not just because of a lack of dawn light. There was a feeling of forboding here. The tree spirits, if any were present, were watchful and still. She saw no activity by solitary Fae, not even a scattering of the insect kind. Rhoswen had described the desert as a prison for Fae offenders, and she wondered if this was like approaching a prison in the mortal world, the surrounding area tailored to discourage the idle traveler. A warning that this was not a place to linger.

The herald pulled up before a pair of trees that formed an archway. Several paces into that archway, all became pitch blackness. Terror and horror emanated from it, such that the herald had to speak twice to snap her attention from it. "Hold out your hand for the entry seal."

When she did, he positioned the silver pestle on the top of her hand. A burning smell warned her a moment before the excruciating agony of the brand. The herald had tightened his grip, anticipating her withdrawal, but she steeled herself to immobility. As she held his gaze, she was mildly satisfied to see him flinch and look away. She knew Jacob had registered her pain, and did her best to send him a brief reassurance. He was staying as close as he could to her for as long as he could, and she didn't mind that. Knowing her as he did, he was staying quiet, watchful, though the helpless rage still simmered in him at how she'd left him bound. But it was for the best, at least until she was where she needed to be. She'd deal with the repercussions later. Actually, she'd look forward to them, if she survived this.

The herald released her, nodded. "Leave the horse behind. Follow the path ahead, no matter how dark it gets. The seal will open the portal."

She held up the brand. "This tells it I'm a prisoner of the desert world, doesn't it?"

"It's the only way you can gain entry. It also keeps anyone from wandering in there uninvited."

"Once there, it's what keeps me locked in. So how do I return?"

He shook his head. "Her Majesty did not give me those details."

Of course she didn't. But Rhoswen wanted that gemstone, so Lyssa expected that was her return passport. She wondered why the queen hadn't sent someone for this long before, but perhaps, once again, it had to do with those rules. Just as Keldwyn had been blocked from being Catriona's rescuer, maybe only one of family blood had any chance of finding and retrieving their father's soul essence. Perhaps Rhoswen had tried before, unsuccessfully. She was beginning to understand what Keldwyn had said, back at Mason's estate. Though the Fae world operated in apparent capricious chaos, there was a rhythm to it Lyssa was starting to anticipate.

She gave the herald a courteous nod. "Your escort is appreciated."

He looked surprised, but after a hesitation, he responded, "Good luck, Lady Lyssa."

Since she was likely to die here, he probably assumed no one would ever tell the queen he'd called her by the honorific. But she still respected his reckless abandon. Giving him a tight smile, she turned and faced that darkness.

She could see in the dark, but even this was a stretch for her mixed race abilities. As she moved into that black corridor, a cold gripped her. Deep, bone-aching, desolate cold, reminding her of the Gaoth Shee. If the desert was as scorching as deserts went, she'd be happy for the air-conditioning in a few moments. At least that was what she told herself. She steeled herself against webs brushing her face, their scuttling inhabitants passing over her hair, shoulders. Then there was a moan, a series of howls, desolate, savage.

The welcoming committee, no doubt. She gripped the pruning knife at her hip, ridiculous as a weapon though it was. She hoped her own magic would function in a world designed for banished Fae, but it wasn't the only resource she had. Jacob, as a trained warrior, had taken over many of her combat requirements since his vampire transition. However, she'd fought in the Territory Wars and knew how to handle a variety of weapons. She was also well versed on hand-to-hand fighting techniques. Since most of them had been employed against vampires of similar strength, at least in her earlier days, she'd had to rely on skill, not superior strength, to win. That would stand her well here. She hoped.

The ground under her feet changed, became unstable. She lurched forward another step and suddenly she went from deathly blackness into startling daylight. It was like birth. A birth into Hell.

Harsh sunlight beat down upon her. Turning around, she saw no evidence of a black tunnel through a cold forest. It was all sandy, blinding desert, at every point of the compass. So eerily flat and devoid of geographic features it had to be an enchantment. The sand burned through her thin boots, telling her they wouldn't be a sufficient protection for long. This kind of sunlight was designed to peel the skin from the body. She thanked all the gods she had dissuaded Jacob from coming, even as she realized she herself might be overcome from the heat in the end.

She couldn't feel Jacob at all. He'd been right. The portal cut her off from his mind, from everything. It was always a disturbing feeling not to have it, when they used that connection like a sixth sense. Pushing aside that sinking feeling, she verified the pouch of Jacob's blood had made it through. Then she reached under her tunic. She'd brought one other item besides Rhoswen's "supplies." She'd showed it to Jacob in her mind when they were discussing how she might find the rose bush, but she hadn't been sure if it would make it through. She'd hoped, though, because she'd felt a strong compulsion to bring it.

Cupping it in her hand, she held the enchanted rose that Keldwyn had given her months ago, the surviving rose from her father's rose bush. At the time, she'd believed that his offering it to her had been motivated by sentiment. Knowing what she now did of Keldwyn, she hoped there were other reasons. *Now's not the time to become inconsistent, arrogant schemer.*

Closing her eyes, she held the rose in her hand and thought about that decaying rose bush, her father's soul beneath it. Almost instantly, she felt a barely there but distinctive . . . pull.

Just like a Ouija board. Her lips curled over her sharp fangs.

Tearing away the hem of her thigh-length tunic, she removed her boots and stuffed the extra fabric down into the soles, standing on each folded boot in turn to protect her feet until she put them back on. Better. Removing the wide brimmed hat from the pack, she fitted it squarely on her head. Three days. She had three days to do this.

Tucking the rose back beneath her tunic, she felt the pulse of its magic like a tiny heartbeat, confirming it could guide her from that sheltered position. Shouldering the pack, she moved forward, made it twenty steps through the deep sand, and then came to an abrupt halt.

Despite there being nothing on any horizon a moment before, three figures had appeared, not anywhere near as far away as they should have been. She could tell they were swathed in a ragtag collection of protective clothing. As the dry wind brought their scent, her eyes narrowed, her pulse quickening. They didn't smell . . . alive.

Putrefaction. As someone who'd walked the earth a thousand years, she well knew the smell of rotting flesh. They began to move toward her more swiftly. She'd also seen an enemy charge before. They wouldn't be pausing to find out her business or seek her as an ally. These were bandits, wanting to take whatever she'd brought through for their own survival.

Reaching deep inside of her, she hoped the magic was there. It was, but there was a price to be paid. Cursing, she kicked at the hot sand, trying to get to a lower point. Even though she only saw more sand, it still put her closer to Earth. There *was* Earth energy here; she could feel it. Fae magic couldn't be spun from something unnatural, no matter how unnatural the results.

Ripping off her boots, she plunged her feet into the hole she'd made, gritting her teeth as the sand that poured back on them burned her flesh.

She saw the gleam of sharpened objects carried by the oncoming attackers, perhaps the Fae form of prison shivs, things taken from previous arrivals. She could also now see the source of the smell. The clothes they were wearing, the layers, had come from the skins of other victims, improperly tanned and leathered. It didn't matter to the wearers, because she was seeing faces that had long ago peeled away into cancerous, tumescent terrain. Blackened lips, swollen places on the throat and around the eyes. The tips of the pointed ears pushed through lank, filthy hair, all of it framing eyes sun-poisoned mad.

She could fight this group off, but how many more like this would she encounter? She'd only gone twenty steps before she'd been discovered. How far would she have to go to get to that rose bush?

"Father, help me," she muttered. Bracing herself for the attack, she reached down through her scorching feet to summon the magic to repel them.

~

With berserker rage fueled by bloodlust, Jacob managed to crack several of the branches by midday. The effort left his arms bloody. He'd given his lady a large amount of blood, so it only depleted his strength further. It didn't make sense, but at times a vampire nature was very much an animal one, particular when goaded by fury or fear. He was smarter than this, but feeling that darkness close around her, the way her mind simply winked out of existence, no longer accessible to him, was more than he could tolerate. He understood her logic, knew he couldn't follow her into the sunlight, but that meant nothing. He was supposed to be with her. His gut was fair screaming it.

Jacob had gotten his upper body free when Keldwyn arrived. He came with one of the serving girls, a wide-eyed waif who'd apparently heard his struggles and gone for help. Jacob had to wonder if he'd paid her to come to him at any signs of trouble, because he didn't figure Keldwyn had been lounging around the castle grounds with nothing better to do. Plus it looked like he'd ridden hard to be there.

At the sight of him, Keldwyn wisely pushed the girl behind him and told her to stay at the door. Moving toward the bed, he lifted his hand and the branches remaining on Jacob's lower body loosened, fell away. As he shoved out of them, he leaped from the bed and charged for the door, not giving a damn about why Keldwyn was here.

He hit a wall. It knocked him to the floor, made him see spots. Keldwyn completed the shield chant, lowered his hand. "If you try again, it will stop you again. You cannot help her, Jacob. The desert world is on a different time scale from this one, anyhow. It has been a few hours here, whereas there it has been two days."

He took deep breaths he didn't need, trying to steady himself. Jesus, his brain was scrambled. And his lady needed him calm. He would have thanked Keldwyn for that sharp blow the floor had delivered to his head, as bracing as a slap, but he wasn't feeling particularly grateful. "So she essentially has more time than she realizes," he managed in a hoarse voice. "Three days here, according to Rhoswen's specifications, could be a week or more there."

"Yes, and no. You are correct about the time, but the conditions in that world . . . it is unlikely she will survive three days, even in that world's time."

Jacob hit the floor the same way again. The girl made a small noise behind Keldwyn. "Send her out of here," Jacob snarled.

"I will not. Once you calm down, you will need human blood."

"I'm not taking it from an unwilling host."

"An utterly irrational response, just like the way you're acting now. But she is not unwilling." Keldwyn extended his hand. "Sellya?"

Sellya was a blond-haired, blue-eyed human delicate enough to pass as Fae. Though she looked pale and a bit nervous, there was a strength to her elfin features. A firm hold to her chin told him Keldwyn was telling the truth.

"It would be my honor, sir." She bobbed a curtsy.

"I'm not a sir," Jacob grumbled, but he slid to his backside, bracing himself against the bed. Pulling his knees up, he used them to hold his elbows as he rubbed his face. Having enough blood would help him think through this, figure it out. He took another deep breath, met her gaze.

"I'm hungry and not entirely stable, Sellya. I need to ask the impossible. I need you not to be afraid. You can't let me smell your fear, you understand?"

"I can entrance her, so she has no fear," Keldwyn noted. However, Sellya surprised Jacob by meeting Keldwyn's lifted hand with her own. Putting her small palm against his larger one, she blocked the entrancement magic before it happened.

"If it's all the same to you, my lord," she said, "I think I can do what he says without that."

"You've fed a vampire before." Jacob recognized it when her gaze turned back to him.

She nodded. "A few years ago, he helped me get away from a . . . bad situation in my world. He doesn't know this is where I ended up, because he had a sorcerer help me, and that was one of the sorcerer's and Lady Rhoswen's conditions, that he not know where I was, just that I was safe, and happy. But while I was staying with Lord Mason, I fed him once or twice."

Son of a bitch. It almost made Jacob smile. Mason and his female projects. "*Are* you happy, Sellya?"

She nodded. "Getting there, sir. I've a better chance of it here than there."

Moving forward, she knelt carefully between his splayed and bent knees. With girlish charm, she put one hand on each of them. "How do you want me, sir?" she asked.

On a sandwich, with ketchup and a side of chips, came his eager brain, his nostrils already flaring at her sweet scent. He had too little control, and he couldn't spare anything for finesse. So he simply slid his arm around her waist, brought her fast and hard against his chest so she tumbled against him. Her arms fell around his shoulders, but then gripped as he took hold of her hair, turned her face into his shoulder and sank his fangs into her throat.

He didn't look at Keldwyn, didn't want to see what look of distaste the tight-assed Fae might have on his face. He needed strength for Lyssa. *She won't survive three days.* What wouldn't she survive? The conditions of the desert? What dangers existed there?

He'd been sensible enough to release pheromones into Sellya's blood, the vampire way of easing the pain and calming panic. True to her promise, though, she had a handle on her fear, though no mortal could have helped a racing heartbeat after that rude yank and taking. The pheromones calmed it, so it didn't provoke his predator instinct.

Of course the pheromones came with another problem. Her hands were kneading his shoulders, and her generous breasts, loose under her servant's dress, pressed into his chest, the nipples hard and needy. She was straddling one of his thighs because of the way he'd pulled her down, and now she was mindlessly rubbing herself against it, dampening him with the slick moisture of her cunt, no underwear under the skirt of course. His cock couldn't help but respond to it, because he was feeding. But he was as likely to fuck a gentle, helpful girl not in control of her faculties as he was to kill her. Plus, his lady was out fighting for her life, while he was getting hard and thinking of rooting on a serving girl like a mindless beast. That was enough to viciously balance the desire.

As Sellya got more aggressive, he made a low growl, startling her enough to tone down some of her reaction. After he'd fed enough, he eased her away, nodding at Keldwyn. Fortunately, the Fae understood, bringing her back to her feet and steadying her as she swayed into him. Her dazed eyes were upon Jacob, her breath fast and shallow. Lifting her, Keldwyn took her to the settee near the bed. He laid her down with a soothing stroke of her forehead. "Sleep," he said. "Dream of your true love."

Her eyes closed, even though that sexy little body quivered with residual lust as she slid off into the place he'd suggested. Jacob turned his eyes away, wiping the back of his mouth with his hand.

"You could have done that at the first."

"She said she didn't want an enchantment. She's given her heart to a Fae, I think. Humans. Always fascinated with others not of their own kind." Keldwyn snorted.

"Well, since she was allowed to live here, I think some of that fascination goes both ways." Jacob gave him a look. "Can I get up now without being knocked back down?"

Keldwyn nodded. "You seem much calmer."

As Jacob began to rise, he glanced down at the floor. Froze. A sunbeam from the window lay across his palm. And all he felt was the mild warmth of the autumnal sun.

From the beginning, he'd noticed he didn't have the same sense of sunrise and sunset here that he had in the mortal world. He'd attributed it to the differences between the two worlds, some kind of Fae jetlag. But a vampire's survival was based on an awareness of when the sun would rise. If survival wasn't a factor, then his sense of it would be like the human one, based on sleep patterns or the clock or looking out the window.

Lyssa had left the curtain drawn, but inevitably a line of sunlight escaped from the sides, depending on the time of day. When he'd landed at the foot of the bed after that last repulsion, he'd been right beside that stray sunbeam.

"You bastard." Striding to the window, he tore back the curtain. As the sunlight streamed in, he flinched, but it was psychological, not physical. The sun poured over his body, giving him nothing more than that mild warmth.

It had been well over a year since he'd felt the touch of the sun, been able to stand fully in its track like this. But that was a fleeting impression, because at the moment, other things were taking precedence. Like wrath.

"I expected an Irishman to remember that all the stories of the Fae suggest their world is underground, such that any sense of the sun or moon would be magically filtered." Keldwyn spoke in a matter-of-fact tone. "However, while the Fae sun here won't hurt you, the desert sun may be an entirely different matter. Fae enchantments can be organic, thinking things. Cruelly duplicitous. Even if it doesn't burn you right away, you could find her, only to have your immunity to the sun vanish, making her witness your disintegration to ash before her."

"Great." Jacob stepped toward him. "So it's like any other normal fucking day. I might die; I might live. Why the hell didn't you tell me about the sunlight?"

Keldwyn looked mildly surprised. The Fae lord never managed to look anything less than diabolically sincere. "You never asked. And my loyalty, my interests, such that they are, are toward Lyssa, not toward her vampire servant."

"Horseshit. If you have any loyalty to her, wouldn't it make sense to give her the benefit of all the resources at her disposal? Like me."

"Lyssa needs to accomplish this quest on her own. Queen Rhoswen decreed I could give her no help to go through the desert, though she made a concession on my small offering of a container for your blood. The Fae queen wants that gemstone." Keldwyn considered the window, the view beyond it. "However, Her Majesty did not prohibit me from helping you. Particularly if you are going in separately, well after Lyssa is on her way."

"Rhoswen really needs to retain a lawyer to deal with you. But thank the gods she doesn't have one right now. Fine. How can you help me?"

"I can get you to the portal, and tell you where to find her. I can also give you weapons to help you get to her side more quickly. However, I can't help you get past Cayden. You must do that yourself. I will meet you at the stables."

Picking up the sleeping girl, Keldwyn moved out of the room, gone before Jacob could even retort.

Quickly, he donned the protective clothing Keldwyn had brought. He tucked the long hooded robe into the additional pack, which contained a couple flasks of water.

He'd almost forgotten about Cayden, until he headed across the courtyard and found the captain of the Queen's Guard at the gatehouse. He sat with deceptive casualness on a stone bench, sharpening his sword. At Jacob's appearance, his eyes got as sharp as the blade and he rose.

Jacob knew Cayden was a soldier, with no patience for Keldwyn's silver-tongued cleverness. Rhoswen didn't want Lyssa helped in any way. That was the intention he'd uphold, no preamble or pretending otherwise.

As Cayden moved into a confrontational position, Jacob strode forward. He came to a halt several feet away from the male, just out of range of his weapon.

"Go back to your room," Cayden said. "Or sit out here and enjoy the rare taste of sunlight, vampire. But you're not leaving."

"You saw the spear go through her chest. She's not your queen's enemy. I'm going to go help her."

When Cayden leveled the sword, Jacob's eyes narrowed. "Centuries ago, the Tuatha de Danaan were defeated by Gaelic warriors, despite all their fancy, enchanted weapons. If you need a reminder of that"—he took a matching stance, armed with nothing but determination and a brace of knives—"this Irishman is prepared to do it all over again."

"She may not be an enemy, but there are many gradations left between enemy and friend. As for you, we have no magical spear to destroy annoyances, so I will have to handle pest control with normal steel."

Jacob sighed, straightened. "Fine." Then he swung the pack at Cayden's sword.

The straps tangled it. Before Cayden could lever upward, cutting through them, Jacob ripped the grip from his hand, sending the blade clattering over the cobblestones. He plowed into him head first, knocking him back against the wall. Cayden struck his back with locked fists, breaking free, but Jacob got in a hard punch to the solar plexus as he went down.

He'd hoped for and counted on Cayden being pissed off enough to make this a soldier's fight, not a magical one, and so far he was getting his wish. But the guy was a seriously good soldier. Jacob landed in the dirt, blood exploding in his mouth, and barely had enough time to roll over and get his legs up to shove Cayden back as he charged in on him. Leaping to his feet, he jumped on the man's back, tumbling them both into the dirt. They rolled and punched, an out-and-out street fight. He wondered where Cayden's men were. Maybe most were part of the ceremonial guard watching over Tabor and Rhoswen. Or perhaps Cayden wanted this to be just between them, which gave Jacob another idea, a faint hope.

He put everything into his next strike, a solid blow to the face that resulted in a payback crunching sound in Cayden's nose, staggering him back. The man bared bloody teeth and roared, charging forward again. Jacob took the attack and fell back with it, going over with him in the dirt. He suffered a few face punches himself but then got in another solid body blow. He put his vampire strength behind it, knocking the wind out of Cayden.

Leaping up, he backed off, wiping the blood off his own face as Cayden staggered to his feet and began circling again. He didn't charge right back in, however, telling Jacob he needed a minute. Good. So did he.

"The only way you're going to keep me from going after her is to kill me. So if you're not prepared to do that, save yourself the beating and step aside."

The captain of the guard gave him a sardonic look. "I am not as thickheaded as you believe me to be, vampire. If you die, so does she. So you will not let me kill you."

Jacob nodded. "I was planning to kick your ass anyway, beat you to unconsciousness, so it's a moot point. But on the slim chance you get the upper hand, to stop me you'll have to take it as close to that point as you dare."

Dropping his arms and offensive stance, Jacob came to a stop. Cayden did as well, eyeing him warily. "You think I don't know what it's like to love a moody she-bitch from hell?" Jacob demanded. "What would you do for her, your queen, if you knew her life was in danger and you weren't with her? She's your heart, your soul, your reason for being alive."

"I serve my queen," Cayden gritted.

"Yeah. And that means sometimes you have to serve her in ways she doesn't even know she needs, but you do. Damn it." Jacob spat out the impatient curse, took three steps forward, coming toe-to-toe with Cayden. "If you want to serve her to the best of your ability, then throw out the fucking etiquette manual and use your heart, your soul, your gut, your cock. Do what *they* tell you to do. That's the only way she'll learn to trust you. Stop doing every fucking thing she says, especially the things you know are wrong. Start loving her. *That's* how you serve a queen."

Cayden stared at him a long moment. The two men were of an equal height. Jacob was aware the man had a backup knife at his belt and his hand was on the hilt. It wouldn't kill him, but Cayden could temporarily incapacitate him, if he didn't move away fast enough, and Cayden was more than capable of moving faster than a vampire.

Cayden let out a sigh, lip curling in frustration. He dropped his hand from the knife hilt. "Go."

"Do you want me to knock you out so it looks less guilty?"

Cayden raised a brow. "I will not lie to my queen, vampire. I take the consequences of my actions."

"Are you sure? I'd be happy to punch you in the face until you're unconscious."

Cayden showed his teeth. "Go, before I change my mind about stabbing you in the chest."

Jacob was already moving. However, when he paused at the dividing wall between main and lower bailey, he looked back. Cayden was staring into space, his face a picture of abject misery. *Damn, damn, fuck.*

Muttering a curse, Jacob took two swift strides back toward him, gaining his attention. "Your queen lost her father," he said quietly. "A thousand years ago or not, in her mind, he abandoned her, turned his back on her mother, though he never promised her anything, except love for the child they'd made. But Magwel rejected that, made that choice for Rhoswen. So in your lady's mind, he turned his back on her for another daughter, another woman. She's afraid of trusting any man, which means you have to teach her to trust. You have to stop playing the game all her way. Instead of following, take the fucking lead."

That was the best he could do for the guy, but something in his gut had said it needed saying, just in case. He took off at a swift jog, headed for the stables. Once he turned the corner, though, the urgency gripped him even harder, such that he accelerated his pace.

He arrived with a gust of wind from his passage, leaving skid marks in the soil near the open double doors. Keldwyn controlled the startled reactions of the horses he held. Taking the reins of the nearest one, Jacob swung up onto the bare back in one lithe move. "I can't touch her mind, but she's in trouble, I can feel it. We need to hurry."

18

Lyssa crouched on the sand, getting her breath back. Despite her chest being slick with sweat and blood, the rose still pulsed against it, telling her she was getting closer. If anyone was following her, she'd left an interesting trail of bread crumbs. She'd turned the first three Fae into cacti, and the next group into a small handful of scorpions. They'd chased her until she outran them. After that, she went for inanimate earth forms. Rocks, dried sticks. The flow of earth magic here was stingy at best, most of it wrapped up into holding the protections and forms of the prison. As her energy and that shifting supply of magic dwindled, like a well spring drying up, the ways she could fight the inhabitants became more and more macabre.

She stared at the last set of cacti, which were not fully cacti at all. They were half Fae, half plant, and the Fae were still hideously, torturously alive, their screams of agony now down to rasping pants, and moans. She was sorry for that. Under normal circmstances, she would have tried to end their pain with a quick throat slitting.

However, the cold and ruthless truth was that the terrifying image of those mangled, half alive bodies, cactus spikes protruding from their bloody torn skin, was keeping the next wave of pursuers at a wary distance. Even so, the newest group had swelled from five to ten members, the largest contingent yet. She'd wondered how any of them had survived to become these desperate packs, if they were so quick to attack newcomers. When she'd fought in close quarters with them, their damaged bodies and dead eyes told her why. Newcomers weren't killed, not outright. Everything of value was taken from the weak . . . repeatedly. From their crawling, avaricious gazes, she also knew why she'd not seen any women. A woman wouldn't survive here long because her primary value was quickly used up by males starved for sexual contact. They were wild, savage beasts with no reason or logic, all of that long ago burned away by the sun.

She was having a hard time believing Rhoswen had ever come here and tried the quest she was attempting now. The fact this place existed was a blight of shame on both monarchs. While the most brutal crime might deserve this kind of judgment, it would taint the judges' souls to give it. A quick execution would be better.

She thought of what Tabor had intimated, that the Fae had experienced a dark period when there was little trust among them, as well as between themselves and humans. Conflict, war between factions. It sounded much like the vampires' Territory Wars and the brutality that had happened then. For all that she was being constantly pursued, there was not a large populace. How long had it been since anyone was sentenced to this? Did those in the Fae world realize any of the condemned still survived?

Though survival was a loose term. Any immortal who figured out how to exist here sentenced themselves to unimaginable hell.

She wished she could tell how far she was from her goal. While the rose's pulse was getting stronger, she had no measure for what that meant. She'd gone through most of Jacob's blood in the pouch Keldwyn had provided, but her body was quivering with exhaustion, because her opponents had gotten in their strikes as well. During one harrowing moment when they'd pinned her, she'd cracked open the earth, a minor quake that threw all of them, including her, fifty feet into the air. When she landed, she'd been fortunate to be the only one not momentarily disoriented, expecting the effect. That had been her first set of mutant cacti, her body too depleted to do the full job, the supply of magical energy too thin.

Those ten were starting to move forward. They'd noticed the trembling, her blood forming a larger stain under her feet. She started moving again. Perhaps they'd trail her for a while before finding the courage to attack her once more. Every step was a possibility she might reach her father's soul before her own departed the world.

Then she realized the shuddering beneath her was not coming from her own body. Whirling, braced for a charge, she saw the ten retreating at a full, stumbling run, dispersing like rats scrabbling on a flat table surface. Realizing the shudder was from the ground beneath her, she started to follow them, to get beyond the point where the desert was violently shifting, the sand rolling away and ground heaving much like it had done when she called up the percussion force. Only this time, an actual *something* was coming up from beneath the earth.

It blasted forth with a loud noise somewhere between a hawk's cry, an enraged lion's roar and a dragon's screech. The explosion knocked her on her ass, but she stopped moving, letting the sand shower over her as a long serpentine neck reared up above. The head that topped it was skeletal looking, with six red eyes and three rows of teeth. This was not a prisoner. This being was indigenous to this place, one of the things put here to ensure nothing survived long. Perhaps the judges' ironic form of mercy.

Her explosion had likely drawn its attention, which meant that movement attracted it. Since its multiple gazes were on the fleeing men, she stayed still, not breathing, not moving. She was close to it, such that it would have to tuck in its chin and look directly down to see her.

Letting out another shrill scream, it took several running steps and launched itself on wings that seemed merely a frame of bones connected by a thin membrane run through by blood vessels. The wings were too thin for this sun, but that might be why it could burrow and travel underground. It might even be immune to the sun.

Unfortunately, those three running steps took him directly over her. She couldn't risk moving, but there was also no time to move away. It pushed into flight off her thigh. The give of the sand beneath her saved the bone from breaking, but the barbed talon tore open her thigh, a long gash that went to the bone. Biting down on a scream, she rolled face-first, pressing her thigh and the resulting geyser of blood into the sand. Hopefully by the time the creature reached and mangled the other victims, it would assume the blood on the talon belonged to them. But she was sure it would be back.

Tearing another strip off the hem of her tunic, she tied it around her thigh to staunch the blood flow. Her neck and ears, any part of her not under the hat or her clothes, was already blistered. She tasted small rivulets of blood from her cracked lips. She'd taken her hair down despite the heat, because it provided some covering for her neck and face.

As she staggered to her feet, moved forward once again, she thought of Mason. When she'd visited him in the desert years ago, he'd worn the elegant tunic and robe of a Bedouin, a romantic figure. It said something that what her memory lingered on was not how devastatingly handsome the male vampire was in such garments, but the garments themselves. If Mason was here, he'd strip them off without hesitation to give them to her, no matter that he'd turn to ash before he even got to her. Her life was full of foolish, noble and chivalrous males.

The sand serpent unfortunately hadn't left a tunnel in its wake. The sand was too soft. When it emerged, the sand had closed in behind it, so following the path it had taken underground was not possible. It was too risky anyhow, not knowing where the next surface break would appear.

She'd held on to one of the Fae she'd turned into a stick and now used it to hobble forward, ignoring the fact she was dizzy and her breath was labored. She'd fought through much worse pain than this to achieve her goals. This would be no different. Of course, when she'd had more vampire strength than Fae, she'd been more certain of what could or couldn't kill her. The wound in her leg, combined with the sun's heat and however many other battles she faced, might end her.

She made it another hundred yards before she heard the serpent's shrieking cry again. It had reversed course. She made a dive for the gully its tail had created and burrowed deep, though she suspected it had already seen her.

As it swooped, she knew that was the case. Even if not, at this range, there was no way it couldn't smell the blood, coating her leg with slick grit. Giving a snarl of pure frustration and exhaustion, she shoved herself out of the gully and took a defensive position. As she did, she reached deep into the ground beneath her. Nothing, no magic left there. The well was dry.

But there was the creature itself, a being of life and earth, no matter how rare or aberrant. As her mind raced over the thought, weighing possibilities, she braced herself, watching it arrow down toward her.

The triple gaping maw of teeth was open, the talons extended. Dropping to a squat, she bit back a moan at the fire that shot up her wounded leg. She had no speed, and even at her best, she didn't have enough strength. It didn't matter. She'd depend on her mind. It had always been her best weapon, coupled with her unstoppable determination to win.

Since Rex's murder, Thomas's death, the Delilah virus and the Council's betrayal, she'd been fighting that damn lassitude. What Jacob had feared was the onset of the Ennui. But suddenly, out here in a barren desert, closer to death than she'd ever been—which, given her precarious life, was saying something—that determination unfolded inside her, like a treasure that had merely been waiting for her to unwrap and remember she possessed it.

She wasn't leaving her boys alone, come hell or high water. Or deserts, Fae queens and sand serpents. Kane and Jacob needed her, and she needed them. She wasn't going to lose this fight; she didn't care what Fate or the law of averages told her about her chances. In the cruel irony that fate often offered, it was truly facing her own inevitable death that gave her a renewed resolve to live.

Looking up into the face of the creature as it swooped down upon her, she got a full face of its fetid breath as it screamed. She screamed back. As she did, she saw the masticated body part of one of her pursuers stuck in the back row of teeth.

Then she ducked and flung herself at its right claw. As the creature closed the talons around her, caging her, she put both hands on the creature's ankle, thick as a young tree trunk. The talons stabbed her like five knives, but she focused, focused, *focused*.

Feeling her magic, the serpentlike beast launched itself again rather than immediately tearing her apart, a vital advantage. High above the earth, dizzying, turning. She pulled the energy from inside that creature, pulled hard. Earth, creation, all of it there, all magic she could use. She could turn it to her will, it didn't matter that her strength was flagging, that there were hazy bands of color shooting across her vision like flashing stars broken free from a rainbow. Two of the talons had hit major organs, because she could feel her body stuttering, losing her grip, her focus.

No. She snarled again, fought it, fought the inevitable. She was not going to be torn apart. She was not going to die like that. Bringing the magic together with the creature's energy, she didn't attempt to control or direct it. She let it go like a suicide bomber tossing an incendiary up over her head and watching it drop with wild, mindless insanity.

The sand serpent, already capable of a symphony of disturbing cries, let out a shriek that pierced her bones, made them ache. The beast shuddered in the air, faltered. Hazarding a look down, she realized they were several hundred feet in the air. She managed a grim half chuckle. The least of her problems, truly. Hanging on to a corner of the magic, she clutched the serpent's ankle as its talons released, her blood painting every claw. Adrenaline pumped through her, making everything numb.

"Damn it, *work*," she growled. She yelled it, gripped that ankle for all she was worth. And beneath her grip, it began to change.

At first it looked like it was turning to stone, a gray tint running up the creature's leg, all the way to the skeletal features and the wings, freezing them in place. As they began to tumble out of the sky, that horrible screech came from its throat again. A terrible shudder and the beast exploded in midair, the inside coming outside, yanked there by her will. Unfortunately, it left nothing to hold. She plummeted to earth among sharp shards of bone, gouts of blood and muscle, and a hailstorm of tiny sand stone, perhaps something it used for its digestion.

A piece of the wing slapped her face, cutting it open. She seized it. She was too close to the ground for it to slow her fall much, but it did help. That, coupled with the last scrap of magic she could command to summon air currents to fill it and slow her descent. As a result, she hit with a dull, bone jarring thud, instead of snapping her spine and paralyzing herself.

She lay there for long moments, wondering if she was about to die. She couldn't seem to move, though that could be her body's way of asking for a few moments to collect itself from the huge power drain of the energy summoning, the blood loss from her leg, or the multiple stab wounds in her upper body. Or the fact she had one enormous, pounding headache. Probably from sunburn.

She hoped that would heal. If she had to emerge from this experience with permanently blistered, unattractive skin, she might choose to die here, with sincere apologies to Jacob and Kane. Family was one thing, a woman's vanity was entirely another. It almost made her smile, remembering how she'd teased Jacob about that not too long ago, at another equally grim moment, when she'd had the Delilah virus.

How many times could she almost die before the Grim Reaper got tired of showing up at the door, only to find she wasn't ready? She hoped at least one more. But she was tired, and she had a plummeting feeling she had no more strength. Perhaps if she just lay here a moment or two more, she could continue. Putting her hand to her chest, she felt a vague sense of alarm. The rose wasn't there. She twisted her head, gasping at the pain. She was surrounded by the debris of an exploding sand monster. It could be anywhere. She looked in the other direction, managed to roll to her side. There . . . was that a flash of red?

Her lips pulled back in a twisted half smile. As she did, she tasted her own blood and that of the creature she'd killed. She'd laugh if it wouldn't hurt so badly. There was her pack, the rose laying neatly upon the top of it as if it had been placed there by a fussy maître d' at a restaurant.

And right next to it was a dried-up rose bush, the sun glittering off the red stone only half buried beneath it.

Her serpent monster had turned out to be a blessing in disguise. In its twisting arc through the sky, it had probably carried her several miles toward her destination, closing that last gap.

Blessings do exist here. In their usual, quite ironic way.

~

At the entrance to the desert portal, Keldwyn swung off his horse, gesturing to Jacob to draw close as he unhooked a saddle bag, tossed it to him. "More weapons, water." Pulling a pendant from his neck, he dropped it over his head. "This makes a ten foot perimeter of invisibility around you, so you will not be slowed down by enemies. It's a limited enchantment, a small magic that won't last much longer than a day or two. I don't suspect you'll require more than that, however. Either your mind connection will bring you quickly to her side to help her finish the quest within the proscribed time period, or you will be dead."

He then pulled out a seal that, as he chanted several words, started to glow red hot. "To get in, you must have the brand of the desert prisoner. It is tailored for Fae blood only, so after I mark you with it, you need to make all haste down that tunnel, because, being vampire, you will heal it rapidly."

"And to get out?"

"That requires an executor on the outside. When Lyssa has what Rhoswen wants, that door will open. Her possession of Reghan's soul essence will allow her to exit. The lack of the brand should allow you to do so, if you maintain contact with her."

"Should?"

Keldwyn lifted a shoulder. "Take your chances, vampire. Unless you are suffering a sudden attack of faintheartedness."

In answer, Jacob extended his hand. His skin was crawling, tingling, every muscle quivering with the need to go, to get through that tunnel and find her. She needed him, now. Actually, she'd needed him now an hour ago. "Do it."

"I will bide here for a time, and leave runners when I must go, in case you need assistance when you emerge with her."

"I still don't trust you," Jacob said, locking gazes with him. "But thank you."

"I'm sure you are aware that thanking a Fae is an insult."

When Jacob merely showed fangs, Keldwyn's lips quirked. "You are correct not to trust me, vampire. It's best not to trust anyone." Gripping his wrist to steady the canvas he was about to mark, Keldwyn jammed the brand against the top of Jacob's hand.

Jacob shuddered, clenching the hand holding the saddlebag and his own pack. It was urgency more than pain, as well as a spurt of rage that they'd done this to his lady. When Keldwyn lifted the brand, he bolted for that darkness.

He couldn't see, an unusual thing for a vampire, but he still ran full tilt forward, assuming that the desert world was hungry for its victims and wouldn't trip him up. It didn't, not until the end, when he stumbled, rolled out of pitch darkness and into blinding day, right into the base of a cactus.

"Ow, fuck." Yanking the needles free that had driven into his side, he pulled out the cowled robe Keldwyn had packed for him. Though it was brutally hot, the sun reflecting the white and ecru landscape like a mirror flashing in his eyes, he wasn't bursting into flames. So far, so good. He squinted, pulled the hood farther over his brow to help cut the glare, then took a closer look at that cactus.

The twisted, distorted shape was eerily familiar. It looked as if it had once been a different being, something humanlike, now forever caught inside the succulent. Two others near it had the same look. He bared his fangs in a savage grin. His lady had been here all right. But that same thought sobered him. She'd had to hit the ground fighting. He studied the landscape, turning slowly to make sure tricks of the light and reflected sand didn't make him miss anything. There. He saw a blot that might have been another set of cacti, then farther on, something like a pile of sticks. A staggering but distinct line of direction, stretching away to the horizon.

Fuck. Panic gripped him as he realized he still couldn't hear her. More than that, he wasn't feeling that buzz of connection that should have been there.

Lyssa? Lyssa, where are you? Help me find you.

Nothing. Tightening his jaw, he started moving, following her battle remains. Mindlinks with servants had a range of a few thousand miles. In this odd world, where it was possible that many magical fault lines existed, he might be in the wrong quadrant to hear her. But she'd left him a trail. Increasing his speed, he focused his energy on that. He was grudgingly grateful for Keldwyn's pendant, keeping him invisible from whatever these things were that had attacked her. Because he sure as hell couldn't waste time hiding. Not that there were a great many options for concealment.

As he ran, he lengthened out to his top speed, his vampire senses taking in every detail around him like the tracking radar of a missile. He saw how the shapes of the cacti changed, his grim forboding growing when he saw how the magic dwindled, creating nightmares. The first time he detected her blood trail, he stumbled and somersaulted across the hot sand. But he forced himself to get a grip on his emotions, started running again. It wasn't the last time he found her blood. Eventually, it was a trail even stronger than the evidence of her skirmishes. It spurred his speed and his temper. He cursed repeatedly as he thought of her here alone for nearly two days, while he'd been trapped in that upper bedroom for six hours.

He would be so fucking glad to be back in a world populated by humans and vampires, normal Greenwich time and Taco Bells that stayed open reliably past midnight.

~

What seemed too many freaking hours later, he passed through another shimmer of energy. It was the second or third time he'd done so, but this time the featureless landscape was suddenly not so featureless. A haphazard arrangement of rocks lay ahead. Even more importantly, he felt his lady.

Though faint, the sense of that connection was a relief so strong it swept through him like a sudden cool shower under the punishing rays. But it was a brief respite, because she was so weak it was like a bad cell connection, a lot of static and dropped dead spots.

Drawing closer, he saw the rocks weren't rocks at all, but bone, organs, and what appeared to be large amounts of scattered gravel. Whatever it had been, it had been very, very large. *Lyssa? My lady? Answer me.*

He shouted it out loud then, as well as thinking it with such intensity that he thought he might have borrowed some of his queen's ability to move the earth. Because after a long, heart-stopping moment, he received a response.

It wasn't a word—merely a sound. A quiet, dying sound. But she couldn't die. If she was dying, he would be dying, too. Because he was her servant, to hell with the changes to the marks.

Jacob ran across that landscape of broken pieces. He saw shards of a jaw with three rows of teeth, some of them like elephant tusks. A portion of a face, the six eyes staring, still eerily sentient. He was fairly certain he saw one of them blink.

When he saw her at last, he was at her side in one quick surge of movement, his hand on her face, her matted hair. "Holy Mother," he murmured. She was impossibly bloody, her skin corpse-pale. She clutched her father's rose, and the other hand lay on the sand next to a desiccated bush, her fingertips nearly brushing a glitter of gemstone that glowed beneath the thin covering of sand. Apparently it was responding to the rose, two splashes of vibrant red in an otherwise colorless landscape. Colorless except for her green eyes, that opened at the sight of him.

"My lady," he greeted her, his voice thick.

She studied him. When her trembling fingertips brushed his knee, it was a touch so welcome he felt it through his whole body. "Hallucination," she said. "My vampire servant, here in the bright sun."

"No. Really here, thanks to a bit of Fae magic. Turns out you needed my help after all."

Her weak cough was so obviously painful he put his hands on her shoulders, trying to hold her together. *Actually, you're a bit late. Could have used you earlier.*

He wanted to smile, but couldn't. "I was busy cutting my way out of tree," he reminded her.

"You want to spend . . . your last moments with me saying . . . I told you so?"

A fist gripped his heart, squeezed. The time to avoid the truth was done. They both knew he wouldn't die with her. When she'd nearly been taken by the Delilah virus, he couldn't walk, the life draining from him with her. He felt none of that now, only the empty, aching sense a vampire experienced from the imminent loss of a servant. The vampire-servant mark she'd given him had in fact been broken. He couldn't follow her into eternity.

Well, fuck that with a ketchup bottle. It was one of his brother's favorite expletives in high school.

I felt him, Jacob. When I touched the stone. I felt my father, as I wished to do. He sensed me, knew me.

"Good, my lady." He swallowed. "That's good." Stretching out next to her, heedless of the sand's heat, he remembered when Jess had almost died and Mason had given her his heart's blood directly. He lifted the sharp pruning knife that lay next to Lyssa, the only weapon other than her magic she'd had to use here. Though he didn't want to flavor this moment with hatred, if Rhoswen suddenly appeared, he'd happily prune out her ice block of a heart, no matter what daddy issues had made her what she was.

"No, Jacob . . ." Her eyes tracked his movements. "We both know . . . I'm almost gone. Much further than Jessica. I've been laying here . . . for hours. Surprised no one else attacked me."

"I think you left a very powerful message that you were not to be messed with. Plus, there seems to be some type of field around this area." He glanced at the rose bush. "I expect because of that. Else one of the other inhabitants of this living hell would have destroyed the bush or taken the gemstone long ago."

As he spoke, he was already yanking off the cloak and the tunic he'd donned. He positioned the knife where it needed to be. As a former vampire hunter, he knew exactly where the heart was located, which ribs allowed access to spill the rich heart's blood. Her hand fluttered up weakly. "Jacob . . . it almost killed, Mason . . . wooden stake or no. Here . . . there's no protection, no help. Kane. Think of Kane."

"With the deepest respect, my lady, shut up." He slid the blade in, smooth as butter. The stutter of his heart was welcome in this situation, and he quickly shifted over her, tilting her head up to position it in that place as the bright, thick blood spurted forth, his left arm briefly trembling as he used it to brace himself over her.

She was so weak. He had to put his fingers in between her mouth and his body, apply pressure to slow the flow, because she didn't have the strength to keep up with the rush. She took small, small sips. Sometimes the pauses between them were so long he grasped at that stuttering spark of life in her mind, making sure she was still with him. Of course, that was irrational, because if her life slipped away, he would feel it, as if that monstrous creature behind him had landed on his body like a ton of bricks. He'd seen vampires lose servants before, servants with whom they had a close bond. There was no mistaking it for anything else.

His fingers were wet where blood had seeped past them, and he knew her mouth and chin were stained with it. He'd have to clean that off. His lady was very fastidious. She had meticulous table manners, didn't believe in gulping blood down like a wolf, even if her life depended on it. He saw tears splotch down on the sand beneath him, and knew they'd squeezed out of his own eyes.

Her body was so limp, her hand lying in that loose curl on the sand. It wasn't enough. She was right; it was too late. He was losing her. She was slipping away from him, into that numb insensibility that came with death, taking away any time for good-byes, a final meeting of gazes.

He believed in an afterlife, knew it was selfish to deny it to his lady when she was so tired, had done so much, but damn it, he'd promised her he'd always be by her side, that she'd never have to leave him again.

That oath was as sacred as a marriage—hell, it was a marriage, in every sense of the word—and he wasn't backing away from it.

She wanted to see her son grow up. She had so much more she wanted to do. And she loved him. For some reason, Lady Elyssa Amaterasu Yamato Wentworth, last Queen of the Far East Clan, loved him, Jacob Green, a drifter and former vampire hunter. Another man might say a gift like that for any length of time was more than he deserved. He should be content with what he'd been given. But when it came to a treasure like that, only a madman wasn't selfish, determined to do whatever was necessary to hold on to it as long as possible.

He thought of the stories of hunters who stole the sealskin of hauntingly beautiful selkies, to make them their wives and keep them with them. And how those same men were left bereft when their Fae wife found her skin and returned to the sea. He wasn't going to let her drift away like that, briefly enjoyed and then given to memory.

Holding his hand on the heart wound, he pulled her up into his arms, into a sitting position. Her eyes were half closed, but sightless. The life spark was distant. Her body had no resistance. Curling his hand in her hair, he pulled it back, and sank his fangs into her throat.

She'd given him her vampire powers. It had been an accident, but she'd told him more than once that foreknowledge of it wouldn't have changed her actions. He'd never tried to turn anyone. All the horror stories of what could happen when a fledgling vampire tried to turn a human rocketed through his mind.

But she wasn't human, and she already bore three marks from him. He had more than a fledgling's abilities, even if he only had a fledgling's experience in handling them. He shot the silver serum directly into her carotid, a flood of acrid taste. As soon as he could no longer taste it, knew it was running through her, he began to drink. He had to drink her almost dry, because that was the way it worked. His own heart seized as she arched up in his arms with a desolate, strangled cry, but he kept pulling on that vein, gulping like a bloodstarved fledgling even as his stomach revolted, heaving.

I'm sorry, oh Jesus, my lady, I'm sorry . . . If it didn't work, and he'd made her last few moments agony, he couldn't bear it. *Please fucking work. Work, damn it.*

He made himself do what needed to be done, watched her grow

paler and paler, even as she bucked and writhed weakly in his arms. It sapped him as well, dizziness taking over, making the world spin around him. The sun dimmed. Was it never night here? What kind of hell would that be? The absence of nighttime, with full moons, chirping crickets and those quiet, solitary moments in bed with his lady, just the two of them in the whole dark universe. There was a spiritual power to joining with her body then, becoming one with her. The universe stilled under the cover of darkness, a time when everyone could experience magic.

Please, my lady. His gut was racked with pain. It was as if his heart had been ripped from his chest. He didn't need to breathe, but he still had the experience of suffocation. He broke free, turned away to retch, though he continued to hold her on his knees. It hadn't worked. That sense of separation was a brick wall coming down, strong and immediate. She was beyond his grasp.

The thought plunged him into pure desolation, worse than even this world. Worse than Hell itself.

No, no, no, no . . . Kane. Was Kane somewhere, screaming and crying, inconsolable, because he could feel that broken connection that nothing could ever replace? Jacob knew that feeling all too well. He wasn't there to comfort his son, just as his own father hadn't been, couldn't be, when he and Gideon lost their mother, lost them both.

Jacob wasn't sure he had the strength and will to give any comfort, regardless. He wanted to die. He knew he wouldn't, that he would get up, and he would do what needed to be done because of that child, her child. Their child. But in this horrible moment, he wanted to die.

He also wanted to stay curled over her. He would protect her from the sun and stay with her. *Lyssa. Sweet queen. Don't go.*

"My lady," he said brokenly, tears running over his mouth. He knew they were falling on her face, but he couldn't open his eyes to wipe them away, couldn't bear to see death at last come to rest on the face of his thousand-year-old Mistress. In the time he'd known her, she'd never revealed her exact age, maybe because she nursed a woman's vanity in that regard. That would be just like her.

As he pressed his forehead to hers, sobs racked him. His whole world was dark. He had no idea how he was going to find the strength to get up, leave this moment. Or keep himself from killing Rhoswen, which would earn him a death sentence, and prevent him from returning to Kane.

"Shhh." Her hand curved over his skull, fingertips in his hair. "Sad Irishman. 'S all right. I'm here. Shhh . . ."

He lifted his head, disbelieving. She'd thought she was hallucinating, when he was here with her in the bright light of day, and now he had the same incredulous feeling. He could feel that emptiness, that loss, pulsing through him like a terminal fever. But she was looking up at him, still weak but alive. It had worked. More than worked. His intuition, honed from vampire hunting, detected the vampire, knew that part of her blood had kindled once more. It was pumping like he'd tapped a well, bringing the waters gushing forth, rapidly filling a dry basin.

She had that stillness in her gaze all vampires had, particularly the very old ones. He had forgotten how obvious it was, when she was truly, strongly vampire. The energy of it pulsed against him with that stillness. She'd recognized it as well, was feeling her way through it. He could still detect the Fae blood, a shifting balance. It wasn't a reversal, though. The Fae blood wasn't being obliterated by the vampire. It was as if they were . . . equalizing.

He felt the restrained strength in her fingers, in the way she touched him. She was reminding herself of the little things. Like that too tight a grip could crush a skull. A fragile, mortal human skull.

He realized it then, a shock that went to his core. His fangs were gone, replaced by normal canines. He was human again. But the emptiness . . . he scrambled through his mind, realized what it was. The second-mark mindlink, the geographic first link, he still felt those threads, but the third, the one that filled his soul with her, it was gone as if it had never been.

When he twitched his shoulders, he felt the physical evidence of the third mark, that serpentine impression. But Brian had said there were reasons for that mark beyond a vampire's ken, beyond what they scientifically knew about the marks. Every time he and Lyssa had faced things that said they could go no farther—*don't step past this line*—they'd let their bond with one another lead them.

It wasn't a vampire bond. It was *their* bond, the one that would exist throughout the ages, no matter what. That was what that serpentine fossil mark meant, and that was why it was still there.

Even so, he wanted that third mark back. It was as sacred as a marriage, holding the same meaning and then some. Though she was weak, he saw the same thing in her eyes. Its absence disturbed her as much as it did him.

She stiffened, her nostrils flaring. "They've found us."

Following the direction her head turned, he saw the small shapes coming across the landscape. Four or five of them.

"Get what you need, my lady. Keldwyn said a portal should open up once you had your hands on what Rhoswen wanted." Glancing down, he was relieved to see his return to mortality had not brought back the desert brand. "I should be able to follow you out that door."

She nodded. "The pack. Get the pouch Rhoswen gave me for the gemstone."

When he did, instead of putting the gem in it, she positioned it beneath the canopy of the small bush. Curious, he watched her touch the closest branch. It dissolved, a cloud of misty ash that drifted into the pouch. She did it to the next branch and the next. Whatever enchantment had held the plant together this long appeared to be directing the residue into the bag, not a single cloud drifting beyond the mouth.

Jacob kept his eye on the advancing attack. "Do you still have your Fae abilities, my lady?"

She nodded, still focused on her task. "It feels as if I do. I don't know if they're the same magnitude or not, but it's a curious feeling, like things have . . . expanded inside of me. The vampire I was is all, fully there. But I don't feel I've lost anything of what I've discovered about my Fae blood. Whether or not that's the case, even with your blood and the restoration of the vampire side, I feel weak yet. I don't know how much I'll be able to do against them."

"Well, a near-death experience can take it out of you." He stroked a hand down her back. "We'll be fine. Please just hurry, my lady."

The last of the plant dissolved into the pouch then, a fickle breeze blowing the sand off that glittering red gem. A tiny teacup rose appeared to be frozen inside it. When Lyssa picked it up, the stone was large enough to fit in her palm.

She clasped it to her breast, her face getting quiet, pensive as it had when she told Jacob she'd touched her father through that conduit. Jacob tied the pouch to the belt loop of her torn and bloody tunic, while she handed him the pack. When they met gazes, he knew she was giving him the supplies and weapons because her exit was more certain than his.

"If I don't come through with you," he said steadily, "Do what you need to do with Rhoswen, then come back for me."

Shadows flashed through her eyes, and with that second-mark link he caught glimpses of the nightmarish memories of what she'd seen for the past two days. "I will not be leaving you behind," she said flatly.

Since they were both wobbling, they helped each other to their feet. As one, they looked toward the approaching enemy. They were much closer. "When the portal opens," Lyssa said, her voice even, deadly calm, "hold on to me, tight and close as you can. If she knows you're here, she'll try her best to shake you loose, leave you behind."

"Like Tam Lin." He looked down at her, stroked back a lock of her hair from her sunburned, bloody face. The bruises and scratches weren't healing. It might be the effect of the Fae world, but it wasn't. Even second-marked, he knew her needs, the pallor of her skin. She needed blood. Lots of it. "To save Tam Lin, the girl who loved him had to hold on to him tightly, though the Fae queen turned him into a variety of frightening creatures to get her to let go. But in the end, she held on, and Tam Lin and she lived happily ever after."

"All the more reason to hold on." Her cracked lips curved, her attention shifting. "Murphy's Law. Looks like they're going to get here before Rhoswen gets around to opening a door."

Jacob bent, found a mace and a short sword in the pack, along with several other knives. Clasping the handles of the mace and short sword together, he straightened and handed her the knives. "They say that things here are capricious, but they seem damn premeditated to me."

"I'll miss eating food," she said calmly. "I hadn't expected to like that so much."

"Yeah. I missed that one a lot myself."

"Well, you'll eat for both of us. But not too much. If you get fat and lazy, I'll have to find myself another . . ."

She stopped before she said it, that final word. Because at the moment, he wasn't her full servant, was he? God damn it, what a crazy thing to be bugging him right now, bugging them both, but there it was.

The oncoming five were less than a hundred yards away now. Carrying scraps of metal, beaten into crude weapons, they were like zombies out of a slasher flick, only with a far more conscious determination to overwhelm whoever stood in their path. They horrified him, even as it increased his admiration for her anew, thinking how many of these she'd defeated to get here.

He tightened his hand on the sword. When they shifted apart, shoulder to shoulder, she gave him enough room to swing the mace. On a second thought, he leaned down, yanked another weapon out of the pack, this one a wicked-looking machete, and tossed it to her. Dropping one knife, Lyssa caught the machete in the same motion. "I'll bet there's quite a story behind how Keldwyn got his hands on this." She considered the blade, flashing in the sun.

"You could write a book of stories about that one, period. Here they come, my lady."

The creatures broke ranks, making a weird noise between a croaking roar and a hiss like a snake as they charged. The sound would flavor his nightmares for some time to come, along with their bloodshot staring eyes and faces bubbled and leathered with sun damage. All evidence of what they'd endured here. Any rational creature would have commited suicide to avoid this fate, but maybe by the time they reached this point they were beyond rationality.

He took the first one with a solid blow with the mace, close enough to get spattered by the blood and brain matter. His lady leaped into the fray with the machete, taking a head off with a smooth stroke. Despite her tough couple of days, she demonstrated such elegant footwork he was almost caught with his mouth open and his guard down. Yes, she'd led small armies during the Territory Wars, but he'd never seen her fight hand to hand. Hell, he might ask her to protect *him* going forward.

He could imagine her caustic retort. *Jacob, I'm not risking my manicure when I have a perfectly good servant to fight for me . . .*

Ducking under his next opponent's lurch, he came back up with a parry and thrust. As the Fae tried to block his sword with a makeshift shield of lashed-together bones, he smashed the shield into shards with the mace, taking out the side of the male's face. The eyes burned into his one last moment, blind pain and fury. Twisting around, Jacob saw a green light limn his lady's figure, the doorway opening where she stood, now fifteen feet away from him.

Jacob.

Another new opponent was coming in fast with two sharp blades, but he managed to backpedal in her direction. She'd taken down her two opponents, but was fighting the pull of that portal as fiercely. Her face showed the incredible strain, her feet planted and arms stretched out wide, holding herself anchored in this world. The green light started to flicker. If they missed their opportunity, Rhoswen might not open it again in time for Lyssa to survive another two days, vampire or no.

Chucking his sword at the last attacker, he spun, snatched up the pack, took two fast strides and sprang. Too slow. He snarled as the blade thunked solidly into his lower back. It didn't stop his forward momentum. Hitting Lyssa mid-body, he wrapped himself around her, tumbling them both through the portal.

~

That absolute darkness again, but he smelled forest floor beneath them. He was on top of her, her heartbeat under his chest, his arm still around her waist, fingers curled in her tunic. When he put his forehead on hers, they drew a sigh of relief together. She felt her way down his back, found the serrated blade. As she pulled it free, he shuddered at the tearing sensation, but refused to let her go. When he'd entered this dark chasm to the desert portal, it had been sinister, no place he'd want to linger. Now, free of the desert world, alive, and yet not quite in Rhoswen's clutches, this in-between place was the best place he could imagine.

Lyssa pressed her lips to his face, his cheekbone, his jaw, then his mouth. He cradled her face in his hands, deepened the kiss, pressing his body down into hers so he felt every curve, the way her thighs spread, a natural cradle for him.

Then her touch slid down his jaw, to his throat. She broke the kiss and used her thumb to tilt his chin up, testing that restored strength, letting him feel the strain in his neck, his shoulders. With a Mistress's natural bent, she demonstrated the ability to hold him as she wished.

When her mouth touched his throat, he trembled, his fingers curling into the torn tunic on her hips.

Jacob, you once again have a choice.

"No, my lady." He murmured it into her hair, the shell of that beautiful ear. "You do. I was always born to be your servant, from the very first time my soul came into this world. You are my heart, and if I'm not fully bound to that heart, then I'm not whole. You understand?"

"It is my choice." She repeated it, her other hand moving to his face in the black, but he knew what her expression was, could tell only by her voice, the way he knew everything about her body language, her emotions, her cravings and darkness.

He swallowed. "Yes, my lady. All choices, when it comes to my life, my will, are yours."

She was feeling a Mistress's pleasure in his words, a Mistress's craving that surged to the forefront, no matter the carnage they'd left behind, or how weak she felt, what she'd been through. It was not just the nature of the vampire, but the nature of the woman herself.

The superior strength and quickness, those powers she'd given him with her turning, they would now reside within her once again, when she reached full strength. While he could mourn those abilities to protect her, and there would be times his alpha nature would deeply regret their loss when he wanted to resist her attempts to be too much the Mistress with him, he knew this was how it was meant to be. She'd tilted the universe to save him, and the universe had been kind enough to allow it. But now it was returning to how it was meant to be.

"Please, my lady. Lyssa."

Her fangs eased in, a hum in her throat, an emotional sound echoed in his aching heart.

I've missed this, Sir Vagabond. Feeding from you as a vampire.

I've missed it as well, my lady. And he had. There in the desert world, he'd almost begged her to take the precious time to reinstitute that mark.

I like it when you beg, Jacob. You know this. "But I also know your heart." She slid her fangs out to tease him a bit as she spoke, pricking his skin. "I feel that emptiness, calling to me. I want that bond as well, enough to make me hesitate, to be sure you're sure. You say it is my choice, and I *will* agree it is, for you long ago surrendered to me as your Mistress, but I will ask you to say it one more time."

"I will do more than that, my lady." Lifting her hand, he placed it upon his chest, over his heart, and spoke the oath he'd taken under Thomas's training. The oath he'd spoken the night he'd been given fifty lashes, part of the Ritual of Binding to a Vampire Queen.

"I am sworn to your service. Compelled by absolute loyalty, I safeguard your well-being before my own or any other ties of family or friendship. I swear it by the giving of my blood to you and before all of divinity, may my life be cursed and my soul be damned if I speak false or ever betray the vow."

She pressed her fangs back into him again then, and this time he felt the release of the serum. He made himself hold still for it, even though he wanted her so badly. He wanted to touch her, to press her body back down under his, reinforce that oath, this re-marking. The craving was so fierce he wondered if he'd somehow retained that ceaseless vampire carnality.

Sexual drive is still very strong in a third-mark, Jacob. A touch of humor, coupled with something deeper, moved through her. *Plus, you have always had a delicious, natural abundance of it.*

Lyssa slid a hand over her servant's chest. Her servant. One taste of her blood away from being her full servant once again. She had to admit it . . . she'd been a vampire for a long time, and though her Fae blood was an integral part of her, this felt more like her real self. In the end, perhaps she was more a vampire with Fae powers, than a Fae with vampire ones. It was good to feel that, to know that. To understand more about who and what she was. To feel a true sense of that, the power and strength of it, for the first time in several years. Even if she was otherwise a bit on the weak side . . . at the moment.

Lying back on the forest floor, she drew him down upon her again. "Brace yourself over me, Jacob," she commanded in a husky voice.

He pressed his palms into the earth on either side of her. In this utter darkness, where neither had the ability to see, it was even more intimate. Though she always liked the pleasure of seeing him, touch had its own special benefits. Opening his laced trousers, she slid her hand over his cock, thick and ready in her hand. It was already turgid from her marking him, the significance of that having its effect on him. It had moved her deeply, how important it was to him, how much he wanted that mark reinstated, to the point it had almost panicked him, not having it. She understood, because she experienced the same feeling, knowing it wasn't there.

The leggings she wore were in tatters, so it was easy enough to slip out of them, guide him into her. "At my pace, my servant," she whispered, and he obeyed, holding back all that delicious strength as she took him slowly to the hilt, then drew him down upon her. His elbows came to rest in line with his palms, surrounding her. He didn't like putting his full weight on her, always worried about her comfort, but she let him see in her mind now that he was not causing her any harm, only pleasure. She wanted his weight as she tilted her head back, guided his mouth to her throat, that delicious feeling of a Goddess nurturing her lover, even as she took him in her body. It reminded her of the ritual she'd witnessed with Tabor and Rhoswen the previous night.

Drink from me, Jacob. Make the mark complete.

He'd remembered how to use his canines, how to bite strong and not hesitate, using the second-mark strength to be decisive about it. Her pussy rippled around him as he did it, welcoming him. During that fight before the portal opened, though the two of them were well coordinated in battle, their mind communication aligned, it wasn't the same as a third mark. She'd felt that absence keenly, a knife in her lower vitals as much as it was for him.

It swept through them both, that disorienting power and heat, the wash of energy that momentarily locked their bodies together in its burn. The third-marking bound his soul to her. She could dive as deeply into him as she wished, owning every part of him, every molecule of blood, every muscle, every thought, every wish, every feeling. It required, no, demanded a level of trust unknown in any world. Human, vampire or Fae. Only vampires and servants had this potential, because once the bond was made, a servant had no choice but to learn to accept it. However, those like Jacob who took the step into that unknown territory willingly, who embarked on that journey, and the vampires who appreciated that leap of faith—a leap ironically that they themselves, as Dominants, did not often have the same ability to take—had a relationship like no other.

As she felt that bond again, she exulted in it, revitalized in a way that might be deceptive, given her many hours in the desert world, but she would accept it nevertheless. She knew he'd miss the ability to protect her to the level that being a vampire had given him, but he didn't realize he'd protected her more than any male who'd ever been in her life. Most of the time, she could take care of herself physically. It was on the emotional terrain she'd always had to defend her own ramparts, guard against ambushes. She'd never been able to relax certain parts of herself enough to fully love. He'd given her that, her brave, reckless Irish knight.

She squeezed down on him then, holding him banded in her arms as she lifted her hips, took him deeper. *Give me pleasure, Jacob. Give me everything.* His back was already healing, the power of a third-marking.

He licked the wound on her neck, suckled her there, then moved up to her lips, letting her taste her blood on his mouth. Slipping a hand under her nape, he held her to deepen the kiss, then braced his hand next to them to obey her, beginning to thrust, slow, easy, then harder, reinforcing the fact they were alive, bonded, unable to be separated. She gasped into his mouth, her arousal building so quickly it startled her. Jacob had once made the joke that a half-dead vampire could still fuck a person to death before they gave out, and she remembered it now, gloriously. Vampire or no, Jacob could make her body sing like no other lover she'd had.

Careful, my lady. You know how full of myself I can get.

Duly noted, Sir Vagabond. She put her smile against his temple, a smile that became a straining, parted-mouth cry as he pushed her up and over the wall of her climax, falling with her only when she gave him leave to do so, something he'd always done, even as vampire.

He was her devoted knight, serving her to the last reserves of his soul.

19

THEY emerged from that darkness into a Fae morning. Since Jacob had explained the sun issue to her, it didn't make her recoil. Instead, she stopped, drew in the scent of the morning air and lifted her face to the warmth, closing her eyes. "I'll miss this as well."

"Maybe if this liaison thing works out, you'll be able to visit again."

"Rhoswen will probably change the environment so I'll be toasted the next time I step into this world."

"True. Queens can be a bit vindictive that way."

She sent a narrow glance his way. He was resting on his heels at a stream edge, trailing his fingers in the water, mesmerizing a small group of fish with large purple eyes and iridescent pink tails. Now, though, he straightened, came to her side. "Looks like we have a visitor."

Keldwyn reined up, two horses following obediently in his wake, mounts from Rhoswen's stable. "Well met, Lady Lyssa," he said. "It appears you succeeded."

His expression remained bland, despite her appearance. She was filthy and bloody, her snarled hair was coated with a fine layer of sand from the desert world. She wore the cloak Jacob had brought with him, covering the tattered and bloodstained tunic and leggings.

"That remains to be seen. I've yet to see Rhoswen. Is she out of the mourning period?"

"Yes, as of a few hours ago. You just made the three-day window." At Jacob's puzzled look, calculating, Keldwyn shook his head. "It's impossible to predict the rate of Fae time between magical portals."

"I expect she would have stretched her deadline if she thought she'd still get what she wanted." But Lyssa's dry tone turned to something entirely different then. His lady still had the ability to cool the temperature around her, a warning of her temper a man would be a fool not to heed. And Keldwyn was not a fool. Lyssa stepped closer, leveling a hard gaze on him.

"My father's crime was *love*. Loving a vampire, getting her with child. How could anyone but a pack of . . . monsters feel that desert was a just punishment?"

"In your own world, what punishments have been handed out to vampires or servants who have loved one another unwisely?" Keldwyn shifted his gaze to Jacob, then back to her. "It is often not a fair world, Lady Lyssa. But love persists, in all its foolishness, doesn't it?" Keldwyn dismounted then, offered her a hand. "Can I help you on your mount, escort you to the queen?"

Lyssa ignored the hand, though she did close the three steps between them. "His death destroyed something in you, didn't it?"

For a long moment, Keldwyn said nothing. Jacob felt the magic the Fae Lord carried within him shift the air around them uneasily, as if she'd stepped on the trigger for a mine. A tiny muscle flickered at the corner of one dark eye. When Keldwyn spoke, his tone was so even it was like a thread pulled perilously taut.

"Yes."

The power of that one word, the pain behind it, was enough to have Lyssa's eyes softening. She laid a hand on his face, a brief touch. He stayed entirely still, a dangerous animal who didn't trust himself, then she nodded, stepped back. "Have you seen Catriona?"

His jaw tightened. "That is hardly your concern."

"No. But it is yours. Since she's behind you, you may want to address it."

It was a rare moment to see Keldwyn startled. He twisted around. The dryad stood at the edge of the clearing. Her short dress of gauzy layers looked like pale blue and green leaves. Tiny shimmers of light sparkled over it, reflecting the same in her wings, soft flickers. Her brown hair was down, waving around her face, her thin face and large eyes young, vulnerable. She looked like a deer that might bolt, torn between trepidation and need.

Leaving Keldwyn standing there, Lyssa moved toward their two horses. Jacob followed to lift her onto the white mare's back. As she adjusted her seat to straddle the mount, freeing her cloak, Jacob swung onto the blood bay next to her. Keldwyn and Catriona had not moved, regarding one another silently.

"We'll see you at the castle, Lord Keldwyn," Lyssa said. As they moved out of the clearing, his horse snorted, but faithfully held his position near his master. Catriona's gaze flickered briefly to them. The dryad gave Jacob a nod, Lyssa a glance, and then she was back to holding that unspoken, emotional communication with the Fae Lord.

"It's like the Dr. Seuss book," Jacob said, his voice pitched low.

"The one where the two characters refuse to step around each other, and stand there for decades while civilizations rise and fall around them?" At his surprised look, Lyssa shrugged. "I like Dr. Seuss."

When she paused at the forest's edge, Jacob reined in and they both looked back. One more heartbeat of stillness, and then Catriona was moving, running across the clearing on dainty feet, her wings lifting her in graceful, urgent bounds of motion. Keldwyn stood motionless until the last moment, when abruptly he stepped forward as if he'd broken out of ice. He barely got his arms open before she hit his chest. He was braced for her, though, his arms wrapping hard around her. Even at this distance, they could tell the male was trembling from head to toe, so hard he went to one knee, holding her folded against him like a ragdoll. Pressing his jaw down on the top of her head, he clutched her like a father welcoming home a long lost daughter, and perhaps he was.

Jacob shifted his glance to Lyssa, saw her eyes glistening. Crying was something his lady had often told him she never did. Now she tossed her head to cover it, in that haughty way he knew well, that he'd missed. Something vital had come back to her, and by God, he loved seeing it, no matter what they were about to face—or the fact they *really* needed to get more blood in her before she fell over. Nudging his horse up against hers as they rode, he brushed her knee in companionable silence when they moved away from the family reunion and headed for Rhoswen's castle.

~

Cayden was on his bench at the gatehouse. Jacob raised a brow at the bruise on his face, a split lip. As the captain rose to take hold of the bridle of Lyssa's mount, he moved stiffly. Jacob's gaze narrowed. He knew that way of walking. "She had you flogged?"

"The queen metes out justice as she sees fit. It was fair. I was told to stop you. I didn't."

Jacob bit down on a retort at Lyssa's warning glance. Following his lady and Cayden through the courtyard, he noticed the staff gave them some curious glances. With their heightened senses, they probably detected their differences, even if not the clear nature of them.

When they reached the main hall, there were no retainers and no throne. No ice sculptures, either. Just fountains this time, filling the wide space with the sound of rushing water. Rhoswen sat on the edge of the largest fountain, one with a life-sized statue of a Fae lord on a horse in the center, the water pouring out from the dais beneath the horse's feet. Floating in the fountain were thick rose blooms, petals jeweled with drops from the fountain. Probably bespelled never to wilt, their life essence captured inside.

His lady stopped, stared at the statue. Rhoswen didn't look up, though she obviously knew they were there. Lyssa glanced at him, nodded, her pale face quiet, serene.

Wait here at the door, Jacob.

Her servant obeyed reluctantly, but when he took up position at the entranceway, Lyssa noted Cayden stayed with him, as if his queen had commanded the same. Interesting. A pace or two away from Rhoswen, she stopped, studied the statue. The noble features, broad shoulders. The planes of his face that reminded her of her own. Her chest tightened, her heart doing a double beat. "Is this what he looked like?"

"Yes." Rhoswen passed her fingers through the water, caressing the roses. She didn't lift her gaze. Her hair was tied loosely on her shoulders. "At Beltane, in honor of spring and creation, there is a competition of sorts. Each contestant brings forth something they have created to honor the new season, and to please the Unseelie queen and Seelie king. The king and queen choose the best of the new creations, and that creation is displayed appropriately until the following year. The year after Lord Reghan was sentenced, Lord Keldwyn commissioned an artisan to do this. He offered it as his entry. A Seelie or Unseelie of his rank wasn't expected to participate in a common competition in the first place. It's typically for the solitary Fae. So it was obviously an act of defiance."

"I take it he was noticed."

"He was lucky he was not killed. It was what my mother wanted. Instead, it was the first time he was banished." Rhoswen stared at nothing, nothing but the past. "For a decade, that time. Of course, by repeatedly banishing him, they ensured that he eventually saw the mountains in your world as more his home than the Fae world."

"Perhaps he found something there that he'd lost here."

Rhoswen turned her gaze to Lyssa then. She took in her appearance without any obvious reaction, then rose. Circling the statue, she trailed her fingers in the water to create a wake from her passing. "In the thousand years of your life, you have seen many horrors, both human and vampire. You fought your Territory Wars, established a Vampire Council to achieve a balance between brutality and intellect. It is a long road."

"Yes. It has been. But some parts have been too short." Remembering the day a knight had helped her against vampire hunters, Lyssa knew the blissful night following had been the shortest of her life. But until Jacob had reentered her life, it had been the most memorable.

"You see me through the eyes of a short period of time, your mortal hours. But there is so much more that has happened. Reasons for how and what we are, that must be."

"There is no reason I can fathom for that desert world except an abuse of power and capricious cruelty. Since my father was subjected to it, I assume many others were put there for similarly disproportionate reasons."

"We have not sentenced anyone there for several centuries. It was barbaric. From a different time."

"Some still survive there. I killed quite a few to reach my objective." Lyssa studied her, pressed her lips together hard. "You know about the survivors."

"There are a handful of Fae laws that are unbreakable, woven into the fabric of what and who we are." Rhoswen frowned. "One is that any judgment handed down from a king, queen or governing Council may not be undone. Ever. It may be approached differently, however." She gave a humorless smile. "From your exposure to Keldwyn, I'm sure you've gained an appreciation for how we twist our way past obstacles. For instance, I can destroy the desert world, but it is a place that has existed long enough to have its own sentience, its own purpose, so I will be snapping strands of Fate if I do that. Therefore, it is not an option, much as I have wished it was. I did rule there would be no more Fae sent there, even those who commit heinous crimes. We execute them instead."

Sitting back down on the fountain's edge, she fastened vibrant eyes on Lyssa, obviously ready to move away from the topic. "Where is it?"

"What do you plan to do with it?"

"Whatever I wish." When the queen shifted her scrutiny to Jacob, Lyssa shook her head.

"You think I'd be foolish enough to bring it here? Why do you think Keldwyn met us? He has free range between two worlds; he can hide it in either of them."

Rhoswen's face froze in pale anger. "I commanded you to bring it to me. To do otherwise breaks our laws."

"I am his daughter," Lyssa said shortly. "Do you really think I'd just turn his soul over to you, whatever consequences you issue—"

"You are *not* his daughter."

The queen snarled, the sound echoing through the hall. She hit the water, freezing the roses on temptestuous ripples of ice that popped, reacting to the water's abrupt transformation.

As she surged up from the fountain, she advanced on Lyssa with such anger that Lyssa braced herself for attack, well aware that Jacob and Cayden shifted into position to do the same.

"Tabor invites Reghan's daughter to the Hunt." Rhoswen spat the words, her tone bitter, mocking. "All the whispers . . . *Reghan's daughter, Reghan's daughter*. They can see Reghan's daughter any day, any moment of their choosing. I am the daughter of his Fae blood, of *pure* Fae blood. And you . . . if it was not obvious before, it is undeniable now. Your Fae blood is not what holds sway in you. It is the vampire. You don't belong here. You may be from his loins, but you are not of his blood. You are *not* one of us."

She drew herself up, and Lyssa noted there was a slight tremor to the hands at her sides. "Here I am known as Magwel's daughter, my mother's daughter. The mother who loved me so little and loved herself so much that she tried to deny me a father. But he loved me. He made me love him, more than anyone I've ever loved. And then, in the end, he chose you. He chose a daughter he never met, and a woman who was not a Fae, who was a *vile*, inferior blood drinker. He died and left me alone, alone with a mother capable of loving no one. In a thousand years, it should mean nothing to me. *Nothing*. The fact that it does, that all this continues to raise its poisonous, ugly head, over and over again, is what makes me hate you, him and her all the more."

Lyssa glanced toward Cayden. There was pain in his face for her, and tension. Jacob was alert but quiet, waiting to see where this would go.

A smooth mask fell into place over Rhoswen's countenance, her tone an abrupt, chilling monotone. "I wish he'd been the cold and unfeeling person my mother tried to make me believe he was. Instead, she left me with the knowledge of what it is to have someone love you, only not love you enough."

Jacob knew he should have anticipated that stillness, the freezing menace, but desert sand, too much stress and trauma made his reflexes slow. With an animal sound of rage, Rhoswen leaped forward.

Bolting forward, Jacob saw she gripped a wooden dagger, runes embedded in the blade and hilt. But he couldn't have matched her speed as a vampire. As a human servant, he knew he was already too late.

He caught his lady's body as she was knocked backward. The next moment was nothing more than a blink, but like Fae time, that blink was an eternity in his mind before he realized the dagger wasn't buried in his lady's chest. Rhoswen hadn't reached Lyssa at all, because there was someone in the room just as swift as the angry queen.

Cayden stood toe-to-toe with her, his large gauntleted hand gripping her wrist, face grim as his arm became coated with ice. Rhoswen screamed at him, incoherent Fae words. He caught her to him with the other arm, controlling her movements and refusing to let her yank back as he used a warrior's training to break her grip on the weapon and send it clattering to the floor.

"No, Your Majesty. Please, cease . . . Damn it, that's *enough*."

The thunderous roar was probably one he used on the practice field. It served its purpose, bringing her up short, shock gripping her features.

The moment he realized he'd distracted her from her purpose, Cayden released her, backed up two steps and dropped to his knees. He kept himself between her and Lyssa, however. Jacob was in a half kneel by his lady's side, ready to move forward to defend her if needed. She probably had better fighting skills than Rhoswen, but despite her apparent vitality, she still hadn't fed or rested enough to stand against a normal vampire, let alone a powerful Fae.

"Forgive me, my lady." Cayden spoke. "But you are far better than this."

"You would turn against me, too?" Her eyes were wild, her body trembling.

When he lifted his head, his face showed his anguish. Pulling out his short sword, he offered it to her. "If you believe that, my lady, take my life. I will not exist in a world where you don't believe that every beat of my heart, every drop of blood in my veins, serves you. But serving you is not following you blindly. It's helping you be everything you've ever wanted to be, for your people . . . and for yourself. So please, my lady. Kill me now or stop torturing yourself . . . and those who do not deserve your wrath."

Rhoswen stared at him, nostrils flared. Letting out a furious cry, she yanked the blade from his grasp and swung it downward. Jacob and Lyssa both leaped toward them, but before they could reach the captain's side, she drove it into the tile before him, cracking the stone and embedding the blade to nearly half its length. Letting go, she stepped back, breathing hard. "Go back to the doorway. Do your job. Guard."

Cayden bowed his head, his great fists clenching, then he rose and obeyed. Rhoswen pivoted on her heel. She stood still for several moments. Then, with precise steps, as if she were walking on ice in truth, she returned to the fountain, folding herself down onto its stone ledge.

Jacob glanced at Lyssa. *That was unexpected.*

But useful. Join Cayden again, Sir Vagabond. I'll be all right.

She squeezed his arm, telling him she knew what she was doing. Though he didn't like it, he obeyed. Before he moved to the doorway, though, he pulled the sword from the floor with a grunt and shower of rock. It was a sign of how upset Cayden was that he'd left it there. Of course, even if the man was stripped naked, he wouldn't be defenseless by a long shot. Still, a warrior didn't leave a blade behind, unless he just didn't care if he was skewered with it.

As Jacob reached the door, he extended the sword hilt first, much as he had on that first day. Cayden took it from him with a stilted expression. Despite the flogging, Cayden was wearing full mail. Jacob expected Rhoswen had ordered it to increase the pain and discomfort, and to remind him of his place.

"Sorry," he muttered. "I didn't say it was safe advice."

Cayden gave him a sidelong glance. Though he said nothing, Jacob caught a curl of the taut mouth, almost a grim smile.

Lyssa moved back to the fountain. "You know, before I came here, Keldwyn said everything else can change, but you can't change someone's fundamental nature, who they are. It doesn't matter whether they're human, vampire or Fae."

"Sounds like his usual cryptic cynicism."

Lyssa lifted a shoulder. "I've been vampire all my life, but I also carry Fae blood. Neither changes who I am, above and beyond both. Like my servant." She glanced at Jacob. "I'm a vampire queen, a fate and destiny that sometimes has been difficult, but it has always been who I am. The moment I felt the strength of it return to my blood, it felt . . . right. Even as I know the Fae part of me is fated to play a role. You say I don't belong here, but you won't let me go, so I think you know it as well."

Cautiously, she moved closer. "Lord Reghan did not choose one daughter over another. He chose honor. As either one of us would have done."

She sank down on the edge of the fountain, despite the fact it was like sitting on an ice block. "I watched you cry for that old man, a mere human, the night in the cemetery. Grief and loss is something we all understand. It binds us. My former servant was there that night, and he told me that . . ." She paused, steadying herself. "Thomas told me that Rex, my husband, weeps over what he did to me. I have forgiven him, but it was very, very hard."

Rhoswen lifted her head, and though it was almost as difficult, Lyssa no more disposed to show weakness than the Fae queen, she let her see the vulnerability, the raw pain that thinking of Rex could still summon. She was glad for the comforting, nonintrusive touch of Jacob's mind. "He did the things he did to me out of illness, but also out of a weakness in character, an innate cruelty."

She took another breath before she continued. "Our father . . . it appears he was an honorable, brave male who did his best to love his family, all of us, and do what he thought was right. If I can forgive a male like Rex, who was so much less in character, then Lord Reghan is worthy of your forgiveness. I expect he would want your forgiveness, not just for his own sake, but as your loyal captain just showed, for yours. He wouldn't want to be an open wound in his daughter's heart."

As a queen herself, she saw Rhoswen as a peer, so Lyssa had no qualms about reaching out and laying her hand on hers. When the Fae's gaze went to that contact, Lyssa wondered how long it had been since someone had touched her without calculated design or permission. She suspected it had been quite a while.

"I know what it is to rule from isolation. To not trust anyone because of betrayal. But if you are brave enough to love, you *will* be a great queen. And there are already those in your life who bear you great love, no matter how sorely you test it."

Lyssa tilted her head toward the doorway. "My Irish wolfhound, Bran, is the only creature I've met as single-mindedly devoted as your captain. Though Bran smells less gamey."

That won a brief flash in the queen's expression that might have been humor. "Tabor would be an extremely strong ally to you in whatever way you need," Lyssa persisted. "And I do not know your history when Keldwyn was your Regent, but I still sense loyalty to you in him, though it is on his own difficult terms."

Rhoswen's lip curled. "I do not trust him."

"It doesn't mean he's not loyal. He was close to our father, right?"

Rhoswen's jaw tightened over the "our," but she let it stand. Looked up at the statue. "Though he had it commissioned, you can see the love there, how every chip of the sculptor's blade was supervised. They were best friends, close as brothers. Perhaps more. There are those who said Keldwyn and he were lovers, off and on. While Keldwyn has never said, I do not doubt he loved Reghan. I was there the day he presented this statue. He was much younger then, of course. But the way his eyes flashed, his expression of utter defiance and grieving rage . . . I'd never seen him exhibit such emotion."

"Then it stands to reason, he would feel a strong compunction to protect and serve Reghan's offspring. Either one of us." Lyssa moved her fingers over the cool hand, drawing her gaze again. "I am your sister, Rhoswen, royalty in my own world, whether or not that world or my position in it has any of your respect. Tabor is offering us a chance to make this a better world on both sides. Let me give you that, and maybe, in time, we can build together what neither of us has. A trusted blood relative."

Rhoswen had lifted her face to stare at the statue again. As Lyssa watched her, her blue eyes glistened, then a tear rolled down out of her eye, freezing on her cheek like single diamond. Lyssa brushed it off with one light finger. Rhoswen didn't move, but when Lyssa touched her hand again, there was a linking of fingers, a tentative gesture that was somehow permissible because Rhoswen kept her gaze averted from it, not acknowledging what her body was doing.

"You don't want to harm his soul," Lyssa realized. "You wanted a part of him back."

"I thought I could put the soul essence into the statue. It would make it a place of power, of strong energy."

"A place for a queen to go and meditate for guidance. This queen, or any of those who succeed her."

"You know I'm barren. Keldwyn told you, of course." Rhoswen's lips curved, bittersweet. "A Fae queen of ice and water, unable to have a child. But there are others who would be suitable heirs to my throne. I shall name one in the coming years, when she is worthy."

At Lyssa's mental prompting, Jacob moved forward again. Cayden came with him of course. When Jacob stopped at Lyssa's elbow, she reached into the pack he brought, withdrew the pouch and the red gemstone.

Rhoswen blinked. "You were bluffing. How did you . . . ?"

"A bit of sorcery I learned a long time ago to protect the location of my underground bedroom at home. Fae magic, of course. I used it then without directly acknowledging it as such, out of stubbornness. We are similar in that regard."

Rhoswen's fingers had closed into a ball. When Lyssa extended the gemstone, she turned her half sister's hand over, loosened the fingers and placed the stone in it. The red stone was held between their palms, their fingers interlaced. The Fae queen closed her eyes. "It's warm. And I feel him. So faint, but I remember him . . . do you feel it?"

"I do. I never had the chance to know him, but to feel his soul essence . . . it's like the cemetery. Painful joy."

Rhoswen kept her eyes closed, but nodded. When Lyssa at last drew her hand back, the queen opened her eyes to see her lifting the pouch for her inspection. "I ask, respectfully, that you let me take the ashes of the bush home with me. The roses I planted in Atlanta were started from the rose Reghan gave my mother. I think he would like it if he were scattered over those roses, so in some way they can be together again."

"I will think on it." After a moment, Rhoswen spoke, with studied indifference. "So Tabor feels you would be a good liaison between our courts."

"He spoke of that, yes. Is he well?"

Rhoswen gave her that faintly scornful smile, though it had less heat. "He makes a good impression, doesn't he? He elicits care from total strangers. It is the type of male he is. Yes, he is well."

Shifting on the fountain, she looked down at the glistening red stone. "I expect, since your vampire and Fae abilities appear to be more balanced, and your relationship with your servant is restored to something the council understands a bit better, a liaison is not a bad idea."

She paused. "To agree with Tabor's recommendation is an acknowledgment that a relationship between our worlds can be beneficial to us, and I'm still not so sure of that. But I am willing to defer to his judgment, wait and see. I appoint you as liaison to the Vampire Council, Lady Lyssa, in addition to whatever other role you will eventually serve for them. My scribes will prepare a formal correspondence from me for you to carry to them. I think that serves both of us, just as it has served Tabor and me to have Keldwyn fulfill more than one role in our respective courts. However, you will come back here three months out of the year. The months that contain Beltane, Samhain and Yule. All Fae court members are required to participate in the rites to honor the Lord and Lady, our blessed Danu and her Consort, and all they represent in our world."

Lyssa pursed her lips. "You issue this as an edict, but by your own laws, by completing this third quest, I have some direction over my own will, my own decisions. I will come for part of Yule, but there are others I honor at Christmas as well. I will want time with them. However, I will give you two weeks of that month. I support the establishment of the liaison role and will champion it with Council. I will hope it benefits both our worlds, and heals some old wounds."

Rhoswen didn't respond, but she did not disagree, either. She took her hand away from the pouch, a tacit acceptance of Lyssa's wishes with respect to it. But as she did, she gazed back down at the roses floating past her in the water. "The old man . . . you are right, that I felt his grief and understood it. But you are wrong if you think I don't understand our similarities. Humans are not so different from Fae, for all that they need their structure. Their structure only hides how truly capricious they are. They vacillate between hate and love, joy and despair, not like a pendulum clock, which is predictable, but like the chaos of shrapnel exploding from a bomb. Much as we do."

She looked at Lyssa now with bright, harsh eyes. "I hate you . . . yet I do not, as well. What I feel toward you . . . it has no order. But I do know . . . I have a desire to see you again, sister. If you would consider coming for a few days in February . . . winters are long here. Your company, the company of your son, my nephew, might be welcome." Now she straightened, speaking as one royal to another. "I swear to you, my oath, that as a child he will never come to any harm here, no matter the tenor of our own relationship."

"I will think on it."

Rhoswen gave her a tight-lipped smile as Lyssa repeated her own haughty words. The Fae queen rose, a dismissal, but she gave Jacob an openly appraising look. "I like you better as human, former vampire. On future visits, I might very well exercise a queen's prerogative to have you share my bed again."

Jacob cleared his throat, sketched a respectful bow. "I'm ever at the disposal of my lady's will, your Majesty."

"Then I shall just have to see what I can do to compel that will."

"You better be capable of making Hell freeze over," Lyssa said politely.

Rhoswen gave her that humorless smile, but it held no more than a shadow of her earlier malice. "My scribes will prepare the correspondence and we will review it tomorrow, so I anticipate you will be able to return home shortly after that. Our dawn will align with your dusk for the next several days. Wait until then to protect your fair vampire skin, sister. Particularly since it needs some time to heal as it is."

As she turned away, bringing the audience to an end, Lyssa rose. "I'd like to ask you a question, sister. About the doll and the child's tea set."

Rhoswen stopped, but she didn't turn back, speaking instead to the sheets of water silently sliding down the wall before her. "He gave it to me, shortly after you were conceived. I have no idea how he knew his child would have dark hair and green eyes, but he was a powerful magic user, gifted with visions of different things. Sadly, his own fate was not one of them. However, perhaps he knew enough, because when he gave me the doll, he told me if I became sad, afraid or lonely, I could talk to her. She would listen, and that would help."

"Did it?"

"Not always. Sometimes I needed her to talk back." Rhoswen looked over her shoulder, gave her a tight smile. "Return to your room with your servant and have the staff care for you as needed. I have some further business to handle here. Captain, please remain."

Understanding that the doll admission was a difficult one, that the whole discussion had been draining for them both, Lyssa was willing to overlook being summarily dismissed. Acknowledging Rhoswen with a nod, she moved toward the doorway with Jacob. Cayden could have been made of stone, his face expressionless.

As they slid out, the double doors closed behind them. Jacob hesitated. *My lady, he defied her on my advice. He's already been whipped. I don't want to leave him in peril.*

"I don't think that's her intent," Lyssa said. "And though your advice may have prompted him, Captain Cayden is very much his own man." At Jacob's look, she sighed, jerked her head to the left. "Come this way. I'll show you something I learned, wandering about while you were sleeping your days away. Unnecessarily I might add."

"You didn't know about the sun any more than I did."

Do I have to do all of my servant's thinking for him? She caught his hand, breaking into a near-silent trot to take him where she intended to go.

A winding stairwell led to a narrow fissure, through which they squeezed into the upper gallery of the main hall. Using her cloaking abilities, Lyssa made sure they blended into the shadows at the rear of it. She warned Jacob to absolute silence, knowing if Rhoswen's attention strayed, they would be found out. After their conversation, Lyssa didn't think the queen would censure them for curiosity, but that curiosity would remain unfulfilled if they were noted there.

Rhoswen had sat back down on the edge of the fountain and now she beckoned. "Come stand before me, Captain."

Cayden complied, maintaining that stolid expression. Leaning forward, Rhoswen took hold of one gauntleted hand. She pulled the heavy glove off, then did the same to the other. His eyes darkened, his mouth tightening as she unbelted his tunic, setting aside his dagger and it scabbard. When she pulled the garment over his head, since he was taller, he had to help. The mail was heavy, so she stepped behind him, lifting it away from his sore back, tugging to tell him she wanted him to help her remove that as well. She dropped it to the floor with a heavy clink.

"My lady?"

"Be still." Now he was clothed in a thin undertunic and hose. Lyssa couldn't deny Jacob the anger that flashed through him at the sight of the dried blood pasting the thin shirt to his back in several raw patches.

Unsheathing Cayden's knife, Rhoswen cut the undershirt he wore, taking a strip from it. She wet it in the fountain then moved behind him again. He shuddered as she squeezed the moisture out of the cloth, dampening those stiff patches and loosening the fabric. His jaw flexed.

"My lady does not need to do that. I can—"

"Your queen will do as she wishes, and you will remain silent, unless I command you to speak. Kneel for me here, where I can sit on the fountain and attend to you."

When he did, she sat back down behind him, her feet placed on either side of his calf. Gently disengaging the cloth from his skin, she removed it, so now he was bare except for his hose, for she cut the rest of the shirt off him, using additional pieces to clean out the wounds. An attendant came in, bearing a tray of salve, evidence that Rhoswen had some telepathic ability to communicate with her staff as Lyssa did. The queen bid the attendant leave the items and go, then began to apply them with her own hands on his broad back. In addition to the wicked scar on his face, Cayden had plenty other battle scars visible under the lashes. Several near fatal blows, making Lyssa remember Rhoswen's reference to the conflicts in the Fae world.

Rhoswen didn't speak as she cosseted her guard captain, but he became progressively more discomfited by this unprecedented behavior. His hands closed into loose fists. She'd set aside the balm, but was still rubbing it in slow circles over the hard muscles in his back. Now she leaned forward and placed her lips on the nape of his neck. She stayed there, her mouth not moving, just touching his flesh. She curled her hands over his substantial biceps, holding him in place. Though he couldn't see her face, her tears had weight. Tiny diamonds of ice pattered against his skin, and hit the tile with a pling of noise.

"My lady," he murmured, his voice broken.

"Sit on the fountain edge," she said, easing her hold.

He did so, but when she slid off of it, going to her knees before him, he clasped her arms immediately, tried to bring her to a standing position. She resisted, moving so she was between his feet, her hands on his knees. He couldn't rise from his seat on the fountain without pushing her away or falling into the fountain himself.

"Lady Lyssa was correct," she said. "You have ever been loyal to me, and though I have punished your disobedience, your actions were driven by what was best for the Fae. Best for me."

"I won't tolerate you on your knees to me, my lady," he said, struggling to rise. "This is—"

"An apology, Captain Cayden. A heartfelt apology." He stopped, caught by the sincerity in her blue eyes. "Cayden, we have known one another for so very long. We've fought together, lost together. I know you love me well. Perhaps too well. If it has become too difficult to serve me, I will give you leave to serve anywhere else in the Seelie or Unseelie world, with nothing but the greatest of praise for you. Tabor would welcome you. Your father was Seelie. You have as much acceptance there as you do here."

"And who would care for you, my lady? Watch over you?"

Cupping his face, she touched his mouth with her thumb. "Though I am quite capable of caring for myself, I'm sure you already have at least five men trained to take your position if ever you fell." Her eyes lifted to his, an intriguing mixture of cool reproach and urgent heat at once. "If that ever happened, I would utterly destroy whoever dared take you from me. Then I would grieve deeply."

Withdrawing her hand, she sat back on her heels and then gracefully rose, stepping back from him. Her face became that dispassionate mask, but one that still managed to convey the strong emotions moving behind it.

"I have abused your service, over and over. I release you from it, and give you the right to ask for retribution from your queen, for the injury she has done to you."

Lyssa glanced at Jacob. From the formality of her tone, and Cayden's stunned expression, it was an offer of unprecedented significance. She lifted her chin. "That means if you want me flogged as you were flogged—"

Surging up from the fountain then, he closed the distance between them in two steps. He didn't touch her, but the effort not to do so was obviously overwhelming. "No one shall ever touch your fair skin, my lady. I would tear off the arm of the first man who lifted a whip."

"But you accept my right to do it to you." She trailed her fingers over his shoulder, touching the edge of an unhealed lash mark. The touch elicited a flicker in his gaze that wasn't pain. "You should be less accepting, Captain Cayden."

Now something trembled in her expression, something that made Jacob remember the armory, when Rhoswen had faced the unexplored but undeniable part of her.

"Perhaps I wasn't thinking of having *someone* do it. Perhaps I was thinking of you. You are a very direct man, one who handles things personally. You might not even wish to use a whip. Perhaps you'd like to use your own hand."

She'd recognized her captain's nature in much the way she had hers. Jacob wondered how long she'd known, and if it had tormented her as he was sure the elusive glimpses of her own nature had tempted Cayden. Now the captain swallowed audibly. While it was hard to tell when the woman was playing a strategic game, Jacob thought Rhoswen might be more nervous than she was revealing.

She is, Jacob. She's trembling. He's close enough to feel it.

"My lady." Cayden cupped her face now, drew her against his bare chest, wrapping an arm corded with battle-hardened muscle around her. "I will never leave your service. If you took away my rank and cast me out, I would sit at your castle gates, sleeping by the moat like a vagabond to be close to you. Whenever you had need of my protection and strength, I would be there. I serve you, in all things."

Another Sir Vagabond. Lyssa was amused but touched as well, Jacob could tell.

Cayden lifted her chin, looked into her blue eyes. There was strength in the grip, command, even as he spoke carefully. "However, if one of the things you need from your servant in private is to force your surrender, to give yourself permission to feel, to laugh, to cry . . . to heal and forget . . . then I am more than equal to that task."

The soldier was now trembling as well, both daring far more than they'd ever dared. Lyssa looked at Jacob. *We've eavesdropped long enough. He is safe from her wrath, for now. But I want exact details about what happened between you two that resulted in this.*

How she connected it to Jacob, he didn't know, but he'd long ago stopped underestimating his Mistress. Of course, he wasn't sure if she was talking about his confrontation with Cayden or the night with Rhoswen. He hoped the former, though by even having the thought, her dangerous curiosity latched on to it like an arrow pointing where he didn't want her to go. He winced. Having been a vampire for a millennium meant she'd picked right back up on how to use all the perks of being one. She could open his mind like a tuna can.

But that was his queen. He didn't want her any other way.

~

She slept deeply. She needed more blood. Since she would only take so much from Jacob, and refused a human donor like Sellya, claiming she preferred to wait to seek more nourishment until she returned home, he sent a note to Keldwyn via Sellya, asking for a favor. Whether or not the enigmatic Fae Lord would accommodate him remained to be seen.

Close to dawn, he left Lyssa nested in the covers to sit in the window seat. He sensed it would be a while before they returned to the Fae world. Surprisingly, Jacob found the idea bugged him. He remembered the dancing in the forest, the sirens and angels. The Hunt. He recalled when they'd chased the hart, being with Tabor and his comrades. His lady's arms around his waist as she pressed against him. Here the fairy tales and legends were real.

He understood Rhoswen's fear of too much interaction between their worlds. The human world, except in its more remote corners, had been irrevocably altered with time, fields and deer tracks replaced by concrete and traffic. Even in its most remote corners, concert T-shirts and soda cans showed up. The Fae world drew on Nature and the elements as a vampire nourished himself on blood. It would not be altered by the wrong kind of change; the magic that was its heart could be destroyed by it. Nevertheless, Rhoswen's realization that there were unacceptable risks in stagnation had made her take a brave step, more indicative of the type of queen Keldwyn's words and Cayden's loyalty had suggested of her from the beginning.

Of course, Jacob expected Rhoswen's response to that would be there was a fine line between a queen's courage and her foolishness. His lips twitched. It was something his own lady might say, in her usual dry tone.

As dawn arrived, Lyssa began to stir. With her vampire blood holding sway, their impending leave-taking seemed to be aligning her to the dusk of their own world. When she was at her peak, she'd sleep lightly, and come out of sleep so alert, it was like she didn't sleep at all. He knew that, not only because he'd seen it before, but because that had been his experience.

Moving to the mirror, he looked at himself, something he'd been unable to do as a vampire. No change of course. Even as a servant, with an average three-hundred-year lifespan, he wouldn't age. When a servant reached the end of his days, the systems started shutting down, like an appliance that had reached the age beyond which it couldn't operate, no matter how shiny it appeared on the outside.

Three hundred years wasn't long enough with her. No amount of time would be. But if she wanted to turn him in the future, he already knew he wouldn't be willing to let her risk the loss of her powers again. Beyond that, just as she'd felt that being more vampire than Fae was her true self, being her servant was his. Of course, he'd as much as said he was that, no matter his form.

Well, there would be a few centuries to think about that, God willing.

"I dreamed Kane was crying."

Moving away from the mirror, he came to her side, slid a hip next to her. Her black hair was soft around her face, her green eyes half open. "If he's crying, then it's because Mason is telling him about women. How falling in love with one makes you insane."

Sliding her arms around his neck, she drew him down to her. "I think he's crying because Jessica is telling him he will turn into a pig-headed package of inevitable testosterone poisoning."

"You've never mentioned having a problem with my testosterone, or its packaging."

Her eyes sparkled as she caressed him through the hose beneath his tunic. "I didn't say it was a problem. Just inevitable." Then she sighed, and drew him down to lie next to her. When she put her head on his chest, he stroked her hair.

"I see the unicorns are out tonight." Her lips curved against his skin. "It will be awhile before I'll be able to say something like that again, won't I? Unless I ask a couple of them to come and live with us, gambol about the estate with the dogs. I wonder what Bran would make of them."

"Are you sorry we're leaving?" He pressed a kiss into her hair.

"Yes and no. I want to go home. I want to be with Kane. But before I can settle into that, there's Council to deal with. That damn letter."

It had been on his mind as well. But when he would have offered comfort, she tilted her head back. Suddenly, he wasn't seeing the Lyssa who'd first read that letter in their Atlanta kitchen with uncertainty and resigned acceptance. He was looking at the vampire queen he'd met over a year ago, the one to whom he'd pledged his eternal life. The one who'd fought to get them both back through that desert portal.

"I'm done with running, hiding, prevaricating and diplomacy. Rhoswen can give us our letter to introduce the Fae end of things, but it's time to remind the Council that the privilege of rule can be revoked. Before we left, I said I want something different for Kane. I'm going to make sure he has it."

Reaching up, she drew Jacob's mouth to hers. In the heat of the kiss, which quickly moved from lazy seduction to outright demand, Jacob felt her core deep strength, something that had nothing to do with how much blood she needed or how pale she was. His lips curved against her, and he surrendered to her passion, even as he made a mental note to send Keldwyn another missive. After all, his job was to anticipate his lady's needs, and he knew of some things that might be useful, given the plans he saw tumbling in her mind.

She'd taken the time she needed and found herself again. Now she was ready to kick some ass.

~

Rhoswen's scribes had drawn up the communication to Council, as the queen had promised. While she and Lyssa wrangled over the wording and shared tea on a verandah framed with flower blooms and overlooking the practice field, Jacob joined Cayden and his men to pass the time and stay in form. Though the need for it had rankled him some, they'd slowed their pace enough to give him a good workout. He told himself they moved faster than a vampire, so it would have been necessary regardless. Plus, Cayden was interested in Jacob's hand-to-hand techniques, enough to want to see them at the slower pace so he could adapt them into his men's considerable arsenal.

When he took a sweaty breather, sitting on a bench next to the captain, Jacob heard Rhoswen's voice rise, snapping. A moment later, Lyssa's dark hair was replaced by clear icicles, sparkling in the sun. In retaliation, Lyssa turned Rhoswen's hair into vines of devil's tongue.

"Look at that." Jacob chuckled. "They really are acting like sisters."

Cayden snorted. "When you encounter sisters in this world, they're usually powerful enchantresses, or witches who share one eye. Always trouble."

Jacob grinned. He'd noticed the guardsman was acting a bit easier, not only with him, but his own men. Since the other guards were involved in a vital discussion of how best to sharpen blades, he quirked his brow at Cayden. "So how *does* it feel to spank a queen? I'm just asking, because I've never had the pleasure."

He was ready for the attack, laughing as Cayden surged up and went after him, quick retribution for the impertinence. But Jacob noticed the captain's face was somewhat flushed, and the glint in his eyes might have been rueful amusement.

"I think you're about to suffer the pleasure, former vampire. Only you'll get the flat of my blade."

"What? I don't get that big, strong manly hand? I'm disappointed."

Jacob had to move fast to avoid the next swing. Hopping nimbly over their wooden bench, he shoved it into Cayden's path, then followed up with a quick parry to drive the man back. Cayden landed a good whack in his ribs. Jacob took it as his due before they settled into earnest practice again. It made him miss Dev, even as he realized he'd no longer have to hold back when he sparred with the Aussie. They would be equal strength again.

He could hear Dev's retort to that. *You just wish you were my equal, bloody Mick.* It made him grin anew, and that was good. It helped him stay away from the less positive side of it. Like the more limited lifespan of a servant, his diminished capacity to physically protect her. It was difficult for a warrior to reconcile the loss of such strength, no matter how short a time he'd had it at his disposal.

But he'd never have to make an annual kill, not for himself. Every vampire had to make at least one human kill a year to maintain strength and mental acuity. It had to be a healthy person, a good person, to ensure the potency and purity of the blood. He'd helped her do hers, the year they'd met, and the experience had torn something deep inside of him.

He was overdue for his own annual kill, something he'd kept putting off, and now he wouldn't have to do it. Could he have done it, year after year? No. And she'd known it. Maybe that was why she'd let him get away with delaying it until it was inevitable.

He was an alpha, a warrior, but he wasn't a predator. Whereas she'd been born one.

Strategically, he now had Cayden at a disadvantage, pushing him back. Then his lady's voice came into his mind.

Would you like to spank your *queen, Jacob? Does the idea of me being over your knee, my pale bottom smarting from your hand, make you hard?*

He missed his opening. Cayden knocked him square on his backside, so that he had to somersault back to avoid being stomped on a follow up kick. He made it to his feet, but Cayden stepped back, giving him the signal to desist. Following his gaze, Jacob saw the queens watching them. Apparently, they'd reached an agreement. The hirsute enchantment had been undone, though Lyssa held one clear icicle, perhaps broken off from her hair.

You did that on purpose, my lady.

I did. Picking on poor Cayden, when he's dealing with all these confusing feelings. I think you retained a vampire's sadistic nature.

Maybe I just picked up bad habits from my Mistress. With a half chuckle, he gave the practice blade back to Cayden and bowed. "You are a credit to your queen, Captain. I look forward to sparring with you another time."

"Not too soon," the captain said, his usual stoicism in place.

"The day you didn't kill me, you and I bonded. You'll miss me."

"I'll miss not putting my dagger between your ribs when I had a chance."

Grinning again, Jacob offered him a parting salute. "Take care of your queen, Captain. We'll see you again near Christmas."

~

When they took their leave at dawn, they had an unexpected escort. Keldwyn and Catriona were waiting in the courtyard, both mounted on Keldwyn's horse. The dryad was curled sideways before him, her slim feet braced on his opposite thigh, her body braced against his shoulder and chest.

"We wanted to take you safely to the portal," Catriona said, looking at Jacob. "You tend to get into trouble."

"I think trouble tends to be attracted to me, not the other way around." Jacob gave her a smile and helped Lyssa onto her mount, then took his own seat beside her. Since he was no longer vampire, the horses had no problem with him, and apparently his lady had enough Fae blood they didn't detect or overlooked the other.

His queen gave him an amused look for that. They'd already said their goodbyes inside the castle, but as they crossed the drawbridge, Jacob saw Rhoswen standing at a window. She lifted a hand, and Lyssa returned it, then the Fae queen disappeared as the waterfall before the opening resumed its course.

As they rode into the forest, Catriona gave them tidbits about it—who the trees were by name, where the gnomes were taking foodstores. She pointed out pretty things, like a small cluster of deep red flowers growing out of a tree's bark, or a family of deer watching them with large liquid eyes, camouflaged by the wood's gray and green background.

She had a timid, hesitant way of talking, probably because she'd been without communication for so long, hidden in her tree. Unexpected movements from any of the three of them could startle her, though it was only quick flinches. Lyssa helped put her at ease by asking her questions.

Keldwyn was quiet, though he'd murmur a word of assent here or there as Catriona asked for confirmation on a point. When they reached the place they'd come into the Fae world, Keldwyn reined up. "You can let the horses go," he said. "They know to go back to the castle."

As Keldwyn dismounted, Catriona maintained her place, shifting to the soles of her feet on the saddle blanket and balancing easily, her wings fluttering. Though Jacob had gotten down and was preparing to assist Lyssa, the Fae Lord stepped up next to him, offered a bow. "Will you allow me?"

Jacob's surprise at being asked almost made him forget to get his lady's assent. When she nodded, he stepped back. Putting his hands to her waist, Keldwyn lifted her down. Next to him, she looked almost as petite as Catriona, but that regal air always made her presence more expansive, no matter how men towered over her. This moment was no different, and yet Keldwyn acknowledged it more directly than he ever had before. He took a knee before her as he kissed her hand.

"Good journey back, my lady. I am sure we will see one another again." He lifted his head, met her gaze. "The queen was right. I have not always been an ally."

"You have not always been an easy ally. But you are an ally, Lord Keldwyn. I won't forget that again."

His fingers tightened on hers. "You do not realize how very much you look like him," he said softly. "Your mannerisms, the way you command yourself and others, even when you do not have the upper hand . . . that quiet core that says you will not be moved where you do not wish to be moved . . . That is all him, Lady Lyssa. And when I first saw you in the forest, those many months ago, that is why I did not drive you from my territory. I knew you were his daughter, and that by some cruel twist of Fate—at the time I selfishly thought it was cruel—you were brought to me."

His jaw flexed, a brief hint of sorrow showing in his dark gaze. "It hurt, that he chose your mother. It hurt me deeply. But though Rhoswen reacted to you as a rival, seeing you as a symbol of old pain, I also saw a part of him. A gift I could choose to hate for what you could not control, or protect because it would honor him, and the fact he always acted nobly, in every aspect of his life. He was ruthless and brutal—ruthlessly honest, and brutally quick—when it was needed. You are all that and more. Wherever he dwells now, he is *very*, very proud of you. And wondering how he managed to create such an amazing creature."

The words overcame her. Leaning down, she pressed a kiss to Keldwyn's lips, a queen's benediction. He closed his eyes, his hands squeezing hers as she murmured against his mouth. "You are a good friend to my father. I hope in time, in addition to being my ally, you will give me the honor of calling you friend as well."

When she straightened, he inclined his head. Then he stood. Reaching into his tunic, he pulled out a velvet cloth, and handed it to Jacob. Opening it, Jacob saw a small, glossy brown stone affixed to a short cord. It reminded him of the pendant Catriona wore, and when he glanced at hers, he saw it had been reshaped, reduced in size. It was a piece of it.

"This is for your son." He looked at Lyssa and Jacob both. "It is intended for a young child. He can not be choked by it, and, once placed upon him, it cannot be removed except by one of his blood parents until he reaches adult maturity. For fifty years, as long as he wears it, no enemy of yours, unless it is an enemy with greater magic than that, can harm him. There are few in the mortal world with magic greater than what has been crafted into that stone. You need to be vigilant, for he can still be taken, but I hope knowing no one can cause him harm while he is in their keeping will give you some peace of mind." His eyes flashed. "And time to retrieve him and punish them soundly for their mistake in judgment."

Jacob nodded. He'd lost his parents young, as had Lyssa, and it was clear this was the type of gift a Fae grandfather or godfather would bestow on a child. Since he knew Fae didn't like to be thanked, he extended a hand. Keldwyn took it, forearm to forearm, gave him a nod and let him go. Pivoting without another word, he returned to the horse. When he mounted up behind Catriona, his normal expressionless mien was back in place, the traces of emotion he'd revealed in his voice gone as if they'd never been.

"Your gateway is opening," he said. Glancing at Jacob, he added, "And I took care of your favor."

20

As Rhoswen had stipulated, it was dark, early evening. Dressed in their Fae garb, Jacob thought they looked like they'd come from a Ren Faire. When he slid the pack with its vital items onto his shoulder, he found himself with an additional weight, a sudden sense of loss. Beyond these trees was the mundane world again, a place of cars instead of horses, lawyers instead of knights and codes of honor. Except for the pull of Kane ahead, he had a near overwhelming urge to pivot and walk right back through the portal.

Lyssa slid a hand through his elbow, drawing his attention. "What favor?" she asked.

"Keldwyn reached out to this world to make arrangements for our transportation home, and additional blood for you once we get there. Aah-aah-aaah." He shook his head, distracting her with the quick staccato protest. "No peeking in my head. I want it to be a surprise."

Though she gave him her arched brow, she indulged him. Ingram was in the gravel parking area, waiting for them. When the majordomo opened the back door of the Mercedes for her, she flustered him with a warm hug, and gave John a smile where he sat in the front seat.

As they pulled out of the park, Ingram glanced at them in the rear view mirror. "So was it as much fun as Disneyland?"

Jacob gave him a wry look, decided not to answer, since the response was more complicated than he'd expected, sticking in his throat. Noticing his lady's scrutiny, he cleared it. "How long have we been gone?"

"Little over a month. We got your friend's message about a week ago."

It wasn't unexpected, based on their discussions with Keldwyn, but Jacob met Lyssa's gaze, covering her hand as her lips tightened. They'd been away from Kane a whole month. A lifetime.

"Where we were, he sent it yesterday."

Ingram gave him a closer look. "Seems like something is different about you."

"Quite a bit. We'll fill you in on the way there." However, from Lyssa's reaction to the length of their absence, and his own surprisingly raw feelings on the matter, Jacob decided something lighter might be needed. "Maybe John could tell us what's been happening here first."

John was a courteous child who didn't try to take over the conversation. But once encouraged, he answered Lyssa's questions with enthusiasm, filling her in about school, Bran and other matters of great import to a just-turned-eight-year-old. When he ran out, his grandfather told him it was time to let the adults talk again. Jacob filled him in on the pertinent points of what they'd been doing, while Lyssa curled up on the seat with a sigh, putting her head on Jacob's thigh.

"You look a little tired out, Lady Lyssa," Ingram noted.

"Just need some rest and more blood."

"I have blood." John eyed her with concern. He'd been besotted with her from the moment he'd come into their lives. The why of it was no mystery, for he had a crack addict for a mother and no other strong female role models in his life. Lyssa had surprised Elijah with how well she stepped into that role, as much as her life could allow. When they'd returned from being fugitives, Elijah had offered to move out of the house, but she wanted them to continue to live in the servant's guest quarters, which gave them as much space as a small house. She'd even had plans drawn up to turn it into a separate living unit, with kitchen facilities and a separate exit and entrance, so Elijah could treat it as their home.

After spending time with John, she'd also made the surprising decision to tell the boy about who they were. She'd discussed it with Ingram, indicating that if they were going to live in the house, it was necessary. She believed the boy was both capable of handling the truth and keeping the secret. Ever a good judge of character, even a very young one, so far she'd been correct.

Another surprise had been Ingram. He'd let Jacob mark John and him with the geographic marker, so his employer could know where he and his grandson were at all times, and if they were in any distress. Council frowned on vampires having human retainers not marked in some way, so it helped with that, but Jacob knew that wasn't why Lyssa had suggested it. And would need to do it again, since his mark had likely disappeared with his vampire abilities.

Now she gave John a smile, reaching out and touching his brown hand. "Thank you, John. I appreciate that very much, but I think Jacob has arranged something special for me."

"Oh. Uncle Gideon."

"Hey." Jacob and Elijah both reached out with a halfhearted swat. The boy grinned at Lyssa, coconspirators.

"That's my boy," she said. Then she looked at Jacob. "You had Gideon come?"

"With Anwyn and Daegan. Lady Daniela was a little far away to handle an escort for Kane back to Atlanta."

She sat bolt upright then, her whole face brightening in a very non-Lyssa way, startling Ingram enough the vehicle swerved and he had to overcorrect. Jacob laughed. "It's been really hard hiding it from you. I've had to exercise some serious distraction measures."

"Oh, is that the excuse you're giving?"

Despite her tiredness, she wouldn't lay back down, her eagerness keeping her body humming with anticipation. Jacob shared the feeling, hand gripping hers. It kept his lingering malcontent at bay, such that his spirits lifted with hers. When they pulled into the driveway, Bran and his pack came charging down the drive, surrounding the car and barking enthusiastically. Elijah threatened to have them all taken to the pound and incinerated, obviously a routine threat, for all the attention they paid to it.

As they got out, she greeted Bran and bestowed warm affection on the others. But when Kane's scent came to them, both parents turned instantly toward the garage entrance.

Gideon stood there, holding the toddler on his hip.

Jacob's brother was harder around the edges than he was, more scarred. While he did have a dry sense of humor, the dangerous glint in his gaze always suggested it was best not to get on his bad side. And that his good side was a very narrow ledge.

The two vampires who appeared behind him had been changing that, somewhat. Jacob still found it a trifle astonishing that his brother, the hardcore, bitter vampire hunter, was the servant of not just one vampire, but two. And one of those vampires was a male.

The three-sided relationship had healed some of Gideon's deep wounds, evidenced now by the faint smile on his face, the sincere warmth in his eyes. They came up the drive toward him, an unlikely procession with the dozen dogs right behind and Elijah and John bringing up the rear.

"Letting a vampire hunter transport a vampire baby," Lyssa commented. "That's the last time I'm letting Mason take care of my child."

Kane was asleep, his head resting against Gideon's neck, obviously just lifted out of his nursery bed when they realized his parents had arrived. It took longer for a child to rouse at dusk than an adult vampire. However, as they got closer, Lyssa noticed the dog yips and growls subsided, as if even the pack knew it was best to let Kane sleep undisturbed.

"Mason didn't have much choice. I threatened to stake him if he didn't turn the kid over," Gideon informed her.

"Yeah, I'm seeing that happening." Jacob snorted. "Forget Mason. Jessica would have cut your heart out with a butter knife."

"True enough," Gideon agreed. "For such a pretty little thing, she can be kind of scary. It's cute."

"Council called a special session, and Mason felt he should attend, since he expected you were going to be one of the subjects," Jacob explained to Lyssa. "He, of course, wouldn't leave Kane. When I used Keldwyn to contact Ingram, I suggested that instead of getting the baby to Lady Danny, that Daegan come and pick him up, and they could bring him here."

Mr. Ingram cleared his throat. "Vincent, Lord Belizar's servant, called the house two days ago, Lady Wentworth. They indicated they expect you to come before the Council within the week, with the child. Since I wasn't sure of your return, and even if I was I wouldn't have guaranteed that pack of vermin anything, I told them I would pass on the message."

Lyssa gave him a quick show of fang. "Mr. Ingram, I'm very glad you took the job here, despite your initial concerns."

Gideon snorted. "Let me guess. He didn't like your longterm health-care plan?"

She turned her attention to Jacob's brother. He hadn't moved from the shelter of the garage, and she knew it wasn't disrespect or rudeness. Most vampire children weren't brought out from under shelter in the first couple hours after dusk, because it was not yet dark enough for them, as it was for an adult vampire. It touched her, though, that Gideon had known how it would feel to have their son present at their homecoming.

"I see being a servant hasn't given you the slightest pretense at manners," she said, moving toward him.

He lifted a shoulder. "If ass kissing becomes a required skill for a servant, I guess Anywn and Daegan'll have to drive a metal stake through my heart and get themselves a new one."

"Since this one is so much trouble, why would we want to start from scratch?" Anwyn stepped out of the garage and gave Lyssa a courteous though wary nod. She was still very new to their world, but wariness of other vampires was not a bad trait to have. Lyssa herself had a natural caution around them, but the fact Gideon was servant to these two helped alleviate the natural mistrust. Plus, she knew Daegan Rei personally, an assassin who'd served the Vampire Council for a number of decades. An honorable male, there was likely not a more dangerous vampire in the world, and that included herself or Mason. Knowing Mason had chosen him to protect Kane in his absence was the best possible choice, and said a great deal about Mason's confidence in the male as well.

She also appreciated the fact Anwyn hadn't hesitated to move into the conversation. Wary, but confident. Not tongue-tied. Of course, they'd spent an evening with Anwyn, Daegan and Gideon on the beach some time ago, and that had helped Gideon's new Mistress feel easier with Lyssa.

She didn't see Daegan right away, and didn't detect him by scent, but Daegan had that unusual trait. Jacob touched her arm, guiding her attention upward. Daegan was squatting comfortably on a thick branch of one of her live oaks. Though her property was well secured, while Kane was outside, he was obviously staying in a position to study all approaches. She nodded to him. "Lord Daegan."

The tall, dark-haired and dark-eyed vampire offered a half bow. The graceful execution emphasized the deadly power of his lean form. "Always a deep pleasure, Lady Lyssa."

She gave him a quick smile, but with the courtesies out of the way, she turned her attention to the one person she most wanted to see, to touch. Laying her hand on the small back, she felt Kane's heat and breath. Hard and thick emotions swam up to choke her, unexpected. Gideon shifted, intending to put Kane in her arms, but her head began to spin. Drawing her arms back quickly before he could lay the infant into them, she swayed alarmingly. *Damn it.*

Jacob had his arm around her, steadying her. She saw his intent to feed her, then and there, but he'd given her more than he should after what they'd dealt with in the desert world. She hadn't let him feed her since, because he wasn't at full strength, either. She wasn't going to weaken him to replenish her, not in a situation that wasn't life threatening.

"I'd try my best to change your mind about that, but it's one of the reasons I asked Ingram to bring Gideon here," he said.

She was being eased down into a chair. Someone had brought it to her in a blink, which meant Daegan. She wanted to be gracious, but she was angry. She wanted to hold her son.

"In just a moment, my lady. Let Gideon feed you."

Four words she never would have expected to hear. *He's all right with this?*

The message I asked Keldwyn to convey to Ingram was that you would need more blood upon arrival. When he was arranging for Kane's arrival, he mentioned it to Gideon, and he volunteered. Other than his Master and Mistress, I think you're the only one to whom he'd ever willingly give his blood.

Gideon had handed Kane to Daegan, who cradled him with surprising expertise and gentleness. From the vampire's relaxed attitude, she knew he had no problem with her feeding from Gideon, but she wasn't expecting any issues to come from him.

As a much older and far more powerful vampire than a fledgling like Anwyn, she had every right to drink from Gideon, even if Gideon or Anwyn opposed it, though Daegan was a different matter. While Anwyn was aware that this might happen, accepting it in concept was a little different from facing the reality of another female vampire taking her servant's blood, an intimate exchange.

Before she'd been forcibly turned to a vampire, Anwyn had been owner and Mistress of a BDSM club, one she still managed. A Dominant's possessiveness had already been strong in her veins before she'd ever grown fangs. While Lyssa wouldn't ask permission, there was a fine line between exercising the rights of a more powerful vampire and courtesy. She met the other woman's gaze. "Thank you for the use of your servant."

In the corner of her eye, she noted Ingram shepherding John discreetly back into the house. Ingram had been around them enough to know when things might become an adults-only situation.

With no self-consciousness, Gideon dropped to one knee, leaning forward to press a kiss high on his Mistress's thigh. He waited for the touch of her hand on his head before he looked up at her. When he turned his face into her wrist, put another kiss there, her expression eased somewhat. Lyssa suspected it had as much to do with whatever he'd said in her mind as well as the gesture.

In a more formal setting, soliciting permission from his lower-ranking vampire Mistress to obey a higher ranking vampire, even silently, would have been an offense. However, Gideon was not the most polished of servants. He acted on his feelings, and they were all driven by his bond with his two vampires.

More than that, Anwyn was a more unstable fledgling than most because of her brutal siring. She contended with seizures during volatile moments. As such, Lyssa knew Gideon was not deliberately perpetuating an act of insolence, but offering needed reassurance. It was the same reason Daegan had shifted to stand at Anwyn's back now, so close he brushed her shoulder as he held Kane. While it obviously discomfited Anwyn to need such support in front of another strong female vampire, she apparently accepted it as a necessity.

Gideon rose then. Moving to Lyssa, he again dropped to a knee. Like Jacob, he was a tall man, so the position put them eye to eye. Stress and violence had hardened his expression over time, but there was a sensual softness to his mouth, a different quality in his blue gaze. Small but significant indications of the changes Daegan and Anwyn's presence had made in his life.

"I seem to remember a time when you were *very* opposed to being bitten."

"Things change," Gideon grunted. "Some people change every damn minute. Vamp one minute, a fairy the next. Flip flopping like a trout. And that doesn't even cover him." He glanced toward Jacob. "Human to vamp, then back to human again. 'Course, that means I can beat on his pretty face without him cheating with that super-fanged strength."

"You can try," Jacob replied.

Despite the banter, Lyssa felt the same intense yearning from him she was feeling toward their son. *Go hold him, Jacob.*

He gets to see his mother first. That's what I promised. I told him I'd bring you back to him. And like his mother, he's terrifying to face when he's not given what he wants.

"Where do you want it?" Gideon asked. "Wrist or neck? I know there are other places, but if you want it from my thigh, you're going to have to wrestle me on that one. I don't think you're up to that."

He shot Daegan a cocky look, apparently in response to something his vampire master had said in his mind. "Blow me."

Daegan gave him a look of predatory amusement, suggesting such repartee was a form of male bonding. Or provocative foreplay. Returning his attention to Lyssa, Gideon explained, "He said if he was close enough, he'd slap my head for being insolent."

She accommodated, a halfhearted thwack behind his ear that earned a grin. "You hit like a girl," he noted.

"After I take your blood, I'll put you through the garage wall."

"That's a hell of an incentive for a good Samaritan." Then he sobered and his voice softened, showing he could be as intuitive as his brother. "Let's get this done so the little man can see his mom. What will work best?"

"The throat."

Nodding, he shifted closer. As he did, he lifted her hand to his shoulder, near that juncture with the throat so she could direct him as she wished. It was so different from the first night she'd met Gideon. Angry, defensive, determined to convince his brother she was a monster. This side of him, the vampire servant and yet still so much the lethal vampire hunter, was quite appealing. As he moved his touch to her wrist to hold her steady, she leaned in and touched her mouth to the strong, corded throat. Daegan moved even closer to Anwyn, his hand on her shoulder as well, though it was a different form of guidance.

She expected Daegan had told Anwyn to go in the house, for she seemed to be visibly taking a firmer stance, her jaw tight, refusing to leave or look away from another vampire female taking blood from her servant. Lyssa didn't blame her. Under similar circumstances, she wouldn't let Jacob out of her sight, either.

While Daegan didn't seem perturbed, she expected it would have been quite different if it was a male vampire drinking from Gideon. Vampires were curious in their jealousies. She didn't expect to see that situation ever happen, regardless. No vampire she knew, male or female, would dare to take something that belonged to Daegan Rei. Not without his full, unequivocal consent. In writing.

It was important not to coddle Anwyn too much, though, because the woman was a Mistress, and had her pride. Being a third-marked servant with that nearly limitless well of sexual response, Gideon could be aroused by Lyssa putting her mouth on his throat, even without enhancement. However, she slipped in a small dose of pheromones. The sensation of her pulling at his throat went straight to his cock.

Anwyn had trained her alpha hunter very well, so he maximized the pain and pleasure response. Though he made a strangled noise of protest, he remained where he was. Lowering her other hand, Lyssa grazed his chest with her fingertips and cruised down to the waistband of his jeans, teasing over his hip bone.

"You're trying to get me in trouble," he muttered.

Lyssa gave Anwyn a gleaming look that didn't convey challenge, but conspiracy. A true Mistress, Anwyn picked up on it. Her tension eased, the beautiful lips curving.

"She wants me to get you in trouble, Gideon." Lyssa licked the flow of blood. It carried an appealing taste, the familial bond with her servant. "It's more pleasurable to punish you."

"Damn vampires." He caught a breath as she closed her hand over him beneath the straining jeans. He was hard and thick, eliciting a little purr in her throat.

"Just as nice as I remember it."

Jacob was a weighted, silent force in her mind. He'd tamped down his reaction with effort because he'd been her servant long enough to understand certain things. He'd expected nothing different from her when he'd called in his brother.

At least I got to choose the donor, my lady.

She gave the challenging thought the narrow look it deserved. Still, he'd been kind enough to arrange for his brother to be here for her, and she wouldn't goad him past bearing. Done with her teasing, she returned to drinking, pulling strong and deep. It felt good to have all those expected compulsions . . . to assert her dominance over other vampires present, to ease that sting with some playful eroticism, to feel the blood strengthening her so quickly she had to relax the grip on Gideon's biceps so she didn't cause him the wrong kind of pain.

She also had to force herself not to rush it, because Kane was waking up. Moving to Daegan at last, Jacob took the baby from him. As Kane recognized his father, his cries became the textbook baby response to an unexpected surprise. He started wailing his lungs out.

It was all show, however. He settled after Jacob gave him a gentle bob in his arms, wagged a finger at the tip of his nose. "What's all this about? A vampire doesn't cry. Your mother's told you that."

As she finished drinking, Gideon was so heavily aroused that standing was somewhat awkward. Leaving him in that state was her gift to Anwyn and a volley back to Daegan, as effective an admonishment as the head slap. Daegan's gaze coursed over Gideon as he turned, heat flickering in his eye. He nodded to Lyssa, tacit appreciation.

Gideon sent her a wry look, well aware of the manipulation. "Still one scary, irresistible bitch."

Though she saw Anwyn's alarmed glance snap from him to Daegan, Lyssa gave the vampire hunter a feral smile. In Gideon's way, he'd just paid her a supreme compliment and reassured her at once. Her momentary weakness due to a need for blood did not diminish her strength in his eyes in any way. And he had very clear-seeing, unsentimental eyes.

Then that was all past. Kane saw her.

He went up several decibels, an ear splitting cry that had his uncle wincing good-naturedly. Leaning down, Jacob put the child in her lap. Kane's little fists immediately closed on her hair, and he leaned back against that hold. His arms spread wide as he swayed, his scream turning to a giggle of delight.

"I suppose you have been a great deal of trouble?" she asked, suffering the yanking with great delight.

Mr. Ingram had returned, having left John occupied in the house. "Not as much as you'd expect, ma'am. All you really need is his uncle. The little man comes to him in a heartbeat and does whatever he tells him to do."

"Big softy," Jacob told his brother.

Anwyn shook her head then. "I suspect part of it is Gideon reminds him of you, Jacob. But Gideon is a very good parent. Very no-nonsense."

"Zero tolerance for bullshit," Ingram added with a faint smile. "Begging the ladies' pardon."

Gideon rolled his eyes. "These vampires are wishy-washy as hell, bro. They spoil the kid rotten if you don't watch them every minute." He jerked his head toward Daegan. "He's the absolute worst. Would probably let the kid get away with actual murder."

"It depends on whether or not the target deserves it," Daegan responded, unruffled.

Gideon scoffed at that. "Before Mason and Jess left for their Council meeting, I told both Mason and Daegan they shouldn't reproduce. They'd have the kind of obnoxious, spoiled kids no one wants to be around."

Jacob's smile turned instantly to a frown. "Mason took Jess to Council? She has no business being there. Has he lost his fucking mind?"

Gideon held up a quelling hand. "Don't jump my ass about it. She made a deal with the devil or something. She gave him those girly doe eyes and said in that sweet-as-a-sugarcoated-knife voice: 'My lord, who is more qualified than you to protect me? And you can't leave Lady Lyssa undefended at Council.' He couldn't argue with either point. The girl has guts *and* brains."

"I would be very upset if championing my cause endangered her—" Lyssa began, but Gideon immediately shook his head.

"Not like that. She's right, if you think about it. The Council's done wanting to harm her, and Mason is the most qualified to protect her, with the possible exception of you and Daegan. The main reason he didn't want her going was because of her past baggage, her fear of dealing with group vampire situations. But he's helped her heal, helped her be stronger, and now she wants the chance to meet those fears head on. Since he loves her, he can't really disagree with that."

"Jesus, my brother has become Dr. Phil," Jacob snorted.

Anwyn chuckled. "He's just repeating what he's heard me say. Like a trained monkey. No real comprehension, just regurgitation. Of course, monkeys actually do comprehend . . ."

Lyssa let the inevitable banter that followed wash over her as she gazed down into Kane's blue eyes. Her heart turned over when he offered a small smile, laughing at all of them. It seemed to her he'd grown exponentially. He'd been doing a little walking before they left, in fits and spurts. Now his legs looked much stronger, sturdier.

She resented having to deal with Council. She wanted to tell them all to go to hell; if they wanted her, they could come find her, and pay the consequences.

She'd thought a lot about that Council missive. She'd also thought about her father, dying in a rose bush in the desert. She wished he could have met his grandchild. She thought about Rhoswen, the way she commanded her world, her strengths and weaknesses. A thousand years had taught her that every challenging situation held a lesson to be learned. Having that confidence required taking huge risks, but sometimes, to secure the future, risk was necessary.

"Kane is going to go with us to Council," she said out loud. "But not because of Council's demands."

Jacob turned toward her. As her servant, he might not always be privy to her mind. But this was not one of those times. In this, he was Kane's father, and she let him fully into her head, let him see what she was thinking. A shadow closed over his face as he considered it, but she also saw him go through the same quick analysis she did. There weren't too many variables to consider. She'd said it in the Fae world. She was done running, and that meant they had to confront the Council as a unit.

He reached into the pack they'd brought, took out Keldwyn's pendant. The stone glowed amber and chocolate brown in the dim light from the garage. Bringing it to her, he knelt at her feet, gave Kane a smile and pressed foreheads to him in playful affection as he let the baby touch the pendant. Then he placed it around Kane's neck. As he did, the cord glowed, a warmth that shone over Kane's fair cheeks a moment before the necklace became an imprint in the child's skin, like a permanent tattoo.

Jacob looked up at Lyssa. "Okay," he said. Despite his initial surprise, he didn't look as if her plan was too unexpected. And then she realized that was the other reason he'd summoned Gideon. Her servant had anticipated her, as he often did, and brought her potential reinforcements.

She glanced at Daegan Rei. Like the others, he was watching them curiously. While she didn't know exactly where his loyalties lay, she knew he'd been at odds with Council directives over the recent year, right before Mason stepped into his position on it. She couldn't imagine Gideon bonding with someone who was dedicated to the current Council's objectives, so she took a chance there as well.

"Lord Daegan, I plan to go into the Council meeting directly opposed to their plans. But I have a proposal for them that I think will be better for us all. Though I do not command your loyalties, would you be willing to attend the Council meeting with us and stand at my back, against them as necessary?"

The powerful vampire studied her. "I don't play politics, Lady Lyssa."

She inclined her head. "I believe you support the vision of Council that I have always had. But I can't stand against you, nor would I. However, if I speak of my plan tonight and you oppose it, enough to inform the Council, then—"

Daegan lifted a hand. "With respect, please let me finish, Lady Lyssa. We are not a democracy, nor even a republic. Council is an oligarchy. However, any governing body making critical, frequent mistakes, the way this Council is, is creating an environment for change. Out of all the vampires I have met through the centuries, I trust your motives as a leader in that regard more than any other." He gave her a bow. "You have my services and guidance, however you may need them."

"Does this mean I get to use explosives again?" Gideon asked.

"Only if we shove them up your ass first," Jacob noted.

"Nice. That's brotherly love for you."

Kane put his mouth to Lyssa's breast, trying to gnaw through the fabric. Holding him close, she nodded to the others.

"I'm going to retire for a while, but later tonight we'll meet and discuss my proposal."

As she received polite acknowledgments from the others, Jacob caressed her shoulder, putting a kiss on Kane's waving fist as he met her green eyes. "I'll be right down."

You are going to tell Gideon about your parents.

Yes. And the other thing.

Her eyes warmed on him, though her hand tightened on his an extra moment as if a concern lay behind it. But whatever the concern was, she didn't voice it. "Take your time," she murmured. "But don't be long."

Jacob smiled at the conflicting commands, typical of his lady. "Count on it."

"Lady Lyssa." Daegan stepped forward. "However you choose to approach the Council, I would appreciate it if Anwyn and Gideon could stay here while we're gone."

"Of course, my lord. They are always welcome here, as are you."

"As kind as that is"—Anwyn directed that polite tone toward Lyssa, though something else entirely entered her voice as she shifted her attention to Daegan—"we're going with you."

"No, you're not," he responded. "Do you remember your last visit to Council? We agreed on a low profile after that. Indefinitely."

Gideon shifted to that aggressive stance Jacob knew all too well. "This Council meeting isn't going to be about us, so it's a different situation. And I'm not letting my brother and my nephew go into it without my help."

"So you are fine with Anwyn deciding to go into a dangerous situation if it suits your own purposes?"

"Don't do that," Anwyn snapped. She moved shoulder to shoulder with Gideon. "You know how it pisses me off when either one of you uses me as a pawn to get your way. Why don't we hear Lady Lyssa's plan tonight and then decide?"

"Fine." Daegan inclined his head. "We will hear it, and then I will decide. I'm going to check the perimeter."

As he strode away, the vampire called over his shoulder without turning. "Gideon, I can see it in your mind when you make a gesture like that."

"Good. I'd hate for you to miss it." Gideon glanced at Jacob. "What the hell are you grinning at?"

Lyssa was moving toward the house, Ingram accompanying her. While Jacob couldn't think of anything more appealing than curling around his lady and Kane while they slept, and catching a few hours himself, he wanted to take a moment with Gideon. He needed to do that.

Gideon sobered, picking up on the change in Jacob's demeanor. "Everything okay, bro?"

His throat suddenly thick, Jacob nodded. He gripped his brother's shoulder, tightening his grasp there in a sudden surge of emotion. "Yeah. Let's go see if Ingram has beer in the fridge. I have to tell you some things about where we've been. Who we saw." Clearing his throat, Jacob added, "Kelpies are real, Gid. And that's not all. You're not going to *believe* where I went the day before we left."

~

Soon after Jacob and Cayden's sparring session, Catriona had arrived at the castle alone, indicating she wanted to show Jacob something, if he could be spared for a couple hours.

Lyssa was busy with Rhoswen, but regardless, Catriona said this was for Jacob's eyes alone. While he rode one of the white chargers the Queen's Guard favored, the dryad chose to fly in low formation next to him. However, after a time, she squatted on the horse's rump, her bare toes and a light hand on Jacob's shoulder balancing her. When they moved out of forest area, right toward a thick sworl of pink and golden mist collecting across their intended path, her grip tightened. "Just keep riding," she said in that soft, breathy voice, a voice like musical chimes. "It's all right."

Since the pitch blackness of the desert world had been his last experience with obscured visibility, he was somewhat wary. However, this was Catriona, and the horse didn't seem concerned. He moved straight into the fog. It was cool, damp on the skin, making it glisten with that same pink and gold shimmer. Catriona's breath was warm on Jacob's neck as she went to her knees behind him, leaning against his back, both hands on his shoulders now.

In several strides, the mist started to clear. He saw they were on the bank of a slow-moving river, the water deep midnight blue, with touches of green and the sparkle of the sun. On the other side of the river, within hailing distance, was an island. Lush green grass, fruit trees with wide canopies, white stone buildings. The setting reminded Jacob of the Spanish monastery where Thomas had trained him to be Lyssa's servant, only even more peaceful and untouched. Women in pale robes picked fruit in the orchards, dropping them into slings on their hips.

"Apples," Catriona said. "So sweet. The priestesses send baskets of them over as an offering to Queen Rhoswen every season and she shares them with us all. Because of those trees, this is called the Isle of Apples."

Jacob swallowed. Something shifted beneath his very foundation. The world tilted. It couldn't be . . .

"Avalon." The word came out hoarse. Catriona's hand tightened on him.

"Yes, Sir Knight. For that is also what your lady calls you, does she not? She has favored Sir Vagabond, but Sir Knight is always what she means, no matter what she calls you. Throughout the ages, no matter the century, there are men who represent the ideals of a knight. Nobility, loyalty, faithfulness, bravery, integrity . . . you cannot turn them from their path. And there is one spirit, one man they honor as the best of all of them, though some believe in his reality, and others only believe in what he symbolizes."

Jacob got off the horse. Catriona used her wings to land next to him, her lyrical voice continuing. "When he died, it is said his half sister, the sorceress, brought him to Avalon to live, until the day he returns again."

Her hand slipped into his. Jacob gripped the slim fingers as two figures appeared, walking down the island beach. One was a tall, statuesque woman with glittering gold hair almost to her knees, her emerald green robes making her look like a jewel in a gold setting. The man who walked next to her wore a plain unlaced tunic and leggings, his feet bare. He swung a naked sword in relaxed fashion as he walked, as if he'd been doing a morning practice before he joined her for the stroll.

As casual as he appeared, no one with eyes could mistake the man for anything but what he was. A king. It wasn't merely the broad shoulders or way he moved. It just . . . was.

It didn't matter that he hadn't looked their way, and perhaps, with

Fae magic being what it was, they couldn't even see the opposite bank. Regardless, Jacob dropped to one knee and bowed his head before he drew another breath. He placed one hand over his heart, and one on the pommel of the short sword still at his hip.

Catriona touched his shoulder again, drawing his eyes up. The two had stopped. King Arthur moved several steps closer to the water, and though they were not within speaking distance, Jacob could see a pair of steady eyes, a firm mouth. The Pendragon raised his sword before him, touched the flat to his forehead and gave a slight bow, an acknowledgment. Then he turned and rejoined the woman, where they continued their walk. As Jacob stared after them, the pink and gold mist rose up on the river, slowly swallowing the island again.

Catriona pressed the hem of her dress to his face, taking away the tears there. "Irishmen are very sentimental," she said, with a tiny ghost-like smile. "I am glad the Lady of the Lake found you worthy. I wasn't sure if she would allow the mist to part and you to see this, but if it was possible, I thought it might be a good gift, for what you did for me."

Jacob cleared his throat. He wasn't sure if he could speak quite yet, but he croaked out a sentence. "It was my lady who freed you. The gift . . . should be hers."

"You are Lady Lyssa's gift. You are her heart. When I honor you, I honor her. She knows this." Catriona put her hem to his cheek again, blotting more tears. "Was it a good gift?"

Jacob nodded, but could say no more. Catriona seemed to understand.

21

When Jacob joined Lyssa in her lower bedroom, she could tell from the flush in his cheeks, the gleam in his eyes, he'd been telling Gideon not only about their parents, but about the Fae world. And Avalon.

As he lay down next to her, he propped himself on his elbow so they could close their upper bodies in a heart shape around Kane, now dozing off after his meal. She caressed Jacob's five-o'clock shadow, enjoying his facial hair again. He'd had a neatly trimmed beard and moustache when she met him, much like the knight she'd met a few centuries before.

"When you came back from Avalon, Rhoswen told me we needed to leave the very next dawn," she said, low. "She told me I should watch over you closely."

That day, she and Rhoswen had been in the main bailey. When Jacob rode back into the courtyard, what Catriona had shown him fairly vibrated from him. Lyssa understood the sheer enormity of it to him. But something about his reaction disturbed her as well. Since they'd returned from the desert world, she'd sensed an odd struggle inside of him, too amorphous to define. Rhoswen had provided the missing piece.

He's human again, Lyssa. This world is an addictive drug to the mortal soul. The moment they step foot here, they yearn to be a part of it, never wanting to leave. He has already started to feel the twisting desire not to depart, though he's balancing it with the love he has for you and your son, both of whom belong to another world. While I expect his desire for you will always be greater than anything else, a heart can be damaged by being torn in two. Leave at dawn. Before you next come here, we will try to figure out how to shield him. Humans whose blood becomes infused with the essence of our world can never return to the mortal world. Their hearts explode from the agony of that separation.

Now she kept her hand on his face. "Will I lose you to the Fae world, Jacob?"

Keeping his blue eyes steady on hers, he curled his fingers around her wrist, kissed her pulse point, making it quicken. "It will never match the yearning I have to be with you and Kane. Being without you is what would truly tear my heart in two. Be easy on that, my lady. I am always yours. What kind of knight would I be if I wasn't?"

~

Later that evening, as Lyssa laid out the plan to the others, she found she'd convened a dangerous strategy team. As hunters, Daegan, Gideon and Jacob all had experience in difficult confrontations, so they provided her a wealth of contingency plans and alternative scenarios if things didn't go exactly as planned—or even if they did. Anwyn contributed her experience as a Mistress, honing the diplomatic approaches into a razor-sharp edge. Lyssa hadn't wanted any household staff other than Mr. Ingram and John present, so was amused when Anwyn took charge of dinner for the four humans. The fledgling vampire enjoyed cooking, though she herself no longer benefitted from it.

Despite the serious nature of their discussion, it was a relaxed environment. Jacob and Gideon helped Anwyn fetch and carry. John, after being called in from the library where he'd been doing his homework, helped set the table. Daegan was absent at the moment, but Anwyn indicated he would join them for dinnertime. Lyssa understood. For the most part, Daegan had been alone and on his own for nearly seven hundred years. When she had Jacob in her mind, available to her as she wished, she often had no need for other company.

Still, after having been in the Fae world, surrounded by strangers, this was a quiet pleasure. John sat on her lap so she could test his spelling for class the next day. Jacob was nearby with Kane balanced on his knees, holding his hands as he pushed his chair back onto two legs and made it bounce like a horse for his son. Anwyn and Gideon were teasing one another in the kitchen. If Mason and Danny were here, she'd feel like she was surrounded by . . . family.

Vampires lived on a pyramid, rating every other vampire as over or under them, and behaving appropriately. They didn't have families, not usually. Even those that got pregnant with their servant or another vampire often still treated the servant or vampire as a lesser or superior, and the child was expected to cleave more to the dominant vampire parent in time, relegating the human back to a servant's status as the child matured.

She glanced at Jacob, watched the boy fall face-first against his father's chest with complete trust as Jacob caught him then held him high in the air, teaching him how to fly like Superman. The idea of ever allowing anyone—whether it was Kane, herself or another vampire—to treat Jacob as less than a full father to Kane, was reprehensible to her, particularly seeing the unconditional love in Jacob's eyes for his son.

When Gideon came into the room, she saw that cautious smile on his face as he looked toward his brother and nephew. This was all new for him, too. Spending time with people he loved without having to always be on guard, emotionally or otherwise.

They were a dangerous group, with bloodlust issues and dominant and submissive sexual proclivities that could be way over the top. So vampires were never going to be a warm fuzzy family, but this worked for them. As Anwyn arrived, her gaze sought out Gideon instantly, and he lifted his head, his eyes warming on her. He kissed his nephew's head, then came around and held her chair for her. As he did, Daegan strode in. When he slid his knuckles along Anwyn's cheek, he also brushed Gideon's body with intimate familiarity, closing his palm on his hip.

Daegan, Anwyn and Lyssa had wine flavored with their servants' blood and a small sampling of the meal Anwyn had cooked. Elijah, Jacob, Gideon and John got steak, mashed potatoes and a Cobb salad. Anwyn had accurately guessed the tastes of the "meat and potato" males, though Lyssa was amused to see John somberly telling his grandfather he should eat only half of the meat and save the rest for later, to watch his cholesterol. Jacob, on the other hand, had attacked the meal with gusto.

You don't have to savor that quite so obviously, you know.

Shooting her a grin, he cut her another tidbit of the well-buttered potatoes and held it out. She took it, well aware of how he watched her mouth as it closed over the morsel.

When they'd all slowed down a bit, she lifted her wineglass, drawing their gazes. Kane had fallen asleep in her lap, and she held him in one arm. "A toast. To good friends and family. Perhaps the changes we make will allow us more times like these, Goddess willing."

"Or we'll all be dead and it won't matter," Gideon added.

She inclined her head. "True. Over the past year, I've learned that there is never an age where you can't learn something new about yourself and the world, and be the better for it."

"Here, here," Daegan murmured, touching his glass to Anwyn's and giving Gideon a fond look.

Lyssa's gaze shifted to Jacob. "Let us hope we can convince the Council of that, peaceably."

"After we stake a couple of them."

This time Daegan did not have to perform the head slap, because Anwyn, sitting between him and Gideon, managed it quite effectively. Gideon gave her a pained look. "You did that because he told you to do it. Puppet."

"We were merely reflecting the same desire," Anwyn responded.

Gideon caught her hand, brought it to his lips to soothe any sting to her palm caused by his hard head. "Just remember our bet," he shot at Daegan.

Daegan lifted a brow. "As long as you remember what you owe your Mistress, regardless of the outcome."

Anywn shook her head at both of them, lifted her goblet toward Lyssa. "I agree wholeheartedly," she said quietly. "Everything I value most is at this table, and I do not want to lose them. Well said, Lady Lyssa."

Elijah sent John off to the den to watch an hour of TV then, while Anwyn sent Gideon to retrieve the desserts. He took Jacob with him. Once they'd left the room, Lyssa raised a brow. "What is the bet?"

"Gideon thinks you'll have to beat Lord Belizar to a bloody pulp to get him to listen to reason. Daegan thinks you'll have to stake him and start from scratch. If Gideon wins"—she glanced at Daegan, confirming he was fine revealing the nature of the agreement—"he wants Daegan to set aside his Master role for one night. Gideon wants to . . . take Daegan."

Intriguing, and more than a little bit astounding. Jacob had fucked men in her service before. It was not his favorite thing, though it had not compromised his male pride to do it. Only extreme circumstances would make her put him in a situation where the reverse was necessary, because of what she knew of him. Since he'd known his brother was of the same bent—innately and often intensely heterosexual—it had been a paradigm shift for Jacob to see his angry, violent-natured brother as the servant for a male and female vampire. However, because of the circumstances that had brought the three together, Lyssa knew this was a significant step for them. It explained why Daegan had agreed to the wager. Gideon actually wanting to be the initiator with Daegan, give his Master pleasure through penetration, rather than being the submissive recipient who could passively deny his own desire, underscored how much he accepted Daegan as his Master.

"And if you win?"

Daegan took a sip of his wine, pressing his lips together over the taste of it, flavored with Gideon's blood. "Wild card. I get to choose."

"Hmm." There were pleasures in peace and contentment. But for vampires, there were darker pleasures as well, ones stirring in her blood now. "What did you mean, he must honor what he owes his Mistress?"

Anwyn answered. "When Gideon surrendered to us, one of my conditions was that, at some point, Daegan takes him down alone, without my participation."

Lyssa privately hoped Anwyn had a diabolical plan to watch that, because she couldn't imagine wanting to miss such a sight, two strong warriors in a sexual embrace, so passionate it would appear like they were in mortal combat. "Now I understand why you sent them both out. Brothers don't need to share everything."

"No, they don't." Anwyn met Lyssa's gaze squarely. Though the woman had been deferential, polite and friendly, there was a gleam in her eye Lyssa recognized. Daegan put a warning hand over hers.

Lyssa smiled, showing the tips of her fangs. "Touché, dear. You're well suited to the vampire world. Just be careful of showing that cleverness in the wrong place, where it won't be properly appreciated."

She sobered then. "Which brings me to an important point. While I expect you will convince Lord Daegan that you and Gideon should accompany him, this could get very bloody. In time, you will be a strong and able vampire. But do not let pride make you foolish. If you are going to be present, obey Lord Daegan's direction to stay safe, so neither Master nor servant will make a fatal mistake, trying to protect you." Lyssa allowed a rare moment of softness in her tone. "He has just found you. His soul is too fragile to survive your loss, but being marked by both of you, Gideon would likely survive your death, Anywn. Physically."

Anwyn nodded, her jaw tight as if she'd already reached the same conclusion, though she found it an unappealing one, standing back in a fight where her two men were in peril. "It's why I hope you're right and neither of them are. I hope reason will prevail."

"Dealing with old vampires, that's not usually the case," Lyssa noted. "But lesser miracles have been known to happen."

"Such as me being wrong," Daegan added. Anwyn flicked a grape at him, which he caught. Giving her a wink, he placed it in his mouth and brought his lips to hers. Cupping the back of her head to hold her still, he used his clever tongue to tease her into taking the fruit from him. It made Anwyn smile against his mouth, as Lyssa was sure he intended, though nothing would completely eliminate the worry of the woman so new to the volatility of their world, and so new in her fierce bond to the two males. However, when Jacob returned, and Lyssa's gaze turned to him, she realized the amount of time didn't really matter. She knew just how Anywn felt.

~

She and Jacob spent a good part of the evening playing with Kane in the library. Gideon stayed with them for a while after Daegan and Anwyn disappeared. Then, when he received a summons from his Mistress, the vampire hunter gave the sleepy Kane a kiss and left them with an affable good night, even brushing a kiss along Lyssa's cheek, pressing her hand.

"He's like an episode of the *Twilight Zone*," Jacob remarked.

"But a good one."

"No argument there." Jacob looked down at Kane, lying on his stomach amid a pile of large Legos, many of which had been scored by sharp baby fangs. "You're worn out, big man. Time to put you to bed."

They went together, tucking him into the soft bed clothes, and then putting the top down on the enclosed crib. The spindles had been done in decorative whorls, twined with sparkling chimes and ribbons to make it look less like a cage. Because vampire infants had the strength to crawl out of a crib at a young age, such measures were necessary. Lyssa studied her son, pushed his dark hair off his brow before they closed it. "He's so you," she murmured.

"No, mostly he's you. I already recognize the haughty look and the indomitable will."

"I think you're mistaking his inflexible stubbornness and hard Irish head."

Jacob drew her close to his side as they gazed down at him together, then he pressed his mouth to her temple, staying there as he spoke. "I love you, my lady. No matter what."

She turned her face up to his, her fingers on his jaw as he adjusted his mouth onto hers, taking her under in that deep, swimming way he had. Unlike her nonbuoyant vampire form, in this kind of ocean she could float and drift, spin with him until their bodies were awake and aching for one another, even as their hearts were cradled and rocked, like Kane's crib.

Slipping her hand down Jacob's back, she cupped the rise of his buttock, dug in, feeling the ache in her womb. She wanted him inside of her, wanted to be gripping his taut ass, feeling it flex as he pumped into her. She'd make him go so slow, until they were both near insanity for that release point, so perilously close.

He drew her out of the room. Knowing her so well, he didn't take her to their bedroom. He took her to the indoor pool, with its moonlit view of her rose garden through the glass wall of windows. She had long stone benches out there to while away the evening in conversation, stretch out and gaze up at the stars . . . or do something far more intimate.

Though Jacob's immediate reaction when he followed her gaze was to look away, giving the threesome their privacy and not impinging on his brother's, Lyssa took a moment to enjoy the view. Gideon was standing, but his wrists were locked to his thighs with straps, making him dependent on Anwyn and Daegan for his balance. The Mistress had blindfolded him as she knelt in front of his naked body and took him in her mouth. While she worked him hard and with obvious skill, Daegan was buried to the hilt in Gideon's tight, muscular ass, his body flush against the hunter's. While Lyssa watched, Daegan put his mouth to Gideon's neck, teasing and nuzzling, and she saw a flash of fang.

Gideon bucked against them, a sensual resistance that seemed to fuel them both. When Lyssa's thighs dampened, she felt that stir of power that came from watching the struggles of a powerfully alpha submissive. Anwyn slid off his cock, leaving it hard, thick and glistening as she bit into his femoral. At the same moment Daegan bit his throat, both feeding from him at once. Gideon's head dropped back on Daegan's shoulder, fingers flexing hard in his bonds, every muscle like steel. He was obviously fighting his climax with every scrap of will.

Jacob knelt before her, not obstructing her view. He slid the skirt she'd worn at dinner up to her waist, put his mouth against her mound, his tongue dragging across the fabric of her panties to stimulate her clit. She let out a low hum of response, let him see what she was seeing, now that she was watching something he'd appreciate. Anwyn was naked, her back as slim and smooth as one of the statues, her bottom a perfect heart shape. She had heavy, generous breasts, the engorged tips rubbing against Gideon's thighs as she nourished herself on his blood. As a servant, Jacob couldn't help but respond to it, and Lyssa knew it. Since both males were naked, she couldn't help but respond to all that flexing male muscle, the power and strength so much like her own servant's.

"Do you think they'll watch us when they're done?" she whispered.

"If they do, I'm not sure I want to know." When he rose, courteously staying somewhat off center so that he wouldn't impede her view with his wide shoulders, she turned full into him, pulled him down for a kiss. As she tasted her arousal on his tongue, she backed him toward the hot tub adjacent to the pool. He'd turned it on, that quiet bubbling roar that could cocoon the noise of the rest of the world. Jacob slid his hands beneath her hair, winding it up on her nape. His blue eyes were intent. "How do you want me, my lady? How can I give you pleasure?"

In answer, she took the hem of his shirt up and over his head. Instead of pulling it off, she left it there. Pressing her body against his bare upper torso, she nuzzled his lips through the fabric as she let her hands course down his body, open the slacks he'd worn at dinner. The garment pooled on his bare feet.

After she removed the shirt, she stepped back, putting some distance between them. *Stay where you are, Jacob.* She slid out of her dress before him. When she was naked, she stepped into the hot tub, went under and came back up wet and sleek, taking a seat on one of the benches. His eyes were good enough to see beneath the bubbling water, and she took full advantage of that now, sliding her fingers between her legs to tease her clit, slip her fingers into herself, making her bite her lip, tremble slightly.

"My lady." His voice was rough, needy, and it shot an additional thrill through her.

"Just watch, Jacob. Think about how nice it would be if I'd let you grip your cock for me, stroke it. I want to see you wanting me, wanting to come inside me."

His cock was high and thick. All the lovely play of muscles were tight, his eyes riveted on what she was doing. *You know you like it better with three fingers inside, my lady. And you like my fingers better, because they're thicker, no sharp fingernails so I can thrust harder. Can you feel them now, just thinking about it?*

In retribution for the sensual teasing, Lyssa gave him more of what was happening outside the pool area, behind him. Anwyn had shifted, so now she was lying on her back on one of the benches. Daegan had brought Gideon down on top of her, and as she spread her legs, revealing a pussy slick with cream, Gideon thrust in slow and deep, causing a guttural sound of pleasure in her throat that she and Jacob could both hear, mixed with the sound of hot, bubbling water. Gideon made a similar noise as Daegan gripped his hips and thrust back into his well lubricated ass. He took his time with it, a tight fit, since Daegan was large. Anywyn writhed, gasping, as their combined force pushed Gideon deep inside of her. Holding her arms to steady her, he gave her a full measure of sensation as Daegan pushed him further to the edge, the two Dominant vampires sensually tormenting their servant as Lyssa was tormenting Jacob now, forcing them to hold out until their needs had been served.

She knew how it drove him crazy, to see her pleasure herself when he wanted to be the one to give her that. When he was a vampire and she finally released him with a sultry, one word command, he'd take her hard, just as she desired him to do. He might not have the vampire blood, but that beast still existed in him. The alpha male need to take over, to attack and devour, was part of his blood, no matter what.

Jacob saw her delight in the contrast between servant and male animal, the jade eyes vibrant, flickers of crimson in the irises. Then she spoke the words in his mind.

Grip yourself, Jacob. Stroke yourself for me, the way a man does it. No finesse, no seduction, just jerking off, watching me do this before you.

When she brought her fingers out from beneath the surface of the water, his nostrils flared, detecting her scent. She tasted them, one at a time. Then she stretched either arm out along the Jacuzzi edge, watching him like some remote sultana who'd called a slave to perform before her. A slave ready to break his chains with any dark magic to remove that remote look from her face, to make her lips part with cries of helpless surrender. She'd rake her nails up his back, punishing and rewarding at once.

Outside, they'd switched. Anwyn was between Gideon and Daegan. She rode Gideon's cock as he stood once more, holding her with sure, strong muscles rippling across his back. Daegan was inside of her as he'd been inside of Gideon, the two holding her between them, taking her up to a pinnacle again. It was how Jacob and Gideon had taken Lyssa that night long ago, at her command and direction. Remembering it now, overlaying it on the image out there, made his cock even stiffer.

My lady, I am going to come all over your nice tile floor.

Then you'll have to clean it on your hands and knees. Naked. Except for a cock harness and a plug that will keep you hard. It will vibrate, so just as you finish cleaning, you will come again, and have to start all over, just for my pleasure.

You've missed being a vampire.

I find I have. Yes. Her eyes glowed again. *But one thing has not changed. I never stop wanting you beyond all comprehension, Sir Vagabond, Sir Knight. Wanting to torment you, love you. Be with you always.*

He stilled, lifting his eyes to meet hers. Because of what he saw there, the implicit permission to change the demand, he moved into the hot tub. Sliding one arm around her waist, he cupped her nape with the other, bringing her up to his mouth. Leaving her arms out to either side of her, she gripped the concrete lip of the tub as he lifted her, pushed her down on his cock, making her moan against his lips and sending a quiver through them both.

"You are my torment. My love. My everything."

At his rough words, she gripped him instead, her fingers digging into his shoulders. When he hiked her up higher, she raked him with those wicked nails, and he felt the blood flow clean and true. In the end, her mouth would find it, taste him, feed from him, and devour his soul. He'd give it to her without hesitation. It had always been that way with her, and whether it made sense to anyone else or not, didn't matter. Faith wasn't a matter of comprehension.

They'd need faith for what they were about to do, but this moment made Jacob ready for it. He'd do everything necessary to protect her and Kane, understanding why his lady had made the choice to bring their son. His lady knew there were things worse than death.

Living life on someone else's terms wasn't living.

22

FOR the past couple of years, the Council had favored an old castle on the outskirts of Berlin as their base of operations. They liked the ancient, stolid darkness of it, the history of war and torment that attended it. At least, that was Jacob's opinion, one he knew his brother shared.

When Gideon, Anwyn and Daegan had gone before Council the first time, Jacob had heard about it after the fact. His brother had intended it that way. If Jacob had learned his brother, the world's most successful vampire hunter, was going before Council as a fledgling's servant, as close to a death wish as possible without simply slitting his own throat, Jacob would have hunted him down and chained him up in a basement until his bout with insanity had passed.

He knew enough details, and suspected the ones that weren't shared, to know it had not been pleasant. But they'd survived. Still, as they got out of the limo in the castle courtyard, he could tell his brother was remembering it, quite vividly. However, that was Jacob's intuition, a brother's insight. To anyone else, Gideon appeared as a silent, intimidating bulwark at Anwyn's back. Daegan shifted a little apart from them, an unconscious flanking maneuver they seemed to favor when it came to being in a protective position around the woman they loved.

Anwyn was acutely aware she was the weak link here, and though she wasn't pleased about that in the least, Jacob admired the fact it didn't show. She looked as composed and cool as Lyssa, just as ready to kick ass. It made him agree with his lady. Once Anwyn gained strength, age and experience, she'd be as formidable a vampire as she was a Mistress, a good match for the deadly assassin who was unexpectedly Master to both her and Gideon.

Jacob waved off the castle staff that came to open the limo's other door, stepping forward to handle it himself. From here forward, appearances were everything. He was dressed in dark slacks and a snug black heavyweight tee that showed his upper body to good effect, as well as the nine-millimeter in its shoulder holster and the steel arrows loaded in his wrist gauntlets. The message was clear. He wasn't here for vampires. He was here to stop human servants. Gideon wore similar attire, only he also had a machete sheath down the line of his spine that contained a blade capable of decapitating a rhinoceros.

Getting ready for this had brought back memories of the nights they'd gone vampire hunting. But some things had changed.

When Gideon had been stripped to his shorts, adjusting his calf rig for extra knives, Jacob had seen fresh scars among the old. The lash marks across his back and ass were new enough to have happened recently, but if they'd been put there after he became a servant, they had to be marked with a vampire's blood; else they would have healed and disappeared. While Gideon was dressing, Jacob saw Anwyn brush past him, her fingernails scraping over one of the lash marks on the upper rise of his buttock, giving him the answer of who'd put them there.

Before he'd become involved with Daegan and Anwyn, Gideon had been furious that Jacob had bound himself to Lyssa. He'd practically demanded to see his servant's mark, which of course Jacob had refused, given the circumstances. Now Gideon got to see all of it. The lashes from his Ritual Oath of Binding, the cross on his hip bone, the serpentine mark down his back. When Gideon moved past him to retrieve his Walther from the duffel of weapons, he'd surprised Jacob by stopping, touching that mark with a quick brush of callused fingers.

Jacob turned, his glance falling deliberately to the trinity of what looked like red teardrops, or blood, high on Gideon's chest. His own servant mark, representing his bond to both of his vampires. He'd acquired it when Anwyn made him her full servant. When Daegan did so later, it remained as the only mark, apparently a confirmation of the trinity that needed no embellishment. The two brothers met gazes. Gideon gave him a bare nod, an expression that said *It's a hell of a kind of thing, ain't it?* making Jacob smile tightly.

Yeah, a lot of things had changed. But one thing was the same. Once they were set, they cross-checked one another's weapons, double-checked the loading. When they disembarked from the plane and went to the limo, they fell in with their vampires without any need for words, as perfectly in sync as if they were in each other's minds, as they'd often been when they hunted.

Of course, though presentation was going to be ninety percent of this op, it probably wouldn't matter if they'd all worn footie pajamas when all was said and done. There wouldn't be eyes for anyone but his lady at this little party.

The last time the Council had seen her, she'd been sick, weak, and then transmuted to her Fae form. Now, as he opened the limo door, one mouth-watering leg came out, embellished by the shimmer of a tempting black stocking and sharp black heel with a decorative strand of diamonds at the ankle. The tails of the anklet crossed and dangled in a glitter of gemstones down the back of the heel. He took her hand when it emerged. He'd done her nails himself, a glossy black with a single diamond chip on each of the three main fingers, outlined by a brush stroke of jade green color.

She'd always been able to make his mouth dry, his heart pound faster. And of course she was always stunningly beautiful, but in the past years she hadn't gone out of her way to make it patently clear she was royalty. When he helped her out of the limo, he expected the castle staff was about to have a panic attack, thinking they should have put down a purple carpet for her to walk the fifty feet to the door.

The dress was a black cheongsam with gold dragons embroidered on it, the frog clasp at the high collar done in jasper. She wore matching gold earrings and her hair was swept up, several long tendrils wisping down over her breasts. The dress fit was perfect, molding her high, small breasts and curve of hip in a way that made every step she took a sensual dance of the female form, particularly with those shoes.

She gave Jacob a cool nod for his help, then released his hand and preceded him. He fell in at her back, three steps behind, watchful of her surroundings and in the proper place as her servant. Daegan, dressed in black from top to toe, including silk shirt, slacks, tie and suit jacket, moved along to her right but one step back, like a silently stalking panther guarding the women. Anwyn was between Jacob and Gideon. Though this show was his lady's, Anwyn had risen to the occasion. She'd worn a complimentary cheongsam, showing clearly where her loyalties lay, the fabric a brown silk embroidered with gold dragons with copper edgings to their wings. It enhanced the sable hair she had clipped loosely on her shoulders. Her blue-green eyes were steady as she carried Kane in her arms, another reason Jacob, Gideon and Daegan were flanking her closely. He'd been fed and was quiet, though his blue eyes were alert and taking in all the new information.

Vincent, Belizar's servant, was waiting at the entranceway. The male was medium height, but compact muscle, his gray eyes steady. His brown hair was trimmed close, emphasizing the strong lines of his face. He'd revealed nothing as they approached, but Jacob knew Belizar wouldn't have a servant who was any less of a cagey bastard than the Council head himself. "Council is in session," Vincent said. "However, you will be summoned from your room when they are ready to address your issue."

His tone was flat, obviously instructed in not only the message but the tenor they wanted to set for this visit. Jacob was reminded of Cayden deliberately withholding his assistance from Lyssa to mount a horse. *Our welcomes have definitely been lacking in manners of late, my lady.*

We shall fix that. "How long have you known me, Vincent?" Her voice was a soft purr.

"Quite some time, my lady." Vincent had the intelligence to execute a deferential half bow, lowering his gaze, though Jacob saw the shrewd servant note how they were armed. He was certain a quick little mental text about that had gone ASAP to Belizar. When he registered Jacob was carrying steel arrows in the wrist gauntlets, he flicked his gaze up to Jacob's face. Jacob met the subtly startled look with cool blue eyes. Vincent turned his full focus back to Lady Lyssa, attending her reply.

"Then you know it would be best if you advise your Master that we are on our way."

"But—" Vincent shifted, as if he intended to courteously block her way. In that blink, he found himself staring down the line of one of those arrows as Jacob leveled the wrist gauntlet at his chest.

"Move out of my lady's way, Vincent."

Glancing at Daegan, the vampire's dark, unfathomable gaze unchanging at Jacob's threat, Vincent swallowed. "Yes, my lady," he said, stepping aside with another bow.

"You are a good servant, Vincent. Thank you."

She proceeded past him and into the front foyer, turning without hesitation toward a wide hallway. Several second-marked human staff came to the doorway of their offices as they passed, retreating just as quickly when Jacob, Gideon and Daegan turned their targeted attention upon them, obviously assessing each for their threat level.

When they reached the large double doors of the Council chambers, they were closed. Jacob moved in front of his lady. At her nod, he turned the latch and pushed the doors open. Before she could step past him, he put himself in front of her. The Council members were seated and staring from behind their half crescent table. Their servants were standing and assembled in a similar shape across the room, none poised with a crossbow. It only took a second to establish the security of the room, and in that second, he'd stepped aside, bowing and gesturing her forward in an attitude of deference and respect that couldn't be faulted. Except by her.

Very presumptuous, Sir Vagabond. If it weren't for the fact I might have ruined this manicure, I would have knocked you out of my way and stomped you with my heels.

You don't push me around when it comes to your safety, my lady. You never will. And from a practical standpoint, I can heal from most things with your blood. If you die, we're both screwed.

She didn't react to his words outwardly, but the current of dangerous warmth was both approval and promise of a Mistress's retribution for the impertinence. He'd be happy to take anything she wanted to dish out after this was over. Now, all his concentration was on this. Warriors of like mind, he could tell Daegan and Gideon were focused on every move and reaction. Per the agreed plan, Daegan took the vampires and Gideon and Jacob divided the servants and entry points into two quadrants for surveillance.

Lord Belizar was in the center position as head of the Council, Lord Uthe to his right. Barbra, the only made vampire on the Council, was at the far end of the table. Mason, as the newest member of Council, held the other end. At the sight of them, a flicker went through the amber eyes, and something remarkably like a smile played around his serious mouth, but then it was gone and he appeared as dispassionate as Lyssa could be in her most guarded moments.

The other five members of the Council filled in the chairs leading up to Belizar's head position. Council sessions often didn't involve their servants, but they might be here for courier purposes, to step and fetch during the meeting.

Or, it could be a reinforcement of older, more restrictive ways, when servants had been required to stand and attend interminably long Council sessions to prove that suffering tedium was an expected part of their role. The servants' positioning was opposite to their respective vampire, so Jessica was diagonally across the room from Mason. Like everyone else, she'd looked toward the door upon their entry, though otherwise she was still and attentive. She looked lovely and well put together, wearing soft slacks that clung to her hips and a thin blouse that accentuated the high curves of her breasts. Her chestnut hair was clipped back on her shoulders, curls soft around her face.

Only the paleness of her face hinted that her first visit to Council might be overloading her nerves, though Jacob expected a lot more was happening below the surface. She was probably a wreck, but determined not to show it. That assessment also took no more than a blink, and then he was back to his post, keeping a full eye on the other servants, a partial eye on the reaction of the Council.

Whatever admonition Belizar might have been about to make, about waiting until Lyssa was summoned, was bitten back. Jacob knew he was far from clueless, and probably realized in a blink that things weren't going to go as they'd mapped them out. However, when he saw Daegan at her side, along with Gideon and Anwyn, a different sort of tension entered the Council chambers. Carefully, Belizar tented his fingers on the table before him.

"What is this?" he asked.

"I am answering your missive, my lord." Lyssa locked gazes with him. "But I am not here as a cowering lackey hoping for your mercy, waiting for judgment. I am here as the Queen of the Far East Clan, the last royal line, the oldest vampire among our kind."

"From what we have learned, Lady Lyssa, you may still have vampire blood, but all your power is Fae magic. You have no authority here. However, as we indicated in our letter, your son would still be considered vampire offspring. At least, we assume he is. He will need to be tested."

"Jacob."

He stepped to her side. Placing an elegant hand on his shoulder, she removed one shoe, then the other, and handed them both to him. "Hold these for me."

Belizar's brow creased. "My lady, this is—"

The Council chamber erupted. Lyssa was no longer next to Jacob. In a movement too fast to follow, she'd cleared the table, seized Belizar by the front of his suit and slammed him up against the stone wall behind his chair. The impact was so hard the stone cracked like a gunshot. The head of the Council snarled. Lyssa dropped him with an answering show of fang and a deft leap that put her on top of the table, in front of his chair, her feet on the stack of papers there. Her jade eyes had gone completely crimson.

"If there's a question about my vampire powers, I will prove them here and now."

With the exception of Mason, the Council members had evacuated their chairs, experienced enough fighters to know that being hemmed in by that monolithic table wasn't a good strategic position. Gideon, Jacob and Daegan shifted, closing in tighter on Anwyn and Kane, turning outward to provide coverage on all sides.

Though Jacob thought the servants should be celebrating the fact the tedium had been disrupted, he kept both wrist gauntlets leveled in their direction, bringing the few who'd started forward to an abrupt halt. Gideon matched his stance with his own weaponry.

Jessica slipped around the wall created by Gideon, Jacob and Daegan to go to Mason's side, obviously at his mental direction. She stood at his chair, a hand on the ornately carved headrest.

Light as a cat, Lyssa pivoted and landed in the open area before the table again. She spread out her hands, an invitation. "You send me a passive-aggressive missive, suggesting I will have no choice but to turn my son over the tender care of this Council, if that is your will. And that I will submit to your judgment about my status as a vampire. So I am here to answer that missive, to prove to you that I am vampire and I am more than capable of caring for my son. But mostly I'm here to deliver my own message. I've had enough."

Her expression changed, eyes becoming hard ruby glass. "I am not here to be judged. This structure is my creation, and since I brought it into the world, I have the right to remove it. I did not fight the Territory Wars and go through utter hell to establish this Council, only to see it destroy itself from within."

Belizar had straightened, his eyes narrowed upon her, rage simmering off him, but he'd not yet made his move. It was too early for Jacob to take that as a good sign.

"We are a species like no other," she continued, sweeping her gaze over the Council members. "We cannot be democratic in nature. We are too brutal, too driven by our predator natures for that. However, the vision I had for this Council was one of fairness, one where prejudices and old fears and hatreds would not stagnate it. I thought things might change in light of what has occurred in the past few years, that you would realize our direction must be adjusted, but I was wrong. If I have to take hold of the helm once again to make sure the vision I had—and continue to have—for this Council, happens, I will do so. If, in order to do that, I must prove I'm still capable of staking every one of you where you stand, with my vampire powers alone, I'm happy to do that."

"With your vampire powers alone?" Belizar took a step forward, crimson shimmering through his gaze as well. He scoffed. "You are too tainted by the Fae sludge in your veins."

"And you are blinded by your prejudices, stumbling into walls such that you can't move forward." She shifted her glance to Uthe. "Lord Uthe, you have ever been a fair force on this Council. Would you say that, if I defeat Lord Belizar, strength to strength, with no evidence of Fae magic, that I will adequately prove my point? Or do I need to kill every vampire in this room?"

Uthe met Belizar's gaze. Lyssa noted the Russian vampire's eyes had gone full flame. He'd been council head for a while, his Cossack background making him a powerful and—up until now—justifiable figurehead. Uthe provided the balance of brains needed for leadership, when Belizar would listen to him, which had regrettably become less and less. The rage swelling up in Belizar was beyond polite, icy missives, and she was fiercely glad to see it. She'd fully intended to take this moment back to their bloody roots, brute strength against brute strength, and apparently she was going to succeed, at least in that.

Letting out another snarl, Belizar stripped out of his coat, providing Uthe's answer. Rolling up his shirt sleeves, he yanked off his tie, an appropriate move since she would choke him with it. Though vampires didn't need to breathe, extreme pressure on the windpipe was uncomfortable and distracting. He cocked a brow at her outfit. "That might be a little constricting, Lady Lyssa."

"I appreciate your concern, my lord, but it's become a world of amazing new fabrics. They stretch and cling at once. Do you want to fight or discuss personal fashion choice?"

He sneered. "I see you've co-opted our assassin for your own use."

"Daegan is a free agent," she retorted. "He chooses his own alliances. I'd say he chose well this time. But he will not interfere in this. This is might-is-right combat terms, what our kind respects above all others. I think there's room for more enlightened thinking than that, but unfortunately the Council's recent decisions seem to have forgotten that. However, you are welcome to prove me wrong, and save yourself a beating. Simply admit defeat now and step down."

Belizar had fought at her side in the Territory Wars, with great capability. They had a history. But he represented the pure traditionalist of the Old World vampires, and he'd not hesitated to want her dead when he found out about her Fae form. His narrow-mindedness and overbearing personality had overwhelmed many of the lesser Council members, keeping the Council on its current path. In watching Rhoswen deal with the consequences of restrictions that had more to do with fear and control than true leadership, Lyssa had become even more convinced such an approach would fail.

As Belizar considered her, perhaps thinking of their shared history as well, she drew herself up, hardly five feet tall without her shoes. Cocking a hip, she tilted her head. "Come, Belizar. Not afraid of being beaten by a girl, are you?"

He gave her a show of fang, a flash of the dark red eyes. Reaching under his shirt, he yanked out two wooden stakes. A warrior like the men behind her, she wasn't surprised he was armed. Mason rose with a scrape of his chair, and Jacob started forward, but Lyssa's sharp voice was a queen's command that reverberated through the room.

"This fight is between the two of us. If he overpowers me, he deserves the kill. That's the whole point, isn't it?" She cocked her head, eyes gleaming. "As it was from the beginning. You'll regret pulling those toys, my lord. You may find yourself on the wrong end of them."

Belizar leaped. With third-mark senses, Jacob could keep up with most of their maneuvers, but some were even too fast for him to follow. At least his lady's speed, while not the fastest he'd ever seen it, was enough to keep up with Belizar. The Council scattered further as they hit the crescent-shaped table, so hard it shattered down the middle, a startling symbolism. Mason joined Daegan in corraling their ranks as Jessica moved back into the knot of servants, the safest place for her now.

Jacob bit back an oath as he saw it was Lyssa who'd broken the table, when Belizar hurled her into the stone. She rolled back, made it to her feet. When he charged upon her, she cut under his guard and hit him hard in the solar plexus, seizing his arm to bend it back. It would have broken with a defining snap if he hadn't twisted free with remarkable agility, turning around to plunge his fist squarely in her face.

He realized he was struggling, Gideon holding him back. Anwyn's hand was on his shoulder as well, gripping hard, even as she held Kane on her hip. His son's uncertain cry jerked his attention back. "Gotta be her fight," his brother hissed. "Can't watch all corners by myself. Get your shit together, bro."

Jacob shook himself free, tried to do just that as Anwyn pressed Kane's head to her neck to hide his eyes, trying to calm him. He was having none of it. His cries were stuttering to a higher level. In a moment it would be full fledged, ear splitting wails.

Lyssa and Belizar's fight took them across the room, Belizar driving her back toward the knot of servants. As the Russian turned, he flung her toward that still group, as if he intended to knock them down with her body like bowling pins.

Too late, Jacob registered Vincent's tense, waiting posture. Saw the gleam of the polished stake in his fist. As Lyssa stumbled, pivoting away from Belizar, Vincent lunged forward. As one, Jacob and Gideon discharged arrows for the impossible shot.

Lyssa fell back into Vincent, and he dropped behind her, providing a cushion as she rolled away unharmed. One of the arrows had pierced Vincent's shoulder. However, that wasn't what had him flailing now. A steel shaft punched through his chest from the back. Jessica had not hit the heart, but she'd hit the spine, immobilizing him. She'd fallen with him so she was on the ground, holding the shaft in place and him against her in a way that looked almost compassionate. Jacob even heard her murmur, "Uh-uh. Nice try. Just sit there for a bit."

Jacob snapped his gaze back to the combatants. They were circling in the center of the room again. His lady's mouth was bleeding, as was her temple, and it looked like Belizar had broken a couple of her ribs. She was limping. Belizar was almost unmarked, but he was holding one arm gingerly, because she'd succeeded in snapping it. His eyes shone with the light of victory. "You may beg my mercy now, Lady Lyssa," he said. "I will be more than willing to grant it. You know you will ever be useful to this Council."

She came to a full stop. Her fangs had lengthened, as they did before she fed. "I have one question for you, Lord Belizar, if you'll indulge me."

"Of course." He nodded magnanimously, though the effort cost him, his face tight.

"Are you done dicking around, or are you ready to fight?"

Jacob didn't know if the street language or the message itself was what threw Belizar. Or if it even mattered. Because faster than Belizar or any vampire he'd ever seen could move, she'd closed the distance between them. He saw the brief flash as she stepped inside his armspan, a frightening moment as Belizar swiped one of the wooden stakes at her chest, narrowly missing her. She turned, her back pressing into his chest, and then she'd caught him by the skull and neck. It was like a lover reaching back to caress his jaw, but she brought him over her shoulder, a graceful choreography that arced him high in the air and then slammed him with brutal force down on the tile floor.

A web of cracks shot out from the impact point. Bones and tile broke together. The male's neck was at an angle that only happened when the neck was snapped. Jacob knew the tile landing would also break ribs, hips and further points on the spine, immobilizing him for however long it would take the bones to heal.

Belizar let out a strangled, agonized grunt, but Jacob saw there was no fear in his eyes. Only shock, anger and frustration, the realization he'd been soundly, clearly defeated. He was at the mercy of his opponent.

The wooden stakes had fallen free from his limp hands. Retrieving them, she laid them on his chest. Squatting at his side, Lyssa lifted his arm and brought his wrist to her mouth. She drank, the ritual spoils of a victor, and though she sank in with a deep, painful clamp, she didn't take long. She withdrew, delicately licking her lips, then took up the two stakes, angling one against his chest. She swept her gaze over the silent, assembled vampires, meeting Uthe's gaze before she lowered her attention back to Belizar.

"I am now head of the Council. I will have final authority on all its decisions, and who serves upon it. You will continue to do so, Lord Belizar. You're an old war horse, like me." A faint smile touched her bloody lips. "And you still fight passably well. But one of my conditions for all who serve on this Council is that I will take the right of a sire's marking. I will have the ability to be in your mind, know your heart and soul. If I sense you resisting any intrusion of my mind into yours, at any time, concealing things from me, then I will remove you from this Council."

"I'm guessing she's not offering a great severance package if that happens," Gideon muttered to Jacob.

He wanted to smile, but there was still too much going on in the room, too much blood and heat. She'd taken Belizar out in one stroke, as if she'd been capable of it all along, but he knew what her state had been only a couple days before, newly transitioned. Right now her mind was closed as a trap, and she might have used the last reserve of her strength to make that move. He wasn't going to make the same mistake twice in his concern for her, though, thank the gods for Jessica. He kept his attention firmly on the servants, trusting Daegan and Mason to handle the vampire end of things.

She straightened then, glanced toward her son, who had tears on his face and was wailing like a banshee. When he saw her looking at him, she pursed her lips, made a soft shushing noise and gave him a half smile, entirely at odds with the violence lingering in the room like the smell of a bomb blast. It startled him enough that he bit off midcry, hiccupping uncertainly. "That's my good boy," she said softly. "Easy there."

Then her attention landed on Vincent, still in Jessica's lap. "You may remove the stake, Jessica. He will need his Master's blood, and his Master needs a great deal as well." Her gaze shifted to Torrence, Helga's servant. The male was built like a mountain, shown to good effect in white shirt and dress kilt. Even as a mere human, he probably could have swung a claymore like a feather. "Go advise the staff that three donors are needed to restore his strength. You others, help carry him and Vincent to a suitable room to use as an infirmary and make sure they are comfortable."

She glanced at the Council members. "If you will not serve under my conditions, then you will not serve. You will be stripped of any territory or overlord titles you carry, and relegated to a territory of my choosing, where I know the overlord or Region Master is loyal to me. I will know the truth of it when I am in your minds, so you might as well speak now."

"She has proven her worth on the field of combat."

Belizar's voice was a weak rasp of sound. His expression showed his agony, on several levels. While a vampire would survive and heal multiple bone breaks, Jacob knew it was not going to be an easy or pleasant few hours for him. "She is worthy to take the leadership. You are all vampire again, my lady."

"I was always all vampire. It is what my soul is, no matter my blood." She gave him a hard look. "I am also Fae. You're going to have to accept that, what it means. I brought a correspondence from the Fae queen, indicating her desire for a liaison between our two worlds. While I was intended to be that liaison, in light of my taking the head position, I will ask that another Fae be assigned that role. I will be recommending the Fae Lord Keldwyn, who already serves as liaison between the Seelie and Unseelie court. He considers this world his home much of the time anyway."

She let her gaze rove over all of them. "We will always be vampires, with predatory drives and dominant attitudes, but there is room for other things. With only five thousand of us in the world, survival is everything. We cannot stagnate. We can be strong, true to our nature, and yet still consider changes that augment that strength and nature. This is one of them."

At her nod, Uthe came forward, as did Lady Barbra and Lady Carola. Lyssa straightened on the other side of the injured vampire, giving them room to check Belizar's injuries so they could instruct the staff when they arrived with stretchers to move him and Vincent.

Belizar made a strangled noise, and Jacob followed the wild flicker of his gaze as Lyssa turned to speak to Mason.

My lady. His warning shot into Lyssa's mind. In the same moment, Barbra closed her hand on one of the discarded stakes and surged upward toward Lyssa.

Once again, Jacob didn't even see her move, which made him wonder if Lyssa had left the stakes there, anticipating Barbra's move. She held the vampire female by the throat, her other hand clamped on that wrist. Her green and bloodred eyes frosted, and that chill Jacob remembered well filled the room. It was a Fae power, yes, but since she'd been known for it even before she'd embraced her Fae side, she didn't mind using it in full force now.

"You are very foolish," Lyssa said. "That might be excused, but I know your heart, Barbra. I don't have to take your blood to know your mind. Thank you, therefore, for making this so easy."

Twisting the stake clutched in Barbra's hand, she shoved it up under the rib cage. Since she held on to Barbra's wrist, she broke her forearm like a twig. Barbra gave a short scream that became violent twitching, bare heels scraping the stone as she fought Lyssa's grip. The death throes kicked her shoes free, one of them rolling across the floor. At length, the life dying out of her eyes, her legs sagged, bending limply. Lyssa dropped her then, several paces from Belizar.

Jacob noticed her gaze shifted to Daegan. As she gave a near imperceptible nod, a look of satisfaction crossed Daegan's face, and Gideon's as well, telling Jacob they'd had unresolved issues with Barbra. Intentionally or not, Lyssa had apparently honored their loyalty by bringing that matter to a close.

The servants shifted back as Barbra's servant, a slim redheaded male, dropped to the floor with a similar strangled cry. A tall blonde knelt at his side, her hand on his shoulder, her face reflecting quiet, neutral compassion as the inevitable happened and he followed his Mistress to the other side.

Kane had started up his wailing again, so Anwyn moved to a corner positioned behind Daegan, a protected place where she could better keep the babe's focus on her. Moving to her side, Jacob brushed his knuckles along his son's cheek, a reassurance to calm him, even as he kept his right wrist gauntlet poised toward the cluster of servants, ready if needed.

The doors opened, Gideon and Daegan permitting the staff to enter with two stretchers, Torrence following in their wake. They all hesitated at the sight of a lifeless vampire and the dead servant, but when Lyssa beckoned to them, they came forward, albeit cautiously. "When Lord Belizar and his servant are cared for, come back and retrieve her and her servant. You may place her in the inner courtyard for sunrise disposal and bury her servant where appropriate for his loyalty to her. Jacob?"

"My lady?" He left Kane with a tug of his short hair, a further reassurance. The toddler was playing with the necklace Anwyn wore, the sparkling amber distracting him. As Jacob stepped to Lyssa's side, he was calmly solicitous as a servant should be, despite the emotions roiling through him. A grim smile slid through her eyes, still more than a bit dangerous. *You have ever failed to have a poker face, Sir Vagabond. There was never anything to worry about.*

If that were the case, you'd let me see all the way into your mind, into your physical well-being.

At the proper time. "Once we deal with things here, contact Dev and advise him his mistress, Lady Daniela, has been appointed to the Vampire Council. I will expect her here as soon as she can choose an acting overlord to handle her territory's affairs. She should plan to stay here several weeks to orient herself as a junior member, until I decide where to move the Council's base. We definitely need a change from this depressing environment." Her gaze flickered distastefully over the heavy stone walls, the ominous darkness of them.

A pained grunt drew their attention. It was Vincent, reacting as Jessica slid the steel shaft out of his back so the servants could move him onto a stretcher. She also removed that one stray arrow from his shoulder, and as she did, she made a small noise of distress. The arrow, shot at such close range, had pierced through Vincent's shoulder and plunged into hers when she grabbed him. Blood bloomed on her blouse, but she gave Jacob a reassuring look as she tossed the arrow aside.

"I will meet with Lord Mason, Lord Daegan and Lord Uthe now," Lyssa told the rest of the Council. "Shortly thereafter, I will visit each of you to mark you as I've designated, so you should go to your personal chambers and remain there until I come to you. Later tonight, we will have a civilized, pleasant dinner, vampire style." She flashed fang. "It will be a celebration, so dress accordingly."

The Council members exchanged glances and moved toward the door with their servants, while those commanded to remain held their positions. Jacob could tell Mason had his attention divided between the retreating vampires and his own servant. Jessica had put herself into one of the few chairs that had not been knocked over. Though she held her hand over the wound in her shoulder, the blood had already slowed. She was healing, and from her internal expression, she was reassuring her Master of that. Jesus, she was tough, but Mason was going to tear him a new one. Jacob decided then and there he'd tell him it was Gideon's arrow.

As the double doors closed securely behind the vampires and their servants, Mason was already going to her. Lyssa nodded once in satisfaction, as if to herself.

Jacob, I'm going to fall now.

He was there in a flash, catching her. Daegan brought another chair, placing it near Jessica. Lyssa glanced at the girl as Mason knelt by her, jerking open the first two buttons of her blouse to push it off her shoulder and see where the arrow had gone through the flesh, just inside the line of her lacy bra strap. "Well played, Jessica," Lyssa noted.

The young woman lifted the other shoulder, turning her gaze to Jacob with a smile. "When it comes to a fight between vampires, *never* forget the servants. That's what he told me."

"And who do you think taught *him* that?" Gideon said gruffly, but he gave her hair a gentle tug where he stood to her left, positioned between both Lyssa and Jess. Jacob's concern for the young servant reflected in his eyes as well.

"My lady, are you all right?" Mason was obviously steadier now that he had his hands on his servant and could physically assure himself of her well-being.

"Nothing draining my servant dry won't cure." She gave a wan smile. "These first few days as a full vampire again, I apparently need three or four on standby."

"Did you know what she was going to do?" Daegan asked Mason.

Mason shook his head, locked gazes with Lyssa. "She told me once she was in range of my mind. We've been linked for several centuries now. She trusted I would follow her lead."

"And my trust in you is never misplaced. Not ultimately. Though for an interminably long time, I do remember you stubbornly refused to support having a Council."

"If you'd done something like this a few decades ago, maybe I wouldn't have."

"You're right." Lyssa's admission surprised Mason, Jacob could tell. "You were always right about their nature. I think it took immersing myself in what the Fae nature is to understand ours better. But I think there will be room for both our viewpoints, in time."

Leaning forward, despite her obvious weariness, she closed her hand on his, while giving Jessica's arm a brief touch. "I am very sorry I put your servant in danger. I would never have asked that of her, or you."

"She pretty much took matters into her own hands." Mason gave Jessica a brooding, stern glance, but one with pride in it. "She does that, no matter how often I beat her."

Jessica had only a smile for that. Caressing her Master's face, she trailed her fingers through the long copper-colored strands of his hair. "Jacob had excellent aim, my lord. Nothing to fear."

Jacob winced, and her eyes laughed at him, telling him she'd intentionally busted him. But if she was teasing him, she was okay. Perhaps Jessica, like Gideon, was more comfortable in a situation where she was fighting, rather than waiting for things to happen to her.

Daegan snorted. "We all seem to have found servants with an incurable streak of disobedience." He gave Gideon a shove. The hunter grunted.

"Yeah, aren't you lucky that way?"

"That is not the word I would have chosen."

"Anytime you want to switch out a pit bull for a fucking arm poodle, nothing's stopping you, Mr. Wear-Armani-to-a-Fight. Good thing you didn't get blood on it."

"The night is still young."

"I have to be able to walk out of those doors as strong as I walked in," Lyssa said. She gave Gideon an amused glance. "I've had enough of your blood for now. Too much of it and I'm afraid I'll start swaggering and cursing like a sailor. I'll get some from Jacob, but I need more. Lord Uthe?"

The quietest member of their group stepped forward now. "My lady?"

"Will you give me the honor of allowing me to drink from your servant?"

"You are head of Council now, my lady. You may demand anything you wish from me."

She heard the mix of emotions in the polite tone. He, too, had known Belizar for many years. They'd been friends, as much as vampires knew how to be, even though their viewpoints differed. In hindsight, she wished she'd put her support behind Uthe as the Council head years ago, though at the end of the Territory Wars, when there was still so much unrest, it had made more sense to put a more warlike figure in that position. Rex had agreed with her, though of course, he would have.

"I am not going to mark you, Uthe," she said. "Though I will let the rest of the Council believe I have done so. You are the type of person I want on this Council, but I want you here fully. If you do not agree with what I have done, I will release you tonight, and strip nothing from you. I will continue to regard you with the highest honor and respect, and seek your counsel."

"If you are saying you want me on the Council specifically for my ability to question and challenge you, with the best interests of our kind in mind, then I accept that privilege." He held her gaze a long moment, then dropped to one knee before her, so she did not have to look up at him. His voice became rougher. "My lady, I serve no one without question, but I have ever viewed you as our queen and would serve you as such. I would be honored if you'd allow my servant, Mariela, to replenish your strength. You will definitely need it for the days ahead."

Mariela now stepped to his side. She was the one who'd comforted Barbra's servant in his passing. Tall and blonde, with dark brown eyes, she had the athletic movements of a female Amazon, and a quiet steadiness and subtle intelligence that complimented her vampire master well.

Lyssa took his hand, squeezed it hard. "Thank you, my lord. I accept. I will draw from Mariela first. Her blood should strengthen me enough to visit each Council member and mark them as I indicated. I will do that alone, with Jacob as my attendant."

She shook her head, anticipating Daegan and Mason. "I have made my point and Belizar has put his support behind me. I used your strength to back me for this key moment, because I did not want my son unprotected in such a volatile environment." *No matter the Fae protection he carries.* She added that in Jacob's mind, saw his imperceptible nod. They'd decided the purpose of the tattooed pendant would not be public knowledge, for concealed weapons were often the most potent kind.

Now she looked to Daegan. "I ask that you continue to watch over him while I take care of that task. Mason, be with Jessica. Give her blood, make her rest to ensure she is fully healed by dinner time. After I mark the Council, I will retire for an hour or two with my servant to feed from him. Hopefully this awful place has a room with a fireplace to ward off the chill coming from the very stones." Her gaze coursed around the room, encompassing all of them. "Thank you. Your loyalty means a great deal to me. I will do my best to deserve it, now and going forward."

A spark of humor went through her gaze as she glanced at Jacob. *And thank all the gods that vampires don't take offense at being thanked.*

23

As the clock moved toward the midnight dinner hour, Lyssa and Jacob finally arrived in the master suite that had belonged to Belizar. She'd of course eschewed the rooms where the Council had originally intended to put her. While she attended to the marking of the Council members, the staff had changed out the bedding, removed all of Belizar's personal effects and moved them to the bedroom where he now convalesced. Someone had thought to add a large vase of vibrant flowers to the room, and kept a fire well tended in the hearth. They brought color and heat to the room, respectively.

Pausing by the flowers, she touched the petal of a bright yellow daisy and glanced at Jacob. "Your doing?"

"I know you hate the darkness here, my lady." Stripping off the wrist gauntlets, he shrugged out of his shirt in a movement of graceful power, leaving him bare above the slacks. He stripped the belt out of it, so they hung lower on his hips, revealing the dark strip of the boxer briefs he'd worn beneath, one of the few times he wore underwear. Since the snug fit helped hold the extra arrows he'd carried along his outer thigh, she'd been more flexible about her requirement today. He pulled those arrows out now, unfastening the top of the slacks to allow him the ability to do so.

She sat down in a wing-back chair, watching the beautiful play of muscle. As he became aware of her close regard, his movements slowed and he looked at her.

Come to me, Jacob.

His stride across the room gave her more of that visual art. She said nothing, gave him no further direction, always enjoying what he would choose to do, how he would anticipate her needs. As he reached her, he bent, slid his arms beneath her in the chair. Lifting her in that easy way of his, he turned and took the seat to cradle her in his arms. His fingers tangled in her hair, tightening. Her alpha warrior. Her knight.

"Drink, my lady," he said. "Take everything you need."

He shuddered as she pierced him, as he often did. Dropping his head to the seat back, a deep sigh slipped out of him as his other hand settled on her hip, stroking that line. "You worried me."

"You worry quite a lot. Enough for both of us."

He grunted at that. Mariela's blood had been sweet, pure, lifegiving. But there was nothing like Jacob's blood, the blood of her full servant. Her arm was around his back, knuckles pressed to the cushioning as she stroked the serpentine shape of that third mark. *Are you worried about tonight, my protective Sir Knight?*

He shook his head. "It's obvious they're on board, at least for today. An indisputable show of strength was what they needed. Overcoming Belizar and staking Barbra more than accomplished that. I'm a little curious how the dinner will go. Given it's a vampire dinner . . ."

She smiled against his flesh. "It's been a while since I've had the pleasure of enjoying my servant during one of those."

"Now I am worried." But she felt the flash of his amusement, followed by a more serious direction. "I'm concerned about Jessica."

"I knew I was right about the protective part. Chivalrous soul. Mason can exempt her if he wishes. He will not let etiquette or seniority stop him. If she participates, it is because she is determined to perform fully as his servant. I expect she needs to prove it to him."

"And he'd allow that?"

"It's amazing what a vampire finds her or himself allowing, despite the fact they are supposed to be Master or Mistress, and the humans the servants. However, if she's convinced him to be a little less maniacally protective, that's not an easy task. She's a remarkable girl."

She was quiet then for a bit, feeding off of him. She stroked his chest, following the appealing flat hardness of his pectoral, the curve of biceps.

"I'll bring Kane tonight," she said. "Let the others pet and play with him."

Jacob chuckled, his voice a little thick, reacting to the intimacy and pleasure of her touch. "If Helga gets her claws into Kane, we won't get him back, short of threatening to stake her."

"He'll love the spoiling. As Gideon says, when it comes to vampire children, we are hopeless. But he does not realize what it is like, to be a species where offspring are so rare that every infant is like a precious, delicate gem. Even without the pendant, I was never worried about Kane being harmed by the Council, not at this age. Only taken away from his rightful parents, who best know how to protect him."

As he made a noise of agreement, she lifted her head. "On that note, I invited Brian to the dinner tonight. When you were talking to the kitchen staff, I visited his lab area. He told me he has some findings on one of his projects he wants to share."

"Good. I've missed the vampire geek."

She snorted. "I dare you to call him that to his face."

"No thanks, I'll pass. I do occasionally understand the benefits of tact, especially around vampires who can throw me through walls."

"Perhaps you can teach your brother such diplomacy."

"Not likely. I'm still kind of amazed he'll be there tonight. I assume he'll have to be gagged, muzzled, blindfolded . . ."

"He has been with Anwyn and Daegan for a few months now. When he knelt before her, that day at our house, it was obvious they've been thoroughly training him in what is expected of a vampire's servant. I would have enjoyed seeing that." Jacob felt a lazy, sensual stir of amusement from her. "But he is still Gideon. He has an unmistakable deference when it comes to his Master and Mistress, though he will never be as smooth with it as you, someone who willingly sought the bond. But it's there. He belongs to them, body, heart and soul."

"I know. I see it. And it still kind of freaks me out."

She chuckled against his skin then, changing the nourishing pull to a stimulating lick, her tongue caressing the puncture. She scraped her nails over his nipple. "I'd like a bath, Jacob. I want you to bathe me, and while you do, I'm going to enjoy touching you however I wish, making sure you are hard and ready for tonight's events, whatever your Mistress wills."

"I'm sure I could do that, even if she decides to avail herself of my cock now."

She rubbed her ass against the mentioned portion of his anatomy, teasing him. "No doubt. I've missed showing you off, Jacob. It's been a rough day, and I plan to enjoy my night thoroughly."

"God help me," he muttered. She turned her face up and slid both hands into his hair, bringing him down for a plundering fuck-me-now kiss he knew wouldn't sway her, even as she'd get so hot and wet he could smell it and it would drive him insane.

His lady was stubborn like that.

Mindful that he had responsibilities beyond tireless and devoted sex slave, Jacob had taken the time to ensure dinner would reflect the new management as best as possible with such short notice. The staff had done well with his direction. The dining room table had a bright white tablecloth, red flower petals scattered over the fabric. A beautiful arrangement of traditional red roses formed the centerpiece, the blooms partially open in that coy, tempting way his lady most preferred. The china was a simple white scallop with solid silver edging. He'd lined up several courses for sampling, foods his lady enjoyed, but ones that would tempt the palates of the others.

Right now, the vampires were still in the study, enjoying pre-dinner drinks, but at a step, he glanced up, pleased to see his brother had joined him. Gideon eyed the table settings. "*Martha Stewart Living* says you should put the napkins on the plates in a fan shape. Adds a little touch of class."

"You still reading magazines in grocery stores? I thought you only did that when you were hunting."

"Anwyn keeps a few subscriptions going in the break room at Club Atlantis. Sometimes I read an article here or there, when I need a few minutes to clear my head."

Jacob gave him a sidelong glance. "You okay with this, bro?"

"Yeah. I can do this." A curl to his lip. "The last Council dinner I attended was a lot more . . . challenging. If the most traumatic thing I have to do tonight is see you naked, I'll live. And if we get to share a pretty girl, well, you gotta do what you gotta do to keep your vampires happy, right?"

Despite the flip comment, Jacob could tell Gideon was tense. He knew his brother, knew that Anwyn was the only woman he wanted in his arms. But it was different with a Mistress, what would pleasure them. They had a unique way of making you want what they wanted. He could tell, as Lyssa said, that Gideon understood that better now. But ultimately it didn't change how either of them felt about the vampires they served.

However, when Jessica slipped in the other door, it was apparent that their concerns were comparatively low level. She looked as if she was going to faint. When she leaned against the door, she closed her eyes, so involved in whatever was happening in her head she didn't even notice them. As such, she nearly jumped out of her skin when Jacob moved, his dress shoe scraping the floor.

Her eyes flew open, took them both in. Drawing a deep breath, she declared, "I can do this."

Jacob nodded, took her hand. "Of course you can."

"I can't have a panic attack. He'll feel it. He's involved with them right now, but if he feels me like this, he won't let me do it. And I have to. I have to show him I can do this. I have to prove to me I can do it."

"You will." Gideon, following Jacob's lead, took her other hand, both of them dwarfing the slim fingers. "You look sensational."

Jessica glanced down at the off-the-shoulder black cocktail dress that was high on the thigh. A simple, classy sheath, sexy as hell. She wore the same choker she'd worn earlier, though Jacob hadn't paid close attention to it then, other things taking precedent. At close range, it was quite obviously Mason's collar, a melding of different metals that had the pattern of a tiger's skin. Copper, bronze and gray, with threads of white glazing that made it an exceptional piece of custom metalwork. The closure looked like a tiger's talon. An amber pendant dangled below it. Jacob drew her desperate gaze up to his as he laid his hand on her shoulder, his thumb brushing that collar, reminding her of its presence.

"Everything that happens in here tonight, everything you do, will be his will," he said, steady. "His pleasure. That's how it works. You get so lost in it, it isn't what you're doing that matters. It's how he reacts to it."

Gideon's attention shifted to him. At one time, Jacob himself hadn't fully understood the words, even after months of training to be a vampire queen's servant. But now he did. All the way to the bone. Jessica held his gaze a long moment, drawing on that authority, and her own strength. Her chin firmed, and a new calmness, though fragile, entered her gaze.

"All right."

"Good. They're coming." He pointed to a chair. "He'll be sitting there, at the other end of the table. She has Lord Uthe to her right and Lord Brian to her left." Belizar was going to be next to Uthe. They'd thought about putting Belizar at the other end, where Mason was, but tonight Belizar was a member of Council only. She wanted him to get accustomed to that before she trusted him as a senior member with advanced standing again.

Moving to Mason's chair, Jessica took her place behind it as Jacob showed Gideon where Daegan and Anwyn would be sitting, so he could position himself between both of their chairs. His brother looked unexpectedly put together in black slacks and a dark blue shirt that stretched over his broad shoulders. Jacob wondered what weapons he was carrying tonight, and if the slacks had been tailored specifically to allow for that. Daegan had probably helped him dress, since Gideon usually bought his clothes based on cheapness and how easy it was to wash blood out of them. Quelling a smile, Jacob took a position behind the head chair, his lady's seat.

As the vampires wandered in, they chatted in a relaxed, amiable fashion, not so different from most cocktail parties. Cocktail parties attended by exceptionally perfect physical specimens of beauty and power, who might have been tearing one another apart only a few hours before.

Some of the servants were with them, while others now slipped in from other doors, taking their place. Helga was on the other side of Mason with Torrence behind her. He and Gideon seemed to have a history because, when their gazes met, Gideon gave him a discreet sneer and Torrence returned a fuck-you look, immediately replaced by bland expressions on both faces. Jacob figured they'd be bonding over football scores by the end of the evening.

He held out his chair for his lady. Every inch of her looked edible in a beaded formal sheath of rich green that went with the emerald and diamond choker she wore on her neck. Her hair was in a simple style, clipped at her neck with a diamond clasp, the ebony curls tumbling down her back and over her breasts. She'd put together the right picture of formidable queen and irresistible, charming woman. It reminded everyone here she could be both, and which side she displayed depended on their behavior.

Belizar was quiet, a little more pale than usual, but seemed recovered. Vincent lingered closer to his chair, but when he saw the positioning of the other servants at the wall, he stepped back so he would not appear to be hovering. Jacob appreciated the male's loyalty, one of those odd quirks of being part of the servants' union, so to speak. Though he would have torn the male's head off if he'd actually succeeded in harming Lyssa, he respected his devotion to his Master, because that was the common bond they all shared. He knew it was why Lyssa had Barbra turned to ash in the main courtyard, but her servant was afforded a respectful burial.

When Mason entered, the vampire's gaze of course went to his servant, taking in her general state. Jessica inclined her head, her lashes brushing her cheeks in a pretty display of submission that won a wry tug of his lips. As he moved past her to sit down, his hand slid over her hip, squeezing her buttocks in an admonishment that had her biting down on a yelp.

However, when his nostrils flared and his gaze cut to Jacob, Jacob realized Mason had detected his scent on the girl. Jessica's fingers brushed his forearm, drawing his gaze back down to her. A quiet mind communication ensued, where Jacob hoped she was making it clear that it had been for reassurance only. Having been the one who'd shot her earlier, he didn't relish finding another reason to be on Mason's bad side.

Don't worry, Sir Vagabond. I'll protect you from Mason.

He stifled a snort. *This could get very interesting, my lady. If it bothers him that I touched her for comfort only, how will he feel about what else could happen to her here?*

We'll find out. And see who's still standing when it's all over.

Comforting. To those who have a chance of surviving his wrath.

Feeling fainthearted, Jacob? My servant usually has a foolish over-abundance of courage.

Pot calling the kettle black, my lady.

As the Council and Lord Brian were seated, Lyssa touched her knife to her glass, the chime drawing their attention. She waited as they all stilled, letting the significance of the moment sink in. "Each of you was chosen for this Council," she said. "And that choice was made because it was believed—I think rightly—that you have the skills and strength to protect our kind and make us better and stronger as a race. What has happened in the past is past, useful only for how it takes us into the future. What is not useful we discard and leave behind."

She met Belizar's gaze. After another long moment, the Russian vampire lifted his glass, inclined his head. The look they exchanged reminded Jacob of what had transpired between them earlier, after the fight. From the other Council members, she'd taken the sire's marking from the wrist, a functional exchange. But when she visited Belizar, in the room they'd intended for her, it had gone a little differently.

The first thing she'd noticed was that the bed was too short for his large frame. She'd looked toward Vincent, standing next to it.

"Vincent, there is a staff member outside the door. Please tell her to prepare accommodations more appropriate and comfortable for your Master. Jacob, please help him."

She wanted a little space around the bed, but more than that, Vincent looked like he needed help walking. Though the removal of the steel spike had allowed his spine to heal, Vincent was still deathly pale. His vampire Master understandably needed to replenish first, and of course no vampire would allow his servant to drink from another vampire because of the mind connection that might be established by accident or diabolical intent. So Vincent would wait for blood while Belizar's strength built from the three donors who'd already visited and fed him.

Jacob figured only his loyalty was keeping Vincent on his feet and wondered why Belizar hadn't ordered the male to sit the hell down. Though in all fairness, the Council head looked as if he'd been poleaxed on a lot of levels today, and didn't have any attention to spare beyond that.

"I will understand if your Mistress deems I should be executed for my part in today's events," the servant said as they approached the door. He spoke in a hushed murmur, but with great formality, giving Jacob a stiff bow. "However, while I have not been his full servant very long, I humbly ask that she wait until my Master is at full strength so the disruption of our link does not add to his current weakness."

Lyssa hadn't spoken on this issue, but Jacob easily knew her mind on it. "We're expected to serve our Master and Mistress before any other," he returned. "You did what you were supposed to do. In your shoes, I would have done exactly the same. My lady has differences with Lord Belizar, but she wants him to remain on Council. She won't be depriving him of a loyal servant." Then, since both their vampires were occupied, Jacob added in a low tone, "We're the one soul in their psychotic world they can trust, right?"

Vincent's gaze snapped up to Jacob. He cleared his throat. "Yes, sir. I expect you're correct about that. Thank you. And if there's anything you need to help understand the workings of the castle staff, please don't hesitate to ask."

It was the first time Jacob realized he was considered head honcho on the servant food chain now. A scary thought. When he returned to Lyssa, he stayed at a respectful distance, though he could hear the conversation.

"You likely should have finished it, you know," Belizar observed gruffly. "Show no mercy to an enemy."

"I think I made my point. And Barbra is far less useful to us than you." Lyssa laid a hand on his thigh, a possessive, relaxed movement. "You're stubborn, bigoted, inflexible. You'll be an aggravation to me, sure enough. But a great many of our born vampires are exactly like you. I have enough of those qualities myself to recognize I need that voice represented on the Council as well. During changing times, you don't do so well in charge. But you'll be of great value as a Council member. Don't worry. I'll make sure you don't become a detriment again."

He gave a half chuckle at that, though his eyes were studied, measuring. It was enough to have Jacob stay on the alert, but he sensed the same level of watchfulness in his lady. She knew the animal she was dealing with.

"I would sit up," he said. "It feels . . . inappropriate for you to have to lean down, my lady."

She helped him, adjusting the pillows behind his head in a way that had her leaning forward, her breasts close to his face, body in intimate proximity to him. It was a vulnerable pose, but Jacob expected it was deliberate. She'd defeated him soundly. Now she was proving she would trust him, if he proved himself worthy of trust.

Belizar's gaze flickered upward as she sat back. "You remember that night Rex, you and I were holed up in that sewer in Italy? We were taking back the Florence territory from Pietro and his fanged thugs."

"We weren't taking it back that night," she said dryly. "You were nearly decapitated, and Rex lost so much blood I was afraid the trail he left would betray us."

"Yet you wouldn't abandon either of us. It was then I realized you were different from other vampires. You seduced a young woman, brought her to Rex and me to feed upon. When she lost consciousness, I remember you lifting her in your arms, tender as your own child, and carrying her up top to a safe place, back to her family home. When you came back, you knelt by Rex, stroked his brow, then came to me. I was wearing that fake beard to look like my countrymen. You tugged on it to tease me, even as I could see the strain in your eyes, the determination."

Belizar coughed, shifted. "The set of your delicate chin told me that before daylight, you would take Pietro down. And you did. Tore him to pieces, scared his thugs into a running retreat with your ferocity. And yet . . . you stroked my beard. You have always been a puzzle to me, Lady Lyssa. Perhaps that is why I often forget why you are a queen."

"I trust it will be a while before you forget again," she said lightly.

"That is so." He turned his head, closed his eyes. "Make your sire's mark. I am yours, to do with as you will."

Leaning forward now, she laid one hand on his abdomen, the other on his throat, fingers slim and petite compared to the massive bull neck. When she placed her mouth on his carotid, she tilted his head up. The way she did it to Jacob, increasing the sense of vulnerability and jolt of sexual awareness at once.

This was his least favorite side of her, this ability to draw men into the sexual miasma that swirled around her like a djinn's magic. It always made him want to pin her up against a wall and fuck her brains out to remind her of his presence.

I am always aware of you, Sir Vagabond. And how you react to this, the fierceness of your want in my mind, makes me wet.

Yeah, it might be his least favorite, but it was nowhere near her least irresistible side. She sank her fangs into Belizar's throat as his fingers curled against the bed covers. His involuntary response was obvious beneath the bedcovers, because he was a well-endowed male. When her fingers stroked his abdomen, he gave a slight jerk, registering the burn of the mark that would make his mind open to her whenever she wished it to be.

Tension was in his face, in every line of his body, for vampires did not open their minds to other vampires willingly, particularly one Belizar's age. There might not be another vampire alive who had the access to his mind she'd just taken.

She gave him a thought to test that link, sharing it with Jacob. *I will tell Brian to look into ways to give male vampires facial hair again. I'd like to see you with a beard, old warhorse.*

As she drew back, Belizar turned his head to look at her, his eyes faintly crimson, revealing the effort it had taken him to submit for her marking. Her hand closed on his forearm. "If you will learn to trust me again, Belizar, as you trusted me that day in the sewer, one day this moment will not be such a painful memory."

Glancing down then, a smile playing on her lips, she stroked high on his thigh, perilously close to the engorged appendage. "It looks like you might have need of Vincent. But give him blood first. He looks a little unsteady. He did his best to protect you, my lord. Though he lacks Malachi's battle skills, he is a good servant."

Belizar grunted at that, though the shadow that passed through his eyes said he still missed the servant who'd been killed at the Council Gathering not too long ago.

Rising, Lyssa moved to Jacob. She placed her hand on his arm, giving him her mesmerizing expression long enough to stroke his nerves before she slipped out, expecting him to follow. He did, conscious of Belizar's eyes following them both.

~

So here they were at dinner, with Belizar answering her toast and the other dinner guests following suit. As the first course was served, Jacob monitored the movement of staff in and out of the room, ensuring everyone was doing their job and the vampires' needs were being met. He caught Gideon making faces at him a couple of times, his brother mocking him acting the proper majordomo. Jacob resisted the urge to send a rude gesture his way. He'd pound him in a sparring match later.

The Council servants were doing what servants did, measuring one another, knowing they might be on far closer terms later in the evening. Gideon, Jessica and he received the most attention, since they were the newest variables. Though Jacob knew some of them in passing, there was one very welcome and familiar face: Debra, Lord Brian's servant. He'd sent her a warm nod when she took her place behind Brian's chair. As usual, she looked too serious and thin, but she'd worn a blue evening gown tonight that accentuated her breasts and line of hip, her hair loose on her bare shoulders. An easier look to her eyes suggested her Master was taking the time to appreciate something other than her lab skills these days. If not, he was a fucking wanker.

He was sure the Aussie derogative had been influenced by his earlier call to Dev. Dev's response to the news of Lady Daniela's promotion had been typically laconic.

"That's going to send her into a blue, for sure. It's near sheep shearing time."

Comparing the formality of this evening to Danny and Dev doing sheep shearing, imagining them sitting out on the station porch afterward to watch the starlight and share a cuppa, was the difference between the sun and moon. Lyssa had chosen well. Daniela's no-nonsense and straightforward personality would be a good element for the Council.

Jacob shifted his gaze to his lady. She was alert and engaged with everyone at the table, missing nothing, not the slightest nuance in conversation or facial expression. In some ways, it was a new side of her for him as well. When he'd met her, she'd been exhausted by everything about the vampire world. Even after the Delilah virus incident, she'd had bouts with that lack of interest and weariness. However, since her vampire powers had been restored, he'd felt that renewed resolve within her. If the turning had somehow contributed to this revitalized queen, he'd never regret the loss of his vampire strengths again.

Kane hit his legs like a little cannonball. Helga had been bouncing him on her lap, making comical voices and faces for him. While Kane had been vastly entertained by the unexpected side to the austere woman, once she put him down, he'd made a beeline for his father. Now the toddler clung to his slacks, swaying on his still unsteady legs, and beamed up at him. "Da . . ."

Jacob picked him up, settled him on his hip, and gave him a warm smile. "What're you doing, troublemaker?"

"Da-da-da-da . . ." He fingered the lapel of Jacob's jacket, his feet kicking his waist. There was a suspicious stain at his mouth, chocolate that Helga had snuck him. He gave Lyssa a glance, and she rolled her eyes indulgently. She'd pushed her chair back to see them, so he lowered their son into her lap. Kane kept hold of them both, rocking on Lyssa's thighs, obviously delighted to have both of their undivided attention.

It felt good to Jacob as well. Then the toddler spotted the chocolate truffle at the edge of Lyssa's plate and went for it like a striking snake. Jacob, anticipating the move, caught his wrist, gave it a little shake, drawing those green eyes up to his face. "No, sir. That's your mother's. And it's bad for you."

Kane's lips settled into a pout. Jacob knew the wheels turning in that small mind, enough that he had to work not to let a grin escape past his stern expression. "Don't think I won't smack your ass here in front of all of them. Behave."

Since Jacob had been vampire ever since Kane's birth, dealing with him as a human servant hadn't been an issue. But it didn't change anything. Even when Kane could outrun him and toss him like a football, or rip his throat out, he wasn't going to be less of a parent. And it was a father's job to teach his son respect.

Kane subsided, recognizing he'd lost. Proving it, he instantly returned to smiling and chuckling at his mother. Straightening, Jacob stepped back to his place at the wall. He discovered a momentary silence had settled over the table, Council vampires and servants alike now staring at them in visible shock. And a lot of that attention appeared to be upon him.

He hadn't really talked about it with his lady, thinking he knew her mind on it, but now he was forcibly reminded that most servants didn't take on an active parent role. Particularly not in front of a vampire gathering like this.

Well, they'd better get used to it. Lyssa didn't look at him, but he felt the warmth in the declaration, her answer to the unasked question. It eased the coil of tension in his gut.

Lord Brian cleared his throat. "My lady, this seems an excellent time to offer the preliminary findings I discussed with you earlier. If you agree."

"I do." When Kane wriggled, wanting down, she let him toddle around to his next target, the somber Uthe. The Council member's eyes lit with a smile as he let Kane examine his cufflink, then clamber onto his knee to examine the Templar pendant he always wore. Mariela made a face at the child when Kane peered over his broad shoulder. Kane's eyes got wide, then his mouth creased in a smile.

Fearless. Jacob hoped he would always be. *Do you want me to ask Lord Daegan to take him to bed, my lady?*

No. We'll wait until after Lord Brian's discussion, as long as he doesn't get overly fussy. I think it could serve a strategic purpose, having him here for this.

Brian rose, nodding to the assembled. "It's a good night to have this discussion, since we have had a . . . perspective shift today. With respect"—he bowed toward Lord Belizar—"I think that shift will be necessary to comprehend the significance of this report, and embrace what it suggests."

Translation—before the coup earlier in the day, Jacob suspected Brian had prepared a report with much more careful wording. It was evident in the easier set of his shoulders, the eagerness in his eyes, now unhampered by concerns about sharp repercussions.

"As you know, one of the most important areas of my research is the low reproduction rate for born vampires. In the past couple centuries, it has dwindled to an alarming rate. At times, this led to various decisions to permit more made vampires, who come with their own problems. With no prejudices intended toward the made vampires who have proven themselves able to overcome these issues, born vampires are more stable, stronger physical stock for our race, and so their continued existence and births are essential for the overall future of our species."

His gaze strayed briefly to Kane as the child appeared at his knee, now trying that high wattage smile on the scientist. Lord Brian gave him a tender look, brushing his hair back from his forehead. When Jacob made a quiet noise that brought the boy back to him, he picked him up, settled him on his hip again.

As he did, he noted Gideon had moved a step closer to Anwyn's chair. Daegan had his arm stretched across the back of it, casual enough, but an obvious reinforcement. Anwyn's expression was fixed and polite, but of course she was the only made vampire present—the other one having been killed by Lyssa earlier in the day. The fact Anwyn still wrestled with unstable blood from her sire made the words more applicable than comfortable. Fortunately, the scientist moved away from the delicate topic.

"Cultures with strong magical versus scientific paradigms, such as the Druids, believed that spiritualism was intimately tied to the practical way life was lived. The outcomes of crop production, fertility, et cetera, were all affected by magical forces or the relationship with the gods. These days, some might call it karma. Whatever name or cause we give it, there does seem to be a correlation between the way we live our lives, and the consequences of those choices, with the expected exceptions. It is even possible that, since we are a very small race, the spiritual forces in our lives are that much stronger to help us survive as a people, to shove us in the right direction, so to speak.

"This is a very odd way to present scientific findings, Lord Brian," Helga noted. "Particularly for you."

He nodded. "If you'll bear with me, my lady, my point will be made clear shortly. So many times, bad outcomes with respect to crops and harsh winters were pinned on individuals, usually community outsiders easy to blame. It is far easier to do that than to consider such difficulties as the result of the way our lives are being lived. Or even considering it a test of Fate, building our strength, helping our adaptability as time goes on."

He nodded toward Helga. "I am perhaps unique from others in my field in that I consider an amalgamation of esoteric factors along with the concrete ones, when the concrete ones reach their limit. When that occurs, testing variables becomes more challenging, but I test all that are available and review experiential data. Let me give you an example."

He looked toward Lyssa. "With your permission, my lady, I would like Jacob to remove his shirt and show us your servant's mark."

At Lyssa's nod, Jacob handed Kane to her. He slipped the buttons of his shirt, turned and let it fall off his shoulders, displaying the fossil-like serpent shape. There were mirrors along the walls of the dining area, a curious decorating choice for vampires, unless one realized how they liked to see their servants at all angles during entertainments. No place to hide facial expressions, but he kept his steady as he watched the Council members' attention turn to his back.

"Every full servant bears a spontaneous impression like this when they receive the third marking. We can't explain why the shapes appear as they do, but they are always symbolic of the unique relationship between the vampire and servant. In this case, Lady Lyssa is the oldest among us."

There was a pause as the Council members exchanged glances. Uthe chuckled. "Best explain quickly, lad. She's close enough to tear off your sensitive appendages."

Light laughter rippled through their ranks. Brian, mired in his science, pulled out of the deep end enough to realize the faux pas. Lyssa arched a brow at him, her jade eyes cool, though Jacob felt her indulgent amusement with Brian's sudden discomfiture. He pressed on hastily.

"I am not comparing you to the fossil, my lady. Not technically. A fossil is an enduring impression of ancient times, of our history, of what has led us to this moment. I think it could be argued that Lady Lyssa does represent that to us. This serpent shape"—he moved closer, followed the track of the mark up Jacob's back with a finger—"has three distinct curve points. Lady Lyssa has made it clear she believes Jacob was a part of her life at three different points, in three different bodies.

"These are just interpretations, obviously, and this symbol is more open to them than others. However, many of you know about Lord Mason's tiger mark on his back, a brand and inked tattoo he put there himself many years ago. When he took Jessica as his fully marked servant earlier this year . . ." Turning toward Mason, Brian had the good sense to clear his throat, ask delicately. "Er, my lord, if you don't mind?"

Jessica waited, her gaze on her Master's profile. Mason gave her a nearly imperceptible nod. Stepping forward, she slid her skirt up almost to the juncture of her thighs, barely covering what was between. Gracefully, she pivoted her toe to reveal her inner thigh, the tiger mark there.

"Thank you, my lady, my lord." He nodded to Lyssa and Mason. Jessica smoothed her skirt back in place. However, before Jacob could shrug back into his shirt, Lyssa extended her free hand out over the side of her chair. While she didn't spare him a glance, he understood the message well enough. Jacob placed the shirt in her hand, and she gave it to Kane to crumple in his fists, bury his face in his father's familiar scent.

"Thank *you*, my lady," Carola said, a sparkle in her eye as she ran an appreciative glance over Jacob's upper body. Giving her a slight bow and a curve of lips, Jacob took up his place on the wall again.

Brian resumed, the sense of expectation in his voice indicating he was about to reach his point of import. "Just like the marks that appear on our servants that we can't explain, but which seem appropriately suited to our relationships, I have found a correlation between those of our kind who are successfully getting pregnant and bearing children now. A significant one."

That stilled movement at the table further, for few things concerned the Council as much as the dwindling population of the vampire species.

"Ten of our nearly five thousand known vampires have children on the way. Eight are born vampires, two are made. Seven others are raising children they have had in the past five years." He nodded toward Kane, dozing off in Lyssa's arms. "I won't bore the Council with the painstaking details of years of data collection on this subject, trusting that you have confidence in my research skills, though of course I always maintain the data for your personal review . . . particularly in this case."

As he paused on those last four words, their attention sharpened. "When biological factors proved no pattern, I chose nonbiological factors. The one common factor every couple had was something I waited to voice until I was reasonably sure of it. What I have found is this: there is an undeniable connection between fertility and those vampires and servants who have a closer relationship than is considered acceptable in our world."

A murmur ran through the assembled Council. Some gazes darted toward Lyssa to see her reaction, but her attention remained on Brian, her expression unchanging. "You may say my research is speculative," Brian noted, "since those vampires and servants who have such a relationship are not likely to reveal it. However, I applied a set of constant factors, and all ten relationships demonstrated them. A higher level of intimacy and trust, some level of *positive* dependence between the couple. Positive, in that the vampire still clearly held the dominant role in the relationship, but he or she valued the servant in a manner that strongly suggests a deep emotional bond there. One that could be defined as deep, romantic love."

At the uncomfortable shifting around the table, the frowns that appeared on more than one face, he lifted a shoulder. "Whenever a scientist dips a foot into such a realm, he is already beyond measurable standards, but I use the term as we define it visually, by intuition and feeling, in our interactions with others.

"I admit I struggled with whether or not to bring this information to the Council, because for as long as we can remember, the relationship between vampire and servant has been strictly dictated. Any sense of a vampire having stronger feelings for their servant than is perceived as appropriate has been dealt with harshly by this Council, as well as Region Masters and overlords. But this is such an important topic for our survival, I think I must trust Council with it."

Though he didn't say it, his glance toward Lyssa suggested the change of governance had aided his decision. Belizar's mouth tightened, but if he thought to accuse Brian of delaying the release of his findings, he apparently swallowed the urge.

Brian bowed toward Lyssa. "It is probably easiest to use your circumstances as an example, my lady, since you have openly declared it. The relationship you have with your servant is much deeper than what is considered usual and acceptable for our kind. You did not conceive for hundreds of years, yet you conceived within a year of being with him."

Lyssa nodded. Jacob knew she had conceived within days of being with the knight he'd once been, centuries before, but she hadn't offered that data to Brian, since that would stretch even his scientific flexibility beyond bearing. Plus, she liked having that memory as a private treasure between them. He didn't mind that, either.

Brian turned his attention back to Council. "It is very possible that there is a biological component here I've not yet located. Scientists know there are chemical forces of attraction that compel males and females of many species to choose one particular mate over another for reproduction. Perhaps when there is a greater level of intimacy and trust, it triggers a chemical change in the female vampire or the seed of the male vampire, to encourage fertility. Science and spiritual forces often overlap in such inexplicable ways.

"As my final evidence for this summary report, I offer the latest data confirming my findings. Yesterday, I took a blood sample from one of my recent subjects. My intention was to run some tests on her fertility levels, but I received a rather direct and unexpected confirmation of it."

Turning to the opposite end of the table, he executed a bow, a smile playing around his serious mouth. "Lord Mason, I'm delighted to inform you that your servant is in the early stages of pregnancy."

There was a pause, then the Council erupted with comments and exclamations. Mason was rooted to his chair, his usually unreadable expression stunned. Jessica's legs began to shake, her eyes wide in her face. Though Gideon and Torrence moved toward her immediately, Mason still beat them there, sliding his arm around her waist and almost lifting her off her feet to steady her. The expression she turned up to him was a mixture of terror and joy.

"This is a simple report of my findings." Brian cleared his throat at length, drawing the rest of the Council's attention back to him and giving the couple a needed moment of semiprivacy. "I am a scientist, not a policy maker. The Council, I am sure, will wish to carefully deliberate on what to do with the information. However, in conclusion, from a purely scientific standpoint, I would suggest this. Though the stringent safeguards on vampire-servant relationships have been set down to good purpose, perhaps they have been twisted in a wrong direction over time, such that it has been harder for those bonds to develop in a way that would encourage fertility."

Giving a short bow to the assembled, he added, "Thank you for your time, my lords and my ladies. As always, I am open to any questions or further discussion."

Lyssa gave Brian a nod as he took his seat, but then turned her attention outward. "First things first," she said.

Handing Kane to Jacob, she rose. At Jacob's direction, the staff had already placed a chair at the wall so Jessica could sit until she was steadier on her feet. Mason stood at her side, his hand on the sweet line between neck and shoulder, his expression full of her and the momentous news. Another staff member had been refilling the wineglasses, anticipating the coming toast. Now Lyssa lifted hers toward Mason, drawing his attention when Jessica squeezed his hand.

"Congratulations, Lord Mason. May your offspring be far less obstinate than you, and as beautiful as his or her mother."

As he locked gazes with the vampire queen, the long history between them was evident in the naked emotion in his gaze, and how her throat thickened over her next words. "You deserve this happiness, Mason. You both do. Blessings upon you both."

The Council members joined in with "Here, here," and assorted other comments of encouragement and good humor. For the moment, the import and potential controversy of Brian's report was put aside. As Lyssa had said, every conception in the vampire world was precious. However, Jacob knew this one was even more personal to his lady.

Putting down the wineglass, she came around the table to the male vampire. With gentlemanly courtesy, he met her halfway, but he walked as if he might stumble, entirely un-Mason-like. When she slid her arms around his wide shoulders, he lifted her off her feet and held her tight, burying his face in her neck, his copper hair falling across his broad shoulder and brushing hers. Stretching out her other hand, Lyssa brought Jessica to them, drew her into the embrace. Jessica wrapped her arms around Mason as well.

As Lyssa spoke in Mason's mind, she shared those words with Jacob.

You know how deeply you are in my heart. Beyond Jacob, you are the one I trust and love beyond any other. I wish you and Jessica all the happiness this child will bring you. And the baby could not have a better mother, one who will love the both of you to the bottom of her soul. For some unimaginable reason, she already loves you that way, despite all your shortcomings.

Drawing back, she gave him a smile through suspiciously wet eyes, pressing a kiss to both his mouth and Jessica's. Then she stepped back, allowing the other Council members to rise and congratulate Mason in their own way. While they would not congratulate Jessica directly the way Lyssa had, Jacob noted they touched her shoulder or gave her a nod of acknowledgment, steadying her further during the earthshattering moment.

During the time they were involved with that, Lyssa returned to the head of the table. Brian sat in the chair at her side, watching the goings on with his usual academic scrutiny. Lyssa tipped her glass to him. "Well played, Doctor. You have a highly unscientific flare for dramatic timing."

Brian shrugged, but couldn't hide a light flush. "Perhaps I have been learning from the company I've been keeping this past year or so."

"They're a dangeous element. You should be careful of that." Her eyes gleamed. "However, you have served the Council well in this instance."

"I credit my lab assistant and servant with this finding, Lady Lyssa. She pointed out the variable to me and backed it up based on some earlier conversations she'd had with your servant, when you were sick with the Delilah virus." He looked toward Debra. She still stood at the wall, quietly watching it all, though there was a shine of happiness in her eyes as she looked toward Jessica and Mason. Once the vampires had been tucked in, Jacob was sure Debra would be part of the servants' group, including himself and Gideon, who would congratulate Jessica more openly, celebrating the young woman's pregnancy.

"Hmm. Yes, I remember some of that, despite Jacob's best efforts to conceal it from me." When she gave him an affected stern look, Jacob offered her a bland expression in return. She almost smiled before turning her attention back to Brian. "You are fortunate in having both a gifted lab tech and servant. Though I admit one question has plagued me ever since that time."

"What question is that, my lady?" His brow creased, concerned.

Before she spoke again, Lyssa made certain the Council was still involved in speaking to Mason. Jacob, picking up on it, shifted his attention to them, watching her back. "I want to know why I gained your loyalty over what you owe to the Council," she said. "And before you answer, know I'm not asking an idle question. As head of this Council now, I require a better sense of what motivates your loyalty. I can take a deeper marking on you to assure myself of your honesty, but I do not think I need that, do I?"

"I am yours to do with as you will, my lady," Brian said, instantly and sincerely. "If that is what you wish, I will embrace having you deeper in my mind."

It was not often a vampire was pressed to state his loyalties so openly. However, he'd responded to the awkward question with an open and raw honesty, at odds with many of the vampires she knew. Debra's gray eyes rested on her Master, the set of his shoulders, as he continued.

"From the night you first marked me, giving me permission to be in your territory, and through everything since then, you've proved to me you are a queen worth serving. You've not yet ever disappointed me in your intentions or in who you are. I am somewhat oligarchical in viewpoint." He flashed his fangs in mirthless humor. "But the best form of governance for our race is a monarchy supported by a fair and intelligent advisory Council, *when* the monarch possesses the abilities you do. The sad fact is few of them do. I believe in our world, the best things that we can be. It is leadership like yours we need to achieve and maintain that. Perhaps, one day, we will be able to be the self-governing Council you hoped we would be. But until then"—he offered a reticent smile—"Long live the queen."

"Here, here." That came from Mason. The vampire had taken his seat at the end of the table again. Lyssa received Jacob's silent nudge of warning toward the end of Brian's monologue, so the Council members who'd also returned to their places hadn't followed the first part of the conversation. However, like Mason, they'd obviously caught the last part. And witnessed what Brian did now.

Rising from his seat, Brian dropped to a knee before her. He bowed his head. "Whatever you need from me, Lady Lyssa—any form of loyalty, be it courage, deception or my very life—you have it. In fact, I encourage you to give me that sire's mark, so you can always have access to my mind if you have need of it, and that I may serve you better."

"I may very well take you up on that, Lord Brian," Lyssa said, touched. Laying a hand on the side of his face, she stroked his dark blond hair back from his ear. "But tonight, I will let your thoughts be your own. That will give you time to banish any incriminating theories, like my fossilized status, from your mind."

A wave of chuckles came from the Council. Though he had the grace to flush again, he also smiled and bowed his head. "Thank you for that mercy, my lady."

Lyssa nodded to them all. "We have many reasons to celebrate tonight. Lord Brian's remarkable findings give us hope for a stronger race, and Lord Mason and his servant will soon bring another strong vampire into our world. In a few minutes, we will retire to the atrium area with our coffee, desserts and Lord Belizar's cognac to enjoy these tidings"—she sent the Cossack a fond smile—"as well as some after-dinner entertainment. If you all will indulge me, I would like to exercise the prerogative of a queen, and dictate what that entertainment will be."

As a sense of anticipation swept over the vampires, Jacob felt that familiar tightening in his lower belly. The first time he'd been part of "vampire games," it had been a nervous, sick feeling, fairly unpleasant to manage. Seanna, Lord Richard's servant, had told him that night that it would become better over time. His very nature, how much he wanted to serve his lady, would make it better. And he found she was right, that what he felt now was an odd mixture of apprehension and anticipation.

Checking on his brother, he thought Gideon was still in that earlier, unpleasant phase. And though she was glowing with her news, such that he hoped it would bolster her courage about it, he knew Jessica would face it with deep trepidation as well. While the babe was not far enough along that Mason could justifiably pull her from such activities, he could exercise his very Mason-like force of will and deny her the opportunity to perform as his full servant. However, it was obvious this night was vitally important to Jess for just that reason. Though she already looked nervous as hell again, she didn't look ready to back down on it.

Of course, if ever Mason was going to allow Jessica to act as his true servant in a mixed vampire environment, there was no better time than this night. The Council members were treading carefully, but many of them knew this version of Lyssa, the all-powerful queen who had helped establish the Council. As such, it told them their world wasn't going to be turned completely upside down, just redirected. While that gave them room to relax somewhat, none of them would be giving one of her inner circle a hard time tonight. If Mason decided he wished to set boundaries on Jessica's participation, it would likely pass unremarked.

Then Lyssa spoke, and Jacob realized he should have known his lady would take care of all of them in one masterful stroke.

"Lord Brian has made some valid points, and we need to consider our response to them cautiously. We should promote an environment where these bonds can happen more easily. However, the bond between vampire and servant is sacred, and sacred things do not happen in an easy flow, but against strong currents. A vampire must ever be assured that his or her servant's loyalty is absolute. We choose them based on an intuitive sense that the desire for service runs deep within them, so deep they themselves may not recognize it until we pull back the layers, with seduction or more forceful means.

"The things we demand of them during a gathering like this is part of that process. However, this is a night of transition for all of us, vampires and servants. I believe our servants themselves can give us a gift to reinforce that. They can show us that, while change might be necessary, some constants will always form the foundation of who we are."

Lyssa let her gaze slide around the table, meeting each Council member's eyes in turn. "While we continue our dinner conversation in the main atrium, I'm going to divide our servants into three different groups and position them around the area for viewing. *They* will determine how best to entertain us. We will give them a limited freedom to prove their understanding of the bond we share with them." She lifted a shoulder. "As always, if we wish to modify the picture, add or subtract a factor, then that suggestion may be made. But let us see what they come up with. Who knows our deepest, darkest cravings better than our servants?"

There were smiles, chuckles at that. "To make it interesting," she added, "at thirty-minute intervals, one servant shifts to the next group, stepping into whatever that previous servant was doing, though you servants may decide to change the scene once an appropriate amount of time has elapsed. Alternate by gender. First shifting person will be a female servant, the next a male, and so forth. At a certain point, every servant must have shifted to each group. If that has not been the case, that particular servant or servants will be called to the center for the entertainment of the vampire master or mistress's choice. For those of you who welcome such punishments, no feet-dragging is allowed."

Lyssa gave Torrence a pointed look at that, eliciting more chuckles. Helga's large servant, a known extreme player, offered the queen a half bow, though his eyes sparked at the challenge. Helga, a fond smile on her face, stroked her hand over his cheek as he bent forward. "No servant is allowed to release," Lyssa continued. "Not until your vampire Master or Mistress gives you express permission to do so. Have fun with it. We shall certainly enjoy watching."

Lyssa didn't need to see the tight jaw or dangerously still expression on Mason's face to know the turmoil within him. *Let your servant do this, Mason. She wants to do it, and it is your confidence in her that will get her through it.*

Lyssa could tell the girl was terrified, the ghosts of past demons dogging her heels, but her resolute chin, the clench of her hands, said she had the courage of a Viking warrior and was determined to face this. It told Lyssa what she already knew—the true problem wasn't Jessica.

There was a reason Mason had preferred the desert sands for so long, and Middle Eastern cultures that were openly territorial about their women. Unlike most vampires, who did in fact get aroused by watching their servant be compelled into play with others, he loathed seeing male hands on his servant. In fact, except in situations he orchestrated completely, it inspired certain homicidal urges that, even for a vampire with his age and control, could be problematic.

I've done the only sanctioned kill today, she noted firmly. *There will be no others.*

How about maiming? Are you fine with that?

She gave him a quelling look and rose. After she broke the servants into three groups, she signaled the vampires it was time to retire to the atrium. Holding Kane in her arms, Lyssa gave Jacob a nod, a curl of that sensual lip, her green eyes as mysterious and compelling as a siren's.

Let the games begin, Jacob thought. *God help us.*

~

The castle atrium had a glass ceiling to allow a view of the sky. The several large fireplaces had been lit to fill the room with warmth. The exotic foliage in the atrium made it one of the less bleak places in the castle, and Jacob was sure that was why Lyssa had chosen it. Scattered throughout it were sofas, chairs and other props to make for comfortable socializing. And viewing.

Daegan had absented himself from the group, agreeing to take Kane to their rooms during the more adult after-dinner entertainments. Since he could see the goings-on through Gideon's eyes or Anwyn's, the vampire would still get an enjoyable view of all that would happen, participating through Anwyn's mind and Gideon's.

As the vampires settled in, talking and considering their dessert and wine choices, Jacob knew he was supposed to take the lead here, get things started. When Lyssa had divided up the servants, he, Gideon and Jessica made up one of the groupings. His lady's ability to think quickly on her feet always amazed him. Gideon's aggressively protective nature toward a fearful female was positively engaged, because he would be directly involved in her first experience, and Jessica knew Jacob the best of any servant here.

"My lady, if I have your leave to begin?" He murmured it as she paused in conversation with Lord Belizar. She gave him a glance, nodded.

Moving from behind her chair, he was conscious of the not-so-casual regard of the assembled vampires, mainly because of who he was about to face. He was probably the only servant brave enough to approach Mason when it was obvious what kind of dangerous vibes were pulsing off him. Well, except for Gideon, and he didn't count, because he'd always had more guts than brains when it came to spoiling for a fight.

Mason had helped him through the difficult months of his transition to vampire. He'd taught him how to manage his power, joining Gideon in keeping Jacob contained when his bloodlust and overwhelming need to be with Lyssa had turned him into a mindless, savage animal. But that Mason was not present in the room tonight. Accordingly, Jacob dropped respectfully to one knee before the vampire, where he sat with all the watchful stillness of a coiled cobra. Jessica stood behind his chair, her hand on the carved head rest near his shoulder.

"My lord," Jacob said. "With your permission?"

He could feel Jessica's apprehension and yet anticipation at once. She had a powerful need to validate herself here, and he'd no doubt she'd made that clear to her Master, but she was equally aware the decision was his. However, if his decision was against it, Jacob knew it would crush a part of her. No matter that she understood Mason's possessive tendencies, the part of her mired and chained to her volatile past would think it was because he didn't think her strong enough to handle the responsibilities of a full servant.

After a long pause, Mason reached up, closed his hand over hers. Guiding her around the chair, he offered the slim fingers to Jacob.

Jessica let out an unsteady breath, her gaze flicking to her Master with love and gratitude, though of course it didn't add color to her pale cheeks, or change the fact that her hand was trembling and cold. Jacob expected it was one of the hardest things Mason ever had to do, because in his shoes, he would feel the same damn way.

As Mason released her, Jacob closed a firm reassuring grip over her. Then he motioned to Gideon. His brother pressed a kiss to Anwyn's shoulder where she was in conversation with Helga. Anwyn paused to give him a Mistress's look, a softly voiced, "Make me proud." Gideon responded with a show of teeth, a quick nip on her shoulder, then he came to join Jacob and Jessica.

The center of the atrium had a platform used for dancing or other activities, like this, that required more elbow room. Perfect. As Jacob moved toward it, the next most senior servant followed suit, gathering his or her group to take up position in a different part of the atrium. Right now, they were not his concern, but he noted the next group clockwise had Torrence. Hopefully, when the first rotation occurred and Jess had to move to that group, Torrence could keep some of his extreme practices in check. Else Jacob expected Helga would need a new servant and the staff would be polishing spattered blood off the leaves of the many plants.

As Gideon joined them, he put his hand on Jessica's waist, a calm caress. "Jesus, girl. You're an iceblock. We'll have to warm you up. Clothes?" he inquired, raising a brow.

Jacob inclined his head, surprised Gideon was so cognizant of what was required. The first rule of most vampire after-dinner entertainments was they preferred their servants stripped, with the exception of any harnesses or other sexual embellishments.

When Jessica swallowed, Jacob met her gaze. "Close your eyes. Just get lost in it. That's the key. Remember, everything you're doing is for the pleasure of your Master. Though he might not realize it, you have the ability to make him feel that way. You can make this work for both of you, Jessica. *You* have that power."

She nodded. Closing her eyes, a shudder ran through her, but also a deep, deep breath. Moving slow and deliberate, but determined not to treat her like a breakable egg, Jacob pushed the clinging fabric of the black dress down her body. He revealed her demi bra that pushed up her breasts in tempting display, then the brief thong panties and gartered stockings. Christ, she was a vision, all toned, smooth muscles from her work with Mason's horses. Gideon dropped to a knee, taking over the removal of the dress over her spike heels. Jacob steadied her as she stepped out of it, though he left on the shoes to make the display all the more delectable.

Good. They all knew what they were doing. Though he and Gideon had a better sense of what would turn the vampires on, Jessica had an intuitive sense of what fascinated her Master.

As Gideon removed the dress, he dropped it to the side and then leaned forward, pressing his mouth to one buttock, nipping her. When she jumped, he turned it into a flick of his tongue over the silky skin, his large hand sliding along the curve, caressing her. Her head dropped back in response, Jacob setting his hands to her waist to hold her. As he did, he bent to those tempting breasts in the demi-cups. Sliding his mouth over the plumped-up curves, he teased her nipple inside the bra, curling his tongue around it, the friction of his tongue and the lace making her draw in a breath.

He was rewarded with the first tentative scent of arousal, her pussy dampening beneath the thong panties. In the meantime, Gideon went right for the intimate act that would warm their nervous girl. Those few months of intense training he'd spent with his new Master and Mistress showed now. Teasing between her buttocks with his mouth, he used his tongue against the thong strap, pushing it against her rim and licking her with that covering to increase the friction and sensation. She gasped. The fact her Master took her often meant her body would respond to skilled lovemaking. Jacob expected she was helping it along by imagining Mason's hands, his mouth. It was what he'd done at the beginning himself, imagining his lady's touch. Her desires.

Even now, what drove him overall, despite the delectable provocation of a female as beautiful as Jessica, was the fact this was commanded by his lady. Despite the casual flow of conversation, he knew Lyssa was watching him, following every movement with razor-sharp attention. In addition to enjoying the visual stimulation of it, she was likely also imagining when he'd done things like this to her. He knew she took a possessive pleasure in it, watching him exercise skills she'd nurtured as he offered them to another servant, by her will. Even as she imagined it would be her later, the one who owned all that skill, taking advantage of it, marking him as hers anew. And that never ending spiral stirred him further as well.

"Undress us, Jessica," he commanded. "Make us hard. Make every male vampire watching you hard, including your Master."

She started with him. As Gideon continued to distract her in ways that had her making little jerks of movement, she unbuckled Jacob's belt, her fingers drifting across the soft stuff of his slacks. When she leaned into him, her mouth closed on his throat, teeth pressing into the jugular.

"Tease," he muttered, and was delighted by the curve of Jessica's lips against his skin. She was pulling out of her fear enough to think about the things that particularly aroused a servant . . . and a vampire. "It will make all the lady vampires get wet," she whispered.

Gideon chuckled against her flesh, bit her hard enough she gave a tiny yelp. "Gotta watch her, Jacob," he said, glancing up at his brother. "She's meaner than she looks."

As she slid to her knees and opened his slacks, Gideon rose behind her, fingers playing in her hair. When the slacks dropped onto the rise of Jacob's buttocks, she kept the belt threaded, holding him to her as she pushed the fabric out of her way. She tongued his cock, stretched out long and thick in front of her.

As good as that felt, she wasn't dealing with two true submissives. After her provocative use of the belt and her taunt, they took the lead away from her. While Gideon removed her hands from the belt, Jacob slid it free of the loops and let the slacks drop. Tightening his hand in her hair again, Gideon held her off his brother as Jacob toed off his shoes, got rid of the pants. She glanced up at him out of long-lashed hazel eyes, her lips moist. Jesus, any male with an ounce of Dom in his blood would kill to have her. And since vampires were all Dom, it was no wonder Mason was so protective.

Gideon guided her so she went back down on Jacob's cock, though she had to do it with mouth only because Gideon knotted the belt around her wrists at her lower back. Stripping off his own clothes, he tossed them aside and then knelt behind her anew, guiding those bound wrists so her hands closed over his own cock blindly to stroke as he pushed her farther onto Jacob. Jacob took over the grip in her hair.

With the brothers' intuitive senses, a pure submissive female was a pleasure to read. The more they subjugated her to their needs, driving up her pleasure, the more she'd get lost in it. Jacob dared a glance toward Mason. He was sitting on the fringes of a group, and it appeared Lyssa was drawing him into the conversation. The subject was mostly about the erotic scenarios around them, since the vampires were fully engaged in the display. Though Mason still had that unfathomable, vaguely homicidal look, it was obvious that watching his servant service two males in ways she'd serviced him was having an arousing effect on him. Jacob hoped Jessica had some energy left when it was all over, because he sensed Mason would later ruthlessly drive her to that mindless edge again and again, imprinting his claim on her once more.

Jessica had a skilled mouth and he was close to coming in no time. Mindful of his lady's order, and again blessing and cursing her insight, he slid his cock free of those sinful lips. Her hands were equally skilled, because his brother looked like he'd been fighting a similar battle for control. But they weren't the only ones. When Gideon removed the belt and helped Jessica up, her mouth was sensually bruised, her eyes dazed.

Jacob had pushed the bra down when suckling her, and her exposed nipples were erect. Slick arousal marked her thighs.

"Want to practice some of those sparring skills I showed you now?" He kept his voice low, teasing. "See what you can handle under distraction?"

She got her breath back enough to manage a spirited look at them both. "I'm not the one carrying a tree branch between my legs. I think I have a shot at landing a punch or two."

She was a scrappy street fighter, for all that he and Gideon could outmatch her. Since they both knew how to pull back to pace their opponent, they could make it an engaging match. One the vampires would enjoy, watching the volatile interplay of naked bodies.

However, before they could move into position to engage, Jessica let out a soft moan, rocking forward. Her eyes closed as she slid one hand to her breast, cupping the curve and teasing the nipple. The other slid down to the juncture of her thighs, dipping into that wetness and rubbing it over her clit with nimble fingers. Lyssa had given each vampire latitude to change up the game as desired, and it appeared Mason had just taken over, to assert his command. Her lips wordlessly formed his name, confirming it.

"Fuck," Gideon muttered, watching her body undulate precariously. "Let's lay her down, so she can keep doing that."

Jacob took the hand that had been caressing her pussy. Lifting it to his mouth, he sucked the honey off her fingertips. She moaned again, throat working. Whatever Mason was saying was sending her close to the edge. If she teetered over it without his leave, then she'd be all his again, subject to his punishment. In a way, it was cheating, but Jacob knew if she was his, he'd do exactly the same.

As they began to lower her down to the ground, she writhed in sudden abandon. It slid Jacob off balance, and as she rolled off his hands, she landed a hard punch to Gideon's side, sweeping his legs from the floor and slamming him down to his ass. Twisting behind Jacob, she knocked him in the kidney with a solid kick before she bounced back on her feet, eyes sparkling.

"I haven't forgotten what you taught me on the beach at Mason's," she told Jacob. "But apparently you have."

"Oh, it's on now," Gideon promised, getting to his feet with an anticipatory grin. "You're going down, girl."

"Thought I just did that." Reaching back to unhook the bra, she shimmied out of the panties, leaving herself as naked as the two of them. She twirled the panties on her fingers, dancing back and dropping them in Mason's lap with a coquettish smile, those lashes fanning her cheeks once again before she came back to the circle. Mason's amber eyes glittered, a near smile at her playfulness.

There'd been appreciative whistles and catcalls from the vampires at the maneuver, and now the three of them held center stage as they circled. With the element of surprise gone, he and Gideon restrained themselves to keep the sparring evenly matched, a fair exchange of blows and maneuvers that highlighted the naked, muscular and toned forms executing them. Of course, they couldn't be blamed for using their superior fighting skills to exercise quick capture and releases that pressed Jessica between them. They did it several times, until Gideon got a lock across her chest, and Jacob caught her thighs up on his hips, both of their cocks angled for penetration if they chose. He met Gideon's gaze, a silent communication and flick of his gaze that his brother followed, giving him a slight nod of understanding.

She was panting, but that vulnerable position had her eyes widening once again. Jacob made a soothing murmur in his throat as Gideon gentled his grip, letting her head drop back on his shoulder as they teased her with the feel of their cocks lodged at her two openings. Reaching between them, Gideon collected slickness from her pussy to lubricate his way into her ass, painting her rim, inserting the tip of a finger. She made a raw, needy noise.

"Such a sweet, willing submissive," Jacob hummed it against her neck, goading her further. "Serving her Master so well. A wet, hot cunt. Wet and hot at his command. Right, Jess?"

She nodded. When she closed her eyes, he knew she was in Mason's mind, that there were likely all manner of equally graphic images between them, making this as much their moment as Jacob and Gideon's.

As he'd planned, just as they had their cocks pressed to her cunt and anus, but not yet penetrating, the thirty minute chime was struck by a staff member. They'd made it through the first round, and Jessica had held her own.

Jacob let her down carefully. In her gaze, he saw her acknowledge the first milestone, and was fiercely glad they'd given her the starting confidence for it. Now if she could just hold on to it. He was amused to see Gideon give her ass a pinch, teasing her a little bit to make her smile. His brother was likely having the same thoughts he was.

As Jacob guided her to the next group, his arousal made his gait awkward as hell, but the vampires were enjoying it, he was sure. She clutched his hand at her waist, glanced up at him.

"You can do this," he murmured. "Remember, your Master is with you, every step. I'm actually more worried about him making it through this than you. You're way tougher than he is."

That won a small smile, a sparkle in her lovely eyes. When he turned her over to Torrence though, he met the man's gaze with a hard warning glance. Helga might want her servant to test Mason's, because that was what vampires did, but things could become pretty bad, pretty fast if it went down that road. Fortunately, he saw no malicious mischief in Torrence's eyes, only appreciation for the wary, aroused female. Hoping the gods would guide Torrence to exercise good sense, Jacob returned to Gideon.

Debra was the new addition to their group. She was flushed by whatever had been done in the last group, and Jacob was worked up enough he was glad no preliminaries were needed. "I've had her mouth on my cock," he told Gideon. "It was sweet as candy, but that pleasure's yours this time. I want something else this round. Lift her around the waist."

Debra made a surprised squeak when they lifted her between them. However, when Jacob guided her legs up over his shoulders and let her head and shoulders drop into Gideon's waiting hands, she understood. Her heartbeat increased. The intoxicating smell of her cream was close to his face. In the downward-sloping position she could take Gideon's cock in her mouth and did. Gideon let out a grunt as she deep-throated him, her nose pushed into his testicles. Jacob set his mouth to her cunt, drinking deep of the soaking wet arousal she had. *Like my lady, so wet and sweet . . . the way she writhes and makes those little helpless noises as I eat her out, and her fingernails sink into my shoulders, drawing blood . . .*

His lady's heat passed through his mind. He knew her well enough now to know the things that would displease her. Pleasuring another servant at her command, that was acceptable. But she could be very jealous about displays of intimacy, so he'd purposefully avoided engaging Debra on that level, setting aside their friendship for other, more clothed times. Fortunately, Debra was gaining enough experience she didn't need the intimacy for reassurance, the way she had when they first met.

She was already crying out. Gideon's face was rigid with concentration. By the time the thirty-minute bell rang this time, despite modifying their pace and rhythm, they were all on the edge of climax. Debra was so close, Jacob thought a current of air would set her off.

"Put ice on her to calm her down," Lord Brian said, gazing at his flustered servant from one of the deep chairs. His eyes were vibrant with pleasure, and they flared up further when Jacob took the ice a house servant brought him and laid it on her clit. Debra let out a short scream, her hands gripping his shoulder and Gideon's. They steadied her, keeping her facing her Master so he could watch her reaction.

And so it went. Jacob had been trained to hold back an inordinate, impossible amount of time, but he got to the same point as Debra and probably all the other servants. It was a mindless, humping, suckling, fucking spiral of energy, a collective state of subspace where they were doing everything they could to please their vampires, to get that permission to release they all sensed wouldn't be forthcoming. Lord Welles's servant was the first to fall, screaming out her climax as she was pushed to her knees and fucked by Torrence's cock, while another male servant lay beneath her and tongued her clit and the slick shaft alternately as it thrust in and out.

To punish her, Lord Welles put her over his lap and gave her a stinging spanking. Then he placed three balls of ice in her cunt and ass and kept them there with a chastity harness. Just like a vampire—as Jacob well knew—a third-marked servant wasn't susceptible to the nerve damage that prolonged contact with ice could cause, so she was laid on the floor at his feet, to writhe and moan against her gag, her body flushed and torn between the pain and pleasure.

They were all required to watch the punishment before they resumed, which just increased the stakes of the game. For that was what it was. Jacob realized his lady was playing a modified version of musical chairs. They would keep going until each servant reached his or her threshold and could hold back no longer. Then his or her vampire would get the pleasure of deciding on their punishment. Torrence was the next to succumb, surprisingly. It amused Jacob that it was Jessica's small mouth—tight on his monster cock—that set him off. Helga tied him over a spanking bench placed among an artful arrangement of foliage. He was flogged with a barbed cat-o'nine wielded by his Mistress, then she offered his ass to two of the male vampires, Walton and Stewart.

When they were done, she pushed a thick, vibrating dildo in the raw opening, strapping it in place so Torrence would continue to stay aroused in his helpless position, his kilt hiked up over his back. She kept him near her so she could run her hand over his taut ass at will, enjoy the straining thighs up close as she continued to place wagers with the other vampires as to which three would be the last standing.

The rotation brought him Jessica again, but the male with him now was Vincent. Jacob had enough brain cells left to know there was another agenda to play out here. Touching his lady's mind, seeing her will in this, he needed nothing further than that to guide him.

"I expect Jessica would like to extend an apology for impaling you," he said. "But you owe me something as well."

Jessica was slick with perspiration, her eyes wild and feral, her pussy deep red and wet, a creature of sex and lust, but there was determination there as well. She was holding, though barely. Glancing at Mason, Jacob suspected he'd continued to employ all sorts of diabolical mind games to push her into climax. Knowing how resourceful the vampire was, and his effect on Jessica, he suspected the vampire was impressed as the rest of them with her stamina and resolve. While wanting to smack her ass for it. His lips twisted wryly. Though he respected Jessica's stubbornness, he did owe Mason something for shooting her in the shoulder.

"Jessica, bend forward and slide your hands around your calves, holding yourself in a folded position."

As she complied, her hair fell forward over her shoulders, the curve of her back and heart-shaped ass a pretty display. He knew she was competitive, but he'd been doing this longer, and he sure as hell knew a woman's body. Jacob beckoned to a staff person standing by with a tray full of sexual aids and picked up a paddle. The *Bad Girl* cutout in the wood made his lips twist, but then he met Vincent's gaze. "You'll use this on her, but when you're done, you'll kneel, take me in your mouth and make me slick for your ass. Got it?"

The new head servant fucking the previous one. The symbolism was strong, an underscore of the day's events. Vincent recognized it, his handsome face resigned. But he was severely aroused, too, and Jacob was certain he could push the man into punishment at his Master's hand. Vincent preferred males, and he couldn't keep his gaze away from Jacob's cock. Even though his grip tightened on the handle of the paddle, indicating he was going to relish dishing out a little pain.

"Don't go overboard," Jacob advised, low. "You can make your point without being brutal about it. The humiliation is the reward here."

Jessica let out a shuddering breath. Jacob had noted no male servant had penetrated her, though Lord Stewart's female servant had used a thick vibrator that almost sent the girl screaming into oblivion. Servants were a savvy lot. Plus, they received direction from their Masters and Mistresses, who perhaps understood the politics of not pushing the boundaries too much with Mason. Not tonight, at least.

Stepping up so he stood beside Jessica, he slid his hand along her spine, soothing her. Her fingers tightened on her calves. "Easy, girl. It'll hurt, but it will equal the scales between you." She'd staked a much more senior servant, and he knew this would ease any future tensions between them.

His lady was amused at his understanding of the maze between politics and pleasure. Even among all the aroused bodies, her scent was a unique perfume. He ached to go to her, give her release.

Keep proving it to me, Sir Vagabond. Fuck him like you'd like to fuck me.

You've a much sweeter, softer ass, my lady.

With the first slap of the paddle, a soft cry split from Jessica's lips. Jacob was aware of the darkness of Mason's gaze, knew that he'd perhaps chosen a bad path, because Mason's dominance was more about deprivation than pain, and Jessica's beautifully tattooed back, a tiger peering through a bamboo forest, overlaid a horrid set of long scars put there by her previous master.

But Vincent showed he was no fool. He made the strikes hurt, satisfying his honor, but he recognized a submissive that responded to a certain level of pain. Jessica's legs trembled, and when he lightly slapped her clit, widening her stance farther, she let out a strangled cry of unmistakable arousal.

Twenty strikes, where *bad girl* was overlaid all over the sweet pale curves, and then Jacob called a halt to it.

He guided Jessica down to her knees, used a gentle hand on the back of her neck to put her forehead to the floor, a resting submissive pose. "Put your hands behind your back and open your mouth," he ordered Vincent. When Vincent complied, he guided his cock into the mouth of Belizar's servant. He had to close his eyes, because he usually did when a male had hold of him, so he could imagine his lady's mouth, though hers and Vincent's were nothing alike. However, Vincent had undeniable skills. Jacob put his hand on the close-cropped hair to hold him still, control his movements so he wouldn't go off like a rocket.

Fortunately, getting him slick didn't take long. He pulled back after only a few moments, turned Vincent so he was facing Jessica's folded-over body. "Take your hips off your ankles, Jess," he said, a quiet order. "Ass in the air."

She obeyed, though he saw her thighs tremble a little bit, but more from arousal than trepidation. He knew she trusted him. Vincent was well lubricated from previous groups, so the cocksucking had been psychological, underscoring the changing of the guard. Jacob drove in deep and hard, taking. He usually kept his lady in mind when having to fuck a male, because it was always more politics than pleasure for him. But there was a primal pleasure in the taking, the control, and he let Vincent feel that. The man grunted, his hands flexing on the floor between Jessica's ankles. He was hanging on by a thread.

"Put three of your fingers inside her ass, Vincent. Go easy."

The male was more than willing to do that, though he fumbled some, responding to the stimulation Jacob was inflicting upon him. The man's ass was contracting hard on him and Jacob knew he was close.

Fortunately, Jessica was also still well lubricated from Gideon's earlier application of oil, so Vincent's fingers slid in easy. When she made that low cry again, Jacob drove her onward with an order. "Squeeze down on him with every thrust, Jess. Make him feel you."

The contraction of the anal muscles affected the clit, made it spasm that much more quickly. As she moved to obey, he kept encouraging her, commanding her. "Squeeze him. Squeeze him hard. Every thrust. Don't miss a single one. It's your Master's cock. Milk him dry."

Vincent let out his own moan as Jacob hit the spot he knew would be the servant's downfall. Hellfire, he had an ass tight as a virgin girl. Belizar was hung like a horse. Vincent probably felt split open when his Master fucked him. "Getting close there, aren't you, Vincent?"

The male cursed him, low, and Jacob bared his teeth in a feral grin. Jessica's fingers scrabbled across the floor, and Jacob recognized the tiny, needy cries, growing in volume. The words, "Please . . . Master . . ."

Mason's eyes were fierce amber, his mouth set into a line. He wanted to punish her, because that was what would please him. Jessica was smart enough to already know it, but she also knew her begging would please him as well.

"Squeeze him," Jacob barked.

Jessica was hurled over that cliff, her admirable attempt to hold back lost in the face of Jacob's expertise and her own lack of experience. She came with a hard scream, her body bucking. Vincent grabbed at his own cock to massage himself furiously, directing the stream of semen toward the floor, away from Jessica. As he twisted away from the girl, Jacob pulled out of him, dropped to one knee and gave Jessica a full completion. His hand closed over her clit, fingers massaging the rippling bud of skin, two other fingers dipping inside of her cunt to thrust, his thumb pressing on her anus. She shrieked, her cream gushing over his hand, a deep pleasure as he slid his other arm under her hips to give her some balance.

He helped her fold all the way to the floor, writhing and convulsing. Vincent was breathing hard, still on both knees next to them. It took both of them a few minutes to wind down, to finish out the climax. A few more to collect their wits again, somewhat. But when they did, Jacob brushed his knuckles over Vincent's shoulder, giving him a nod and glance to show they were square. In return, he received a deferential gesture, devoid of malice. Belizar's servant also touched Jessica on the hip, a similar communication.

Good. He was proud of himself for keeping the politics in play despite the fact his cock felt like a fucking aluminum baseball bat. With one word, his lady could probably make him spew all over himself.

You never cease to be a charmer, Sir Vagabond.

His lips twisting, he lifted Jessica in his arms. She was still shuddering, her skin so sensitive that even his carrying touch had her making soft cries and writhing.

He brought her to Mason, keeping his eyes down as he settled her between her Master's feet, her naked back braced against the male vampire's leg. Mason slid his fingers into her hair, tipped back her head so she had to look into his face. She'd cried during her climax, and her mouth was parted and moist. It had been difficult, but she'd done it. That triumph was in her eyes, as well as the heartache and past pain that had made it so important to her.

"You disobeyed me, Jessica."

When she reached up with a shaking hand, he closed his hand over her wrist. She touched him anyway, eyes adoring. "Yes, Master. Please forgive me. P-punish me as you see fit, please."

"Later, *habiba*." His tone softened, his eyes reflecting some of the same pain and suffering, mixed with pride and love. He gave her a kiss then, his mouth a brief tease on hers. "When we are alone, I will torment you in ways that make this seem like child's play."

Jacob returned to his position to find only three of them were still standing. Somewhat. Him, Gideon and—surprisingly—Debra. The servants who'd lost were variously engaged now, each the center of one or more vampires' attentions, the after-dinner play turned into a sexual bacchanalia. It made the heat in the room even closer, made it difficult for Jacob to look at anything but his lady. Her lips were parted, eyes that glowing green color like a cat hunting in the moonlight. But she ignored him, making him harder.

"You may return to your Master," she told Debra, then glanced at Gideon, a faint smile playing on her tempting lips. "And to your Mistress. Well done."

Gideon dropped to his knees next to Anwyn, sitting in a nearby chair. As she slid a hand around his neck, a Mistress's fierce demand was in her gaze. Though her voice was soft, Jacob heard her clearly enough. "Daegan says he wants you to pleasure my pussy, make me come. When we go back to the room, he will fuck you and finally—if you've pleased me—he'll let you come."

Gideon put his hands on either arm of the chair, caging her as he captured her mouth in a demanding kiss that showed her all he was feeling. But when she pushed him back, his broad back curved, his palms bracing himself on the floor between her sexy stilettos as he worked himself beneath her snug skirt, into the dark fragrant valley between her shapely thighs. She threw her head back, sable hair fanning out over the fabric of the chair. As he obviously made contact, burying his face in her pussy, the sounds of licking and suckling her reached Jacob's ears. It made him want to do like Vincent, wrap his hand around the fucking tree branch of his erection, give the aching some relief, but he'd hold out forever if it meant his lady would do it instead.

To all appearances cool and remote, she emitted that molten heat beneath, those jade eyes fastened on his. When he reached her, he swept his gaze down before he dropped to a knee before her in the winged-back chair. "How may I serve your pleasure, my lady?"

"You will serve it in our chambers. Follow me."

They left the atrium, passing out of sight of those left behind, though it probably little mattered, since they were involved in their own pleasure. Once they made that first corner, Jacob caught her arm, whipped her around and pressed her hard to the wall, devouring her mouth with his own. Her arms slid around him, her hips lifting to push against his. Since he was naked, she was rubbing herself against his bare cock, but the beaded fabric of her skirt was a rough and frustrating barrier. It was all part of the pleasurable cruelty, and he dragged it out, giving her every bit of his need in that kiss, feeling the dampness of her cunt through the cloth, the stiffness of her nipples, the strong clutch of her arms, all that bountiful hair tangling over his fingers. One heel dug hard into the back of his calf, her nails scoring his back.

Put me down, Jacob, and follow me to our room.

He did, and saw her eyes were fierce, wild, her mouth wet with his. She led the way, the sway of her hips driving him insane, so that he dared the insolence of cupping one silk-clad buttock. She sent him a warning look beneath those mink lashes, but it was pure tease now, a predator allowing the prey to toy with her. He was fine with that, because he sensed her mood, what she needed, wanted, and it matched his mood perfectly.

When they got into the room, he attacked again, sliding an arm around her waist and another under her legs, lifting her off her feet. She twisted free and, in a flash, had shoved him hard against the wall, face-first, his cock mashed uncomfortably against the rough stone.

"Who do you serve, Jacob?"

"You, my lady. Always you." Her fingers teased his rim, and he fought her, to no avail. Her strength was at peak form, and he no longer had the ability to overpower her. So he strangled on a curse as those sharp nailed fingers slowly glided down his rectum. "No . . . I don't want to come that way."

"But whose wishes matter? Have you forgotten?"

"Yours, my lady. But let me fuck you. Let me spill my seed inside your cunt."

"Such language." She pressed up behind him, letting him feel every curve as those fingers continued to play. She scraped her fangs over his mark. "Though you might be the alpha servant now, you still answer to your Mistress."

"Always. My lady." He closed his eyes tight, muscles straining against the stone.

"Then why are you still fighting me?"

"Because tonight you want me to fight."

She chuckled then, a sultry sound. "Clever, clever knight."

Suddenly, she released him. When he turned, she was ten steps away, in the center of the chamber. The look in her eyes stilled him, made the chamber itself seem suddenly quiet, the air filled with a sense of silent expectation. "Perhaps it is the Crusades again." Her voice was a whisper. "You are part of an invading army. You are merely a foot soldier, a poor knight. Yet you breach the walls of the sultana, and for the next few moments, she is all yours, before your generals or kings find her. For this moment, she is your treasure."

The dress molded every curve, and it made his mouth dry, but he saw the tenor of it change in her mind. Her fantasy merged with the reality from long ago. "There you stand," she continued softly. "Dusty, bloody. Sir Knight. And my heart opens in a way I didn't know it could."

He swallowed, but instead of taking her to that other time, he brought her back to her fantasy. “The sultana is perfect, disdainful of me,” he said, in the same low voice. “But as I look at her, I see her tremble, just a bit. I watch her press her lips together, moist, and I know she could be mine. If only I reach out to take.”

Her mouth curved. Power emanated from her. Every inch his queen. He moved forward. When he reached her, he dropped to his knees, looking up at her face for a long moment from that reverent position. The slope of her abdomen, rise of her breasts, the line of her hip and thigh, so close. He'd been with her when she'd given birth to Kane, had seen those thighs tremble, her stomach contract, her throat arch back in a cry of pain but of determination as well.

Bending forward, he brought his lips to her insole, her ankle. When she shifted, he was ready. The foot that would have planted itself on his chest and shoved him back slid under his left arm. He caught it there, tugged the other one out from under her. When she fell to her back, trusting, he used a servant's speed. Her skull fell into his waiting palm, his body stretched over hers, one knee between her thighs. Lifting her chin, she regarded him with sparkling eyes. “Clever knight,” she repeated.

“I have no cleverness left. Only need. I want to use you, and use you hard. Then I want to build you back up again and make you scream. I want your tears, your laughter. I want the softness in your eyes as well as the violence.”

“I will come before you do, Sir Vagabond,” she said in a near whisper, looking up at him. “Because I can hardly bear another moment without you inside of me. Your sultana is helpless beneath you. For the moment.” Her eyes consumed him. “Do your worst. Or best, as the case may be.”

He knew how much the dress cost. He didn't care. He tore it to tatters on her body, exposing breasts in one impatient rip, letting them spill out for his hungry attack, tongue and teeth moving over them. Cradling her hips, he tilted her up, lifting his upper body enough that he could gaze down at her as if she was a prize he'd conquered in truth. Then, when her lips parted, he drove into her.

Sheer, utter bliss. No one knew the power of denial the way a vampire did. Everything he'd done tonight at her behest had been about this. She had her arms above her head, mock surrender, though he knew he was the true slave here. He thrust deep, and forced himself to the rhythm he knew would take her with him, no matter that he wanted to rut upon her like a beast. She arched up to him, her pupils dilating so the green was almost gone.

She was true to her word. No more than a dozen thrusts, and she rippled around him. Her fangs elongated, and the cries in her throat became that helpless little symphony as she squeezed around his cock.

"Let go, my lady," he urged in a hoarse voice. "Give me that gift. Let me hear your pleasure."

You with me, Jacob. You come with me.

He could refuse her nothing. They went over that cliff together, and at the pinnacle of it, she reared up and sank her fangs into his chest, just above his heart. They were of one mind, a pair of winged creatures falling into pleasurable oblivion tangled together.

And the way they felt for one another, they'd let the ground break them before they let go.

~

Once they'd ravished each other to exhaustion, his lady wanted two things: her son, and a cup of tea, in that order. Had it not been for those desires, Jacob knew she would have chained him to the wheel rack, a standard amenity in Belizar's old chambers. The way her gaze lingered on it overlong, told him her desires clearly enough. Sometimes he didn't need to be in her mind to read her thoughts.

The first night they'd met, Lyssa had chained him, giving him an unforgettable lesson in accepting submission. He'd changed a bit since then, the idea of her putting him on the device and making him wait on her pleasure making him more aroused than apprehensive. But perhaps she'd changed as well, since she ruled in favor of Kane and her tea. Either path would bring her pleasure, so both worked for him. And knowing his lady's diabolical mind, she'd probably mapped out a later time for the wheel rack.

Jacob found Kane up on the castle walls, with Daegan. The assassin was holding the toddler on his shoulders and jumping the wide spaces between parapets, making him think they were flying. Kane was delighted, whereas Jacob hoped Lyssa never saw it in his mind or she might decide to beat the assassin to a pulp. He gave Daegan his thanks. The vampire touched the boy's head fondly, nodded to Jacob, and then was gone, probably moving swiftly to join Anwyn and Gideon, to make good on the erotic threat he'd issued earlier. Given that it involved his brother being naked and at the mercy of two Dominant vampires, Jacob banished that visual from his mind pretty quick.

Instead, he hugged the boy tight, rubbing his back, inhaling his baby vampire smell and enjoying the small hands on his neck. The boy's cheek pillowed against his shoulder as Kane settled down and started feeling the exhaustion that came with being the center of attention for the past few hours. Delivering the toddler to his sleepy lady for a feeding, Jacob headed for the kitchen. The sooner he brought back the tea, the sooner he could enjoy the domestic bliss of being in bed, dozing with and holding the two people he loved best.

He was surprised to find Mason already there. The male vampire wore a dark robe loosely tied so his chest was exposed, his long hair tied back carelessly to keep it out of his way. He didn't turn as Jacob entered, but Jacob knew he'd heard him approaching the moment his feet turned down the corridor to the kitchen.

Smelling the aroma of rich hot chocolate, he saw Mason drop a handful of marshmallows into the mug. "You know, I've heard that chocolate depletes male virility."

"Hmm."

"Is she okay?"

Mason locked gazes with him. As the silence drew out, Jacob was keenly reminded that, while he considered Mason a friend, he was still a vampire. Lyssa had warned him countless times that humans should never forget that. His brother had told him the same thing. He understood that. But, as Dev might say, he wasn't a wuss, either. He wasn't going to dance around this.

"If you want to take a piece out of me for it, take a piece out of me," he said. "But she held together tonight. She's a fucking incredible woman, and she loves you enough to do anything to stay by your side. That's what we do. That's what being a servant is about. And she knows it."

Mason continued to study him with that dispassionate expression that could hide a variety of things, including whether or not he was considering breaking Jacob in half like a pencil. At length, he turned back to the chocolate. "The hot chocolate is for her. And no, I didn't care to bother a house servant to make it for me. It's been a long and exciting night for everyone." He paused. "It helps with nightmares. She did well tonight, but this has been difficult for her. Her sleep has not been easy. There is such a thing as too much courage, and loving someone past the point of good sense. Past the point they deserve."

Jacob's jaw tightened. "Singing helps my lady," he ventured after a pause.

Mason turned around, his brow lifting in surprise. "Lyssa has nightmares?"

"How can you see all she's seen, and not have them occasionally?"

Mason acknowledged the truth of that with a grunt. "I haven't tried singing. I have a passable voice."

"Doesn't matter if you're off key or not. It's your voice that makes the difference. It even works when she's asleep and just starting to get restless. I learned that with Kane. If you start singing when you see the signs, it'll sometimes work without waking her up."

It was an odd moment, sharing common ideas for soothing the women they loved. For Jacob, it was his Mistress, the woman who owned his very soul; for Mason, it was the woman whose soul *he* owned, who belonged to him utterly. But in the end, Jacob knew it was all the same.

As if reading his mind, Mason gave a faint smile, lifted the cup. "Good morning to you, then." As he reached the door, he stopped, looked back at Jacob. "What Lyssa did yesterday—it gave me a few bad moments, her and Jessica both in the line of fire, but it was needed. She has my full support, unquestioning."

"I don't think she'd ever doubt it, but good to hear it out loud. And congratulations on the baby, my lord. She and Kane can grow up together."

"If Allah be merciful," the male said. "But Allah preserve me if it's a girl."

Jacob grinned. "I'm sure Kane will watch out for her."

"That's what concerns me." A quick flash of fangs, and then Mason disappeared down the hallway.

A smile still playing on his lips, Jacob downed the glass of ice-cold water he'd been seeking for himself, then prepared a chamomile tea for his Mistress. Shutting off the kitchen lights, he headed back to his own favorite female, knowing there was no where else he'd rather be.

~

Lyssa had taken Kane out of his crib and lay with him on the bed. She wore a loose robe, and the toddler had pushed aside the silk impatiently to nurse, giving Jacob a pleasurable view of her breast. When Lyssa reached out to him, Jacob came to the bed. Sitting with his back against the headboard, he slid his lady and son in the space between his bent legs, holding them both.

After he placed the tea on the side table, she pressed her cheek into his heated palm. Catching her fingers in the waistband of the jeans he'd pulled on, she teased the muscle there while he stroked her wrist, feeling the steady thud of her pulse.

He shared Mason's message with her, and she nodded, thoughtful. "You remember what I said a while ago, that I don't want Kane to have to face the challenges we have?"

Jacob made an assenting noise. Kane was just mouthing her now, and Jacob reached down, caught a drop of blood and painted it on the small mouth. Kane made a satisfied noise, his eyelids heavy and almost closed. "I'm not sure we should remove all the challenges for vampire-servant relationships," she said. "If we do, I think it would be a disservice to vampires and servants in the long run. This relationship shouldn't be easy. I think there are some obstacles that exist because they are the purpose, in a sense. The journey we've taken, the things we've learned about each other . . ."

She looked up at him. "If it had been easy, I'm not sure either of us would have understood it the same way. We *will* have harsher laws to deal with things like what happened to Jessica, but the intention of vampires and servants, the shape of their relationship, I think it essentially needs to stay the same. Do you disagree? Your counsel on this matters to me, Jacob."

He stroked her hair, thinking for long moments under the weight of her soft gaze. Truth, when this journey had started, he'd almost left her a couple times, not sure if he could handle a vampire's ruthless nature, particularly one a thousand years old and dealing with all the politics she handled. But he couldn't deny the truth of her words. It was in everything he'd seen, not only in himself but in those around him. Jessica,

Dev, Vincent . . . even Gideon. It was like they were part of a train, and once that connection was set, the lock was true, no matter how the train raced toward an unknown destiny.

Vampires and servants, there was a balance there. It needed to be the way it was. The wisdom that had driven the decisions over the century had proven it. Yet he was certain, with her hand at the helm, there would be more room for relationships like theirs to grow. And as Brian had said, that would ultimately save the vampire race, keep it from extinction.

Looking down at his son's small skull, he laid his own hand over hers upon it. When she tilted her face to his, he gave her his answer in a kiss.

And in that heated, lingering connection, in the energy he felt between them, he was even more certain such relationships wouldn't merely survive—they would thrive, for centuries to come.

Don't miss

SOMETHING ABOUT WITCHES

by Joey W. Hill.
Coming soon from Berkley Sensation.

Ruby Night Divine is a gun-shop owner. She's also a witch who knows magic can fail. She's experienced it firsthand, with full-blown tragic consequences. Smith & Wesson is a whole hell of a lot more reliable, and nothing's as cathartic as the ability to put a few holes in the things that piss you off. Like Derek Stormwind.

A powerful sorcerer, Derek is determined to get to the bottom of why Ruby pushed him away and ran three years before. He also needs her help. A coven needs training to fight a demon and his minions. While Ruby is willing to do it, she's sure it's just a ruse to get back in her heart—and her bed. The thing is, that's where she wants him. Unfortunately, her bed's already made, she's this close to losing her soul and she fears nothing can save her. Not Derek. Not even Smith & Wesson.